# UNDAUNTED

# DIANA PALMER

## UNDAUNTED

HQN™

Recycling programs
for this product may
not exist in your area.

ISBN-13: 978-0-373-80246-3

Undaunted

www.HQNBooks.com

**Printed in U.S.A.**

In memoriam:

Robert (Bobby) Richard Hansen, Jr. 1951–2016

He leaves behind a daughter, Amanda; a stepson, Johnny; sisters, Helen, Darla, Marlene and Lavonna; a brother, Bruce; four grandchildren; a niece, Elizabeth; and numerous other relatives. He was preceded in death by his parents and a brother, Terry Hansen. He was a Vietnam veteran. We will miss him very much.

Dear Reader,

It seems that I am dedicating more and more books to loved ones who have passed away. This one is no exception. Our nephew Bobby was a character. When James and I had been married about a year, there was a knock on the door late at night. Disturbed, we ran to answer it—usually bad news at that hour. So we open the door, and there stands Bobby with two sandwiches from Dairy Queen. He just wanted us to taste these wonderful new sandwiches he'd discovered! That was Bobby: full of fun and unpredictable.

He'd served in Vietnam. He told me some stories about his combat experiences that I've never shared, and never will. I was a newspaper reporter. Things we see and hear about on the job aren't shared with civilians, as a rule, because they're pretty horrible. Bobby saw a lot of those things. Despite his experiences there, he went on to marry our Betty and had a daughter, Amanda, and a stepson, Johnny, and several grandchildren.

We also lost our sweet nephew Tony and our brother-in-law Doug within a space of months. You never know how long you've got to appreciate the people you love. Never go out the door without hugging your family and telling them that you love them. You just never know.

I hope you enjoy reading *Undaunted*. It's a little offbeat and mostly takes place on a Georgia lake. I truly enjoyed writing it. (I used to spend a lot of time on the lake in the book, fishing). I loved the hero, but I did want to clobber him by chapter three! The heroine is from Comanche Wells, Texas, and you might recognize Cash Grier and one of his unmarried brothers in this book, also.

I am still your biggest fan,

Diana Palmer

# ONE

Emma Copeland was sitting on the end of the dock, dangling her bare feet in the water. Minnows came up and nibbled her toes, and she laughed. Her long, platinum-blond hair fell around her shoulders like a silk curtain, windblown, beautiful. The face it framed wasn't beautiful. But it had soft features. Her nose was straight. She had high cheekbones and a rounded chin. Her best feature was her eyes, large and brown and gentle, much like Emma herself.

She'd grown up on a small ranch in Comanche Wells, Texas, where her father ran black baldies in a beef operation. She could ride and rope and knew how to pull a calf. But here, on Lake Lanier in North Georgia, she worked as an assistant to Mamie van Dyke, a famous and very wealthy writer of women's suspense novels. Mamie's books were always at the top of the *New York Times* bestseller list. That made Emma proud, because she helped with the research as well as the proofing of those novels in their raw form, long before they were turned over to editors and copy editors.

She'd found the job online, of all places. A Facebook friend, who knew that Emma had taken business courses at her local vocational school, had mentioned that a friend of her mother's was looking for a private assistant, someone trustworthy and loyal to help her do research and typing. It wasn't until she'd applied and been accepted—after a thorough background check—that Emma had learned who her new boss was. Mamie was one of her favorite authors, and she was a bit starstruck when she arrived with her sparse belongings at the door of Mamie's elaborate and luxurious two-story lake house in North Georgia.

Emma had worried that her cheap clothing and lack of social graces might put the older woman off. But Mamie had welcomed her like a lost child, taken her under her wing, and taught her how to cope with the many wealthy and famous guests who sometimes attended parties there.

One of those guests was Connor Sinclair. Connor was one of the ten wealthiest men in the country—some said, in the world. He was nearing forty, with wavy jet-black hair that showed only a scattering of silver. He was big and broad and husky with a leonine face and chiseled, perfect lips. He had a light olive complexion with high cheekbones and deep-set eyes under a jutting brow. He was handsome and elegant in the dinner jacket he wore with a spotless white shirt and black tie. The creases in his pants were as perfect as the polish on his wing-tip shoes. He had beautiful hands, big and broad, with fingers that looked as if they could crush bones. He wore a tigereye ring on his little finger. No other jewelry, save for a Rolex watch that looked more functional than elegant.

Emma, in her plain black cocktail dress, with silver stud earrings and a delicate silver necklace with a small inset turquoise, felt dowdy in the glittering company of so many rich people. She wore her pale blond hair in a thick bun atop her head. She had a perfect peaches-and-cream complexion, and lips that looked as if they wore gloss when they didn't. Light powder and a soft glossy lipstick were her only makeup. She held a champagne flute filled with ginger ale. She didn't drink, although at twenty-three, she could have done so legally.

She was miserable at the party, and wished she could go

somewhere and hide. But Mamie was nearby and might need an iPad or her phone, which Emma carried, ready to write down something for her. So she couldn't leave.

From across the room, the big man was glaring at her. She squirmed under his look, wondering what she could have done to incur his anger. She'd never even seen him before.

Then she remembered. She'd been out on the lake in Mamie's speedboat once. She loved the fast boat. It made her feel free and happy. It was one of the few things that did. She'd been crazy about a boy in her class at the vocational school where she'd learned administrative skills. When he'd asked her out, all her dreams had come true. Until he'd learned that her father ran beef cattle. They were even engaged briefly. Unfortunately, he was a founding member of the local animal rights group, PETA. He'd told Emma that he found her father's profession disgusting and that he'd never have anything to do with a woman who had any part of it. He'd walked out of her life and she'd never seen him again. After that, he ignored her pointedly at school. Her heart was broken. It was one of the few times she'd even had a date. She went to church with her father, but it was a small congregation and there were no single men in it, except for a much older widower and a divorced man who was her father's age.

Her home life wasn't much better. She and her father lived in a ranch house that had been in the family for three generations and looked like it. The furniture didn't match. The dishes were old and many were cracked. Water came out of a well with an electric pump that stopped working every time there was a bad storm, and there were many storms in Texas. Her father was a rigid man, deeply religious, with a sterling character. He'd raised his daughter to be the same way. Her mother had died in childbirth when she was eight years old, and she'd seen it happen. Her father had drawn into himself at a time when she needed him most. That was before he'd started drinking. He'd rarely been sober in recent years, leaving most of the work and decision making on the ranch to his foreman.

He'd never seemed to feel much for his only child. Of course, she wasn't a boy, and it was a son he'd desperately wanted, someone to inherit the ranch after him, to keep it in the family. Girls, he often said, were useless.

She dragged herself back from her memories to find the big man walking toward her. Something inside her wanted to run. But her ancestors had fought off floods and cattle rustlers and raiding war parties. She wasn't the type to run.

She bit her lower lip when Connor Sinclair stopped just in front of her. He wasn't sipping champagne. Unless she missed her guess, he held a large glass of whiskey, straight up, with just a cube of ice in the crystal glass.

He glared down at her from pale, glittery silver eyes. "I had a talk with the lake police about you," he said in a curt, blunt tone. "I told them who you worked for and where you lived. Pull another stunt like yesterday's on the lake, and you'll find out what happens to kids who take insane risks in speedboats. I've had a talk with Mamie, as well."

She drew in a shaky breath. "I didn't see the Jet Ski!"

"You weren't looking when you turned," he bit off. "You were going too fast to see it at all!"

She was almost drawing blood with her teeth. Her hand, holding the flute, was shaking. She put her other hand over it to steady it. "There was nobody out there when I started…"

"Your generation is a joke," he said coldly. "Unruly kids who have no manners, who think the world owes them everything, that they can do whatever the hell they please, do whatever they like, without consequences! You go through life causing tragedies and you don't care!"

She felt tears stinging her eyes. "Ex-excuse me," she said huskily, turning away.

But he took her firmly by one shoulder and turned her back around. "I never make threats," he said coldly. "You remember what I've told you."

Tears overflowed her eyes. She couldn't help it. And it shamed her, showing weakness before the enemy. She jerked away from him, white-faced and shaking.

He frowned, as if he hadn't expected her reaction. She turned and ran for the kitchen. She put the flute down on a counter and went out the back door into the cool night air, desperate to get away from him. Nobody knew where she was. Nobody cared. The tears tumbled down over her cold cheeks. She'd grown up without love, without the simplest display of affection after their housekeeper Dolores left the ranch, except for an occasional hug from the women in her church. She'd lived alone, had her dreams of romance shattered. And now here she was, her pride in shambles, hounded out of her home by a relentless enemy who seemed to think she was a juvenile delinquent bent on killing people. All that, because she went a little wild in the speedboat.

By the time she got herself together and eased back in, Connor Sinclair was nowhere to be seen. She went back to Mamie's side and stayed there the rest of the night, hoping against hope that he wouldn't return.

It had been a sobering confrontation. She hoped she never had to see Connor again. Sitting on the dock, she moved her toes in the cool water, laughing softly at the tiny fish still nibbling on them. The lake was glorious in autumn. Leaves were just beginning to turn, in every single shade of red and gold the mind could imagine. There was a soft breeze, lazy and warm, because autumn had come late to North Georgia. Emma, in her long cotton dress, with its brown and yellow and green print, looked like part of the scenery in a postcard.

"What the hell are you doing on my dock?" a cold, angry voice growled from behind her.

She jumped up, startled, and grabbed her shoes, too unsettled to think of putting them on. "Your dock?" She'd thought the house was closed up. She hadn't seen any lights on in it for days and she'd never considered who might own it. The dock had always been deserted. She'd been coming here for several days to enjoy the minnows and the view of the lake.

"Yes, my dock," he said angrily. His hands were shoved deep in the pockets of his tan pants. He wore a brown designer polo shirt, which emphasized the muscles in his chest and arms.

"I—I'm sorry," she stammered, her face turning bright red. "I didn't think anybody lived here…"

"Funny girl," he shot back. "Mamie knows that I'm here three months of the year. You knew."

"I didn't," she bit off, feeling tears threaten all over again. She moved away from him. "Sorry," she added. "I'm sorry. I didn't know…"

"I come here to get away from people, reporters, telephones that never stop ringing. I don't want my privacy invaded by cheap little girls in cheap dresses," he added insolently, sneering at her off-the-rack dress.

Her lower lip trembled. Tears threatened. But her injured pride wouldn't let that insult go by unaddressed. "My dress may be cheap, Mr. Sinclair, but I am not." She lifted her chin. "I go to church every Sunday!"

Something flashed in the eyes she could barely see. "Church!" he scoffed. "Religion is the big lie. Sin all week, then go to confession. Sit in a pew on Sunday and hop from one bed to another the rest of the week."

She just stared at him. "From what I hear, bed-hopping is your choice of hobbies. It is not mine."

He laughed shortly. "Women will do anything for a price."

As if in answer to that cynical remark, a beautiful brunette in a fashionable dress stuck her head out the door of his lake house. "Connor, do hurry," she fussed. "The soufflé is getting cold!"

"Coming." He gave Emma's dress a speaking look. "Did you get that from a thrift shop?" he asked insolently.

"Actually, I bought it off a sale rack. And for a very good price."

"It looks cheap."

"It is cheap."

"Stay off my dock," he said coldly.

"Don't worry, I'll never walk this way again," she murmured as she turned to leave.

"If you take that speedboat on the lake again, you pay attention to where you're driving it. The lake police will be watching."

She didn't turn around. Her stiff little back told its own story.

"Impudent upstart," he muttered.

"Overbearing pig."

She thought she heard amused laughter behind her, but she didn't turn around. She kept on walking.

Mamie looked up as Emma walked into the living room. The house was two stories high, overlooking the lake. It had a grace and beauty much like Mamie herself. It seemed to blend effortlessly into its surroundings. She was smiling, but the smile faded when she saw the younger woman's face. It was flushed, and traces of tears marred her lovely complexion.

"What's wrong, sugar?" she asked gently.

Emma drew in a breath. "I didn't know Connor Sinclair owned the house down the shore," she said. "I've been sitting on the dock, dangling my feet off the edge. He caught me at it and ordered me off the property."

Mamie grimaced. "I'm sorry, I should have told you. He spoke to you at the party, about the boat, didn't he?"

"Yes, if you can call threats and intimidation a conversation," she replied with a wan smile. "I wasn't being reckless at all. I just didn't see the Jet Ski. It came out of nowhere."

"You have to anticipate that people on Jet Skis do crazy things. So do other motorboat drivers. We had a tragedy here on the lake a few years back. A speeding motorboat hit a houseboat and killed two people."

"How horrible!"

"The driver had been drinking. He was arrested and charged, but the passengers on the boat were still dead."

"I'll be more careful," Emma promised. She grimaced. "I don't understand why he dislikes me so much," she murmured absently. "He was horrible to me at the party. And he looks at me as if he hates me," she added.

Mamie had a feeling about that, but she wasn't going to say what it was. She only smiled. "I'll have a dock built on the lake, just for you, sweetheart, so you can dangle your little feet." Mamie's was one of the few homes on the lake that didn't boast a private dock. Emma had to drive Mamie's car over to the marina to use the boat. Or walk, if Mamie was away, as she often was, since Mamie was eccentric and only kept one luxury car at her lake house. It wasn't that much of a walk for someone as young and athletic as Emma was.

Emma laughed. "You don't have to go to that trouble. I'll walk over to the marina and dangle my feet off the docks there. It isn't as if I can do it much longer, anyway. It's October already."

"With your luck, the dock you choose at the marina will be the one where Connor keeps his sailboat." Mamie chuckled. "Docks don't cost that much—they're mostly empty drums with planking on top. I'll have someone see about it next week." She waved Emma's protests away, then said, "Come on in here, will you, honey? I want to dictate some chaotic thoughts and see if you can inspire me to put them into an understandable form."

"I'll be happy to," Emma replied.

"Who was the girl on the dock?" Ariel asked as she and Connor shared the overcooked soufflé she'd taken out of the oven.

"One of the new generation," he said coldly. "And that's all I want to say about her."

She sighed. "Whatever you say, darling. Are we going out tonight?"

"Where do you want to go?" he asked, giving up his hope of a quiet night with a good book and a whiskey sour.

"The Crystal Bear," she said at once, naming a new and trendy place on the outskirts of Atlanta, near Duluth, where the main attraction was a huge bear carved from crystal and a house band that was the talk of the town. The food wasn't bad, either. Not that he cared much for any of it. But he'd humor Ariel. She was beginning to get on his nerves. He gave her slender body a brief appraisal and found himself uninterested. He'd felt that way for several days. Ever since that little blonde pirate had almost run into him on the Jet Ski and he'd given her hell for it at Mamie's party.

The girl was unusual. Beautiful in a way that had little to do with her looks. He'd seen her, from the porch of his lake house, usually when she didn't see him. There had been a little girl who'd wandered up on the beach. The blonde woman—what was the name Mamie had called her? He couldn't remember—had seen her, bent to comfort her, taken the child up in her arms and cuddled her close, drying her tears. He'd seen her walking back down the beach, apparently in search of the missing parent.

The sight had disturbed him. He didn't want children,

ever. Countless women had tried to convince him, practically
trick him into it, for a decade, but he was always careful. He
used condoms, despite assurances that they were on the pill.
He was always wary because he was filthy rich. Women were
out to ensnare him. A child would be a responsibility that
he didn't want, plus it also meant expensive support for the
child's mother. He wasn't walking into that trap. He'd seen
what had happened to his only brother, who lived in misery
because of a greedy woman who'd gotten pregnant for no
other reason than to trap him into a loveless marriage. That
marriage, his brother's, had ended in death, on this very lake.
It chilled him to remember the circumstances. The blonde
woman brought it all back.

Still, the sight of the blonde woman with the child close in
her arms, her long, shiny hair wafting in the breeze, made him
hungry for things he didn't understand. She had no money,
and wasn't even that pretty. It puzzled him that he should have
such an immediate response to her. That night, at the party,
he'd stared at her, hungered for her, wanted her.

He'd made her cry, frightened her with his reckless anger.
He hadn't meant to. She didn't seem like other women he
knew who pretended tears to get things. Her tears had been
genuine, like her fear of him. He'd been shocked when she
backed away from him. It had been a long time—years—since
anyone had done that. And never a woman.

Then he'd found her sitting on his dock, laughing as she
dangled her feet in the water. The sight had hit him in the
heart so hard that it had ignited his temper all over again.
He had no need of this blonde woman. He had Ariel, bright
and beautiful, who would do anything he asked, because he
showered her with the expensive diamonds she loved.

The blonde in the cheap dress had been wearing even
cheaper jewelry. Her shoes had been scuffed and old. But she
had a regal pride. It amused him to recall her cold defense of

her morals. Which were of no concern to himself, he thought, and promptly shut her out of his mind.

Mamie called Emma to her office a few mornings later as she was sealing the last of several envelopes that contained the neat little notes Emma had typed and printed for her. Mamie had just finished signing them.

"I would have done that for you," Emma protested.

"Of course you would, but I had some time." She put the envelopes in a neat stack. "You can stamp them and put the address labels on. Here's the thing, sweetie, I'm going to be away for about two or three months. A sheikh has invited me to stay at his palace and see the sights in Qawi with his family. We'll watch horse races, attend cultural events all over the Middle East, even spend some time on the Riviera in Monaco and Nice on the way home. Do you want to stay here or go home to your dad?"

Emma swallowed. "Well…"

"You're welcome to stay here," she said gently, because she knew how Emma's father treated her. Emma had often lived with another family in Texas, but she'd said that she didn't want to impose on them. "I know how much you hate to travel. It's why I've never taken you overseas. But you'd be doing me a favor actually, because I wouldn't have to close up the lake house. What do you think?"

"I'd love that!"

Mamie smiled. "I thought you might. Okay. You know what to do. You can drive the speedboat, too, but no speeding," she added firmly. "You don't want to make Connor angry. Really, you don't."

Emma frowned at her employer. There was something odd about the way she'd said it.

Mamie sat down and folded her hands in her lap. "I wasn't always a famous author," she began. "I started out as a news-

paper reporter on a small weekly paper. From there I moved to
entertainment magazines, doing feature stories on famous people." She grimaced. "One of them was Connor Sinclair. His best
friend—who turned out to only be a distant acquaintance—had
assured me that he had Connor's permission to tell me things
about his private life. So I quoted the man as my source and
ran the story."

"This sounds as though it ended unhappily," Emma said
when her companion was very quiet.

"It did. The man who gave me the quotes was a business
rival who hated Connor and saw an opportunity to get even
for a business account he lost. Most of what he told me was
true, but Connor's fanatical about his privacy. I didn't know
that until it was too late. Long story short, the magazine fired
me to keep him from suing."

"Oh, no."

"It was a bad time," Mamie recalled quietly. "I was just divorced, with no money of my own. I depended on that job to
keep my bills paid and a roof over my head. I landed another
job, with a rival magazine, a couple of weeks later. Luckily
for me, that publisher didn't like Connor and wasn't going
to be forced into putting me on the street for what another
magazine printed."

"He tried to have you fired from that job, too?" Emma
asked, aghast at the man's taste for vengeance.

"Yes, he did. So when I tell you to be careful about deal-
ing with him, I'm not kidding," Mamie concluded. "I would
never fire you, no matter what he threatened. But I still work
for publishers who can be threatened."

"I see your point," she said quietly. "I won't make an enemy
of him. I'll make sure I stay out of his way from now on."

"Good girl," Mamie said gently. "You're very special,
Emma. I trust you, which is more than I can say about most

people I know. I wanted children, but my husband didn't."
She smiled sadly. "It's just as well, the way things turned out."

"Why is Mr. Sinclair so bitter?" Emma asked suddenly. "I
mean, he never smiles and he's always upset about something
or someone. It just seems odd to me."

"He lost his brother, his only sibling, in an accident on this
lake. A drunk driver in a boat hit him and his wife in their
houseboat and left the scene. They both died." She swallowed. "Connor spent a fortune, they say, searching for the
man's location for the police. He was prosecuted and sent to
prison. He's still there."

"Did the drunk man have family?"

Mamie nodded. "A wife and a little girl. They lost their
home, their income… The child had to go to social services.
The mother ended up dead of a drug overdose. It was a tragic
story, all the way around."

"Life is so hard for children," Emma murmured, thinking
of the poor little girl. Connor Sinclair was vindictive.

"It is." Mamie looked around. "Well, I'd better be on my
way. Come help me pack, Emma. I have a couple of evening
dresses I want to give you. They're too small for me, and
they'll suit you very well."

"I never go anywhere to wear evening dresses." Emma
laughed. "But thank you very much for the thought."

Mamie glanced at her. "You should be dating, meeting
men, thinking about starting a family."

"I haven't met anyone I felt that way about, except Steven."
She shuddered. "I thought he was the perfect man. Now I'm
not sure I'll trust my judgment about a man ever again."

"You'll get over it in time, honey," Mamie said, a gentle
smile on her face. "There are plenty of handsome, eligible
men in the world, and you have a kind heart. You don't think
so right now, but men are going to want you, Emma. That
nurturing nature is something most men can't resist. They

don't care as much for physical beauty as they do for someone who's willing to sit up with them when they're sick and
feed them cough syrup." She grinned.

Emma laughed, as she was meant to. "Well, one day.
Maybe."

Mamie left in a whirlwind of activity, met by a stretch limousine with a stately driver in a suit and tie. She gave Emma a
handful of last-minute chores, a research assignment to complete for her next book and an admonition to be careful about
going out after dark. Her parting shot was to stay off the lake
in the speedboat until Connor went to his home in the south
of France as he did most years just before Christmas.

Emma promised to be careful, but no more. The speedboat had become her solace. When she was out on the lake,
with the wind blowing through her long hair and the spray of
the water on her face, she felt alive as she'd never felt before.

She hadn't told Mamie, but she was still wounded by Steven's
rejection several years later. She'd been too wounded to ever trust
another man. She'd felt close to Steven, felt a sense of belong-
ing to someone for the first time in her young life. His rejection
had been painful. She'd always been shy, lacked self-confidence.
Now she distrusted her own judgment about people. Steven had
seemed so perfect. But he had prejudices she hadn't known about.

Ideals were worthwhile, certainly, but it had been her father's choice of vocations that had alienated him. He hadn't
considered that she might not feel as her father did. He simply walked away, without a backward glance.

For several weeks, she hoped that he might call or write,
that he might apologize for making assumptions about her.
But he hadn't. In desperation, she'd written to a former girlfriend in San Antonio, where Steven had moved to, a mutual
friend from high school. The friend told her that Steven was
involved with a new organization—a radical animal rights

group, much larger than the one he'd belonged to when Emma knew him. He and his friend were apparently still living together, too. Neither of them dated anybody. Steven said that he was never going back to Jacobsville, though. That was when Emma finally gave up. She wasn't going to have that happy ending so beloved by tellers of fairy tales. Not with Steven, anyway. She walked idly through the woods, a stick held loosely in her hand. She touched it to the tops of autumn weeds as she walked, lost in thought.

She almost walked straight into the big man before she saw him. She jumped back as though he'd struck out at her. Her heart was beating a mad rhythm. She felt breathless, frightened, heartsick. All those emotions vied for supremacy in her wide brown eyes.

She bit her lower lip. "I'm sorry," she said at once, almost cringing at the sudden fierce anger in his broad face.

His hands were jammed deep in his trouser pockets. He was wearing a beige shirt with tan slacks, and he looked, as usual, out of sorts.

He glared at her from pale glittering gray eyes, assessing her, finding her wanting. His opinion of her long brown checked cotton dress with its white T-shirt underneath was less than flattering.

"Well, we can't all afford Saks," she said defensively.

He lifted an eyebrow. "Some of us can't even afford a decent thrift shop, either, judging by appearances," he returned.

She stood on the narrow path through the woods that led to the lake. "I wasn't trespassing," she blurted out, reddening. "Mamie owns up to that colored ribbon on the stake, there." She pointed to the property line.

He cocked his head and stared at her. He hated her youth, her freshness, her lack of artifice. He hated her very innocence, because it was so obvious that it was unmistakable. His whole life had been one endless parade of perfumed, perfectly coifed women endlessly trying to get whatever they could out of him. Here was a stiff, upright little Puritan with a raised fist.

"You're always alone," he said absently.

"So are you," she blurted out, and then bit her tongue at her own forwardness.

Broad shoulders lifted and fell. "I got tired of bouncing soufflés, so I sent her home," he said coolly.

She frowned, searching his face. He showed his age in a way that many older men didn't. He pushed himself too hard. She knew without asking that he never took vacations, never celebrated holidays, that he carried work home every night and stayed on the phone until he was finally weary enough to sleep. Business was his whole life. He might have women in his life, but their influence ended at the bedroom door. And nobody got close, ever.

"Can you cook?" he asked suddenly.

"Of course."

He raised an eyebrow.

"My father has a little cattle ranch in Texas," she said hesitantly. "My mother died when I was only eight. I had to learn to cook."

"At the age of eight?" he asked, surprised.

She nodded. Suddenly she felt cold and wrapped her arms around her body. "I was taught that hard work drives out frivolous thoughts."

He scowled. "Any brothers, sisters?"

She shook her head.

"Just you and the rancher."

She nodded. "He wanted a boy," she blurted out. "He said girls were useless."

His hands, stuffed in his pockets, clenched. He was getting a picture he didn't like of her life. He didn't want to know anything about her. He found her distasteful, irritating. He should turn around and go back to his lake house.

"You had a little girl with you a few days ago," he said, startling her. "She was lost."

She smiled slowly, and it changed her. Those soft brown eyes almost glowed. "She belongs to a friend of Mamie's, a young woman from Provence who's over here with her husband on a business trip. They're staying at a friend's cabin. The little girl wandered over here, looking for Mamie."

"Provence? France?"

"Yes."

"And do you speak French, cowgirl?" he asked.

*"Je ne parle pas trés bien, mais, oui,"* she replied.

He cocked his head, and for a few seconds, his pale eyes were less hostile. "You studied it in high school, I suppose?"

"Yes. We had to take a foreign language. I already spoke Spanish, so French was something new."

"Spanish?"

"My father had several cowboys who were from Mexico. Immigrants," he began, planning to mention that his grandfather was one.

"Their families were here before the first settlers made it to Texas," she said, absently defending them.

His pale eyes narrowed. "I didn't mean it that way. I was going to say that my grandfather was an immigrant." He cocked his head. "You don't like even the intimation of prejudice, do you?"

She shifted on her feet. "They were like family to me," she said. "My father was hard as nails. He wouldn't even give a man time off to go to a funeral." She shifted again. "He said work came first, family second."

"Charming," he said and it was pure sarcasm.

"So all the affection I ever had was from people who worked for him." She smiled, reminiscing. "Dolores cooked for the bunkhouse crew. She taught me to cook and sew, and she bought me the first dress I ever owned." Her face hardened. "My father threw it away. He said it was trashy, like Dolores. I said she was the least trashy person I knew and he…" She swallowed. "The next day, she was gone. Just like that."

He moved a step closer. "You hesitated. What did your father do?"

She bit her lower lip. "He said I deserved it…"

"What did he do?"

"He drew back his fist and knocked me down," she said, lowering her face in shame. "Dolores's husband saw it through the window. He came in to protect me. He knocked my father down. So my father fired Dolores and him. Because of me."

He didn't move closer, but she felt the anger emanating from him. "He would have found another reason for doing it," he said after a minute.

"He didn't like them being friendly to me." She sighed. "I felt so bad. They had kids who were in school with me, and the kids had to go to another school where Pablo found work. Dolores tried to write to me, but my father tore up the letter and burned it, so I couldn't even see the return address."

"You should have gone with them," he said flatly.

She smiled sadly. "I tried to. He locked me in my room." She looked up with soft, sad eyes. "Mamie reminds me of Dolores. She has a kind heart, too."

There was an odd vibrating sound. She frowned, looking around.

He held up the cell phone he'd kept in his pocket. He glared at it, turned the vibrate function off and put it back in his pocket. "If I answer it, there's a crisis I have to solve. If I don't answer it, there will be two crises that cost me a small fortune because I didn't answer it."

"I don't even own a cell phone," she said absently. It was true—Mamie paid for hers.

How would she pay for one, he almost said out loud. But he didn't want to hurt her. Life had done a good job of that, from what he'd heard.

He nodded toward the sky. "It will be dark soon," he said. "You shouldn't be out alone at night."

She managed a smile. "That's what Mamie says. I'm going in."

She turned, a little reluctantly, because he wasn't quite the ogre she thought he was.

All the way down the path, she felt his eyes on her. But he didn't say another word.

# TWO

Emma wondered about Connor Sinclair. She was curious why he was so angry, because she saw it in him, felt it in him. She didn't want to think about him so much. He disturbed her, fascinated her, in ways she didn't understand. Probably, it was because he was so hostile toward her. It had to be that.

Tired of the lake house, she walked to the marina and got into Mamie's speedboat. Nobody saw her leave, but then, she had the key and she could come and go whenever she wanted to.

It was a beautiful early October morning. All around the lake, mostly trimmed with pine trees, a few hardwoods were beginning to show their lovely fall colors. The leaves turned more slowly here, in the foothills of the Appalachian Mountains. Up in North Carolina, people said, the leaf season was in full swing, attracting tourists from all over the piedmont. Around the North Georgia lake where Mamie's house was situated, the maples were going to be glorious in their reds and golds. This was Emma's favorite season. She loved the bright beginnings of the season, the many different shades that combined to turn the whole world bright and new in its last feverish gasp before winter.

She turned the boat toward the wide-open part of the lake and revved it up. She laughed as the wind blew her hair back, bit into her face, made her feel alive and young, as if the whole world was hers.

The sun was low on the horizon, making a bright trail in the water as she whirled the boat and sent it spinning toward the distant shoreline. It was so early that nobody was on the lake. She had it all to herself. She could step on the gas and never have to worry—

There was a horrible scraping sound, a horrible jolt that shook the boat and Emma.

"Damn it!"

The angry curse came out of nowhere, like the Jet Ski that she hadn't seen in the brilliance of the morning sun that blinded her for just a few seconds.

She let off the gas, shaking from the collision and fear of what she'd done. She stood up in the boat, her eyes searching the water around her. There was a Jet Ski on the side of the boat toward the small cove.

"Oh, no, oh, no!" she cried. "I'm sorry!"

There was no answer. The Jet Ski revved and headed toward the distant dock. She knew at once whom she'd hit, and her blood froze. But he seemed to be all right. He got to the dock, and climbed off the Jet Ski. He sat there, seemingly disoriented, and called to someone.

As Emma watched, three people spilled out of the huge, luxurious lake house and ran toward him.

Unseen by the people in the cove, Emma eased the boat into motion and moved it back toward the marina. Her heart was racing like mad. She'd hit Connor Sinclair. He'd be out for her blood. He'd warned her. He'd threatened her. When he found out who'd hit him, she'd have no safe place to hide in the whole world.

She had no place to run. She couldn't go home. Her father would want to know why she'd come, why he wasn't getting the money she was supposed to send him every month. He'd be furious. Mamie was overseas and she'd called just once to tell Emma that she'd be in places where she wouldn't have cell phone service for a few days.

Emma had all of a hundred dollars in her bank account and less than two hundred in savings. Not nearly enough to run and hide from a multimillionaire who'd want her arrested.

She drove the boat back to the marina, aware that it had a dent on one side where it had hit the Jet Ski. It was a sturdy boat. It didn't seem any the worse for the collision. She drove it into the slip and got out, pausing to ask the custodian if the boat could be dry-docked, because Mamie was going to be away for the rest of the year and it was turning cold.

The older man smiled and said of course they could, and did she want him to beat out that dent in the hull? She smiled back, very calmly, and said that would be very kind; she'd hit a stump in the water too close to a cove.

That happened more often than folks realized, he said, chuckling. When the dam was built, and the land flooded, which created Lake Lanier, many trees had been covered with the water that became the lake. He'd do the work and send Mamie the bill, he promised.

Emma walked back to the lake house, prepared to find the lake police on the front porch waiting for her.

But they weren't. She spent a sleepless night worrying about it, waiting for it. Connor Sinclair was her worst enemy. He'd never stop until he made her pay for what she'd done.

She hated her own cowardice. She was hiding from him, from retribution, from punishment. She hoped he wasn't badly hurt, but what if he was?

On the second day after the incident, she got up enough nerve to call his lake house. It wasn't listed under his name, just under its own designation: Pine Cottage. Only local people knew it was Connor Sinclair's home.

Emma called the number and let it ring. Her heart was running wild as it rang once, twice, three times, four...

She was about to hang up when a female voice answered.

"Pine Cottage," she said, using the name local people gave the sprawling vacation home.

"Is Mr. Sinclair available?" she asked in her most business-like tone.

"Connor?" the woman replied. "Oh, no, he's at the hospital. He fell off the Jet Ski and hit his head. Poor thing, he has no idea how it happened...is this Jewell?"

"No, this is Adrian Merrell's personal assistant. Mr. Merrell was hoping to speak to Mr. Sinclair about an upcoming conference they're both attending," she lied.

"Merrell? I've heard that name. No matter, Connor won't be going anywhere anytime soon, I'm afraid."

"I'm very sorry to hear about his accident. I'll tell Mr. Merrell. Thank you. Goodbye."

She hung up. Connor was alive. He'd hit his head. Why wouldn't he be going anywhere soon? Emma groaned as she wondered just how much damage she'd done. There hadn't been anybody on the lake, she was certain of it!

But the sun had been in her eyes. She'd been daydreaming, not paying attention. How could she not have realized where she was, whose cove she was near? She could have cried at her lack of good sense, at her own recklessness. She hadn't meant to hurt him. But would that matter in the end?

She agonized about it for the rest of the week. On her walks, she got near enough to the big house to tell that people were still coming and going. There didn't seem to be any frenetic activity. She didn't see lake police or ambulances there. Perhaps he knew it had been Emma who hit him, though, and he was just biding his time, waiting to let her worry about what he was going to do about the accident.

She finally realized that it was doing no good to wear ruts in Mamie's carpet. She was hiding, like a coward. Whatever the consequences, she had to apologize and beg him not to press charges. She'd offer to work for him, free, to do anything within reason to help make up for injuring him. Surely he'd realize that she hadn't done it maliciously. Then she recalled his warnings, his anger at her for earlier near-misses. He wasn't going to be merciful. He'd want blood.

But hiding wasn't helping her, either. She was a nervous wreck. She might as well face the music. She didn't want Mamie to suffer for something that was her own fault. However painful, she had to face the music.

She walked slowly toward Pine Cottage. It was late afternoon on Saturday. There were boats scattered on the lake. The sailboats were elegant and beautiful. Emma loved to look at them. She wondered if Mr. Sinclair ever sailed. Mamie had said that he owned a sailboat. If only he'd been in it the previous week, and not on that stupid Jet Ski—

"Oh!" she exclaimed as she almost ran right into a huge man standing on the lakeshore. "I'm so sorry."

Her voice caught in her throat as she met Connor Sinclair's pale, glittering silver eyes. She bit her lower lip. She'd forgotten how dangerous he was. That cold gaze brought it all back. He'd probably call the police as soon as she told him what she'd done.

"My fault," he returned. "I can't see you."

"You can't…see…me?" she gasped. The horror of what she'd done made every muscle in her slender body clench. She'd blinded him. She'd blinded him!

He shrugged. "Concussion," he said, turning toward the lake as if he could see it. "I fell off a Jet Ski and hit my head. Or so they say. I don't remember any of it. They said it was a miracle that I made it back to the dock at all."

"I'm…so sorry," she choked. "Your sight…will it come back?"

"They don't know. Five thousand dollars' worth of tests to tell me that they're not sure if I'll see again. No more Jet Skis, for sure. Either way."

She paused beside him. "I thought Jet Skis were dangerous," she began.

"They are. I like dangerous things," he said curtly. "Skydiving, race cars, testing planes, Jet Skis," he added with a faint smile. "I had my housekeeper lead me down here. I'll have to find my own way back. As I said," he added whimsically, "I like dangerous things."

"Why?"

Both thick eyebrows went up. He turned toward her voice. "What the hell do you mean, why?"

"Life is precious," she said.

"Life is tedious, monotonous, maddening and joyless," he shot back. "It's hard, and then you die."

"You stole that line from a retro television show," she accused involuntarily, with a muffled laugh, and then flushed.

But he chuckled, surprised. "Yes, I did. *Dempsey and Makepeace*; you can find reruns of it on YouTube."

Then he frowned. "Who are you, and why are you here?"

She had to think fast. Confession was good for the soul, she thought, but not yet. "I'm staying with a girlfriend for a couple of weeks. I'm sort of in between jobs. I got lost. I thought her cabin was this way, but nothing looks familiar here."

"What do you do for a living?"

"Brain surgery," she said pertly. "I took this mail-order course…"

He burst out laughing.

She was surprised, because he was a man who hardly knew how to laugh.

"Pull the other one," he invited.

She grinned. "Okay. In my spare time, I make custom harnesses for frogs. So you can walk them."

He let out a breath, and grinned. "What do you do?" he persisted.

She shrugged. "I'm a copy typist for a law firm. Or I was."

"Why?"

"I was made redundant. Laid off sounds better, though." She glanced at him. "It's getting dark. Should you be out here by yourself when you can't see? The lake is very deep."

"Should you be out by yourself when you're lost?" he shot back.

"No, I shouldn't," she said. "But you shouldn't, either."

"Want to lead me to my door?" he invited.

"I might as well. At least you're not lost," she added.

He held out his hand.

Odd, how it felt to hold his hand, to feel the warm strength of that big, beautiful hand against her skin. She had to fight to keep her confusion from showing.

"Where do you live?" she asked, because she wasn't supposed to know.

"Pine Cottage. There's a sign."

She let out a breath. "Oh, it's there. I see it."

He hesitated. She tugged, just gently.

"It's this way," she said softly, letting him catch up without making an issue of it. She walked very slowly, very carefully, so that he was on the path and didn't walk into obstacles like rocks that could throw him off balance. "Three steps," she said. "This is the first one."

He went up them with no seeming difficulty and stopped. "You're quite good at this."

"I practice on little old ladies who can't find their glasses," she returned, tongue in cheek.

He smiled. It wasn't a cold, formal or social smile, either. And he hadn't let go of her hand.

"Who are you?" he asked.

"The Energizer Bunny?" she suggested.

"Try again."

"I'm Emma," she said, having fought the impulse not to lie to him. But there had to be a zillion women named Emma. He wouldn't connect her. He probably didn't even know her name. He'd have no reason to want to know it. He'd connected her with the near-miss on the Jet Ski before Mamie's party, when she'd been driving the boat, but that was just physical recognition. Mamie had said that he didn't know Emma except as her assistant. He hadn't asked for her name.

"Emma what?" he asked.

"Copeland," she replied.

His lips pursed. "Think you could find your way back here?"

She hesitated. "I found it because I was lost."

"I'm having Barnes drive you home," he said surprisingly. "He can pick you up where he drops you off, yes?"

Her heart was racing. "Why would I want to be picked up?"

"Breakfast," he said simply.

"Breakfast?"

"Eggs, bacon, pancakes…strong black coffee," he added.

"My friend has Pop-Tarts." She groaned.

He grinned. "Eggs, bacon, pancakes—"

"Don't! You're torturing me! What time?"

"Eight a.m."

"Okay."

"You don't sleep late?"

"I go to bed at nine," she said. "Eight a.m. is late to me."

He chuckled. "Fair enough. I'll see you soon, Emma."

"Who are you?" she asked, because she couldn't give herself away. Not yet.

"Connor."

"Connor. It's nice."

"I'm not," he cautioned, his silver eyes flashing at her.

"Pop-Tarts might not be so bad…" she began.

He grinned. "I'll try to be nice. Just for breakfast."

"Okay."

"Barnes!" he called.

A short, older man came in, smiling. "Yes, sir?"

"Take Emma back to her roommate," he said, indicating Emma. "And make sure you remember where you drop her, so you can pick her up in the morning and bring her back for breakfast."

"Yes, sir. Are you ready to go, Miss Emma?" he asked in his slow, sweet Georgia drawl.

"I am."

"Good night, Emma," Connor said with a smile.

"Good night."

She had Barnes drop her off at the Frenchwoman's house. She waved him off and then asked Jeanne Marie if it was all right that she pretended to live there. She couldn't explain, she added, but she promised it was nothing illegal or immoral.

Jeanne laughed and said of course it was all right. When Emma told her about the next morning's appointment, Jeanne said that was fine, as well. She was curious. Emma just blushed, and Jeanne asked no more questions.

All night, Emma agonized about going to breakfast at Connor's. It seemed like a sound idea, to get to know him, just a little, and then confess what she'd done. If he knew her, he might not jump to conclusions that she'd hit him on purpose.

But it was risky, just the same. She couldn't go back to her father. She couldn't go to her friends in Jacobsville, either, without putting them in the line of fire. She knew they wouldn't mind, but they'd already done enough for her.

At eight the next morning, she got into the expensive sedan with Barnes at the wheel and let him take her to Pine Cottage.

"Eggs, bacon, pancakes," she enthused as she walked into the dining room and took a long sniff. "What a delicious smell!"

Connor was sitting there at the head of the table, his broad face smiling, his head cocked slightly to one side. He wore a green polo shirt with tan slacks and deck shoes. He looked expensive and so sexy that he made Emma's toes curl.

But those thoughts were destructive. He was just a man she'd met on the lake. That was all he could ever be.

"It tastes as good as it smells," he assured her. "Edward has cooked for me for over a decade, but he didn't want to live on a lake in Georgia. So I left him at my house on the Riviera years ago and hired Marie," he indicated an older woman with silver hair and a bright smile, "who has a way with herbs and spices."

Emma started to pull out a chair for herself when Barnes came out of nowhere to do it for her. "Miss," he said politely, bowing.

"Thanks," she replied shyly.

"Barnes practically came with the property." Connor chuckled. "His mother kept house for my father, on his rare visits here." His face tautened, as if the memory wasn't a pleasant one.

"It's true," Barnes said, smiling. His eyes twinkled. "He's a terrible boss," he added suddenly. "You should see him when he loses his temper."

"Shut up while you still have a job," Connor muttered, but his eyes were twinkling, too. He waved a hand. "Go build something."

Barnes winked at Emma and left, grinning.

Connor chuckled. "He weaves baskets as a hobby. He picks up vines out of the woods and twists them into all sorts of

shapes. There's one of his on a side table. Over there, I think."
He indicated an elegant-looking basket on a side table.

"It's really beautiful," she said, surprised. Her knowledge
of baskets was scanty, but that one looked professional.

"He could make a living with them if he wanted to," he
said. "He has his own website. He sells to designers all across
the country." He shook his head. "When he makes his first
million, I'll have to have a stranger drive me everywhere." He
raised his voice. "I'll probably be killed in a horrible wreck!"

"I will never make millions!" Barnes called back. "And if
I do, I'll still drive you!"

"Okay," Connor called back. His sightless eyes were twinkling. Barnes threw up a hand and went out the back door.

"He drove me mad at first. But I tend to get moody. I don't
like strangers in my house, as a rule."

She fingered her empty coffee cup and remained quiet.

"I didn't mean you, if that's what the silence is about," he
mused.

She laughed softly. "Okay."

He looked in the direction of her voice. "Well? Are you
pouring coffee or meditating on it?" he chided.

"I, well, I wasn't sure if you said grace or..."

"Grace?"

Her eyes widened at the venom in his tone.

His pale eyes glittered with bad humor. "I'm not much on
religion. Just pour the coffee. And if you want to say grace,
say it silently, please," he added curtly.

She didn't know what else to do. She nodded. Then she
realized that he couldn't see her, and guilt washed over her
like a wave.

"Well?" he prompted, his tone cutting.

"Sorry. Coffee?"

"Obviously I want coffee. Hence the empty mug right
here." He fumbled for it and rattled it.

"You are a very unpleasant man!" she pointed out.

"And I work hard at it, too."

She grimaced as she poured his coffee.

He reached for it, managed it on the second try and lifted it to his mouth. "I want bacon and eggs. No pancakes."

She got up and ladled them onto a plate. She put the plate down in front of him, caught his big hand and put a fork in it. "Bacon at three o'clock, eggs at nine o'clock. Buttered toast?" she added.

"I don't eat much bread." He dug into his breakfast, downed a swallow of eggs and coffee and put the cup down. "How did you learn to do that?" he asked.

"What?"

"The positions on the plate."

"Oh. We had a blind lady who went to our church. I used to sit with her when we had picnics. She taught me. That was how she managed her food. She was eighty-six and she could ride a bike and play the piano. I was very fond of her."

He finished eating, then leaned back with a sigh and pursed his lips. "Did she teach you anything else about blind people?"

"That you never grab them. It disconcerts them." She told him about the guide dog the woman had, and her determination to learn Braille.

He was smiling faintly. "You learned a lot."

"I listened," she said simply. "People mostly don't listen. They want to tell you about themselves, they want to discuss the latest vote on the reality shows and the latest fashions." She sighed. "I never cared about those things. I don't watch much television."

"I listen to the news. I don't follow anything except the stock market."

There was a brief, companionable silence while she finished her coffee.

"You said you were in between jobs."

"Just briefly. I'm going to put my name down with one of the temporary agencies in Gainesville…"

"Come work for me."

She almost dropped the cup. "What?"

"Come work for me," he repeated. "I have secretaries in all my corporate offices, but I don't have a private secretary. Administrative assistant. Whatever the hell you call it. Someone to take dictation, answer the phone, make appointments and see to it that I keep them. Things like that. I used to have the Atlanta office send someone up, but I don't want my condition to get around."

She knew what he meant. Any bad news about his health would probably drop stock prices. People gossiped.

So he was offering her a job. She didn't dare. She couldn't. But she wanted to. "For how long?" she asked breathlessly.

"We'll give it a month's probation to see if we suit each other. How about that?" he asked, and his face tensed, as if her reply really mattered.

She smiled. A man like him wouldn't care whether she said yes or no. It would be insane to agree. If he ever found out who she was, if he ever recognized her voice…

On the other hand, she could help him, take care of him, try to make up for what she'd done to him. It pained her to realize the price he'd paid for her stupidity. If only she'd never gotten behind the wheel of the stupid boat, if only she'd looked where she was going!

"Well?" he prompted curtly.

"I…I would like to," she heard herself saying with absolute horror. It was nuts!

His face relaxed. He drew in a breath. "Fine. You'll live in. Marie can show you to a bedroom later and help you get settled." He named a salary that was six times what Mamie paid her.

She blanched. Her gasp was audible.

"Not enough?" he chided.

"Not enough?" she burst out. "I don't make that much in a year!"

"You'll earn it," he said, and his pale eyes twinkled faintly. "I'm a difficult man, Emma. You may wish you'd said no."

"If you get too troublesome, I'll push you headfirst into the lake and use my alligator whistle."

He thought for a minute, and then burst out laughing. "If you can find an alligator in any North Georgia lake, I'll double your salary," he mused. "All right. We'll give it a month."

The first few days were hectic. There was a learning curve, because he wasn't as flighty as some of her bosses had been. He was studious, methodical, exacting and sometimes maddening. He wanted files in a certain order. He wanted letters done exactly as he said, even if they weren't always polite. He wanted routine in everything. Emma found it exasperating.

"You're making that sound again," he said curtly from his desk. "Now what?"

"I feel like I need to ask permission to change my clothes," she muttered. "Organization. Heavens! I've never been able to organize anything in my life. I'm too scatterbrained."

"You'll learn. You can pretend you're in the military."

"I'm not going on military time, and I'm not saluting you," she shot back.

He chuckled. "Okay."

"You've got two thousand unanswered emails," she added.

"Go through them and delete the ads. That should get rid of ninety percent."

"I need a program that does that automatically," she murmured.

"Then go online and download one," he said.

She almost sighed again, but he was looking surly this morning. "Yes, sir," she said instead.

"How sweet that sounds," he snarled.

"Sweet like vinegar, sir, the better to douse you with," she muttered.

He chuckled.

The phone rang and she answered it.

It was a woman. She asked for Connor. Emma had no idea who the woman actually was; she just handed the phone to Connor and went back to work.

There was a terse conversation. It ended with a short curse and the phone being slammed down on the desk.

"Don't ever put that woman through again, do you understand me, Emma?" he snapped.

"Yes, sir!" she said at once, reddening.

He ran a hand through his hair. "Damn women everywhere!" he cursed. "I gave her a mink and a Ferrari and a diamond the size of a hen egg, and she can't understand that it was to get her out of my hair!"

"Poor man, stalked by women, not safe even in his own home," Emma mused. "Perhaps we should build a fence."

"Damn it!" he exploded. He stood up, his eyes blazing, furious. "Do you think I'm kidding?"

She drew in her breath. He looked formidable when he lost his temper. She sat quietly, waiting for the rest of the explosion.

"She wants to make up," he snarled. "Which means she wants more presents from me, and she's willing to do anything, absolutely anything, to get back into my life. I would rather feed myself to a shark!"

She wanted so badly to invite him to, but that way lay disaster. She just sat still, like a statue.

"I don't want marriage. I don't want a family. I'm happy with my life just the way it is. She said that I needed a son to inherit what I've got. A son." He slammed his fist down on the desk and Emma jumped. "What she meant was that she wanted to get pregnant with my child and have me support her for the next eighteen years! No damned way!"

She didn't say a word.

"I've always been careful," he said through his teeth. "Always prepared. They said they were using birth control, but I never believed it. All my adult life, I've dodged women trying to trap me into marriage. All I wanted was brief affairs. They wanted forever. There is no forever!" he ground out. "Only damned fools believe there is!"

She was almost shivering now. The force of his rage was intimidating, even when he was sightless.

"And you put her through," he added, looking toward where he thought she might be. "You put her right through to me without asking if I wanted to talk to her. By God, you do that again, and I'll throw you out on the front lawn in your damned nightgown!"

She fought back tears.

"Do you understand? Talk to me!"

"I understand, Mr. Sinclair," she said shakily.

"Good!"

She tried to type, but her hands were shaking too hard.

"Get me some coffee," he snapped.

"Yes, sir." She got up from her chair, still wobbly. Her voice had sounded shaky.

"Emma!"

She stopped. "Yes, s–sir?" she stammered.

He hesitated. Frowned. "Emma, come here," he said in a tone like velvet, soft and gentle. "Come on."

She went to him slowly, disturbed and shivering.

He felt for her shoulder and pulled her suddenly right into his arms, folding her close to that warm, magnificent strength. She laid her cheek against his chest and the tears stained the fabric.

"You're crying," he chided. "Come on, Emma, I'm not an ogre."

"Yes, you are," she said through tears. "You're scary like one."

"So people tell me." He kissed her hair. She made him feel guilty. It had been ages since a woman had accomplished that. "Come on. Stop crying. I won't yell anymore."

"I didn't know who she was," she sobbed.

He held her closer, burying his face in her throat, petting the soft, long hair that ran down her shoulders. Then his big hands smoothed gently along her spine. "I didn't realize that." His mouth moved on her neck.

She gasped. Her heart raced. This close to him, she was feeling odd sensations, ripples of pleasure that she'd never experienced, not even with Steven. This man had a sensual magnetism that was uniquely his.

"You like this," he teased.

"Mr. Sinclair…" she protested.

He laughed, deep in his throat.

"I have to go…"

His cheek slid against hers. "Do you?" he whispered as his mouth moved close to hers, hovered over it.

"I should…" she choked.

"Should you?" he whispered.

She didn't know what to do. There had only been Steven in her life, and he'd barely touched her. Theirs had been a cerebral sort of relationship until he found out what her father did for a living and dumped her. She had no experience at all with the sort of flirting Connor was subjecting her to. She stiffened in his arms.

He drew back, his eyes narrowed. He wished that he could see her face. Her young body was stiff as a board. But her breath was fluttering at his collarbone. He could feel her heart beating like a butterfly. She was attracted to him. Very attracted, by the feel of her. But she was also frightened.

He frowned. "What are you afraid of, Emma?" he whispered.

Both her hands pressed against his broad chest, feeling the hard, warm muscle under his shirt. "Please," she faltered.

He let her go. He didn't seem to be angry anymore. He looked more puzzled than anything else.

She almost ran out of the room. But she didn't. She stood her ground. And went back to her desk.

# THREE

Emma took dictation on a letter he was writing to his attorney. She was barely aware of what she was writing down. It had upset her, that blatant, unbridled anger. But what had followed it had upset her even more.

She was vulnerable with him. It was surprising, because he was so much older than she was, almost a generation. But when he touched her, the years fell away. She felt far different with him than she'd ever felt with Steven, and it scared her.

She tried to tell herself that he was just very experienced with women. That was what it was. But there had to be an attraction in the first place. He'd been amused by her reactions, but then he'd gone silent. He was still silent, in between dictation. He was frowning, as if he was worrying a puzzle in his mind.

"Read that back," he said when he finished dictating.

She read the letter to him.

He drew in an irritated breath and ran a restless hand through his thick, wavy hair. "I hate not being able to read my own damned letters," he muttered.

"It will get easier as you go along," she said quietly.

His head lifted and turned, as if he was trying to see where she was. "Do you think so?" he asked with a rough laugh. "I very much doubt it."

"We all have trials in life," she said simply. "We get through them. Everything passes away—grief, anger, hope, joy, all of it. It's both a blessing and a curse."

"What have you gotten through? Are you even old enough to have had trials at all?"

She started to tell him about her father, then quickly bit her tongue. There were going to be pitfalls, working for him. Here was one of the biggest. She remembered telling him, when he was sighted, about Dolores, and her father, and the boy who'd broken their engagement when he found out her father ran beef cattle.

"We all have trials," she replied.

"How old are you?" he asked suddenly.

She knew she'd never told him that. She doubted that Mamie had, or that he would have bothered to ask. "I'm twenty-three," she said softly.

"Twenty-three." His face was impassive. His eyes were narrow. His lips compressed. "Twenty-three."

She couldn't see into his mind or she might have been surprised at why he reacted that way to her age. He was seeing doors closing. She was twenty-three. He was thirty-eight. Her life was beginning. He was approaching the middle of his. Even if he'd been interested—and he was—her age put him off.

He leaned back in his chair and drew in a long breath. "My brother died on this lake," he said abruptly.

"Your brother?"

"He and his wife were on a houseboat. There was a party. It was late on a Friday night. A couple of teenagers in a motorboat came flying around one of the coves and hit it broadside. My brother and his wife drowned in the time it took rescue people to get here and start looking for them."

"I'm so sorry," she said as she understood, too well, too late, his overreaction to her speeding in Mamie's boat.

"He was the last living relative I had," he replied. "We were close." He glanced her way. "Do you have family, Emma?"

She hesitated. "Yes. My father lives on a small farm in North Carolina." There was no reason for him to check that out, after all.

"Are you close?"

"Not so much. He's very independent. But my mother and I were. She was very sweet and gentle."

"How did she die?"

She swallowed. "She died in childbirth."

A shadow passed over his broad face. "Unusual, isn't it, in this day and age? Any decent obstetrician should be able to call in specialists if there are problems."

"She was in labor for a long time and she had a hidden heart condition. She died of a heart attack."

"I see. And the child?"

"A little girl. She was stillborn. They said she'd been dead for several days. They couldn't save her." That wasn't the whole truth. She wasn't telling him that her father had let her mother lie in childbirth for two horrible days, or that she'd died, ironically, while he was delivering a calf out in the pasture several miles from the house. By the time he finally got home to a sobbing Emma and a still, cold wife, it was too late to save her.

Emma's father had delivered Emma at home, and he'd planned to do the same with his second child. Apparently it had never occurred to him that he should have taken his wife to the hospital when she started complaining of chest pain. She'd had an undiagnosed heart condition that the stress of prolonged childbirth had caused to go critical. She'd died of a massive coronary.

It had hurt, so badly, to lose her mother, especially at such a young age. Emma had watched her die, helpless to do anything. She had managed to live at home until graduation, but the minute she had a job, she moved to town and never looked back. Emma had nothing to do with her father at all these days. She wasn't certain that she'd even be willing to ask him for help in a dire emergency. Or that he'd give her any. He was rarely sober enough to care about anything, anyway. He did manage to go out to work on the ranch, enough to keep it going, but his drinking was such a problem that he now had a huge turnover in cowboys.

Emma was ashamed of the way he behaved. Although his ranch was in Comanche Wells, everybody knew about him in nearby Jacobsville, where Emma had worked at the local café. At least she hadn't told Connor about the drinking when he was sighted. She'd been too ashamed to admit it, even to a stranger.

"Emma?"

"Oh. Sorry. I was…lost in the past," she confessed.

"You were with her when she died, weren't you?" he asked suddenly, as if he knew.

She hesitated. "Yes."

He crossed his long legs. "My sister-in-law was pregnant when she died." His eyes glittered. "She didn't want the baby. She said so, often."

"Then why…?"

"My brother would never have married her if there hadn't been a child on the way. She bragged about it, about how she'd snared him with the child, and that he'd have to support it, and her, until it came of age. She'd have everything she wanted, she'd said, and she laughed at him." His eyes closed. "He was a sweet man. I tried to tell him what she was like, but he was naive. He'd never been in love before, and she was a good actress. He only found her out when it was too late."

"That's a shame, for a woman to do that to a man," she said quietly. "We had a sweet old fellow in our church who'd been married to the same woman for fifty years. When she died, a widow down the road sweet-talked him into marriage. Then she took him for everything he had, even sold the house out from under him. He went to live with his son, and she called him every night to laugh at how gullible he'd been." She sighed. "He killed himself."

"Why?" he asked, shocked.

"He loved her," she said.

"Love," he scoffed. "I fell in love when I was a teenager. I soon learned that it's just a euphemism for sex. That's all it is, a chemical reaction."

She sighed. "You're probably right," she said. "But I'd like to keep my illusions until I grow as crotchety as you are."

His eyebrows arched. "Excuse me?"

"Crotchety. That's what you are," she explained patiently. "You're rude and overbearing and your temper could curdle milk."

He chuckled softly. "Feeling brave, are you?"

"I can type."

"That's an excuse?"

"A woman who can type can always get work," she explained. "So if you fire me, I'll just go right out and look for another job."

He stretched lazily, still smiling. "Always the optimist. Doesn't anything get you down, young Emma?"

"Worms."

He blinked. "What?"

"Worms. You put them on a hook and drown them in an attempt to catch fish that you also have to kill in order to eat them. It's so depressing. Imagine how the worm feels," she teased.

He burst out laughing.

"You look nice when you laugh," she said softly.

"I don't, often," he said a minute later. "Perhaps you're corrupting me."

"That's my evil influence, all right. I'll have to look up my pitchfork."

"Back to work, my girl," he said. "Read me the next letter in the stack."

"Email doesn't have stacks."

"Sure they do. Get busy."

She grinned. "Okay."

That night, something woke her. She couldn't think what. She sat up in bed, frowning, and looked around. The house seemed quiet. There was nothing going on outside, either. She got out of bed in her flowing cotton nightgown with its puffed sleeves and slipped on her matching housecoat, tossing her hair in a pigtail over the back of it. She crept to her door and opened it.

Maybe it was her imagination…no! There it was again. A moan. A harsh moan.

She walked down the hall, frowning. The sound grew louder. She stopped at a door and knocked.

"What the hell do you want?" came a rough, angry voice from behind the door.

She opened the door a crack. "Mr. Sinclair?" she called softly.

"Oh. Emma. Come here, honey, will you?"

She hesitated. "Do you…wear pajamas?"

He laughed even through the pain. "Bottoms, yes. Come in."

She opened the door and walked in, leaving it open behind her.

He was sitting on the side of a huge, king-size bed. A brown paisley duvet was thrown back from brown sheets. Pillows were scattered everywhere. His head was in his hands, propped up on his broad thighs.

"Are you okay?" she asked.

"No. I hurt like hell. Go into the bathroom and look in the medicine cabinet. There's a bottle with blue-and-white capsules in it, for migraines. Bring me one, and a bottle of water out of the minibar in the corner."

"Mini what?"

"Minibar." He lifted his head. His eyes were bloodshot and his face was drawn with pain. "Like a small fridge," he explained kindly.

"Sorry. I've never seen one."

"They have them in most hotels," he pointed out.

"Well, I've never stayed in a hotel. Or a motel." Which was true. Mamie traveled, but Emma stayed home and took care of the house and typed drafts for Mamie's new books. She walked into the bathroom, unaware of his raised eyebrows.

She found the bottle, read the directions, popped one out into her palm and closed the lid. She put the bottle back, then went to find the water.

"Open up," she coaxed. He opened his mouth and she put the capsule on his tongue. It was intimate. It was also sexy, to feel his mouth that way. She tried not to react as she opened the bottle of water and put it carefully into his hand.

"It's open," she said.

He then lifted the water to his chiseled lips and took a long swallow. The feel of Emma's fingers near his mouth affected him, even through the pain. He winced. "Do you have migraine headaches, Emma?"

"No."

"Anyone in your family have them?"

"No." She was going to mention that her employer, Mamie, did until she realized that she wasn't supposed to know Mamie. "I had a friend who had them," she managed. "They were pretty awful."

"Awful is a good word to describe them. They make you

sick as hell, and then they give you a headache that makes you want to bounce your head against a wall."

"I never get headaches," she said.

"Mine weren't this bad until I was blinded," he said.

She winced. She hadn't realized how it was going to feel, watching him suffer and knowing that she'd caused it. She'd blinded him. It was very hard, trying to live with that. She wanted to tell him the truth, but every day she waited made it more impossible.

"Sit down," he said. "There's a chair by the bed. Stay with me for a minute, until it eases."

"Of course."

He hadn't moved much. She noticed the faint olive tan that covered him from the waist up, the muscles in his big arms. He was gorgeous without his shirt. A thick mat of hair ran from his chest down to the waist of his burgundy pajama bottoms, and probably past it. She flushed. She'd never seen a man in pajamas before, except on television or in movies. He was very sexy. And he didn't look his age at all.

"You don't talk a lot, do you?" he asked after a minute.

"I figured that talking wouldn't really help the headache."

"Good point."

"Have you had them all your life?"

He nodded and winced, because the movement hurt. "My mother had them. Terrible headaches. We had to drive her to the emergency room a lot, because they got so bad."

"Wouldn't a doctor come to the house for you? I mean, you're very rich…"

He smiled. "I wasn't always."

"Really?"

"I inherited a small private air service from my father. I studied business management and parlayed it into a bigger private air service. I absorbed a company that made baby jets, and added a regional air taxi service that had gone bankrupt. It took a long time, but when I hit it big, I hit it big."

"Empire builders."

"What was that?"

"You're an empire builder," she said simply. "I read about them when I was in school. Men like Carnegie, Rockefeller, Sinclair. Men who started with nothing but had good brains and strong backs and earned fortunes."

"It was a little easier in their day." He chuckled. "No income tax back then, you see."

She cocked her head. "You own one of the biggest airplane manufacturing corporations in the world," she recalled. "One article said you test-flew the planes yourself."

"I did."

"Why?"

His eyebrows arched.

"I mean, you're rich. It's risky, right, testing planes?"

"Very risky."

She was silent. She didn't push. She just waited.

He drew in a long breath. He didn't usually discuss personal things with staff, not even with Barnes or Marie. But she was different somehow.

"I got married when I was eighteen," he said after a minute. "She was beautiful, inside and out. She had black hair and blue eyes, and I loved her beyond measure. At that age, I thought I was invincible. I thought she was, too. We went on this vacation. It was before cell phones were popular, when you usually had to have a landline to talk to people. We were on an island with no outside communications except a line to the mainland, to be used in emergencies. It was a quiet place just for honeymooners. The boat ran once a week. We had the time of our lives, lying on the beach, cooking for ourselves. She was five months pregnant with our child."

Her lips fell apart. She stared at him.

"She'd been healthy, perfectly healthy. The doctors said it was risky, to go off like that, but we were young and stupid. Something went wrong. She was in agony and I didn't know what to do. I tried to call for help, but there was a storm and the lines were down to the mainland. I couldn't even manage to build a fire and signal, because of the rain." He lowered his head. The memory was still painful. "She died in my arms. The baby died with her. At least, I suppose it did, because I had no idea how to save it. It would have been too soon in any case. When the boat came to bring supplies, I was half-mad. They took me off the island, put me in the hospital and sedated me. My father and mother, and her mother, came to make the arrangements for her and to bring me home." His face hardened. "I never wanted a child after that. I hated the whole idea of a baby, because a baby cost me Winona."

She grimaced. What a tragic life he'd had. Now she understood his attitude about love. He'd had one great love, and now he'd convinced himself that love and sex were the same thing. It was a shame. "I'm so sorry," she said softly. "I can't even imagine how that would feel."

He hesitated a minute before he spoke again. "I've had brief affairs, but I never let a woman get close again. And I make sure there will never be another child. I thought about having a vasectomy, but my doctor talked me out of it." He shrugged, then clenched his jaw. "Every woman who came along wanted a child. I told them that if they got pregnant, I'd insist on a termination."

The words chilled. He was the sort of man who would love a child if he had one. But he was obviously determined never to let that happen. To Emma, who loved children, it was a blow. She caught herself. Why should it bother her? She was just his assistant. She sat up straighter. "It's sad, to blame a baby for something that wasn't its fault," she said very quietly.

"The baby killed Winona," he said harshly.

She felt his sorrow, his rage. "You know, we think we're in control. That we can decide what happens to us by the actions we take. But life isn't like that. We're like leaves, floating down a river. We can't even steer. We have the illusion of control. That's all."

He sat up. "And now we can talk about God and how He loves people and takes care of us," he scoffed.

"No. We can talk about how there's a plan to every life, and that what happens to us is part of it. If she'd been meant to live, she would have."

His eyes began to glitter. "Twenty-three, and already a philosopher," he said sarcastically.

"I'm not bitter, the way you are," she said. "I haven't had bad things happen to me." That was a lie, but she couldn't tell him the truth. "So I see things from a different perspective."

"Pollyanna."

She smiled. "I guess I am. Optimism isn't expensive. In fact, it's cheap. You just have to take life one day at a time and do the best you can with it."

"Life is a series of tragedies that ends in death."

"Oh, that's optimistic, all right."

A half smile touched his hard mouth. "Happiness is an illusion."

"Sure it is, if you think that way. You're living in the past, with your heartache. You don't trust people, you don't want a family, you don't have faith in anything, and all you live for is to make more money."

"Smart girl."

"Now you're all sarcastic," she said. "But what I'm trying to say is that you don't expect any more from life than a struggle and more heartbreak."

"That's what I get."

"And are you happy?"

He scowled.

"It's an easy question," she persisted. "Are you happy?"

"No." His jaw tautened. "Nobody is happy."

"I am," she said.

"What makes you happy?"

"Birds calling to each other in the trees. Leaves rustling when they turn orange and gold and there's just the faintest nip in the breeze. White sails on the lake just after dawn. Crickets singing on a summer night. Things like that."

"How about nights on the town? Dancing in a nightclub? Going to a rock concert? Watching the Grand Prix in Le Mans?" he mused.

"Martians playing in dust storms? Because I'm just as likely to see the latter as the former. Not my world."

"I'll take my dancing in a nightclub before your crickets on a summer night," he said sardonically.

"Glitter. That's what you have. Glitter. It's an illusion."

"So are crickets. I'm sure they only exist in cartoon form and star in Disney movies."

"I give up."

"You might as well. You'll never change my perspective any more than I'll change yours." He chuckled.

"How's your head feeling?"

He blinked. The question surprised him. "Better."

"Probably all the talk about crickets and rustling leaves," she said pertly.

"More than likely the hilarity over your concept of happiness."

"Whatever floats your boat," she told him. She stood up. "If you're better, I'll go back to bed."

"You could stay," he pointed out. "We could lie down and discuss sailboats."

She laughed softly. "No, thanks."

"Have you ever been in love, Emma?" he asked, curious.

She drew in a breath. "I thought I was once," she said. "We got engaged. But it didn't work out."

He didn't like that. It surprised him, that he was jealous, when she was far too young for him and an employee to boot. She'd been engaged. Even religious people had sex when they were committed. It changed the way he thought of her.

"Why didn't it?" he asked.

She didn't dare tell him the truth, because she'd told him about her ex-fiancé before he was blinded. "We discovered that we didn't think alike in the areas where it mattered," she said finally. "He wasn't at all religious…"

"And that matters?" he chided.

"It did to me," she said stiffly.

He cocked his head and looked toward the direction of her voice. "You're a conundrum."

"Thanks."

"It wasn't a compliment."

"Now you're getting nasty. I'm going."

"How about bringing me another bottle of water before you leave me here, all alone and in pain, in the dark, by myself?"

"Oh, for heaven's sake, you're a grown man! You're always by yourself in the dark," she muttered as she opened the minibar and pulled out another bottle of water.

"Not always," he said in a deep voice that positively purred.

She blushed, and she was glad he couldn't see it.

"Okay," she said. "I'm putting it right here on the night table… Oh!"

While she was talking, he'd reached out and caught her around the waist, pulling her across him and down onto the bed with him.

He was very strong, and she felt the warmth of his body as he made a cage of his big arms and trapped her gently under the light pressure of his broad, muscular chest.

"Mr. Sinclair," she began nervously.

He lifted one big hand and touched her hair. "Just be still," he said quietly. "I want to see you. This is the only way I have, now."

Guilt made her lie still in his arms as his fingers traced her eyebrows, her forehead, her high cheekbones and straight nose. They lingered on her rounded chin and her soft, bow-shaped mouth. From there they went down to her throat and stilled on the pulse that was surely visible as well as if he'd been able to see it. Her heartbeat was almost shaking her and she had to fight to get in a breath of air.

"You're nervous," he said softly.

She bit her lip. "Yes."

"No need. I'm curious. Surely you did this with your ex-fiancé?" he chided.

She pushed gently against his chest. Her fingers tingled in contact with the hard, warm muscle. "What I did with him is not your business, Mr. Sinclair," she said uneasily. If he could have seen it, her face was flaming red.

He didn't like her assertion that it wasn't his business.

"I'm just curious," he said sarcastically. "Did that religious thing tie you in knots when you slept with him?"

"Religion is all I've had most of my life, Mr. Sinclair. Please don't ridicule me because I believe in something more powerful than human beings."

She was so devout. But he'd never felt closer to anyone. The thought shocked him. She was an employee. She was a glorified typist. She had no knowledge of sophisticated living, of men, of the world. Or did she? He'd had too much of women who pretended innocence and were more experienced than he was.

He traced her soft mouth and felt her teeth on the full lower lip. "Stop that," he said, tugging at it.

She swallowed and drew in a shaky breath. The feel of him

was like a narcotic on her senses. He smelled of soap and the
faint, lingering scent of aftershave or cologne. He was muscular without being blatant, and as his chest rose and fell, it
seemed to her that his own breathing was none too steady.

"Are you on the pill?" he asked suddenly.

She pushed at him, growing frantic when she couldn't move
out of the cage of his arms.

He laughed. "All right," he said. "Calm down. I get the
idea. First you fall in love, then you get in a committed
relationship, then you have sex."

She almost corrected him, that nothing short of a wedding
ring was going to get her into any man's bed, until he laughed
again. "It's not funny," she muttered angrily.

He took a long breath. There was a lingering smile, but
no more amusement. "You fight for your ideals, don't you,
young Emma?" he mused. "I don't agree with them. But I
respect you for them."

"Thanks. Can I get up, now that we've agreed that I'm
living in the past?"

His fingers traced her soft mouth, feeling its helpless response. The house was very quiet. The only sounds were her
quick breathing, and the furious beat of his own heart. The
medicine had relaxed him a little as it took the pain away.
Perhaps it had relaxed him too much.

"I'm hungry, Emma," he whispered, bending slowly to her
lips. "I want to see how you taste."

The last word was almost a groan as he found her mouth
with his and possessed it with a tenderness he hadn't felt since
Winona. He could feel Emma's uncertainty as his mouth
teased hers, explored it softly, parted her lips and moved
against them with slow, sweet sensuality.

Emma wanted to fight. But it was like a drug. He was tender, and methodical. He didn't rush. He didn't demand. He
enticed. He coaxed.

Her lips were parting on their own now, following his as they lifted and tempted her, taunted her. He laughed, deep in his throat, at her sudden yielding. So much for her high moral tone. She was as hungry for this as he was. He drew in a quick breath as he felt her hands flatten in the hair over his muscular chest, and reacted to it helplessly. It had been years since he'd been so quickly aroused with a woman.

He wanted to drag her against him and let her feel his hunger, but he hesitated. Even if she was only doing lip service to her morals, he didn't want to dampen the hunger she was beginning to reveal. He caught her upper lip in both of his and tasted it underneath with his tongue, brushing and lifting. He felt her hands on his upper arms now, her nails digging in involuntarily as she lifted toward him.

His hands slid under her back, under the robe, and he eased down against her, the pressure of his chest even through her gown causing odd, sweet sensations all over her untried body.

One big, strong hand came around to toy with the cotton under her arm. She caught it with a tiny gasp, because even through her robe and gown, his touch was electrifying. But his mouth covered hers again and her fingers relaxed more and more until they moved away. She didn't want to stop him, anyway. He was making her body sing. He smoothed his fingers over her rib cage, his thumb brushing just the side of her firm breast and making her quiver. He slid it around, over her hips, down to cover her flat stomach.

Why should he suddenly think of babies? His own breath caught against her mouth. A child. He groaned. His mouth became suddenly insistent, demanding. He moved down against her.

Through the gown and robe, she could feel his chest rubbing against her pert little breasts, brushing his chest, arousing him. His hips brushed hers and she felt the changing contours of his body.

A sound worked its way out of her throat and up into his mouth. He recognized it for what it was.

So did she. Even as she heard herself moan, she knew she had to stop him. This could never happen. He was a man who had disposable lovers. She was the woman who'd blinded him. She couldn't—didn't—dare let this go any further.

Her hands pressed hard against his chest and she drew her mouth from under his, not without a little shudder of anguish. "Please," she whispered brokenly. "Please don't...!"

He lifted his head. Odd, that he had a sudden image of white roses and lace flash in his mind.

He moved away from her and fought to catch his breath. It was hard to let her go, because she tasted like heady wine.

He felt her begin to relax as he lifted himself away from her. But his fingers still moved on her rib cage, very slowly, teasing near her breast. He felt her reaction to even that innocent touch. She wanted him. She might not be ready for intimacy, but she wouldn't resist long, if he insisted. He was sure of it.

Emma was torn between what her body wanted and what she knew she had to do. His touch kindled a hunger that was totally unfamiliar. New. It wasn't the lure of sex, either. It was something more, something sweeter.

He drew in a last, steadying breath. "You're very slender, Emma," he said softly. "How much do you weigh?"

She laughed. "A hundred and ten," she said, surprised.

"You're tall."

"Well, not so very. Just five feet and six inches."

His hand lifted, reluctantly, and found her hair. It was braided down her back. He smiled. "You don't let it loose at night?"

"It tangles."

"I suppose so. What color is it?"

"Blond. Pale blond."

"And your eyes?"

She smiled. "They're brown. Dark brown."

"An interesting combination."

"I'm not pretty," she added quietly. "I have regular features, but they're not beautiful. Nothing like…" She bit her tongue. She was going to say, like that woman who'd cooked him a soufflé once that he complained about. She'd been beautiful. But the woman he'd hated, who'd blinded him, had remembered that. The woman she was pretending to be wouldn't have known about the soufflé, and he'd have snapped at the memory like a fish biting a worm. She had to be careful about what she said to him.

"Nothing like…?" he asked.

"Nothing like the sort of women you probably know," she said instead.

He shrugged. "They all start to look alike after a while. Feel alike. Sound alike." He sighed. "I suppose I've gotten jaded in my old age, Emma. Women come and go. Mostly they go. I'm thirty-eight. I'm slowing down. I sent the last one away a couple of weeks ago. The one you put through to me recently," he added with pursed lips.

"Oh, dear."

"You'll learn who gets to talk to me and who doesn't."

"Do they take numbers and stand in line?" she wondered.

He chuckled. "Not quite."

It felt comfortable, lying in bed with him. She liked it very much.

"I should go to bed," she said.

"I guess you should." He sat up and felt for her arm, pulling her up gently with him.

"Is your head better?" she asked as she got to her feet.

"Much better." He cocked his head and smiled wickedly. "If I get another migraine, will you come back?"

She laughed softly. "Not without some promises from you first."

"Coward."

"You bet."

He drew in a breath and stretched lazily. Watching him, Emma almost moaned at the way he looked, half-dressed. He was beautiful, like a painting. Like a sculpture.

"I'll see you in the morning, then," she said abruptly, because she realized she was enjoying the sight of him a little too much.

"Thanks, Emma," he said suddenly.

"You're welcome. I'm glad your head's better."

He just nodded.

She went out and closed the door.

He groaned and put his head in his hands. His body was in agony. She wasn't like his other women, and he wanted her. But she'd expect a commitment, a wedding, the whole nine yards if he gave in to his urges. So what the hell was he going to do now?

Down the hall, Emma was wondering the same thing. She loved kissing him. She loved having him hold her. She should have resisted more. Instead, she'd enjoyed everything he did to her.

It had felt like descriptions she'd read in one of the romance novels she loved to read. She'd dreamed of a kiss like that from a man who'd love her and marry her and make a home with her.

But she had to keep in mind that Connor was a millionaire—maybe even a billionaire. He lived life in the fast lane. Casinos and shows on Broadway and all things glamorous. She'd never fit into that world. And she'd better remember that he didn't want marriage or children. It would be madness to get involved with him, even in an innocent way.

Beneath all that was the memory that she'd blinded him, that he couldn't see because she'd gone wild in a speedboat on a lake where one had killed his only brother. She shivered as she thought of the vengeance he was likely to take if he ever found out who she really was. It had been insane to do this, to think that he might soften if he got to know her, that she could tell him and he'd forgive her. This was a man who never forgave anyone, who repaid in kind every transgression. This was a man who didn't know what mercy was.

She didn't sleep much. By morning she'd made a decision. It wasn't an easy one.

# FOUR

Emma went to breakfast the next morning, dragging her feet. She was going to put in her notice. It made her sick to think of leaving him. It was the last thing she wanted to do. But she was susceptible to him. Vulnerable, and he was used to women who thought nothing of climbing into bed with him. She couldn't do that. It wasn't who she was.

She walked into the dining room, head high, determined. And...he wasn't there!

Confused, she sat down. There was only one place setting, for her.

Marie came in with a platter of eggs and sausage. She knew that Emma loved sausage best of all the breakfast foods. She added buttered biscuits to the platter and pushed a jar of homemade blackberry preserves toward Emma.

"My favorite foods," she exclaimed. "Wow! Thanks, Marie."

"You're very welcome," the older woman said gently.

"Where's Mr. Sinclair?" she asked with her eyes lowered.

"He actually went to a conference." She laughed. "It's the first time since he was, well, you know, that he's left the house at all. He said it was time he got back into the swing of things and took care of business. He took his attorney with him. You'd like him. Alistair Sims. He's British."

"Oh, my," Emma exclaimed. "This is a small mountain

community. He's British and he wanted to live here? Well, Bear Lake, where we are, is a small town. But we're near Gainesville, which has over fifty thousand people."

"Closer to thirty-five thousand." Marie laughed again. "Yes, Alistair married an American woman and moved here years ago. She died, but he never went home. He said he felt closer to her here, where she's buried."

"What a sweet man he must be," she replied.

"He's very kind. He can keep secrets, too. That's important to a man like Mr. Sinclair. You wouldn't believe the problems money can make for someone who's wealthy."

"I can't, and I don't mind it at all." Emma beamed. "I'm happy with my life."

Marie stared at her. "You make people around you happy, too, Miss Emma," she said softly. "Mr. Sinclair actually laughs now. He never did before, even when he could see. He was always somber and cold. You'd never know he had a sense of humor. Not until you came along."

"That makes me feel very good," Emma confessed. Inside, the guilt was still eating her up, though. Not even what Marie was saying made a lot of difference.

"Well, I'll get back to work. Call me if you need anything, Miss Copeland."

"Just Emma," she corrected, smiling.

"All right, then. Just Emma." Marie smiled back.

The house was suddenly empty. Cold. Haunted by memories. Emma walked into the study that Connor used for an office and felt the emptiness like a living thing. When Connor was here, his very presence filled the world. He brought color and life to the house. He seemed larger than life.

Now, without him for the first time since she'd accepted the job, Emma began to realize just how much the big man meant to her. It was dangerous, those feelings. For one thing, she couldn't afford to become involved with him, in any way. She lived in fear that she'd slip up, and then he'd finally realize who she was. Even though nobody had seen her in the boat the morning of the accident, he was rich. If he wanted to, he could afford plenty of detectives to seek her out.

But he didn't remember how he'd been hurt. That was her only solace. It gave her the opportunity to look after him, take care of him, make up a little for what she'd done. But if he ever found out…

She shivered, even in the warm room, thinking about how vindictive he was. Mamie's words rang in her ears. Connor always got even with anyone who crossed him. His vengeance, if he realized that the same woman who'd blinded him was working for him, would be absolute. He might even think she'd done it for another reason, that she was playing him, trying to get money out of him. She knew already that he'd give her anything she asked for, because he was fond of her.

But she hadn't asked for anything. She never would. She worked for what she got. It would never occur to her to be like the women he knew, greedy, grasping women who only wanted what he had.

She wondered why he liked that sort of woman, like that brunette who made soufflés, or so he said. He knew them to their bones. Perhaps that was why he never got attached to them, because he knew what they were about.

She recalled what he'd told her, about his late wife, and the way she'd died in childbirth. It helped her to understand him, just a little. He blamed the baby for killing her. But that was just God's will, she thought, and was saddened that he didn't share her belief system. She smiled. His wasn't a unique viewpoint. In today's world, many people thought that God was just a myth.

She recalled things she'd read about in history books, about other periods of time when men had become fixated on their own power—only to have some natural disaster remind them that men were less powerful than they believed.

In the winter of 1811–1812, there had been a devastating earthquake on the New Madrid fault in Missouri (which was pronounced New Mádrid, not New Madríd). It had caused damage in many surrounding states, including Georgia. Part of the Mississippi River had run backward. Sand blows—areas that liquefied and sand rushed to the surface in huge circles— had been everywhere in the impact zone. There were a few eyewitness accounts. Not so many people had died, because in those days the area wasn't as populated as it was today. But after the earthquakes, the churches were full. It just went to show, Emma thought, that people sometimes got reminded that they weren't all-powerful.

She sat down in the big chair behind Connor's desk, her fingers caressing the armrests. She missed him. It was insane to let these feelings get a grip on her heart, because inevitably she was going to have to leave. Her great plan to gain his confidence and then tell him what she'd done had gone to pieces. She realized now that she could never do it. She didn't want to leave. She couldn't bear the thought of his outrage, his disgust, if he knew who'd blinded him. He would hate her...

She got up from the chair as if it had turned red hot, and walked out of the room. She closed the door behind her, almost overcome with silent fear. She had no one to blame but herself. She'd parked herself in the lion's den and now she was waiting to be devoured.

In a panic, she went to her room and got out her suitcase. She could run. She could go home to Jacobsville. Not to her father's ranch; she never wanted to go back there. But the Griers would certainly take her in again. Cash and Tippy had given her the affection she'd never gotten from her father. It was just that she felt she'd imposed on them too much. She had a cousin in Victoria, near Jacobsville, where she could live until she got a new job. Cousin Ella would let her share the big house she'd just inherited, and there was always work at the big ranches nearby; or maybe get a job cooking in a restaurant somewhere.

Even as she thought about it, as her fingers touched the cold vinyl of the hard-shelled suitcase, she realized that she couldn't do it. She thought of Connor here with nobody to help him with the tangle of daily email, or with routine things like where food was on his plate, how many steps he had to walk down to go to the shore of the lake, where Emma led him almost every evening when he was home. Who would sit with him when he had the horrible migraines that plagued him? Who'd tease him and wipe away the broodiness that hallmarked his personality?

She moved her suitcase back into the closet and slowly closed the door. Until now, she hadn't realized how much she cared for him. That had been a huge mistake. But he was the sort of man who attracted women. Not only for his amorous technique—which was formidable—but also for his wit and courtesy and the soft heart he hid from most people.

He cared about the people who worked for him. Marie told her how much he'd done for her family and Barnes's. He'd done that for other people, as well. He was generous to a fault. He was that way with Emma, too. He'd wanted to buy her things, but she'd refused every attempt. There would inevitably come a time when he'd find her out—hopefully, long after she left him. She didn't want him to remember that she'd accepted expensive presents from him. It would look as if she had ulterior motives for coming to work for him. Her only motive had been to try and make up just a little for the horrible thing she'd done.

She had nightmares about the boat hitting him. Now that she knew him, had feelings for him, she was tormented by the memories. She should have stopped the boat, gotten out, helped him, apologized, tried to explain. Even if he'd sent the sheriff's department after her, which he would have had to do since the lake house wasn't within the city limits, she'd have dealt with the consequences, whatever they were, bravely.

Instead, she'd let him give her a job that she never should have taken under false pretenses.

But look what she'd have missed, she told herself. Quiet evenings by the lake. Breakfast with him every morning. Working together in the office, listening to his deep, velvety voice while he dictated. Easing his headaches with medicine and companionship until he fell asleep. Just being with him. Looking at him. Loving the handsome face and muscular physique that defined the man he was. She never saw the millionaire. She saw the man.

She wandered out to the deck overlooking the lake. There was a flat area between this lake house and Mamie's place, right on the shore. There was a log there where Emma liked to sit. It was where she'd been sitting that first time, when Connor had found her and railed her out about trespassing. It was near where he'd offered her breakfast later, when he lost his vision. She'd teased him and he'd laughed.

Marie said he hardly ever laughed before Emma came to work for him. It made her proud that she could give him a few light moments in his darkness. She wished she could go back and undo what she'd done.

He'd gone away so suddenly. Was it because of last night? Had it meant something to him, beyond just the physical attraction that was so evident to both of them? Did he regret his behavior because she worked for him? Was he embarrassed? Ashamed?

She laughed. He was never embarrassed, and he would hardly be ashamed. Nothing much had happened. She'd struggled away from him before anything could. But she recalled the sudden hardness of his body. He'd wanted her, badly. Did he think she'd let him touch her for ulterior motives, that she wanted something for being with him? She was horrified that he might think she was pretending to be clueless. She'd told him she was engaged once. Did he think she'd slept with her fiancé as many women did before the wedding?

Her mind flew ahead to his return. How would he act when he came back? She hoped he wouldn't pursue her, because she knew she wouldn't be able to resist him. She loved being in his big arms, she loved kissing him. That was unwise for many reasons. She hoped she could get her hormones under control before he came back. Because she absolutely could not let him get close to her. The thought depressed her so much that she skipped lunch and went to wander the lakeshore like a lost soul.

There were a few emails left that he'd wanted sent, so she took care of those. After that, there wasn't much to do. She helped Marie in the kitchen. The older woman liked to make exotic dishes and freeze them, for when company came.

Not that there'd been many visitors lately. Connor had been famous for his lake parties when he was sighted, Marie commented a few days later. The house had been alive with light and music and the sound of conversation.

"I guess he knows a lot of important people," Emma said as she chopped fresh herbs for the omelet Marie was making them for supper. They had light meals since Connor wasn't in residence. Marie did the cooking, a chore she'd shared with Connor's chef, Edward, who stayed in France at Connor's other home on the Riviera. Emma loved omelets, for any meal. This one had lots of herbs, with tiny muffins to accompany it.

Marie heard the wistful note in her voice and glanced at her. "Too many, it seems sometimes. You know, I always felt that he hid in people, in droves of people, to keep from facing his personal demons. The house was full, but he was alone, even then."

"He told me about his wife," she confessed.

Marie's eyebrows lifted. "He did? My goodness, he never speaks of her to anyone, that I know."

Emma laughed softly. "People tend to confide in me. It's always been that way."

"It's because you listen. You really listen," Marie emphasized. "Most people want to talk about themselves. They aren't quiet enough to listen to what other people say to them, they're thinking ahead to what they want to say next."

Emma grinned. "I never thought of it that way."

Marie laughed softly. "Mr. Sinclair's women don't listen, they talk," she said.

Emma groaned inwardly at the reminder of his women. Of course he had women. She'd seen the glittery woman who made soufflés. She'd almost blurted that out to Marie. It would be fatal, if she ever said such a thing to Connor and he made the connection. He'd remember that the woman who'd blinded him had seen the woman at the lake house. She'd almost let that slip to him, the night before he'd left the lake house.

In a way, she was sorry that she'd taken this job so impulsively. Her motives had been noble, at the time, but they would lead her to tragedy if she wasn't careful. Mamie had told her how dangerous Connor was, how vindictive. Mamie wasn't the only person he'd hounded relentlessly for crossing him. If even the memory upset Mamie, it must have been very bad.

"All right, dump them in," Marie cut into her thoughts.

It took Emma a moment before she remembered that she was helping with supper. She tossed the herbs into the bowl where Marie was whisking the eggs.

"How did you come to work for Mr. Sinclair?" Emma asked.

Marie smiled. "My husband died and I had nowhere to go. We'd lived on a poultry farm for years, ever since we first married. When he died, I didn't want to do the job alone, so the company he worked for wanted to move another family in. I came here, to the lake house, on a whim, because a friend said there was an eccentric millionaire who needed a local cook. I was scared to death of him. You know, I have a thick Southern accent, I'm a countrywoman, all that. He didn't mind at all, despite his very French and very elegant chef, Edward. Barnes is sort of like me, too—he's local, so you could never say that the boss was biased toward people who don't have money."

Emma laughed as she pictured poor Marie on her first interview. "I was scared of him, too, when I first came here," she confessed.

"It was only supposed to be for a few months a year, while he was here. But he liked me, so I stay year-round. Usually by myself—" she grinned "—since he takes Barnes with him when he goes overseas. We have temporary people come in to help out when he throws parties, but there's just me and Barnes when he's alone. When he leaves, it's just me and the telephone, really. It rings constantly when he's not here. Reporters looking for a confidential story, rivals tracking his movements overseas, business associates trying to track him down. And women." She groaned. "I didn't understand why he lived on the Riviera for several months a year. Now I do," she added wryly.

"What does he do there?" Emma wondered.

"He swims. He sunbathes. He has house parties. Or he did," she added quietly. "Now—well, I'm not sure." She turned up the heat on the front ceramic burner of the stove and placed the pan to warm before she added the eggs. "You know, I often thought that he needed people the way some people need alcohol." Emma knew all too well some people's need for alcohol. "He doesn't like his own company."

"He hasn't had people here since I came to work for him."

Marie added eggs to the pan and began to move the mixture to the center as the edges bubbled. "He doesn't seem to need other people when you're around, Emma," came the soft reply. "He's like a different person with you, and I don't mean that in a bad way. He's at peace. Yes," she added, turning the eggs. "That's the word I wanted. He's at peace."

Emma didn't say another word. She felt a kind of quiet pride. At least she was of some worth to Connor, even if she was a dead loss as an amorous substitute.

Perhaps that was why he'd gone away. To find a woman who'd do for him what Emma wouldn't. The thought depressed her beyond words. She finished her supper, made some excuse about a book she wanted to read and went to bed early.

Emma wandered the shoreline, tapping tall autumn weeds lightly with a twig she'd found. It had been a whole week since Connor had left. She'd done what little work he left her, helped Marie, brooded in his office, haunted the lakeshore where she'd spent so much time with him when they weren't working. Nothing helped. It was like being separated from an arm or a leg. Funny, how much he'd come to mean to her in the short time she'd worked here.

She wondered if he missed her, then laughed out loud. Sure he missed her. He was probably drowning in attractive brunettes, helping him enjoy whatever casino was nearby wherever he'd gone. He liked glitz and glamour. And she'd heard that conventions were breeding grounds for all sorts of wild behavior.

The thought of that big, muscular body with a woman in

a bed drove her crazy. She hated the thought of him with other women.

She told herself for the hundredth time that she was never going to have any permanent place in his life. She worked for him. Yes, he'd kissed her, but he was only curious. He'd said so. He wanted to see how she tasted, and she'd better hope that she tasted like bad medicine, or she was going to be in big trouble very soon.

She stared across the lake, enjoying the cool breeze that ruffled her hair, the nip of autumn giving it a flavor all its own. She closed her eyes and smiled. Such a simple thing, to bring such pleasure.

"Emma! Where the hell are you?"

Her heart jumped. Connor was home! She turned back toward the lake house, running in her joy. "I'm here!" she called back, laughter in her voice.

The man standing on the deck didn't smile. He stiffened as if a bullet had hit him. He'd gone away to forget that she went to his head like alcohol, that he wanted her with an obsession he'd never felt in his life. And here she was, laughter in her voice, excitement in her steps he could hear clearly as she approached.

She stopped in front of him to catch her breath. But the joy she felt at his return wasn't shared. He was as cold and unreachable as he'd been the first day she'd talked to him, when he'd chewed her out about speeding in Mamie's boat. This wasn't the kind, mischievous, teasing companion of recent weeks.

"Come with me. We have work to do," he said coldly, and turned back toward the door.

He reached toward a chair that had been moved and almost lost his balance. "Who moved my chair?" he demanded as he stopped in his tracks.

"We have a woman who comes in to do the heavy cleaning—"

"Hell, I know that! I want to know why it wasn't moved back!" he said curtly.

She drew in a shaky breath. "I'm sorry, sir."

He breathed slowly, deliberately, while he got his temper under control. "Get Barnes," he said shortly. "I'll need help to get to the office."

"Sir, I don't mind…" she began, putting a soft hand on his arm.

He shook it off violently. Pale eyes looked in her general direction. "Don't touch me!" he snapped. "Get Barnes! Now!"

She took a deep breath to steady herself. She was shaking from the aggression in his voice. "Yes, sir," she said. Her voice shook, too. She hated that.

He heard it and his body tensed. He didn't want to hurt her, but she was getting too close. He couldn't let her. He had nothing left to give.

Barnes led Connor to his office. Emma, her face flushed with embarrassment and grief, followed slowly along behind, because he hadn't told her what to do, now that he was home.

"Thanks," he told the other man.

"Anytime, sir," Barnes said politely. He looked at Emma's disturbed face and grimaced, then tried to smile.

She nodded and didn't meet his eyes. He went out, closing the door.

"Are you in here, Emma?" Connor snapped as he sat down behind his desk.

"Yes, sir." She sounded calm again, thank goodness, even though she wasn't.

"Good. Let's get to work."

She might have mentioned that he was just home from a business trip, and wouldn't he like to get out of the very becoming charcoal pin-striped suit he was wearing with a white shirt and blue tie, and change into something comfortable? But that grizzly bear wouldn't take kindly to any such personal remark; she knew it at once. She wasn't risking his temper again.

He dictated letters to two congressmen and a senator. They concerned some upcoming legislation that would, apparently, impact aviation. She didn't ask questions. She just took dictation.

"I'll want those printed out on paper for my signature," he added when he finished. "Half the time they do the same thing I do with email—they just ignore it. It's harder to ignore a registered letter. That's how you'll send them, too. Registered mail. I'll have Barnes drive them to the post office in town."

"Yes, sir."

He got up, drawing in another breath. "Call Mrs. Harris at Bear Lake Florist. I want flowers sent to Ariel Delong in Atlanta." He gave her the address and the telephone number. "Have them put 'I have sweet memories' on the card. Got that?"

Her heart was dying. "Yes, sir."

"Send her two dozen red roses," he added.

"Yes, sir."

He smiled sarcastically. "Had you forgotten that I have women, Emma?" he chided. "The rest of the world moves on, while you sit in your room at night and dream about white picket fences and happily-ever-after."

She didn't comment. She thought she might choke on her own words. Besides that, she wasn't trying to justify her ideals to a man who only ridiculed them.

"Nothing to say?" he persisted.

"Not a thing, sir."

"I'm taking her nightclubbing tonight," he added with a sensuous smile. "It's her birthday. We'll do the town and then

I'll take her home. Barnes will go with me. I won't be back until tomorrow afternoon, so get those letters done ASAP."

"Yes, sir." She was a parrot. She needed to make a recording of her voice saying that, so she could just hit Play when he asked a question or made a statement.

"She likes to dance," he said. "So do I." His face hardened. "It's hard to do anything more than a lazy two-step now, of course. I can't see! I can't see a damned thing!"

She bit her lip. He wasn't accusing her; he didn't know who she was. But the pain was like a knife in her heart. She'd done that to him!

He struggled for composure. "I love Viennese waltzes," he said. "I danced with a countess in Vienna once, at a ball given by the American consulate. I danced the tango in Argentina with the daughter of a titled count. And now I can't walk if someone moves a damned chair into a position I don't remember!" His fist hit the desk so hard that Emma jumped. "I hate being blind! I hate it!"

She swallowed. "Mr. Sinclair," she said softly, "I'm more sorry than you know, for what happened to you. But you have to go forward. Life doesn't have a rewind button."

He leaned heavily on the desk for a minute, a caged lion roaring at his fate. After a minute, he moved away from the desk and slid his hand along the back of a leather chair. "Tell that cleaning woman that if she moves another piece of furniture in this house, and doesn't move it back, she's fired."

"Yes, sir."

He got almost to the door. "Tell the florist to add a box of chocolates to that order," he said. "She likes sweets."

"I will." The "yes, sir" was wearing thin.

"You don't dance, do you, Emma?" he chided, turning his head back toward her. "God forbid you should have to get that close to a man! Dancing is sinful, isn't it? Anything that gives people pleasure is forbidden!"

Actually, she danced quite well. There had been a party that she'd gone to before she took the job with Mamie. Cash Grier, Jacobsville's police chief, had heard from his wife, Tippy, that Emma couldn't dance. He took it upon himself to teach her, and he was great at it. Tippy had grinned at her with the new baby boy in her arms, laughing when Emma tripped and said she was going to kill him with her two left feet and go to jail. They'd all laughed. Emma had gone to a party soon afterward, and she'd been the belle of the ball.

So Emma could dance. But she wasn't giving the big man any more chances to taunt her. She just remained silent.

He cursed under his breath and left the room.

Emma didn't understand his changed attitude. Or maybe she did. He blamed her because he'd gotten out of hand. He wouldn't remember that he'd pulled her into bed with him, that he'd been the pursuer. He was angry because he'd given in to a hunger he should never have entertained for a young woman who worked for him. But he didn't make mistakes like that, so naturally it was Emma's fault. She'd tempted him.

Or maybe it was just that the new woman in his life had made him realize that he was desperate for sex. Emma had been handy and he'd been hungry. As simple as that.

Either way, the joy was gone from the lake house. Emma knew in her heart that it was better this way. She didn't dare get involved with him. But she'd had dreams. Stupid dreams. Why would a man like that, urbane and rich and sophisticated, want anything to do with a countrywoman who bought clothes off the sale rack and valued morality above fun?

She finished his letters. She'd had some idea that he'd have her help him sign them. It was dangerous to be that hungry for contact with him. She remembered too well how it felt to be held close to that muscular body.

But he brought Barnes into the office with him and had the other man help with the signature.

"They have electronic signatures now," Emma ventured, braving his temper. "You sign up with the service, and then you just push a button on the screen to make legal signatures on documents."

"That's something we'll look into later," Connor replied. There wasn't an edge in his voice this time. He sounded worn-out.

She wanted to say that, to say a lot more. He shouldn't try to go nightclubbing when he was so obviously fatigued. She knew, because of Mamie, that too much excitement, along with any number of other triggers, could bring on a migraine. She remembered how bad the last headache had been. She hated seeing him suffer.

But it would be worth her job to say so.

"What time is it?"

Barnes looked at his watch. "Just going on four thirty, sir."

"Take those letters to the post office as soon as Emma finishes with them. Then come back and help me dress," he said, and smiled. "I've got a hot date."

He ignored Emma completely as Barnes opened the door for him and he found his way down the hall to his own room.

Emma watched him go. Then she went back to the mail, carefully folding and inserting the letters in addressed envelopes. She stamped them. When Barnes stuck his head in the door, she had them ready to go.

He gave her a sad smile. "It looks like you'll have the night off, Miss Emma," he said. "You should go see a movie with Marie. She likes movies. It would do you both good. Go talk to her."

"I'll do that. Thanks, Barnes," she added softly.

He just nodded. He was mentally comparing sweet, kind Emma with the sort of women Connor brought home. What a shame that the boss was even blinder than he looked. Emma

cared very much for Mr. Sinclair. He imagined it cut the heart
out of her to hear him boast about his date. But there was
nothing he could do to help her.

Connor wore a dinner jacket with a white shirt and black
tie, immaculate slacks and polished black shoes. He had a
Rolex watch on one wrist, and a ruby ring on his pinky finger that probably cost as much as the lake house.

Emma had to bite her tongue not to tell him how devastating he looked.

"I won't be back until late tomorrow," he repeated. "That
doesn't let you off work in the morning, Emma," he added
curtly. "There will be emails to delete and some to answer.
Set aside the ones I need to address and we'll see to them
when I get back."

"Yes, sir." She really did sound like a parrot. But her voice
was light and breezy. She did that deliberately. He couldn't
see the pain in her soft brown eyes, and that was just as well.

Marie saw it and grimaced. She didn't understand what
was going on. The Ariel that Connor was going nightclubbing with was the same brunette he'd sent packing because
he'd gotten tired of bouncing soufflés. Now he was dating
her again, and he was really rubbing it in. Did he know that
he was hurting Emma with just the mention of the woman?

She studied his hard face as he looked toward Emma's voice.
Yes, he knew it, she realized suddenly. He was doing it deliberately. He wanted to hurt her. But why? She'd been kinder than
any woman Marie could ever remember seeing with Mr. Sinclair. What reason would he have to grind into Emma like that?

There was one pretty obvious one. He liked variety and
he had no religious leanings, while Emma was conservative
and religious. Perhaps she'd said something to him about
his lifestyle and he hadn't liked it. He was getting even. No.
It had to be more than that. He was taunting her with an-

other woman. Had he been too forward with Emma and she'd knocked him back? That would certainly explain what was going on. Marie thought privately that he'd do far better with Emma than with all the glittery women, as Emma called them, he was used to. Emma would love him. She'd take care of him. Even if he lost everything, which was unlikely, Emma would never leave him.

But he was going out with a woman he could buy. It was such a shame. Not her business, she told herself.

"You've got the night off," Connor told Emma. "I guess you can read one of your romance novels and dream about Prince Charming, can't you?" he taunted.

"I'm going to see a movie with Marie," she replied quietly.

"Better than books, I guess, as romance goes."

"It's about a group of commandos rescuing a hostage," Marie said coolly.

He registered her disapproving tone. He thought about Emma in the city at night. Most of the theaters were in areas that could be dangerous in the dark. "Marie, call the limo service I use and get a car to take you to and from the movie," he said curtly.

Marie's eyebrows arched. He'd never done that before. "I can drive us," she began.

"Do what I tell you," he returned. "Barnes, let's go." He hesitated at the door. "Be careful of your surroundings," he added to the women.

"Mr. Sinclair..." Marie began.

"I can't cook," he said, as if by way of explanation. "And I sure as hell can't type."

Marie laughed. "Yes, sir."

Emma didn't say anything. It made her feel warm inside, that even in his ill mood he cared about her welfare. Well, about Marie's, too. Apparently even grizzly bears had hearts, she thought with faint amusement.

# FIVE

The movie was exciting. It was even funny. But all Emma could think about, while she munched popcorn and tried to pay attention to the screen, was Connor in bed with some other woman.

He'd ridiculed her idea of fun, listening to night sounds on the lake and enjoying the quiet landscape. He wanted noise, excitement, glitter. They were worlds apart on the things that really mattered in life. He had no faith. Her faith was all she had. He wasn't going to settle down. He hated children. He was obsessed with making sure that he never fathered any. Emma loved kids. She wanted them more than anything.

In retrospect, she should have stayed in Jacobsville and gotten married. There were plenty of bachelors there. She could have married and lived on a ranch. She'd loved her father's livestock, the cattle dogs he kept. If he hadn't been so cruel, her life might have been very different. She'd been the only stability at home. Her father drank so much in her last years of high school that she often had to set jobs for the cowboys, even take care of payroll and things like shipping cattle and helping with branding. It had been like that for so long. He'd always been tight with money, but she didn't remember him drinking so much when she was little, when her mother was still alive.

The last year she'd lived at home had been troubling. She

hated to leave, but she couldn't take any more of her father's rampages. When he had too much to drink, she got the back of his hand for any imagined slight. He'd hit her just after graduation.

The bruise had been visible, and Cash Grier had gone out to the ranch to have a talk with her father. She'd worked for Barbara Ferguson in the café part-time while she took business courses at the local vocational school. Cash and Tippy saw her at lunch most days. She was like family to them. Cash was livid when he saw the bruise on her cheek, and the almost pathetic way she'd tried to hide it with makeup.

He came back with Emma's suitcase, the very one she had in her closet right now, and he'd moved her in with his own family. She'd been nervous and shy and ill at ease the first day. But then Tippy's brother Rory had taken her fishing, and Tippy had let her help with the baby boy and little Tris. And after that, she'd truly felt part of a family for the first time.

She'd probably have stayed there, living with Cash and Tippy, cooking for Barbara. But then she'd met Steven at the vocational school and started dating him. He'd just moved to town, with his friend Willie Armour. He'd been applying at the school when he and Emma started talking and found a lot in common.

Steven and Willie moved into an apartment in downtown Jacobsville. Steven didn't start classes right away, but Emma was working at the café, and Steven and Willie went there for most of their meals. Soon afterward, Steven's mother and father bought a small house near their son and moved there, as well. Emma liked Steven's mother. In fact, she and her husband went to the same Methodist church that Emma attended.

Steven wasn't much on church. But he and Emma seemed to have a lot in common. They started talking and Steven seemed to find her really interesting. Only two weeks after they started dating, he proposed. He didn't buy her a ring.

His people were well-to-do, he could have, but he said he
didn't really believe in all that stuff, so they could just let it
be known that they were engaged.

He'd never mentioned a wedding date, and never asked
questions about Emma's family, even though he knew she
lived with the Griers. Cash made some odd comments that
never really registered about how close Steven was to his
roommate, but they went right over Emma's head. She was
head over heels in love, probably because Steven was the first
man who'd ever paid her any real attention. Besides that, he
loved to plant flowers and trees and he loved coming to the
Griers' house, with Willie, of course, and watching a real-
life fashion designing show on television that Tippy enjoyed
so much. A famous model, Tippy had given up her career to
marry Cash. Steven was fascinated with that world and was
always asking her questions about clothes and makeup.

Cash was supportive, even when she got engaged, although
he and Tippy were uneasy. Emma assumed that was because
Steven was so vocal about animals being used for food, and
he'd never asked about Emma's real family or what they did
for a living. She wasn't sure Steven would understand if she
told him her father kept cattle. There was another odd thing,
that Steven insisted they have his friend Willie with them
wherever they went. Honestly, there were times when she
felt positively left out. She liked Willie. He was a kind, sweet
man, very like Steven. But it seemed odd that an engaged couple would take the man's best friend everywhere they went.

It didn't matter, she reflected, because Steven hardly ever
touched her. He said he liked her so much but he had a really hard time kissing her. He did it very rarely and even reluctantly. He thought such things should wait until after the
wedding, he said once. But he wasn't religious, didn't go to
church and hardly ever mentioned actually getting married.

They were just talking one day in the café on her break

when it came out that her father owned a ranch. Steven, who'd been acting oddly for days, suddenly burst out that he couldn't marry a woman whose family killed helpless animals to eat. He said he was very sorry, but he was moving back to San Antonio with Willie and he wouldn't see her again.

He'd walked out without another word. Emma shuddered even now as she remembered how humiliated she'd been. Cash, strangely, didn't seem surprised about the broken engagement, although he was sorry for Emma. He and Tippy did everything they could to cheer her up.

Jacobsville was small, like Comanche Wells, where Emma's father ranched. Everybody knew what had happened. Nobody spoke of it to Emma, but everyone who ate at Barbara's looked at her with sympathy in their eyes. It didn't help that Steven's mother was still around, making sure everyone knew that Emma and her son had been engaged, and wasn't it such a shame that things didn't work out for them? She was sympathetic to Emma and often apologized for her son's odd reaction, but, she reminded the younger woman, he was an animal rights' activist. However, Emma seemed to remember that he loved steak more than any other food, and never seemed to see anything wrong with eating it, despite saying he'd helped found the local branch of PETA.

Emma went on with her life, going to work and to church and trying to forget the heartache. But it wasn't easy. She grew more and more depressed.

Tippy saw what it was doing to Emma. She had a Facebook friend who knew Mamie van Dyke, a very famous author who'd just lost her longtime secretary. She'd messaged her friend, who'd talked to Mamie. Tippy had told Emma about a job ad—a white lie, there wasn't one—for a typist, and did she want to apply for the job? It was in the North Georgia mountains, far away from Jacobsville and all the painful notoriety.

Emma had agreed. Tippy, who'd saved Emma's pride by not confessing that she'd interfered, had gone with Cash to put the girl on a plane for Atlanta. They'd arranged for a car to meet her at the airport, as well.

"But what if she doesn't like me?" Emma had worried at the gate.

Cash chuckled. "She'll like you."

"Yes, she will," Tippy assured her. "If she doesn't, you come right home." She hugged Emma. "I'll miss you."

Emma hugged her back. In a life desperate for female comfort, Tippy had been her fairy godmother. "I'll miss you more," she wailed.

"Enough of that." Cash hugged Emma, too. "Get on that plane and call us when you get to Mamie's, so we know you got there all right."

"I will." Emma looked at them with sad eyes. "Nobody was ever...so kind to me," she said in a wobbly voice.

"Go on, before I start bawling, too, for God's sake," Cash said, and he wasn't totally kidding. He and Tippy had become very fond of the shy, unassuming young woman they'd more or less adopted.

"Okay. Thanks. For everything," she added.

She got on the plane. Mamie, delighted with what she'd been told and even more with what she saw when Emma arrived on her doorstep, hired her on the spot.

So Emma learned about clothes and deadlines and rich people. She called home every night for a week. Then she began to feel at home on Lake Lanier. She still missed the Griers. She talked to Tippy on Skype often, but she had to stop when she went to work for Connor. He'd mentioned once that a West Texas rancher named Cort Grier was a fellow investor in some new technology, and he knew him fairly well. Cash had a brother named Cort who ranched in West Texas. The name might be a coincidence, but if Cort was Cash's brother, and Connor knew Cort, he might know Cash. She couldn't risk having Connor find out that her family lived in Texas, because he might remember that the woman he'd warned about the speedboat also came from there. It might clue him in that his secretary was actually the woman who'd blinded him. So she sent emails and text messages to Tippy instead, explaining that her boss was eccentric and didn't like her telling other people about him. She never said who he was, in fact. She simply told Tippy that she was doing a favor for this friend of Mamie's who was blind and needed a temporary secretary while Mamie was out of the country.

She hadn't contacted her father at all. When she'd moved in with the Griers, he'd washed his hands of her. People said he was still drinking like a fish. But in his sober moments, he managed to keep the ranch going. Gossip traveled into town. There was a woman, someone he'd met through an agent for one of the bigger meat packing companies, who'd moved in with him. So maybe she was keeping things running so he wouldn't go bankrupt.

Emma put all that to the back of her mind and tried to forget the cloud under which she'd left home. She was still wounded by her memories of Steven. Their breakup had hurt her, especially in a small town where gossip ran rampant. Everybody knew he'd dumped her. It was heartless. She'd been in love with him, and he'd just walked away. She'd been crushed. It was as if her femininity was faulty, as if she wasn't woman enough to keep a man. So she hadn't tried again, after Steven, to attract men. On the rare occasions when a young man tried to flirt with her, she'd been shy and standoffish and not encouraging in the least.

Not so much since she'd gone to work for Connor. But he was wounding her even more. She'd never been this upset by Steven. She hadn't cared this much…

She tamped down hard on those thoughts. She didn't dare

let herself get involved with Connor Sinclair, in any way. It was easy to forget why she worked for him. He was blind. He might never see again. It was Emma who'd blinded him. If he ever found out, her life would be hell. He never forgot people who crossed him, and he always got even.

Her heart fell as she realized how hopeless her situation was. She'd been driving a speedboat too fast and she'd run over Connor in the lake and blinded him. What would he do to her if he knew? She recalled how Mamie had felt when he went after her, and that was just about a newspaper article he didn't like. Emma had cost him his eyesight. He would be out for blood. Her eyes closed and she shivered.

It was late afternoon the next day when Barnes guided Connor through the house to his bedroom.

Emma hovered, but he didn't ask for her. He sent for Marie instead.

The older woman came out of his bedroom silent and uneasy. She glanced at Emma and made a face. Apparently his date hadn't gone well. He didn't act like a man who'd found satisfaction with his slinky brunette. Not at all. Emma tried very hard not to care.

In the middle of the night, she heard Connor groaning. The pain must be very bad, she thought, and wanted to get up and go to him. She even started to. But then she remembered how furious he'd been when she'd tried to guide him to his desk, and he'd bellowed for her to get Barnes. She wasn't risking his temper again.

She lay back in the bed with a sigh. Poor man. It was a migraine, she guessed. He'd pushed himself very hard, then he'd gone nightclubbing. He liked places with loud music and that's probably where the brunette had taken him. Combined with the pressure, that had probably brought on the headache.

She tried to go back to sleep, but couldn't. She heard a door open down the hall and another door open. Voices, one loud and angry. She winced. She recognized that voice.

The door closed. Another door closed. Peace again. Until the groaning got even worse.

She heard another door open, closer to hers. Marie, she guessed as she heard soft footfalls go past her door. She knew that Marie had an intercom that linked to Connor's room. So did Barnes, but apparently Barnes had failed to help his boss.

A door opened again and the loud voice sounded a little calmer. Minutes later, there was a soft tap at Emma's door.

"Come in," she called, turning on her bedside lamp.

It was Marie. "Can you come?" she asked gently. "I don't know where his migraine medicine is or how much to give him, and he can't tell me. He's very sick."

"Of course."

Emma got her robe on and followed the older woman down the hall. Connor was in the bathroom, apparently losing supper and everything before it.

"I'll take care of him," she told Marie gently. "Go back to bed."

Marie hugged her. "Thank you."

Emma went into the bathroom and wet a washcloth. Connor was on the floor with one arm across the toilet seat, his forehead propped on it. His face was ashen.

She cleaned him up and flushed the toilet.

"The sink is three steps to your right," she said softly.

"Emma?"

"Yes, sir."

He groaned again. "I told Marie not to wake you!"

"She doesn't know about the migraine medicine and I do. Here. It's mouthwash." She handed him a cup with a little in it to rinse his mouth. He made a face as he handed her back the cup.

"Come and lie down. I'll get your medicine. Do you think you can keep it down?" she asked matter-of-factly.

"There's ginger ale in the minibar. That usually works," he said heavily.

She helped ease him down on the bed and back onto the pillows. "I'll be right back."

She got the capsules out of the medicine cabinet and paused long enough to get ginger ale before she sat down beside him on the edge of his bed.

"Maybe if I hit my toe with a hammer it will take my mind off how badly my head hurts," he muttered.

"Then you'd have a sore toe to go with your headache," she returned. "Here. Open."

He opened his mouth and she put the single capsule on his tongue. He sat up. She handed him the ginger ale. "Top's off," she said.

"What, the ginger ale's or yours?" he asked sarcastically.

She just sighed.

He swallowed the capsule and a little of the ginger ale before he handed her back the bottle. "That was crude, I suppose."

"I have never considered that ginger ale was crude," she said blithely.

He managed a faint laugh. He drew in a long breath, his hand over his eyes. "God, it hurts, Emma!"

"I'm sorry."

"Are you? Why? It's not your fault."

It was her fault. She'd blinded him. It ground into her conscience like a hot poker. But she could hardly admit it now. "Figure of speech."

"You don't have a clue what's wrong with me, do you?" he asked heavily.

"If I had to guess, your date threw cold water on you and put you on the porch."

His sightless eyes opened wide and he laughed out loud suddenly, wincing when it hurt his head.

"Sorry," she said demurely.

"You pain in the butt," he accused. "I'm your boss."

"You're a grizzly bear in pin-striped suits."

"Shame on you."

"Nobody else will tell you the truth. They're afraid you'll fire them."

"And you aren't?"

"I'm temporary," she reminded him. "That's why I work for temporary agencies. I don't want to be shackled for life to a man who thinks of women as disposable napkins."

He laughed softly. "I've missed you, Emma," he said.

"I've been right here," she reminded him.

He leaned back with a long sigh. "I guess you have." His pained eyes narrowed. "Just don't build romantic dreams about me, Emma," he added surprisingly. "I don't believe in happily-ever-after, and you do."

She was shocked that he'd say such a thing. He was a millionaire and she worked for wages. Worse, she worked for him. It was embarrassing that he knew how she felt about him.

She looked for a way to save face. "It's the movies."

"Excuse me?" he asked, scowling.

*"Jane Eyre,"* she explained. "I've seen the movie half a dozen times. You're Mr. Rochester, with a permanent scowl and bad attitude. All you lack is the dog."

He chuckled. "Is that so?"

"Yes, sir. I've been watching too many old movies on late-night television, and when you had the headache, I remembered that Jane Eyre saved Mr. Rochester from a fire in his room in the middle of the night. Except that I'm saving you from headaches in the middle of the night."

"And you made romantic connections, is that it?" he asked, smiling.

"Absolutely."

He managed a laugh. "Well, it's one way of interpreting things. But we'd both do well to concentrate more on the aircraft industry than late-night romantic trysts, even if they're provoked by headaches. Right?"

"Absolutely."

"You'd better patent that word if you plan to continue using it," he jibed.

"I'll phone the copyright office first thing in the morning," she promised. "Head any better?"

He shifted in the bed a little. "Somewhat. You'd better go back to sleep before Marie and Barnes start talking about us. We do need to stop meeting this way."

"Yes, sir," she agreed.

He laughed. "Friends again, Emma?"

"Friends again, sir."

He had a whimsical look on his face. "I've never had a woman mop me up in a bathroom before," he said.

"We all get sick sometimes," she replied.

"Thanks, just the same."

"You're very welcome." She got up, returned the prescription bottle to the bathroom, cleaned up the sink and turned out the light.

She paused beside the bed. "Doing okay?"

"Yes. I think I can sleep now. Good night, Emma."

"Good night, sir."

"Something I've been wondering…"

"Yes?"

He looked toward the sound of her voice. "Who broke the engagement?"

She hesitated. "He did."

His eyebrows arched. "Why?"

"My parents had a few farm animals that they raised for food. He was an animal rights activist."

"Didn't he know that when you got engaged?"

"I guess not."

"I suppose you missed the physical closeness when he was gone," he fished, because it would help explain why she was so vulnerable with him.

But she wasn't going to tell him anymore. It hurt her pride too much. "Yes, I did…miss it a lot," she lied.

So she had been in bed with her fiancé. He'd suspected it, but it hurt him in some odd way to hear her say it. He closed up again.

"Good night, then."

"Good night, sir."

She went back to her room. It was good that he was speaking to her again. Maybe they could get back to the way things used to be between them. And maybe, someday soon, she could tell him the truth about why she'd taken this job. Maybe she could work up enough courage to admit what she'd done and ask forgiveness for it. Maybe.

Connor was more animated at the breakfast table than he'd been in days. He talked about a new design his team had come up with for a baby jet, a basic refit of a popular one. Emma wondered why they didn't do a whole new design. He told her that lawsuits were supported when a completely innovative project came out. It was far safer, for many reasons, to adapt an older design than to create a new one.

"So that's why they all look alike," Emma began.

"Good Lord, woman, they don't look alike! Any idiot can tell a Cessna from a Learjet!"

"I can't," she replied.

He sipped coffee. His expression was hard to read. "I can't tell them apart anymore, can I, Emma? Only people with eyes can do that."

She grimaced. "Mr. Sinclair…"

His fist hit the table. "Damn it!" he exclaimed. "Oh, God, why? What use am I without eyes? I can't fly a plane, much less design one!"

Emma felt the guilt all the way to the soles of her feet. "You might regain your vision," she said weakly. "Miracles still happen, if you believe in them."

"I don't believe in anything," he said flatly.

"I know." She bit her lower lip. "I'm so sorry," she added huskily.

"Why? I wrecked the Jet Ski." He put a hand to his head. "I remember that. I wish I could remember how it happened. It's all a blur, everything."

"Perhaps you will remember, one day," she said soothingly, and then recalled that if he ever did, she would have to run for her very life.

He leaned back in his chair. "Maybe." He was brooding again.

"There are about a hundred business emails sitting on the computer," she began.

He grimaced. "That never ends. The damned phone's been ringing off the hook since five a.m.," he added. "It's mid-morning in several other places around the world. They don't even look at the time difference when they phone me."

"Why don't you turn your phone off at night?" Emma asked, aghast. "People have no right to disturb you when you're trying to sleep."

"They think they do."

"Just turn it on Silent."

He chuckled softly, then drew in a breath and stretched, the muscles in his chest and arms rippling with the movement. He was so sexy that Emma felt a shiver go down her spine.

"I feel like a change. Got your passport with you?" he asked Emma.

She blinked. "Well, I do have a passport," she ventured.

"Steven said we might go to somewhere in the Caribbean for our honeymoon so I got it, just in case. Why?"

"I thought we might fly down to Cancún for a few days and soak up some sun," he replied.

Her lips parted. "Mexico?"

"Or we could go to Jamaica or the Bahamas…"

"I would love to go to the Bahamas!" she exclaimed. "I've wanted to see them my whole life!"

He chuckled amusedly. "Why?"

"Pirates," she returned. "Woodes Rogers was governor of the Bahamas back in the late 1600s and early 1700s, and he started out as an English sea captain and became a privateer. In fact, Henry Morgan was a notorious Welsh pirate in the 1600s, and became lieutenant governor of Jamaica."

"You like pirates."

She shrugged and smiled. "Well, yes."

He pursed his sensuous lips. "Your favorite character in the *Star Wars* movie was Darth Vader, I'll bet."

She grimaced. "Actually, yes, he was. I always thought he was just misunderstood. So I bought this T-shirt that said Vader Was Framed. I wore it until the letters faded out."

He chuckled. "You're full of surprises, Emma."

"I guess I am."

He didn't react visibly to the mention of her fiancé being the reason she had a passport. He hated the whole idea of her fiancé, and he didn't understand why. She worked for him. That was why he felt protective about her. Now, if he could just manage to keep his hands off her! But even if he couldn't, she'd already admitted that she missed intimacy with her fiancé, so maybe he could coax her into his bed if he took his time. He couldn't remember a hunger so sweeping, not in his whole life.

Connor felt for his cell phone. "Barnes, have them get the

jet ready. Tomorrow morning, first thing, we're leaving. Do what you have to before then. Everybody hear that?"

"Yes, sir," Marie and Barnes replied together, and then laughed because they had.

"You, too, young Emma," Connor said with a smile.

"I'll be ready!" she promised. "Do we take the office laptop with us?"

"We'll have to," he replied. "It's my lifeline when I travel. There's a case for it in the closet in the study."

"I'll find it today," Emma promised.

"Barnes, you'll need to drive me into town after breakfast. I need a new bathing suit. Have you got one, Emma?"

She did, but it was at the Griers' house in Texas. "No," she said baldly.

"What size and what color? We'll pick you up something."

"Medium," she told him, "and I like blue."

"Done."


He came home with a bag from a famous department store and held it out for Emma. "I hope you like it. We had to go almost all the way to Atlanta to find the shop I wanted. It's not that long a drive. Here."

Her heart jumped when she pulled it out of the bag. It was a symphony of blue, a one-piece maillot with high-cut legs and a low-cut neckline.

"Don't fuss," Connor told her. It was a designer suit and probably cost more than she made in a month.

She sought for the right words. "Okay. Thanks, Mr. Sinclair."

"Barnes says it's a little risqué, but we'll be on a private beach. Nobody will see you." His face hardened. "Not even me."

"It's beautiful," she replied.

"If you don't like the colors, you can blame Barnes. I had to take his word for it."

Barnes laughed. "Well, it is blue," he defended himself. "I'm sorry about the style, Miss Copeland, but I had to take the saleslady's word that it was the most conservative bathing suit they sold."

"He doesn't swim," Connor said with faint sarcasm.

"Neither do I," Marie called.

"Well, I swim," he returned. "Emma may have to save me from sharks, but I'm not going to sit on the beach!"

Emma's heart jumped. She laughed. "Not to worry, sir. I can take on three sharks at a time if I have to."

"Liar," Connor purred.

"I can take on one shark, if it's been harpooned," she amended.

He chuckled. "That, I'd believe."

It wasn't a long trip to Nassau. Emma was fascinated with everything, starting with the small jet that Connor owned. He didn't like public transportation of any kind, Barnes had whispered, so he never used commercial airplanes.

Emma was grateful, because she didn't like crowds. Her first airplane trip had been from Texas to Atlanta, and she still got nauseous remembering it. She'd been sandwiched in between a fighting couple and a mother with two toddlers. By the time the plane landed, she'd been listening to the in-flight radio with the volume turned up to maximum. She'd worried that she'd probably go deaf from it, but it was so much better than screaming preschoolers and cursing couples.

"You're very quiet," Connor remarked.

"I'm awed," she replied. "I've never been on a private plane. I've never been over the ocean. I've never been anywhere, really, except Georgia and…" She hesitated. "North Carolina," she added quickly. She was about to say Texas. Big mistake.

He smiled, apparently overlooking the hesitation. "It's been a long time since I experienced anything for the first time," he said. He leaned back in his seat. "But it's nice to be free of the phone for a couple of hours."

Just as he said that, his phone rang. He was laughing as he answered it.

Emma's first glimpse of New Providence left her speechless. "It's true," she burst out as they started to land. "The water really is that color! I thought it was just a bad picture! It's turquoise and dark blue and light blue and almost neon blue, all at once!"

Connor chuckled. "Yes. The water startles people seeing it for the first time." His smile faded. "I used to love to watch people on the beach."

"You still can," she promised. "I'll describe them all to you. Everything."

His bad mood left him. "I'll hold you to that, Emma."

"Okay," she replied. "You know, I'd give you my eyes, if I could," she said so solemnly that his silence made her uncomfortable.

He drew in a long breath. "Thanks," he said. It had just occurred to him that not once in his life had a woman nurtured him as Emma did. He remembered her holding a cold, wet cloth to his head when he'd gotten sick from the migraine, never leaving him until the pain eased. She kindled emotions in him that he was certain he'd never felt before, even with his first wife.

He wasn't sure he liked it.

# SIX

Emma loved the feel of the hot, sugar-white sand under her bare feet. The water crept in from the bay, swirling around her feet as she walked along the beach. There were plenty of people, but Connor had stayed in the villa while he dealt with a crisis at one of the companies that manufactured his aircraft.

It was lonely without him. She listened to the gulls calling as they flew overhead and laughed as they dived and soared. She closed her eyes and listened to the rhythm of the surf rolling in from the bay. Nearby, tall casuarina pines swayed gracefully in the breeze that seemed constant and eternal on the beach.

Connor owned a huge villa on the bay. It was a symphony of white and royal blue, with graceful arches and stone patios and floors. All around it, blooming flowers loosened a scent more delicate than the finest perfume.

Emma hadn't put on the swimsuit Connor bought her. They'd only just arrived, and she wanted to settle in before she tried swimming in the salt water. She could swim, just barely, but she couldn't float. She sank like a rock. Not that she'd been swimming that much since she was a little girl.

The Bahamas had to be close to paradise, she thought as she walked. She'd never been anywhere like this. She'd dreamed of seeing foreign places, but this surpassed her imagining.

Pirates had walked here in centuries past. Travelers from all over the world came to Nassau to vacation. It was incredibly beautiful.

Connor had promised to take her on a tour tomorrow, to see the forts and downtown Nassau. They might, he teased, even take in the casino on Paradise Island, across the bridge from Nassau. She could try her luck with the one-armed bandits.

She'd buried her nose in a travel brochure while Marie unpacked for him. He was on the phone again. He'd been yelling at someone when she dived out the door to go for a stroll. He was the man in charge, and the aircraft corporation, from what she'd gathered during her tenure as his secretary, was enormous and worldwide. Something was always going wrong, and many times he couldn't delegate when problems arose. There were decisions that only he could make.

"Emma!" he called, breaking into her thoughts.

"I'm right here." She ran up to the porch, where he was standing, waiting, in the shade of the eaves. He was wearing white shorts with a red-and-white button-down shirt, open down the front. She'd never seen him quite that undressed and she couldn't help eating him up with her eyes. He was the most beautiful man she'd ever seen, perfect physically, powerful and sensuous. She had to clench her teeth not to reach out and touch that broad, muscular tanned chest with its pelt of black, curling hair.

"What are you doing?" he asked. "Gone in swimming already?"

"I don't swim that well," she confessed. "I've just been walking along the beach, drinking in the sounds and smells. It's the most beautiful place I've ever seen!"

He laughed softly at her enthusiasm. "I'm glad you like it. My grandfather built this estate. I like France better, but this is close to the States when I want to get away for a few days."

"Why do you like France best?" she asked, curious.

"My grandmother was French," he said simply. "I was raised by my grandparents. My mother died when I was four or five. My father was too occupied with making money to care what happened to his two sons. William and I were dumped on our grandparents. They lived on the Riviera. Old money." He chuckled. "They had ancestors who were beheaded in the French Revolution."

"My goodness!"

"We all have skeletons in our ancestry," he teased.

"Well, we had a horse thief who was hanged, back in the 1800s," she confessed.

"See?"

She laughed. "Do you want to come walk on the beach?" she asked.

He shook his head. "I'm overseeing some changes in the design staff at our northern Atlanta facility," he said darkly. "I gave orders that weren't followed, so heads are going to roll."

"I guess you have a lot of employees."

"Too many, sometimes. Don't stay out in the sun too long. It can be deadly."

"I won't. I'm just exploring."

He managed a smile for her. "Okay. I'll have some letters to dictate in about an hour. You're free until then."

"I'll be back in time," she promised.


It was lonely when he left. Odd, how his very presence seemed to color her world, she thought as she dragged her bare feet through the sugary sand. He wasn't the man she'd thought he was when she first met him. He was surprisingly personable and kind, for a millionaire.

She picked up a few shells and carried them inside when Marie announced that lunch was on the table.

There was conch soup and a mango salad with chicken and macaroni, followed by lime custard pie.

"This is wonderful!" Emma exclaimed as she tasted each dish.

Marie laughed. "Thanks. Mr. Sinclair had a chef from one of the local restaurants come and teach me how to make all the island dishes. He was very good."

"I like local fare when I travel," Connor said easily. He finished his coffee and stretched, rippling muscles in his broad chest. "Okay, Emma, let's get some work done if you're through."

"I am," she said, finishing up her last bite of pie. "Thanks, Marie!"

"You're most welcome."

Connor paused. "It really was good, Marie," he added.

The cook arched both eyebrows. She'd worked for him for years. That was the first time he'd really complimented her on a meal. "Thank you," she said.

Connor turned and made his way to the big study, where an oak desk and several bookcases and leather chairs made up the furnishings. There were wooden blinds at the windows that fronted on the bay, and beige carpet on the floor. There was also a huge wooden ceiling fan with lights, and it was turning lazily, moving the air around.

"This is grand," Emma murmured as she took in the furnishings.

He chuckled. "I always liked it. Barnes said he put the laptop on the desk."

"Yes, he did." She pulled it around in front of her and sat down in one of the roomy leather chairs that surrounded the six-foot desk.

Connor felt his way around the desk and into the enormous chair behind it. He sat down gingerly and let out a breath. "Well, that's something, I guess," he mused.

"What is?"

"I left standing orders that not a stick of furniture was supposed to be moved before I got here. The cleaning crew was
briefed." His face hardened. "I'm still learning my way around
places I used to be able to see."

She bit her lip. "Isn't there some chance that your sight
could return?" she asked.

He leaned back in the chair. "One of my doctors is a famous neurosurgeon, another is a famous neurologist. They
did every test known to man and I passed them with flying
colors."

"Then there's no physical damage?" she asked hesitantly.

"Of course there's not! That's why I'm blind!" He hit the
desk with his fist, his mood gone sour in an instant. "Tests,
damned tests, and the damned tests didn't show anything! If
I'm all right, why can't I see?" He groaned and drew a hand
over his face. "Oh, God, why can't I see?"

"You don't remember...anything?" she persisted.

"No." He flexed his shoulders and sat up straight. "I remember pain. They said my head was bleeding. There was a
mild concussion, but nothing serious enough to cost me my
sight. I was alone on the lake. There were other boats, but
they were far off. If one had hit me, surely it would have to-
taled the Jet Ski," he added irritably.

"It wasn't hit?" she fished.

"Well, yes, it was," he said after a minute. "I'd forgotten
that. There was a dent in the side. So maybe something did
hit me." He frowned. "There was an incident. I think I was
angry at someone, for speeding on the lake." He ground his
teeth together even as Emma cringed inwardly. He scowled.
"Damn it, I can't remember!"

She was almost holding her breath by now. She wished
she hadn't brought up the subject. But she needed to know

if there was hope, if she might someday find absolution if his eyesight returned. "What did they think it was?' she asked.

He clenched his fists together on the desk. "Oh, this is good," he said, his smile a study in sarcasm. "They say it's hysterical blindness."

Her heart jumped. "But you're the least hysterical person I've ever known," she blurted out.

That brought a faint smile to his face. "Thank you."

"It's some long scientific name, isn't it, like short-term amnesia or something," she guessed.

"They said that if I saw something coming toward me and expected to be blinded, that my senses might trick me into believing that I was. But it's been weeks, Emma," he added. "If I were going to see again, I'd be able to by now. No, I think there's something else, something they missed." He clasped his big hands together. "Maybe they'll find it eventually. I have to hope so. I can't bear the thought of living in this darkness for the rest of my life."

Her heart sank. What he said made sense. If it was psychosomatic, it probably wouldn't have lasted this long.

"We won't solve the problem today, at any rate, so let's get to work. Read me the message from Cybernetic Systems. They produce the computers we use in our executive jet, the one we're having problems with."

She obliged him, her voice soft and quiet in the stillness of the office. But when she finished, she had no idea what the message meant. "It's Greek to me," she muttered.

He chuckled. "Not quite. We've got a glitch in one of the backup systems, an error that keeps cropping up in the software. That's what he and his team are trying to address. Ready? Here's the reply…"

They worked for a solid three hours. Emma was learning volumes about the aviation industry and its components. She hadn't realized so many different companies were involved in the construction of an aircraft. But when she thought about it, there was the fabric used in the seats, the material that constituted the storage bins, the oven in the small kitchen, the plumbing and hardware in the bathrooms—and all that was separate from the engines, the electronics, the endless wiring and computer systems that actually made the plane fly.

"How in the world does an airplane ever get off the ground with so many things that can go wrong?" she wondered when she'd sent the last email message out.

"It was easier for the Wright brothers," he agreed with a chuckle. "In fact, before World War I, aviators had no way to land the plane unless they could get a few cars to line up and light the landing strip."

"My gosh!"

"My great-grandfather flew with the Lafayette Escadrille in France during the First World War," he recalled. "He was still alive when I was a boy. He could tell some stories. Like the time when he shot off his own propeller and went down behind enemy lines. It was before the days of proper machine guns that fired through the propeller by syncing the action."

"I'd love to have heard those stories." She sighed. "It must have been a great adventure."

"To hear him tell it, certainly. He said that when the Red Baron crashed his triplane, the Brits flew over and dropped a wreath on enemy headquarters in his honor. They were a special breed, those first aviators. It was a gentleman's war in the air."

"I've read about the Red Baron," she confessed.

He nodded. "So have I. Those first planes fascinated me. I think it's why I went into manufacturing in the first place. I wanted to build something new, something innovative. I guess I did. The first baby jet I designed won awards and made my first millions."

"I'd never be smart enough to design anything," she said.

"I was always good at math," he said simply. "Electronics was a breeze. I learned everything I could from men like my great-grandfather and improved on their designs. But I got a degree in business from Harvard," he added. "I needed to know how to manage what I had. I didn't like to delegate." He leaned back in his chair wearily. "I still don't. But I have to now. I can't even see the designs, much less approve them. I have to count on my executives not to bankrupt us."

"If your executives are like Marie and Barnes, they must be wonderful at what they do," she said. "You have a knack for picking the right people for the job."

He smiled. "They're great, aren't they?" he mused. He cocked his head. "You're not bad yourself, young Emma. You take dictation very nicely. At the computer, too."

"I had to learn that at my first job," she said. "The lady I worked for didn't bother writing notes. She just started talking and expected me to write it all down. So I did."

"What sort of work did she do?"

*Tricky question, Emma,* she reminded herself, *be careful.* "She was an attorney," she prevaricated. "She said that going in front of a jury was like storytelling, and if you told a better story than the defense attorney, you could win the case." Actually, she'd learned that from one of the Griers' friends, Jacobsville's district attorney, Blake Kemp.

"It is like storytelling, isn't it?" he agreed. "But I'll tell you a secret, Emma. It's usually the client with the most money who wins the case. Innocence or guilt is relative."

"That's very cynical," she pointed out.

He shrugged. "I'm a cynical man." His sightless eyes stared straight ahead, full of the disillusion he felt. "Most people are out for what they can get. Especially women."

"Not all of them."

"Little Miss Sunshine," he chided. "Don't you want a sports car to drive?"

"I don't like sports cars," she said simply.

His thick eyebrows lifted. "What do you like?"

"Pickup trucks." She grinned. "That's what I drove back home, a twenty-year-old pickup truck with a dent in the fender and a straight stick with a clutch."

"My God! Poverty row!"

"I lived within my means," she pointed out.

"And liked it?" he chided.

"Yes." She smiled at his expression of disbelief. "I told you, I like crickets. You can have your casinos and your flashy lights. I'll take a quiet night anytime."

"You really need corrupting," he said. "I'll have to work on that."

"Do your worst, you won't change me," she dared. "I'm just a simple country girl. Anyway, you're a millionaire and you can get all the beautiful, glamorous women you like. I'm much too plain for someone like you, even if I weren't poor and uneducated."

"Did you graduate from high school?"

"Sure," she said. "But I never went to college, unless you consider vocational school higher education. I went straight to work and took courses on the side."

"Typing."

"Actually, my first job was cooking," she confessed. "I made all the cakes and pies and pastries for a restaurant."

"I hate sweets." He chuckled.

"No wonder you have such perfect white teeth." She sighed.

He pursed his lips. "And a great dentist," he added, tongue in cheek. He got up from the desk. "How would you like to go to the casino tonight?"

Her lips parted. "I've never been in a casino." She grimaced. "And honestly, I don't have the clothes for it…"

"You've been watching too many James Bond films," he scoffed. "People wear anything from shorts to blue jeans."

"Really?"

"Really. So. Want to go?"

"Yes, please," she replied.

"We'll go first thing after dinner," he told her.


"Oh, my goodness, it's like...like Christmas," she exclaimed as the limousine took them over the bridge to Paradise Island. "The boats in the marina light up!" she enthused. "And the city looks like a Christmas tree!"

He laughed softly at her enthusiasm. She was wearing jeans and a button-up blouse and sneakers. He had on navy twill slacks and a white sports shirt. It made her less inhibited. He didn't actually look like a millionaire tonight.

"Wait until you see inside the casino," he told her. "It has crystal chandeliers and imported cut-glass accents."

"You've been there before."

"Yes. The owner of the Bow Tie is a friend of mine. His name is Marcus Carrera. His wife is from Texas."

Emma felt as if she'd been slammed in the stomach with a bat. She knew Marcus Carrera's wife, the former Delia Mason. Delia had done repairs for the dry cleaner in Jacobsville, where Emma had worked in the café, and was a gifted dressmaker, as well. She'd made a dress for Emma to wear to the one dance she'd attended with Steven before he broke off their engagement.

If Delia saw Emma, she'd recognize her on sight, and that would lead to questions she couldn't answer in front of Connor. He thought she was from North Carolina. The joy drained out of her like water through a sieve.

"You've gone quiet," he said, looking in her general direction. "What's wrong?"

"Nothing," she assured him. "I'm just drinking in the view. Will we get to meet Mr. Carrera?"

He hesitated. There was an odd note in her voice. He couldn't quite place what it was. "I don't think so. Not tonight, anyway. He and Delia took their little boy to see his aunt in California. She's a commercial artist. She was married to Marcus's late brother. They had two children."

"Maybe some other time, then," she said, and tried not to let the relief she felt show in her voice. "Oh, we're here!"

She held Connor's hand unobtrusively, and whispered directions to him. The contact was electric. Just touching him made her giddy. He was broad-shouldered and husky. His presence made him seem much taller than he was. She loved the faintly callused touch of his big hand in hers, the spicy scent of his cologne. His hands were perfectly manicured, as well. He was a fastidious man, for all his ruggedness.

As they walked, heads turned toward them. Connor drew women's eyes. One of them, a gorgeous blonde, gasped and made a beeline for him.

"Connor!" she exclaimed, and grasped his arm so hard that she almost overbalanced him. "It's so good to see you! How have you been?"

"I've been well, Grace, how about you?" he asked, smiling toward the sound of her voice. "Sorry, but we're short on time. I'm showing Emma the casino."

"Oh." The blonde's perfect mouth pouted as she met Emma's eyes. "Well, I'll just get back to my friends. So good to see you! Call me!"

"Sure," he said.

She dashed off as quickly as she'd bounded up to them. "Sorry," she said softly. "I didn't see her in time to warn you." She knew that suddenly being clutched was unnerving to sightless people.

"It's okay." He drew in a steadying breath. "She didn't notice that I can't see, did she?"

"No."

"I've kept it quiet. Reporters love to pounce on imperfections," he added coldly. "I don't want to feed the gossip mill."

"I'll make sure nobody notices," she promised, and whispered instructions that took them to the one-armed bandit.

"Here," he said, tugging a twenty-dollar bill out of his pocket. He'd had Barnes slip several in a clip for him earlier. "Get some quarters and go to work. I'll wait right here."

He leaned up against the vacant machine while she ran to get change. It only took a minute. Then she sat down.

"Here goes nothing." She laughed.

"Good luck."

She fed it and fed it, pulling the handle and hoping for success. She lost more than she won. But she kept getting free rounds with matches, which let her play for a longer time than she'd expected. Then, on her last quarter, the machine rang wildly and flashed the winnings.

Connor laughed. "Jackpot."

"Yes! Oh, my!" She was beaming from ear to ear. "It's a fortune!" she exclaimed.

"How much?"

"Five thousand dollars!"

He was thinking that it was pocket change, but Emma seemed to think her ship had come in. He laughed indulgently. "Ready to cash in, or want to play some more?" he teased.

"No, I'm done. This is great!"

"Okay. Let's go."

She held his hand and guided him unobtrusively through the crowd to the payout booth, where she handed them the ticket and collected her winnings.

"Now that you're rich, are you planning to leave me?" he teased as they walked out into the warm, breezy night air.

"Not at all." She laughed. "In fact, I know exactly what I want to do with this. Can the driver take us into downtown Nassau?"

"Of course," he said, letting her guide him into the waiting car. "Tell him where you want to go. But most of the shops aren't going to be open this late…"

"It's not a shop." She told the driver her destination before she let him put her in beside Connor.

"I couldn't hear what you told him. Where are we going?" he asked.

"It's a little church, right downtown," she said. "I noticed it when we drove by."

"A church."

"Yes. It will have a poor box inside," she added. "That's where I'm going to put my winnings."

He was silent for so long that she thought she'd said something wrong. "It's…it's all right, isn't it?" she asked after a minute.

"Why don't you want to keep it?" he asked.

"Because it was easy money," she returned. "I put in twenty dollars and won five thousand dollars. I like working for what I get. My mother taught me that things you get without effort aren't worthy of you."

He let out a breath. In his entire life, he'd never taken a woman to a casino and had her offer to even share her winnings, much less want to give them away.

"You aren't mad?" she added, worriedly.

"I'm not mad, honey," he said softly.

He was silent the rest of the way into the city. He stayed in the car while Emma went inside the small church and stuffed her winnings into the poor box. He said very little all the way back to the estate.

"I've upset you," she worried when they were inside the house.

He found her shoulders and rested his big hands on them. They were warm and comforting. "The sort of women I'm used to don't share anything," he said quietly. "They take."

"Mama always said that giving was much more noble than taking."

He smiled gently. "I think your mother must be a wonderful woman."

"She was," she said.

"Dead?"

"Long ago," she replied.

He frowned. "I thought you told me that your parents both lived in North Carolina."

She'd told him that her father lived there. She knew she'd told him that her mother died in childbirth. "My father has a girlfriend," she said. Well, he did have that woman living with him. "She's very nice," she added, hoping that wasn't a lie. She'd never met the woman.

"I see."

"Thank you for taking me to the casino. It was really exciting!"

"I'm glad you liked it. Tomorrow, we'll make time for one of the other tourist traps."

"That would be great!"

"But we'll have to do some work first," he said, smiling in her general direction.

"God forbid that I should become a worthless layabout," she agreed.

He chuckled. "Sleep tight."

"You, too."

She watched him go down the hall with soft eyes. She

didn't care so much for bright lights, but she loved going places with Connor. She slept soundly all night.

The next morning, she found a growling grizzly bear in the study. He was on the phone, obviously furious.

"I told you," he was raging at someone. "The cost overrun was unavoidable! If we hadn't made the design change, the jet would never have passed inspection! I was barely able to land it myself, and I've been flying for twenty years!...Yes. Yes! I know all that. You tell the board of directors that if they can find someone to replace me who can guarantee the profit I've given them, go for it. And that's my final word." He cut off the phone and tossed it onto his desk, where it landed with a thud. Foul language ensued.

"Boss?" she asked hesitantly.

His black mood began to fade. He grimaced. "Damned pencil-pushing, backbiting sons of larceny," he muttered. "Questioning a decision I made that sent profits up ten percent, and they're angry about a cost overrun! In this economy, they're lucky they have a company to employ them!"

"We all have these difficult times to get through. Why don't you come walk on the beach and pretend you're a vagrant with no money?"

He hesitated, then suddenly burst out laughing. His pale eyes were alive with humor. "A vagrant with no money?"

"Sure! Then you can enjoy the beach with no money worries to haunt you."

He drew in a long breath. "Why not? Lead on."

She took his hand and tugged him along with her, describing the lay of the land and the distance to the beach.

"You're really quite good at this," he remarked.

"Necessity is the mother of invention," she quoted. "Now. Just stand here with your feet in the surf and drink in that delicious air!"

He did. He seemed to relax more with every breath. "I never have time to spend like this," he remarked after a minute. "There's always a meeting or a dinner or a working conference or a phone call…"

She looked up at him and was glad that he couldn't see her face. She absolutely adored him, and it showed. He was the most masculine man she'd ever seen in her life, and it wounded her that she could never have him. Over and above her feelings, there was always the fear that one day he'd learn her true identity. She knew how vindictive he was. There would be no place she could run where he wouldn't find her. Retribution would be terrible.

She bit her lower lip. They said confession was good for the soul, didn't they? Perhaps now would be the time to tell him the truth, and throw herself on his mercy. If he didn't already know what sort of person she was, he never would.

"There's something I need to tell you," she began hesitantly.

He turned to her, big and sensuous and teasing. "Is it something shocking?"

She shifted. "Well…"

His hands went out to her waist and he lifted her off her feet, holding her up against him—close, very close—and nuzzled her face with his.

"You can tell me anything, Emma," he whispered. His lips smoothed down her soft cheek to the corner of her mouth. "Anything at all."

Her heart raced like a wild thing. She slid her arms around his neck, just to hold on so he didn't drop her, she rationalized. "I can?" she whispered back.

The sound of the surf was very loud. Or was it the loud beat of her heart, echoing so that he could hear it.

"Yes," he murmured as his lips feathered across her mouth. "You can."

The teasing motion made her hungry. Unconsciously, she

began to follow his lips with her own, tempting them to press down harder.

His hands tightened on her waist. He let her slip, just enough to let her feel his thumbs teasing under her breasts, to make her arms pull him closer.

She was barely breathing. She was afraid to move, afraid to break the spell. He smelled of coffee and spicy cologne, and she wanted nothing more than to feel his sensuous mouth open, pressing her lips apart, grinding into them in the silence that hung like a silken veil around them.

"Hungry, Emma?" he whispered at her mouth.

She swallowed. "Yes," she admitted.

"Show me…" His mouth opened on her lips, pressing them apart, and he groaned as the hunger mushroomed inside him. "Emma!" His arms went completely around her, and he kissed her with such anguished desire that she moaned under the crush of his mouth.

He heard the hunger in her tone and felt it to his bones. "It aches, doesn't it, Emma?" he breathed into her mouth.

"Aches," she whispered as he kissed her again.

His body was making an emphatic statement about what it wanted. It wanted hers. He didn't try to hide it, although he felt her gasp softly and resist him, just for a few seconds. He was curious about her reticence. She'd been engaged. She knew the score. He was imagining things.

"Connor," she moaned as he deepened the hard kiss.

"Soon, baby," he breathed into her mouth. "Soon!"

Soon…what?

But before she could ask, before he could turn toward the house, Marie's voice called out from the tree-lined arches.

"Mr. Sinclair, there's a call for you from the States!"

"Oh, damn," he ground into Emma's welcoming mouth.

She drew in a shaky breath. "They want you to save the world," she teased on an unsteady breath.

"I'd give it away to carry you to bed, Emma," he breathed into her lips. "I want you. God, I want you!"

She shivered a little. "Oh, but—"

"Mr. Sinclair, are you out there?" Marie persisted. "They say it's urgent!"

He muttered under his breath as he put Emma back on her feet. "Okay, lead the old blind horse back to the barn, Emma," he muttered.

"You're not old," she said huskily. "You'll never be old."

He chuckled and his gray eyes twinkled. "Oh?"

She cleared her throat. "We should hurry."

"Just what I was thinking," he said, and the tone of his voice was enough to make her feel panicky. What had she done?

# SEVEN

Unfortunately, the phone call led to two more phone calls, and those led him to a meeting in downtown Nassau with a group of investors who wanted Connor to join their ranks.

"I'd love to be able to turn it down," Connor said as he waited for the limo. "But it sounds like a good investment opportunity, and with the cost overrun, I can't really afford to ignore it."

"Do you want me to come and take notes?" she asked.

He reached out and clutched her hand tight in his. "Not this time, honey. They have a stenographer with them." He lifted her hand to his lips. "I hated being interrupted," he whispered. "But we've got all night, haven't we?" he purred.

"About that..." she began.

"No more teasing, Emma," he said quietly. "You can have anything you want. I mean that."

"But I don't want anything," she protested.

"Diamonds?" he tempted. "Emeralds? A beach house down here and free frequent flyer miles so that you can come whenever you like?"

"I don't want anything," she repeated.

He tugged her closer. "You want me," he said under his breath, bending his head toward her face. "You want me as badly as I want you."

"I can't," she moaned.

"You know you want to," he said softly. "I won't let anything happen to you. I promise."

Her face flamed. He was talking about preventing a pregnancy. Heavens, what had she led him to think?

"It was just a kiss," she faltered.

His fingers linked slowly with hers. "You told me yourself that you missed the closeness you had with your fiancé. I don't have a woman in my life right now."

"You have...her."

"Her?"

"That glittery brunette you took out on the town and stayed all night with." She tugged her hand free and stepped back.

"Ariel?" He remembered he'd had Emma send her flowers and chocolates, wanting Emma to believe he'd been sleeping with Ariel, that he was getting what Emma denied him somewhere else. His chest rose and fell. "She's like all the others, Emma," he said after a minute. "They numb the ache for a little while. Then they're gone."

"Like I'd be gone. After I numbed the ache."

He scowled as he heard the car stop at the front steps. "We can talk about it later. I have to go."

He turned and went out the front door, allowing the driver to help him inside the limousine.

Emma went back inside and jotted down talking points from the emails he'd received during the morning.

He didn't come back to the house until after dark. He bypassed dinner, assuring Marie that he'd had dinner with the other investors.

"Emma, have you eaten?" he asked.

"Yes, sir," she said. She'd eaten very little. She'd spent the day brooding, worrying about what he was going to expect from her when he came home. She adored him, but she wasn't going to sleep with him. She knew he thought she'd been intimate with Steven. She'd have to tell the truth. It was the only thing that might keep him at bay. She'd give in if he put on the pressure, and she couldn't afford to. Her heart was involved, but his definitely wasn't. It was his body that ached for her, and only until it had the satisfaction it craved. He'd said as much. He wanted her to numb the pain. Nothing more. And then she'd be gone, as all the others were gone.

But Emma…loved him. She loved him. She knew that now, and she couldn't give in to him, then just go on with her life. Not only would it go against everything she believed in, it would be a memory that would haunt her for the rest of her life. He'd go on to the next woman, but Emma would be bound to the memory. Without him, she would have no life.

"I need to dictate a letter to the investors. I'll meet you in the office. Barnes! Come and help me get changed."

"Yes, sir," the older man said at once.

Connor had two letters to dictate, both about the investment group—one to the chairman of the board of his aircraft corporation, the other to his stockholders. It was an explanation of why he was going to tie up some of the company profits in a new, innovative software that might revolutionize cockpit navigation.

He also named some of the other investors. One was a man from West Texas with a name that Emma recognized. It was Cort Grier, Cash's brother. If he was in Nassau, she had to make sure that she didn't meet him. He'd never seen her, but she was certain that he'd have heard about her from Cash and Tippy. That would never do. If he mentioned the connection to Connor, he might remember the troublesome neighbor who'd almost hit him with a speedboat. That might jog his memory in a deadly way.

He didn't remember who hit him, who caused his blindness. But once he knew who Emma really was, it would be easy for him to make the connection and then make other connections. Hit-and-run was a felony, and that's what she'd done. She'd hit him on the lake and hadn't stopped to see if he was all right. Worse, he might think she'd done it on purpose, which could lead to another felony charge. He could have her arrested and prosecuted, and what defense would save her? It had been foolish, taking this job. She should have gone back to Texas at once.

"You've gone quiet again, Emma," he teased.

"I'm sleepy," she lied, with a smile in her voice.

"At this hour? God forbid! Wait up for me," he added gently. "I may have some emails to get out after the meeting. With the time difference, I can be doing business yesterday and tomorrow with the rest of the world, even if people in the States are sleeping." He chuckled.

"Okay." She wished she hadn't agreed so quickly. There was an odd, smug, almost predatory look on his broad face as she replied. He thought she'd be a pushover. He was right. She had to start thinking up excuses right now.

But before she could come up with anything useful, he was on his way out the door. "Barnes!" he called. "Let's go."

"I've already had them bring the limo around, sir. It's waiting on you."

"Thanks." He paused long enough to whisper something to Barnes, who looked toward Emma with a worried expression. But he was well trained, and he quickly erased the emotion from his face.

Connor went out. Emma went back to the office, to deal with the usual clutter of emails that came from his various department heads. He kept an executive assistant at his office in Atlanta, and he had another at company headquarters in Chicago. Emma learned their names and was careful to read anything they sent to Connor as soon as the messages were received. Then she made summaries, talking points, of each one, so that it didn't tire him so much to listen to dozens of inquiries. Anything she could refer to his executive secretary in Chicago, Tonia, she did. Apparently Tonia was practically his second-in-command. She coordinated the management people and reported back to Connor about any decisions that were needed on his part.

The aircraft corporation could have been called international, but it was more fitting to say that it had overseas affiliates. There were divisions in most of the European nations, along with competent managers who could function without being micromanaged. Connor pretty much left the managers alone until problems cropped up. He hired them for their ability to take charge, he'd told her once, and they were good at their jobs. He had a chain of command in each division, and Tonia knew who to call in an emergency if she couldn't get hold of Connor. She'd been with the company for twenty years. Emma thought of her as an administrative assistant, but Connor said that Tonia was more of a division-level manager. Even the in-house flight management people answered to her as much as to Connor.

She noticed that even though he kept a fleet of corporate jets, most capable of international travel, he didn't go to a lot of meetings. He told her that meetings were usually non-productive, and expensive. Unless he was closing a deal, he let his executives deal with day-to-day irritations. The fact that his face was so well-known was another reason he disliked being visible. He'd purchased the lake house in Georgia with the idea that its very isolation would protect him from the press. And it had. It was a gated community, so journalists would have had to go through the very formidable security guard who manned the gatehouse. So far, nobody came in who wasn't on the list of approved visitors.

She slid her hands slowly over the top of the desk, tracing where Connor's big fingers had rested while he was dictating letters. It was pathetic, she told herself, being so moony over a man that she coveted even the touch of his fingerprints. She laughed softly at herself and went back to work.

He was back late. It was after ten o'clock when the limo dropped him at the front door. Barnes had already gone to bed. So had Marie. It was unusual for them to retire as early as they had, but perhaps they'd both been tired, she rationalized. She didn't dare think of another reason they might have been told to keep out of the way when he returned.

He paused in the living room, one big hand on the back of the sofa, his face lined with fatigue. "Emma?" he called.

"I'm right here, sir," she said in her soft voice.

He let out a breath. "Come outside with me. I need some fresh air."

She slid her hand into his. "It's this way. Two steps forward, turn right."

He followed her directions, chuckling. "You've got this down to a science, haven't you?"

"I'm working on it."

"Just a sec." He slid out of his jacket and handed it to her. His tie followed, along with his belt. "Much better," he said heavily. While she was putting his things on the back of the sofa, he unbuttoned his shirt. "I could do with a few minutes of peace. Put this somewhere, too." He pulled out his cell phone and handed it to her. "Turn it off. I've been available enough for one day."

"Yes, sir."

She shut off the cell phone and laid it on the end table. Then she took his hand and led him out onto the patio, where a breeze ruffled the tall palms and the casuarina pines.

"There's a big divan, large enough for two," he said. "Where is it?"

Alarm bells went off in her head, but the feel of his hand in hers made her reckless. "Over here."

"I feel like a glass of wine. Don't we have some white that's chilled?"

"Yes. Marie put it in the fridge."

"Know how to use a corkscrew?" he teased.

"I think I can figure it out."

"Bring me a glass. And pour one for you." He smiled, as if at some private joke. "Don't be long. I might trip over something," he added as he felt his way down on the big, cushioned divan on the patio, near the huge swimming pool at the back of the estate.

"I won't."

She found the corkscrew. After two tries, she managed to get the cork out. She poured two small glasses of wine and put the cork back in, sliding the bottle into the fridge.

She went out onto the patio and handed Connor his glass, retaining her own.

"Ideally, we'd have an ice bucket and champagne," he mused. "Sit down. Here, beside me."

"I've never had champagne," she replied.

"Or wine, from the sound of things. I'm not trying to get you drunk, just in case you wondered," he purred.

"You're still corrupting me, you bad influence," she chided.

"Sip the wine. It's a chardonnay. Like drinking sunshine."

She was dubious. But she put the glass to her lips and took a sip. She made a face. It wasn't a sweet wine, like the blackberry wine her mother had soaked a cloth in and put on the fruitcake at Christmas. It was dry. But after the first sip, the next one didn't taste so bad. By the fifth, she liked the taste.

"No complaints?" he teased.

"It's really nice," she said, surprised. "I thought it would taste like medicine. My father liked…hot toddies," she lied. Her father had liked straight whiskey and she'd tasted a drop of it once. It hadn't been pleasant at all.

"There's a world of difference between whiskey and wine, honey," he said softly.

She smiled. The endearment made her tingle all over. She was feeling very good, in fact.

"What are you wearing?" he asked.

"My yellow sundress," she said without thinking. "It's so hot, even with the air-conditioning on…"

He chuckled. "Why do you think I've got my jacket off? There's always a breeze out here. It feels nice. Here. Put this down, will you?" He handed her the Waterford crystal glass.

She put it, and her own, on the glass-topped table nearby.

"Now come stretch out with me and we'll count crickets."

"Crickets?" She laughed, surprised.

"Do we have crickets here?" he wondered as she slid onto the divan beside him. "You know, I'm not sure. We'll have to ask a native."

"Good luck finding one at this hour of the night," she mused, yawning.

"You're not sleepy?" he asked with mock surprise.

"Wine makes me drowsy apparently," she murmured, letting her head slide sideways onto his broad shoulder. That felt good, so she turned and slid her hand over his broad, hair-covered chest. The feel of his skin shocked her and her fingers stilled.

He pressed them closer. "It's all right," he said. "I'm not afraid that you'll try to have your way with me."

Laughter bubbled out of her. "Okay."

He turned slowly, so that she was suddenly on her back and he was leaning over her. But he didn't make any aggressive moves. His hand went to her face. "I can't see you any other way. Is it all right?" he asked softly.

"Yes. But there isn't much to see," she said sadly.

His big fingers, callused and warm, moved over her oval face, lingering on her long lashes, her straight nose, her bow of a mouth, her rounded chin. They slid lower. "You have a long neck," he said.

"Like my mother."

"And tiny ears," he teased, tracing them.

"Like my grandmother."

His hand slid lower, to the edge of the shirred bodice, but when she stiffened, it lifted, and moved to her waist, her flat stomach and down over one leg. "You're not tall, are you?" he asked.

"I come up to your shoulder," she reminded him. "But you're tall."

"Compared to you, I am, shrimp," he teased.

"I'm five and a half feet tall. That's not shrimpy." She laughed at her own phrasing, a bubbly, uninhibited sound in the darkness.

"Not so much, perhaps." He moved closer. His breath was scented with wine and coffee. His chiseled mouth brushed over her forehead, her closed eyelids. He moved it over her nose and down to linger, teasing, at her lips.

He heard her breathing change. His mouth opened, tempting, taunting, so that the contact just made her hungry for more.

While he tempted her mouth, his hand was smoothing up her rib cage. His fingers explored just under one firm breast in a touch that wasn't intimate but felt like it.

The other went under her head and hesitated at the ponytail he found there. "I don't like your hair bound up. Let it loose, Emma."

"But—"

His mouth slid softly over hers. "Take it down, sweetheart," he whispered into her parted lips.

That voice! It was sweeter than honey, drugging, deep and soft in the quiet of the patio. It was impossible not to be affected by it. She dragged the tie from her hair and let it fall like silk around her shoulders.

"It's very long," he mused, tracing its length as he lifted and separated the strands. "What color is it?"

"Pale blond," she said, her voice a little unsteady.

"Pale blond." His cheek nuzzled against hers. He caught a thick swath of her hair in his hand and tugged her face around. "I never liked blondes, until you came along…"

She felt his mouth settle on hers, felt the hunger and restraint in it. His hand tightened in her hair, angling her face so that he could press her mouth with his. While he kissed her with mounting passion, his other hand slid up her rib cage and right over her small, firm breast.

She wanted to protest. She wanted to stop him. But the wine and her own hunger tied her hands. She shivered with the pleasure his touch engendered in her untried body. She'd never been touched so blatantly, with such hunger.

He moved closer. His mouth touched and lifted, teasing hers as his hand moved up and then suddenly down, under the dress and her lightweight bra, right onto her soft flesh.

She arched helplessly at the pleasure that shot through her like fire. She gasped with the stark hunger it provoked. Her hands went into his thick black hair and she moaned.

"You like that?" he whispered. "You'll like this more…"

As he spoke, his mouth slid down over her chin, her throat, her collarbone, under the fabric, right onto her bare breast. Before she could manage a protest, he had her breast in his mouth and he was teasing the nipple with his tongue, making it hard.

She cried out softly as she felt real passion for the first time in her life.

Connor found her responses puzzling. She accepted whatever he did to her, if reluctantly, but she didn't respond like the experienced women he knew. It didn't matter. He wanted her so badly that he was grateful for every acquiescence.

He rolled over, his body heavy on hers as his mouth lifted. He tugged down the bodice of her dress and the flimsy bra. His mouth found hers as he levered down, between her legs, his bare chest against her bare breasts.

Her nails bit into his back. She lifted up to him, whimpering a little at the unexpected shock of desire he provoked in her. Involuntarily, she tried to get even closer to the heavy body lying so close against hers. He was aroused. She'd never been close to an aroused man in her life, and she really should be protesting now, because he had her hip in one big hand and he was pushing her hard against the thrust of his body.

She shivered, clinging harder.

"Emma," he groaned. His mouth ground down into hers as his body moved helpless on hers, rhythmic and arousing, against the layers of cloth that separated them.

He drew in a sharp breath. "It's no good. We can't have each other here. We'll have to go inside."

He got to his feet and drew her up with him. His face was flushed with desire, his body rigid with it. "Are you on birth control? If you're not, it's all right. I keep what I need in the drawer beside my bed."

She panicked. He thought she was going to sleep with him. She didn't know what to do. He was so hungry that he'd go through the roof when she refused; she could see it in his hard face.

Prevention. He was talking about prevention. Of course. He didn't want children. She wanted a child with him, so badly. But it was impossible. He just wanted a few hours, not a lifetime. She had to think. What to do?

"Emma?" he asked harshly.

"I have…to stop by my room for a…a minute," she stammered.

He relaxed just a little. "All right, then. Help me inside. I can get to the room without you."

"Sure."

She let go of his hand in the hall. "I'll just be a minute," she lied.

He pulled her to him and bent to kiss her hungrily. "Don't keep me waiting too long," he whispered.

"Okay," she agreed.

He let her go and moved slowly down the hall toward his room. She went into hers and closed the door. When she heard his door close, she locked hers and ran into the bathroom. She put the lid on the toilet down and sat there, trembling, cursing herself for letting things go so far. He'd be furious. He'd probably fire her. She should have told him the truth, all of it, the first day she saw him after he was blinded. Now it was too late. She'd burned her bridges. He'd hate her forever for tonight, and she couldn't blame him. She should never have let things go so far!

A few minutes passed. She heard a door open. There was a tap on her door. She thought she heard her name called. The tapping turned into a rap and then a hard banging. It was followed by some of the foulest language she'd ever heard, and she was grateful that Marie and Barnes had rooms on the other end of the house. Hopefully they couldn't hear him, because they'd certainly guess what had happened.

Finally, he gave up and went away. His door slammed so hard that the floor shook. She relaxed. She'd gotten away. But at what cost?

She went to bed, guilt-ridden and shamed. She'd led him

on. It was a cold, cruel thing to do. It was mostly the wine, but not completely. She loved him. He was the moon and stars to her. She didn't want anything he had. She just wanted him. But after tonight, he'd hate her. She dreaded getting up the next morning. It was going to be horrible.

*Horrible* was a mild word for the arctic chill at the break-fast table. Connor barely said two words, and nothing to her.

"We're going back to the lake house," he said curtly. "Marie, call Brent. Tell him to get the caretakers back in tomorrow. Have them fuel the jet, Barnes."

They went to get their tasks done, leaving her alone with Connor.

"I'm so sorry," Emma began miserably.

"Pack up the laptop," he interrupted her in a businesslike tone. "I've invited some people to the lake for a few days. I'm giving a party for the investors in my group. Marie will take care of the particulars, but you'll be needed to take notes periodically."

"Of course, sir," she said quietly.

"Did you send those emails yesterday?"

"All of them. There were some queries that I couldn't answer..."

"I'll deal with them when we get home. Get packed."

She hesitated, but only for a minute. "Yes, sir."

It was a warm day, but she felt the chill all the way to her bones. He'd iced over. He probably thought she was playing hard to get, that she wanted something, that she was bartering her body. It wasn't the truth, but those were the kind of women he was used to.

She wanted to tell him what she felt, why she'd drawn away from him. She wanted him to know how innocent she was. He probably wouldn't have believed her if she'd told him.

Anyway, he wasn't disposed to listen to her at all. He'd made that clear. She went to her room and packed.

It was like the other time he'd held her and kissed her, one of the times he'd had migraines. He'd been furious for days afterward, and treated her badly. But this was worse. He wasn't impatient or sarcastic. He simply ignored her. He treated her like a piece of office furniture. It hurt more than when he was furious.

One of the first guests to show up was Ariel Delong from Atlanta. She was the woman he'd taken out on the town. Emma had sent flowers and chocolates to her. But when Ariel walked in the door, Emma noticed something worse. She was the woman who'd called Connor in to eat the souf-flé, the day Emma had talked to him on the beach. That was after he'd called her down in the speedboat. She prayed that Ariel wouldn't recognize her voice. She'd phoned Connor's house to see how he was after the accident, pretending to be another businessman's secretary. Her South Texas accent was still noticeable, although she'd tried to hide it.

Ariel gave her a long, insolent look and made an amused sound before she went running to Connor. She wrapped her arms around him and drew his head down to kiss him ex-pertly.

"It's so good to see you, lover," she said huskily. "I've missed you!"

He chuckled. "I've missed you, too. What are you wear-ing?"

"Over? Or under?" Her voice dropped suggestively.

He pursed his lips. "Come walk with me. You can de-scribe it to me."

"I'd love to!"

She took his hand and pulled him toward the door. Emma ground her teeth together. The woman was going to unbalance him and he'd fall. She had no idea how to guide or direct him. But Connor didn't seem to mind. He went along with her.

She didn't realize that she was glaring after them.

"You need a pin and a voodoo doll to do that properly, you know," a British-accented voice said from behind her.

She turned abruptly, catching her breath. "Oh. Mr. Sims." She laughed. "You startled me."

"Sorry," Alistair Sims said, smiling. He was tall, with a receding hairline and nice dark eyes. "You were rather giving her the evil eye."

"It's not my place to approve of the boss's friends," she said softly.

"She's a gold digger of the worst sort," he replied somberly. "He sent her packing a few weeks ago. I can't imagine why he's letting her back into his life. She's a lawsuit looking for a place to happen."

"A lawsuit?"

"If she can entice him, and then claim to be pregnant..." He stopped at once when he saw her face. "Sorry. That was blunt. Comes from too many hours spent in court as a prosecuting attorney."

"I thought you were a...a corporate attorney," she stammered.

He laughed. "I am now. But I was an assistant DA in Fulton County before I moved up here, after my wife died." His face hardened with grief.

She moved a little closer. "Marie told me about her. I'm so sorry."

He grimaced. "It's been years, you know," he said. "But I never got over her."

"My grandparents were like that," she recalled. "She died first. He mourned her for years. Then one morning, he sat up in bed, smiling, and he said, 'Anita's coming to get me today!' None of us understood what he meant. But that afternoon, he just…went to sleep and didn't wake up." She smiled sadly. "We figured Granny came back for him. There was an old saying when I was a child, that the person who loved you most would be sent to fetch you when it was your time to go."

"That's rather a nice thought," he mused.

"It's time."

He blinked, then raised both eyebrows.

"Time is all that separates us from the people we loved who have left us. If I could go back twelve years, my grandparents would be still alive."

He cocked his head. "If I could go back, my wife would be here."

She smiled sadly. "Now, if we could only find a way to move time," she began.

He chuckled. "So they say."

Car doors slammed outside, followed by the sound of voices.

"Company's here," Alistair Sims said with a long sigh. "I hate these parties he gives. I'm not a social animal. I wish I had an excuse to leave, but I'm needed for contract negotiations, I'm afraid."

"And I'm needed for note-taking," she added.

"Kindred spirits." He chuckled.

She just smiled. But her heart wasn't in it.

Ariel never left Connor's side for a minute. She might as well have been glued to him, and he seemed to dote on her. The only time they were apart was when one of them had to use the restroom. Not only that, Connor made a point of talking about her wonderful attributes anytime he thought Emma might overhear.

Marie shot her sympathetic glances. The older woman never interfered, but Emma thought she might have suspected what happened. She knew Connor a great deal better than Emma did, and she'd know how he reacted to being rejected.

The sad thing was that Emma hadn't wanted to reject him. She just had a belief system that didn't allow for casual relationships. Connor wasn't a forever kind of man. He was a here-and-now man. He needed women. He went through them like potato chips. Emma wanted a home and a family. Connor couldn't give her that. She knew why, and she didn't blame him.

All she could think about lately was how it had felt to be held and caressed by him, to be needed, wanted, by him. He was probably a fantastic lover, judging by the tenderness he'd shown her. He was experienced. Emma wasn't. But even she could recognize the sophistication of his touch. She thought of the women who'd given him that sophistication and tamped down a surge of jealousy.

It was ridiculous to be jealous of a playboy, she told herself firmly. He'd never be able to settle for just one woman. He'd probably start wandering the minute the ring was on her finger. He wouldn't like captivity.

Emma would have loved it. Just Connor and a house on the lake and several children playing around her. She closed her eyes. *Wish for the moon, you fool,* she told herself. *You'd have a better chance of getting it!*

She went into the study he used for an office and closed the door to drown out the buzz of conversation in the living room. He'd invited several people who hadn't even shown up yet, so it was going to get crowded. She hoped the next few days wouldn't drag on. She wanted things back to the way they had been, when it was just Marie and Barnes and Emma and Connor. But those days seemed gone forever.

He didn't say a word to Emma if it didn't concern some aspect of the work she did for him. The rest of the time, he and Ariel were inseparable. Emma watched them with agony in the eyes that Connor couldn't see. If he continued to treat her this way, she was going to have to leave.

That might not be a bad idea, either. Because sooner or later, his memory was going to come back. And then all her troubles would begin.

# EIGHT

The music was almost drugging to Emma, who'd rarely heard a live band. She smiled as she listened, thinking it helped soothe the pain of watching Connor smooth his big hands over Ariel's bare back while they danced lazily to the music. Even though he couldn't see, he moved with sensuous grace.

She turned away from him and moved closer to the band, her smile faintly dreamy as she thought back to happier times at the lake house. Times when Connor liked her. When he wanted to be with her. When she was enough, without a house full of people, and one especially glittery woman.

"You look lonely," came a friendly voice from behind her.

She turned. The man was one of Connor's new business associates, she supposed. She didn't recognize him, and he'd come late, arriving just before the band did. He was lean and rangy, and he had a way of looking at women that made Emma uneasy. She could see the faint contempt on his hard features as he looked at her. She pegged him as a player who found little mystery left in women, but was always on the lookout for a midnight snack. His very experience was threatening to her. So she used her best defense. Humor.

"Loneliness is a state of mind," she returned in a pleasant, but not encouraging, tone. "I don't live in that state. The property values are far too high for my purse."

He blinked as if he hadn't heard her right. Then, when what she'd said sunk in, he started laughing. "That's a good one."

"Thank you," she replied with an exaggerated, simpering look. "I do try so hard to fawn over rich people. Are you rich? Because I really don't want to waste my time on you if you turn out to be just a cowboy or something."

The twinkle in her eyes gave away her mood. He chuckled. "Well, I've met my match," he mused.

"Sorry, I don't marry men I've just met," she mused.

He frowned. Then he got that remark, too. His whole mood lightened. "Are you sure?" he asked. "Because I think I've got more than enough money to appeal to you, and I still have most of my own teeth."

She grinned at him. He turned out to be more interesting at closer acquaintance. "I'll reconsider you between sips of coffee," she promised.

Now his eyes were twinkling, too. "Do you dance?"

"Sorry," she said. "I have two left feet."

He looked down. "They look all right to me. I won't even complain if you stand on my boots."

She looked down, too. He was wearing very expensive cowboy boots. He had big feet.

"Stop comparing my feet to shoe boxes," he chided.

She laughed. "Was I that obvious?"

He just grinned. "Who are you?"

"I'm Emma."

He moved a step closer. That made her nervous. She laughed a little hollowly and moved a step back.

"Who are you?" she replied.

"Cort," he told her, and now he was plainly interested.

The name went right by her. She was intent on his feet. "Those are really nice boots." She was a connoisseur of boots, having lived in a town full of cattlemen who only wore the most expensive, hand-tooled ones.

"I could buy a car for what I paid for them," he returned. "I own a purebred Santa Gertrudis ranch in West Texas."

"I have…" She stopped. She couldn't tell him her father had a ranch in Comanche Wells, Texas, when she'd told Connor he lived in North Carolina. "I have a cousin in Comanche Wells, south of San Antonio," she amended.

"I don't like East Texas," he drawled. "Too much grass and trees and flat land."

"We have mountains," she protested.

"You have molehills," he shot back.

"You have dirt and salt," she returned.

His dark eyes had grown warmer in his deeply tanned, lean face, and the smile got bigger, displaying perfect teeth. "Would you like to learn how to dance? I'm no expert, but I could teach you the basics." His deep voice had dropped into a purr.

Emma was so intent on him that she didn't hear the couple coming to a halt behind her.

He'd had Ariel search for Emma. She'd described Emma's chumminess with her new friend, and he was livid.

"Emma!"

Connor's voice shocked her so much that she jumped and almost spilled her cup of coffee. She turned quickly, flushing. "Yes, s-sir?" she stammered.

Connor was glaring toward the man he couldn't see. Beside him, the brunette was holding his hand, obviously guiding him around the room. "I need you to take some notes for me. If you're not too busy," he added sarcastically, glaring at where he hoped her companion was.

"Yes, sir," she replied in a subdued tone.

"Emma's my secretary," he added, obviously having been told about Emma's new acquaintance by his companion. "She isn't here to mingle with the guests."

"Well!" the ranch owner said heavily. "When you said you had a homely little assistant, I took you at your word."

Emma flushed at the description Connor had given of her. It was unkind. A lot of what he said to her lately was unkind, and she was getting tired of it.

Connor's face grew harder. He recognized the voice. He knew the man from business connections with a mutual friend. "Cort Grier, isn't it?" he asked the cattleman.

"Yes."

Emma's heart jumped. Cash Grier had a brother who ranched in West Texas, and everyone called him Cort. She'd heard Connor talk about him, in Nassau. She'd been so intent on his boots that she hadn't recognized his name.

"I think the man you came to see is Matt Davis. He's interested in that mining consortium you belong to. He's over by the punch bowl." Connor's deep voice was cutting.

"Then I guess I'll look him up. It was nice to meet you, Emma," he added softly, and with a genuine smile. "I hope I'll see you again later."

"Thank you." Her reply was friendly, but not overly so. She hadn't given him her last name, and she hadn't confided in Cash and Tippy, whom she wrote infrequently, that she was working for Connor. Hopefully, her secret was safe. If anyone mentioned her ranching connections to Connor, who thought her family was from North Carolina, he might make some uncomfortable connections between the Emma who worked for him and the woman he'd called down on the lake for speeding in the motorboat who was from Texas.

"She'll be busy later," Connor said icily.

The rancher's sensuous lips pursed and he glanced at Emma with a knowing smile. "Too bad." He put just enough feeling into the words to make Connor's broad face contract with anger. "See you, Connor," the rancher added, and gave Emma a wistful look as he passed.

Connor was seething. Emma tried not to notice, because it was affecting his companion, who suddenly saw her as a rival.

"Well, he did like you, didn't he?" the brunette asked with a little laugh. "He was just eating you up with his eyes." She gave Emma a taunting look that Connor didn't see.

Connor's pale gray eyes flashed, unseeing. "Was he, now?" he snapped. "Just for the record, Miss Copeland, these are my guests, not yours," Connor told Emma firmly. "I pay you to work, not flirt with rich cattlemen!"

Emma managed not to flinch. She was flushed and shaken, but she wasn't breaking down in front of that brunette. "Yes, sir," she said curtly.

Connor was almost vibrating with bad temper. But even angry, he was devastating. He looked elegant in evening clothes. They outlined his muscular body without being too obvious. The white shirt he wore with a black bow tie emphasized his olive complexion. He was a handsome man who didn't begin to look his age.

"Ariel, get me a refill, will you?" he asked. He held out the glass that contained what looked to Emma like a whiskey sour. It wasn't like him to drink so much hard liquor. Maybe the throng of people unsettled him.

"Where are you, Emma?" Connor asked her a minute later.

"Right here, sir."

He followed the sound of her voice. One big hand caught her around the waist and pulled her close to his broad, warm chest. When she just stood there, he guided her arms up around his neck.

"If you want to learn to dance, I'll teach you. Dancing is easy," he said at her ear, his deep voice slow and sensual. She could feel his warm breath against her skin when he spoke. "You just let go and listen to the music. You don't even have to look at your feet."

"Please," she whispered, almost panicking at the pleasure

that shot through her at the almost intimate contact. "I... I really...don't want to dance...!"

He nuzzled his cheek against hers and both big hands slid up and down her waist, smoothing her body against his. "Shut up, Emma," he said, but his voice was deep and soft, the words sounding far more like an endearment than a command.

Her body, starved of him, shivered a little and suddenly went soft in his arms. She felt him stiffen for just a second before his hands slid around her and held her closer. She felt his thighs brushing hers as they moved to the lazy rhythm like one person. His breath at her temple was whiskey scented and it came a little too fast. His fingers bit into her back, involuntarily contracting as the feel of her began to arouse him.

Emma felt him reacting to her closeness. She tried to pull away, but his big hands spread out on her back and pulled her back.

"No, you don't," he whispered, his voice deep and just faintly unsteady. "Move with me."

She really wanted to jerk away and run, but it would have caused a scandal. She'd never felt such sensations in her life. Her body reacted to him involuntarily as they moved to the music. She had to bite her lip to keep herself from moaning. She wanted to kiss him. She wanted to feel that chiseled warm mouth biting into hers as it had the night when they'd lounged on the divan at his Nassau home. She wanted to strip off her black cocktail dress and his shirt and feel his bare skin under her hands. She wanted to lie down with him and let him do anything he liked.

It was one long, slow ache to feel him moving her lazily to the music, to feel his breath on her forehead, her nose, her lips, as he bent his head toward her while they danced. Desire seemed to be addictive. She didn't want to feel it, because he was playing with her. She knew this wasn't romance. It was revenge. She'd been socializing with one of his rich male guests and he didn't like it. He didn't want her. But Emma belonged to him. He was proving it to her.

She shivered as his hand fell to her hip and moved her against him with blatant seduction. He felt her helpless response. He hated her for it. She'd been flirting with the cattleman from Texas. He didn't like that. She was his. She was off-limits to other men, to any other men. His hands moved to her waist and began to move up and down in a lazy, expert caress, his thumbs dragging up just below her breasts in a move that made her want to moan out loud.

His mouth hovered just over hers. "I thought you wanted him," he whispered huskily. He laughed, deep in his throat. "But you don't, do you, Emma? You want me."

"M–Mr. Sinclair," she stammered, trying to draw back.

"Don't be shy with me. Come closer," he whispered. His mouth taunted hers as he moved against her. "Do you like this?" he asked as his thumbs found the silky soft underside of her firm breasts and touched them.

"Oh, please," she bit off, glancing around worriedly. "People will see…!"

His cheek rubbed against hers. "Come outside with me," he bit off. "I'll ease that silky dress down around your waist the way I did in Nassau, and suckle your pretty little breasts until you scream!"

"Connor…" she whispered.

"You want me. I want you," he said at her ear. "Let's get out of here!"

Emma was desperate to get away from him. She had no pride, no sense of self-preservation. She wanted what he wanted. Her body ached to know him, to lie with him, to be under him…

"Oh, for heaven's sake," the brunette said harshly as she came back with Connor's drink. "You can't imagine how the two of you look!"

Emma flushed and jerked away from Connor.

"How do we look?" he asked Ariel with a rakish grin. "Jealous, honey?" he teased.

The brunette glanced from Emma's flushed, embarrassed face to Connor's taunting one.

"Yes, I'm jealous," the brunette muttered.

He chuckled. He let go of Emma and turned toward the brunette. "Then come show me," he said huskily. "Got my drink?"

"Yes, darling. Here it is." She thrust it into his hands, disconcerting him. Emma eased things into them. Ariel didn't have a clue how to deal with a blind man. But he had to put on a good act. He could imagine how Emma looked. He knew that he was much harder for people to read, even at close quarters.

"Dance with me," he told Ariel, and slid an arm around her and pulled her close while he took a large swallow of the whiskey and felt it sting on the way down. He could have gone through a bottle at the moment. Emma was that potent.

Emma turned away as Ariel pressed herself even closer to Connor. "Why, darling, you're so hungry!" She laughed, her voice sultry.

"Starving." He chuckled, and moved with her to the music.

Emma slipped away from the party and into her room, sitting on the foot of her bed, shivering. She was appalled at how easily he'd controlled her.

She had to get herself together. He hadn't meant it. It wasn't even personal, and that was the most sickening thought. He didn't like other men flirting with her, and he was showing his dominance. Emma loved birds. She spent her life watching them. It was the same principle as what birders called "pushing" with doves. Male doves used it to control their mates around other male doves. It was natural. But it felt uncomfortable between a man and a woman.

If Connor had meant the things he said, if he'd really been jealous and he wanted her that much…

But he hadn't. He was only showing her that he could control her—not only in working hours, but after them. He was making a public statement that she was his possession. Which meant hands off as far as other men were concerned.

Her face burned, like her temper. He had no right! She should march right back out there and dance with Cort Grier and dare Connor to do anything.

Sure, she thought with a sigh. That was Ariel's sort of tactic. It just wasn't Emma's, as much as she might have liked it to be. And if she started something with Cort, he might mention her to Cash. She couldn't risk having anyone know that Emma's father had a ranch in Texas, especially Connor.

She dangled her feet from the high bed with a sigh. If only she could just go to bed and plug her ears to the music coming from the living room. If only. But Connor would miss her and send someone to get her. She was working, as he'd reminded her. No matter how much it hurt to see him with Ariel and know they were lovers, she had no choice if she wanted to keep her job. He probably knew how much it hurt her. After all, her emotions were not easily concealed, and he knew how she reacted to him.

She got off the bed, fixed her face, checked her hair and reluctantly went back into the living room.

Ariel came looking for her. The older woman was wearing a very contented smile. "Connor wants to see you," she said. "There are some notes he wants you to take down. He was very angry that you'd run off somewhere."

"All right," Emma said, without looking at the other woman.

"As if he'd want you," the older woman said with a disparaging laugh. "He told Cort you were homely, and he didn't mean it in a nice way. You aren't even pretty. Not many men would find you interesting. Especially not one of the richest men in the world. You're just poor white trash."

Emma just looked at her. She didn't say anything. Her expression was more of pity and sorrow than of anger.

It made the other woman so uncomfortable that she walked off without another word.

Emma made her way through the crowd of partygoers to Connor, her heart in her shoes. Nothing like having the truth rammed in your face to change your perspective on life, she thought philosophically. She'd been dreaming if she thought Connor would find anything about her attractive except her body.

"I found her, darling," Ariel said with a purr in her tone, curling under Connor's shoulder.

Connor's face was hard. "Cort went missing when you did. Were you luring him into your bedroom?" he asked with icy sarcasm.

"I haven't seen Mr. Grier," Emma said softly. "I had to go to the bathroom."

Connor was almost vibrating with frustration. Just the sound of her voice filled him with desire. He wanted her so much. More than he wanted anyone since his first marriage, so long ago. She'd been engaged. She knew the score. If she was keeping him at arm's length, it couldn't be for any religious reason, despite her often quoted moral principles. She wanted something from him. That had to be it. She was bargaining with her body. It made him furious.

"Matt Davis has some figures on the mining consortium he wants to buy into, along with Cort Grier. I'm interested in it myself. Go and talk to him and let him give you the cost estimates and stock projections he's come up with."

"Yes, sir." Emma wouldn't have dared tell him that she had no idea what he was talking about. She hoped Mr. Davis was a kind man who wouldn't gallop through all sorts of numbers without explaining what he was talking about. Connor did that sometimes, and he was impatient when Emma had to stop and ask him to translate it.

"Tell him you don't know anything about finance," Connor added reluctantly, "so he won't go too fast for you."

"I will, sir."

"And stop calling me sir, damn it!" he snapped.

"Yes..." She swallowed, aware of the brunette's amusement. "I will."

"Go on," he muttered, pulling Ariel close as the music started up again.

Emma found Matt Davis to be elderly, kind and patient.

"You don't know a lot about this, do you, young lady?" he asked when he'd helped her get his facts and statistics into some order that she could type up later.

"No, sir, I don't." She laughed. "I'm very grateful to you for being patient. Mr. Sinclair can be... Well, he sometimes goes a little fast for me when he's dictating."

"You haven't worked for him long, have you?"

"No, I haven't."

"He has a secretary at his headquarters office in Chicago," he replied. "Antonia. We call her Tonia. She's been there for twenty years, knows the business inside and out. Have him give you her number, and call her if things get too much for you. She'll help. She's got a kind heart."

"I do know about her," she chuckled. "But I wouldn't have dared asked him for her number tonight. I'm afraid my ears wouldn't withstand the request."

He chuckled softly. "Gives you a hard time, doesn't he?" he mused.

"I'm afraid so. I'm sure it's mostly my fault. Until now, the dictation I took was always in the form of letters and—" She caught herself before she blurted out "fiction manuscripts" and gave herself away. "Well, what I did wasn't financial stuff."

"Connor loves numbers. Always did. He loves the marketing people. He loves cost projections and sales estimates, things like that. He handpicks his tech reps. He wants young people, people who think outside the box, who are innovators. He's thinking of going into aerospace, space shuttles, things like that."

"Wow!" she said softly. "I didn't know. He never talks about it. Well, why would he? I mean, I'm just an assistant."

He pursed his lips. "I'll take that with a grain of salt," he mused as he sipped his drink.

Emma didn't understand. "Sir?"

"You didn't see him while you were talking to Cort Grier. I thought he was going to explode. He's quite possessive of you, isn't he?"

Emma, flustered, searched for words.

Matt Davis saw more than she realized. He became serious. "He isn't a man who wants a settled future. He's dated many women since his wife died. He was very young, and he's cloaked himself in the illusion that it was the greatest love ever." He shrugged. "She was a rounder, like that saucy brunette he's parading around the dance floor right now. Her family had money, but not like his. She loved life in the fast lane, and she married him more for what he had than who he was. I've never mentioned it, and you mustn't. But he's feeding himself on illusions."

"He said he hated children. She died in pregnancy. He blamed the baby."

"She died because she was a foolish, young woman," he returned. "She knew the risks. She talked Connor into going to some romantic primitive island where they could be alone. When complications arose, there was no help. He's blamed himself for years. That's why he doesn't want children. He uses the baby as his excuse for avoiding commitment. But the truth is, he doesn't like being reminded that the trip was as much his choice as hers. It's guilt that makes it hard for him to leave the past behind."

She raised her eyebrows. "You see deeply."

He nodded. "I'm old," he said, smiling. "I've lived hard, and I've learned a lot in my life. Connor is a fine man. He's running away from himself, with women like that party decoration he's squiring about. But she'd only last as long as the money did, just like the other handful that came before her." He was watching the brunette with cold eyes. "She's the worst kind of opportunist."

Emma bit her lip. She wondered if he was thinking the same thing about her.

He looked down and saw that expression. He laughed. "Not you, young woman," he said softly. "You're the sort who would go into battle with her husband. Did you know that Libbie Custer lived with Colonel George Custer right on the battlefield during the Civil War?"

"No! But isn't it General…?"

"The General part was a brevet promotion that he got on the battlefield. His actual rank when he died was Colonel."

"I don't know much about him," she confessed. "But his wife sounds very interesting."

"My grandmother was from Michigan, and she actually knew Libbie. The Custers lived near her family home. She always said it was her claim to fame." He chuckled. "I have autographed copies of every book Libbie wrote. She lived through some fascinating times during her travels with her husband. Good reading."

"I'll have to check those out."

"She was far more competent than she's made out to be. Not a pretty wallflower at all. She was a woman with grit."

"I can see why, if she lived on the battlefield with her husband!"

He smiled. "You should get out there and dance. The party's winding down. You've done enough work for one night, haven't you?"

She grimaced. "Mr. Sinclair wouldn't like that. He's already said that he doesn't want me mingling with the guests."

Mr. Sinclair was jealous as hell, was what Matt Davis thought. But he didn't say it out loud. Instead, he went over his figures again with Emma, so that she'd have them down precisely when she transcribed them.

The band was packing up. Connor looked odd. Worn. Ragged. But his temper hadn't calmed a bit when he told Emma she could go to bed.

"Just in case you wondered, Cort Grier's on his way to the airport," he told her with a cold smile.

Ariel was still hanging on his arm, her head against his broad shoulder. "Too bad, dear," she told Emma with taunting eyes.

"He was a very nice man," Emma said involuntarily.

"Nice?" Connor asked, scowling.

"Very nice. He told me about West Texas and his ranch."

Connor seemed perplexed. Nice. Emma hadn't been impressed by the cattleman, who drew women in droves everywhere he went? It surprised him.

On the other hand, he was still trying to forget the way she felt in his arms. He couldn't get Nassau out of his mind. Her response had driven him mad. It had been the longest, most anguished night of his life. She'd tricked him. He hated her for that. It was cheap. Somehow, it was unlike Emma. She was straightforward. She didn't play games like all the other women in his life.

Nevertheless, he didn't like his body's immediate reaction

to even her lightest touch, and he was smarting because he couldn't control it. For the first time in his life, he was at the mercy of his own raging hormones, and he didn't have youth as an excuse.

"I'll want those notes you got from Matt Davis transcribed first thing in the morning," he told Emma curtly.

"Yes, sir."

"Make sure the band has a check and that the caterers get the mess cleaned up before they're allowed to leave."

That was more Marie's duty than Emma's, but he was obviously bent on making as much work for her as he possibly could. Maybe he thought Cort Grier might suddenly fly back and ask to stay the night.

The thought amused her, but it wasn't worth her job to voice it, or show any humor. "Yes, sir," she said instead.

"Have Barnes make sure he's hired enough limos to get my guests to the airport in the morning in time to catch their flights," he added.

Emma was making notes on her iPhone, the one he'd purchased for her. So they were leaving tomorrow. About time. Thank God! "I will." He could have just asked Barnes, but that would make less work for Emma.

"Make sure that damned chair in my office hasn't been accidently moved again," he added curtly. "I meant what I said about the woman losing her job."

"I know that, sir. I'll make sure."

"What chair is this?" Ariel, being sidelined, made sure he knew she was still there.

"Someone in the cleaning crew moved my damned chair around in the office. I tripped and almost fell over it."

"Careless, dear," she said to Emma. "You should watch when you're cleaning things."

Emma started to tell her that she wasn't the cleaning lady, but Connor beat her to it.

"Emma is my personal assistant," he said shortly. "She doesn't do cleaning."

"Oh. I must have misunderstood. Sorry, dear." The words were only on her lips, certainly not in those cold, cobra eyes.

Emma didn't answer her.

"Go to bed," he told Emma. "We'll start early tomorrow, so don't think you'll get to sleep in."

"No, sir," Emma agreed meekly.

Her complacence seemed to infuriate him. "Go on, then." He turned to Ariel. "We can have a nightcap. Everyone else has gone to bed, so we'll have the living room to ourselves." His voice was almost purring.

"How delightful!" she whispered huskily.

Emma turned and went into her room, red-faced and furious. Connor had sent the brunette to her room the other nights she'd been here. Now, it seemed, he had something besides sleeping on his mind.

She couldn't bear the thought of that glittery brunette wrapped around him like a body stocking. She couldn't bear it!

Tears ran down her cheek. She couldn't stop them. They were hot and wet and copious.

She got up to find a tissue. There were voices outside the door, loud enough for her to hear inside her room.

"Now that your tedious little secretary has gone to bed, we can have some fun." Ariel was laughing. "Are you hungry, lover? Oh, yes, you are!"

He laughed, too. "My secretary is just temporary. She'd never manage to handle anything more complicated than correspondence, and she lives in some dreamworld of her own. The sooner she's gone from here, the happier I'll be."

"Poor girl, are you going to fire her?"

"Sooner or later," he muttered. "I don't want to talk about

Emma. She's the most boring woman I've ever known. I want
to talk about you, sexy. Come here…"

Emma felt her heart drop. Boring. Lives in a dreamworld.
Couldn't manage anything more complicated than correspondence. Going to fire her.

The phrases ran around in her mind like rats on a tread-
mill. But far and above those cold insults were the sounds of
kissing right outside her bedroom. She couldn't bear it!

She went into her bedroom and closed the door, drowning
it out. She couldn't stay here another day. She had to leave.
It was going to hurt, but it would only be worse the longer
she put off the decision.

Connor didn't want her. She'd known it, of course she had,
but it hurt to have it put so bluntly, and in front of that brunette who wanted nothing more than what was in his wallet.
Just the same, he was taking her to his room. He did it deliberately, pausing by her door so Emma would know.

Well, let him wallow with his special woman. Emma wasn't
going to take it anymore.

She got down her suitcase and started packing.

# NINE

Emma waited until she was certain that she wouldn't be seen. She carried her suitcase to the study, where she penciled a note that Marie could read to Connor. With it, she left last week's uncashed check. She asked Marie to tell him that she'd forfeit this week's check as well, so that she could leave without working notice. She said she was sorry. She didn't dare say why she was leaving.

She picked up her suitcase, left the note and check on the kitchen counter for Marie, went out the back door and locked it behind her. She'd walk to Mamie's house. She still had her key. Mamie's house could barely be seen from here, so Connor wouldn't know Emma was staying there if she kept the lights in the front of the house off. And she'd be careful about being seen outside. Then she'd find another temporary job until Mamie came back.

It was easy to plan her next moves. But it was painful to leave Connor. In just a few weeks, he'd become the color in her world. Without him, everything was gray and sad. It felt as if the heart was being torn right out of her.

But she couldn't stay and watch him and that brunette in each other's arms all the time. She was sure Ariel wasn't leaving tomorrow. After all, she'd gone to Connor's bedroom with him tonight. She was sure that they hadn't spent their time talking. It broke her heart.

Her suitcase was so heavy she couldn't pull it. She had to carry it. She made it to the big log on the lake between his property and Mamie's, where she'd been sitting the time he'd come upon her and they'd talked. That was long before she blinded him and later went to work for him.

She sat down on the log with a sigh. It was going to be a long walk. She might as well rest for a few minutes. Everyone at Connor's house would still be asleep, except Marie. But the older woman had been in the bathroom when Emma sneaked out. So nobody would know she was leaving. Not until the next day, when Connor would have the note read to him.

It was the saddest thing she'd ever written.

The house was very quiet, except for faint sounds in the kitchen where Marie was clearing away the last of the party dishes.

Connor had sent a disappointed Ariel to bed alone. He couldn't forget the taste of Emma he'd had while they were dancing. Her anguished response to him had made it impossible to feel anything for Ariel, except the lingering desire for Emma that hardened his body. Ariel thought she'd provoked it. He felt nothing when he held her past a basic hunger that any man might feel. She was beautiful and experienced. But tonight, she couldn't interest him less.

He'd been cruel to Emma. He was sorry. He wanted to apologize, but he couldn't think of a way to do it that wouldn't savage his pride. He didn't trust her. Yes, that was it. She responded to his advances, acted as if she would die to have him. And then she ran. Every damned time. It was like trying to hold something ethereal.

He couldn't sleep. His brain kept humming like an engine. He got up, leaving the phone turned off on his bedside table, slipped on his loafers and felt his way to the door. He was still wearing his slacks and the white shirt, open down the front. It was no use dressing for bed when he wasn't sleepy.

He paused by Emma's door. He tapped on it lightly and called her name. He frowned at the sudden emptiness he felt, something of the senses that was unexpectedly strong. He opened the door and felt for the light switch. It was on.

"Emma?" he called.

Marie heard him and came to the end of the hall. "She's gone, Mr. Sinclair," she said quietly.

"She's what?"

She walked closer to him, so that he wouldn't wake the rest of the household. He looked furiously angry.

"She's gone. She left a note for me to read to you. She said she'd left you last week's uncashed check and she wouldn't expect one this week, in lieu of severance pay. She took her suitcase and started walking down the shoreline."

"In the middle of the night? God knows what she might find out there! Black bears come up near the lake...!"

"I'm sure that she knew the dangers, Mr. Sinclair." Her tone was as disapproving as the expression he couldn't see.

The panic he felt was unexpected. Emma was gone. A cold emptiness lodged in his chest at the thought that she wouldn't be at the breakfast table with him, in the office where they worked together, sitting with him when he had a migraine and was too sick to take care of himself. Emma was necessary to him. He'd come to depend on her, for so much. She'd quit her job because he'd humiliated her in front of his guests. And it was all his fault. He'd been getting even because she wouldn't sleep with him. It seemed a very flimsy and unworthy reason to hurt her. She was gentle and kind, not demanding or overbearing or greedy, as most of the women in his life had been.

He drew in a breath. "Wake Barnes for me, will you?" he asked in a subdued tone.

Her eyebrows arched. He didn't even sound like himself. "Yes, sir."

Barnes joined him shortly. "Yes, sir?"

"Lead me out to the shoreline," he said gruffly. "And we'd better hurry. Emma's leaving." He was hoping that the suitcase would slow her down, depending on how much she'd packed.

"Sure thing, Mr. Sinclair."

"Which way was she going, Marie?" Connor asked. "Did you see her?"

"I did, just after I found the note. She was going toward the road."

"Thanks."

Barnes guided his boss's hand onto his arm and he led him outside, using the method Emma had taught him. The road that led around the lake was near Mamie van Dyke's house. It was a long way. Connor only hoped that they could catch her in time.

He had no idea exactly where in North Carolina her people lived, or where she might go when she got to the road. She might be desperate enough to hitchhike, which would put her in danger, even in a rural area like this where most residents knew their neighbors.

"Do you see anything?" Connor asked Barnes, and he sounded almost desperate.

Barnes was peering ahead through the darkness. There was a full moon, so he could see a good ways from them. There, in the moonlight, was Emma, sitting on a big log near the shore with her suitcase beside her.

"She's over there, sir," Barnes said. "Sitting on a log."

"Thank God," Connor said under his breath. "Let's go!"

Emma heard footsteps and jumped to her feet, frightened. Then she saw who was approaching, and her heart clenched in her chest.

"Okay, Barnes, leave me here," Connor said quietly. "If I'm not back in an hour, it will mean she's pushed me in the lake," he added with a grin.

"Yes, sir."

Barnes walked back toward the lake house. Connor stood a little away from Emma and tried to choose his words. He didn't want to do any more damage than he already had.

"Are you going to push me in the lake, Emma?" he asked softly. "I won't say that I don't deserve it. But I want to talk to you."

He was asking, not ordering. That was new. But she didn't fancy that he was here because he cared. He needed her. She'd become like part of the office equipment, to be used and put away.

"There's nothing to say," she replied in her soft, quiet voice. "I'm sorry. I can't...I can't go back."

"Where are you?" He contrived to look helpless, something she knew he wasn't.

"I'm on the log."

He cocked his head. "Something a little more specific?"

She drew in an audible breath. "Three paces forward, turn right, sit down."

He followed the instructions, feeling for a place on the huge log. "Funny," he murmured. "I think I remember this place. It's a little blurry. There was a woman. She'd done something to irritate me, and I upset her," he recalled, unaware of his companion's sudden rigidity. "I felt guilty. I made her cry, at a party Mamie van Dyke gave." He grimaced. "It's hard for me to admit guilt. It's a matter of pride. I never did one damned thing that pleased my father," he recalled curtly. "He drew back his fist when I did something he didn't like. Then he made me apologize, in front of as many people as he could find on the spot. He enjoyed humiliating me."

"That's sad," she said quietly. The reference to Mamie's

party upset her. She hoped against hope that he wouldn't remember any more about that time.

"One day, I came home from school. I guess I was about fourteen. He drew back his fist, and I drew back mine. I threw him to the floor and beat the ever loving hell out of him. And made him apologize for what he did to me and my brother." He leaned forward, lost in time and pain. "He stopped hitting me after that. But he got even. He threatened me with William." He smiled softly. "I loved my brother. I'd have done anything to spare him what I'd gone through. That was wrong, to punish you that way. I learned early that the people closest to you are the most dangerous."

"I learned that, too," she said, without elaborating.

"From whom?" he asked quietly.

"Someone in my family who drank to excess. It was hard to forgive what he did to one of my female relatives." She didn't add that the female had been her mother. "But I wasn't big enough or strong enough to protect her. I guess I've been nervous about men for a long time."

"You were engaged once."

"Yes."

He rested his elbows on his knees and looked, sightlessly, straight ahead. "You said you missed the intimacy," he began.

"I missed having somebody I thought cared about me," she corrected. "Steven didn't... Well, he didn't really find me attractive in any physical way."

"Why not?"

"I never knew," she confessed. She shifted on the log. "He said that we were soul mates, that he cared about me. But it was like he had to force himself just to kiss me. He...never wanted me. Not physically."

Connor felt his heart stop and then start again, racing. "You weren't intimate with him?" he persisted. "You didn't sleep with him?" he amended.

She drew in a breath. "No."

"Why?"

"Mainly because he didn't want to. I used to go to church every Sunday," she added slowly. "Religion was what got me through the hard times, and there were a lot of them. We learn that there's right and wrong. And what's wrong doesn't change, no matter how society changes. I don't sleep around because I was taught that decent people don't do that." She shifted again. "Go ahead, laugh at me. Most of my friends did. They thought I was crazy."

His heart was racing. "You've never had a man, have you, Emma?" he asked in a subdued tone.

"No," she said simply. "In my world, you fall in love, get married, have kids, live together until you're old and then you die with your family around you."

He laughed coldly. "In my world, you take what you can get and you never let emotion get in the way of a good time."

"Crickets and casinos."

He felt for her hand and slid his fingers in between hers in a slow, sensuous motion. "There's nothing wrong with casinos. You liked the slot machines. Admit it."

She smiled to herself. The touch of his big, callused hand made her feel safe, comfortable, valued. She felt shivery inside at the warm contact.

"I guess casinos aren't so bad."

"Maybe I could get used to crickets."

"Not a chance," she chided.

His fingers clasped hers closer. "You can't leave me, Emma. I need you."

"You replace computers and printers all the time," she returned. "Think of me as an obsolete piece of office furniture."

"No. I can't." He took a long breath. "I thought you were playing me."

"You what?"

His hand contracted. "Tease. Retreat. Indulge a man and then run away to make him want you."

"I'm not like that," she faltered. "I mean, I don't know how to play games like that…"

He brought her hand to his mouth. "I didn't know you at all, did I, Emma?"

"You thought you did," she said.

"I saw what I wanted to see. Pardon the irony. I can't see anything."

Guilt swept over her. "One day, you will," she said. She was going to pray for it every single night. "One day, you'll see again."

"Think so? I'd take that bet and get richer if you had money."

They were quiet. Crickets grew noisy around them. The faint slosh of the water coming up onto the shore was peaceful, like the distant baying of dogs.

"Come back," he said gently. "I won't ever put you in that position again."

"I'm in the way," she argued.

"That's not it." He could hear her breathing. It was fast. Unusually fast. He nudged her fingers with his. "It's Ariel. Isn't it?"

Her teeth ground together. No way was she admitting that she was jealous, possessive, of him.

She couldn't have known that her silence was an admission. It made him feel things he'd forgotten long ago. He was protective of her. And yes, possessive. She belonged to him as no other woman ever had.

"I didn't sleep with her," he admitted curtly. "I sent her back to her own room."

Her heart jumped. "It's none of my business!"

While she was talking, he drew her to him and found her mouth blindly.

★ ★ ★

It was always the same. She loved him so much. More than anyone or anything in the world. He touched her and she melted into him. It was a response she couldn't help.

He knew that. His hands were gentle, but not invasive. He kissed her with a tenderness she'd never had from him before.

"A virgin," he breathed into her mouth. It excited him to think about being her first man. He'd never been the first with anyone.

Her hands touched his face hesitantly, feeling the jutting brow, the high cheekbones, the faint stubble around the mouth that was teasing hers.

"I should have shaved," he whispered.

"I don't mind," she replied huskily.

"Don't you?" He drew her across his lap and sat, just holding her, in the quiet moonlit darkness. "My first wife," he said slowly, "was a debutante. She and I were just in our late teens when we married, but she'd been sexually active for a long time. I've never been a woman's first man."

"Listen," she began worriedly, "I can't..."

He drew her up so that his face was in the long hair draped across her soft, warm throat. "You won't have to." His arms tightened. "You make life bearable for me. I've never had tenderness from a woman," he added softly. "Passion, aggression, all the usual things. But I don't know a single woman who would have been willing to nurse me through a migraine headache." He kissed her warm throat gently. "If you leave, nobody will know what to do for them."

She was weakening. She loved being close to him. If he wasn't demanding, if he'd stop pressing her... She swallowed and drew closer to him. "Can't you go somewhere else with Ariel?" she asked miserably. "If she isn't at the house, I guess I could go back."

"You're jealous."

She swallowed. "She's beautiful and cultured and experienced. She's been with you for a long time."

He scowled. "How did you know that?"

"Marie told me," she lied.

"I see."

"You're my boss," she added, trying to salvage what was left of her pride. "I guess I don't like sharing you with other people. That sounds selfish."

It sounded delightful. His dark mood lifted. He smiled against her throat. "I don't mind."

Her heart jumped. "But you can't seduce me," she said bluntly. "You'll just walk away, but I don't get over things easily. I'd never get over that."

His arms contracted. "Whatever you want, honey," he whispered. "Anything."

She drew in a long breath. He smelled of cologne and soap, scents she always associated with him. The words warmed her as much as the embrace. She felt safer than she'd ever been.

Connor was feeling something similar and fighting it. She was something out of his experience. That had to be why it was so difficult to think of letting her go. He was fond of her. He loved kissing her. She was tender with him, efficient, great at reducing huge amounts of data into talking points that he could grasp easily.

"You're one of the best PAs I've ever had," he said unexpectedly. "I can't handle the weight of business if I don't have you to help me."

She smiled sadly. "Office furniture. That's what I am."

"Precious cargo," he whispered. His head lifted, his cheek slid against hers in a bristly caress. "The most precious thing in my home."

She felt her heart racing at the words. Maybe he needed her for business, but the way he was holding her was new, sweeter than honey. "You don't mean that. Not really," she whispered back.

"I mean every word of it." He lifted his head and looked down, wishing he could see her. Touch and hearing and smell told him that she was desirable, but he wanted to know what she looked like. He wanted to see her eyes while he touched her, see the visible proof of her attraction to him.

His fingers drew down her cheek, over her full lips, to her rounded chin. "I'd give anything to see what you look like right now, Emma."

"You told that West Texas cattleman that I was homely," she said, wincing inwardly at the way he'd worded it.

"I was being a jerk, and you know it," he bit off. "You ran from me that night in Nassau. I went to bed expecting... Well, something more than I got. I was getting even. Ariel heard me talking to Cort on the phone and she couldn't resist bringing it up when we were together at the party." He sighed. "I'm sorry," he said, and it was one of the few times in his life that he'd said it. "Truly sorry. It was a lie. I don't even know what you look like, Emma."

"I'm plain," she said quietly, resting against him. "It was the truth."

"No ego," he mused. "None at all. You're soft and warm and desirable. You make me ache all over when I kiss you."

"I do?"

He brushed back her disheveled hair. "Your engagement put you off men, didn't it?"

"Yes," she confessed. "I thought it proved that I wasn't woman enough to make a man want me. It hurt so badly that I was afraid to try again. I did my job and went home."

"Surely you were asked out again."

She smiled against his broad chest. "I didn't get asked out much. When Steven dated me, I was so excited by the attention that I didn't question why he wanted us to get engaged so quickly. Looking back, I think his mother pushed him into it. She'd met me at the café and liked me. She introduced us."

His hand tangled in her hair. "Maybe she just liked you."

She grimaced. "She wanted to tell everybody about the engagement. She made sure it was in all the newspapers. When Steven dumped me, everybody knew about it. It was so humiliating. I couldn't stay there and face the pity. Even Steven's mother was upset. She told people her son was an idiot for letting me get away—like I'd left him, instead of him leaving me."

"Odd," he mused.

"She and Steven's father moved away when he went up to San Antonio with his friend."

He was getting a good picture of her engagement, and it did no credit to the boy. He wondered if she really knew what was going on? For his mother to push him into an engagement, she must have been desperate to protect her son, or herself, from gossip. After a moment of stillness, she said, "You're very quiet."

"I'd like to punch your ex-fiancé," he said frankly.

She nuzzled her face against his chest. "That's nice. Thank you."

He chuckled. Under her ear she could feel the heavy, fast beat of his heart. "You're welcome. So. Are you coming back home?"

He made it sound as if she really would be going home. Because home was wherever he was.

"Well…it's a long way to the road, and my suitcase is very heavy," she murmured.

He turned her face to his and drew his lips slowly, tenderly, over hers. "Yes, it is," he whispered huskily. "And you might meet a bear along the way or a coyote, or even a person with ill intent."

"I guess I could stay. For a while longer." She panicked,

thinking that Mamie would be coming home in less than two months. What would she do then? She worked for the famous author. Could she just quit and stay with Connor? She went cold at the thought of leaving him forever. She couldn't even bring herself to tell him the truth. She should have told him right after the accident. She should have gone to him and confessed, regardless of the punishment. By working for him, staying with him, she was digging her own grave.

If he ever regained his memory, he'd think she'd stayed to play him, as he'd said before, that she was out for what she could get. She would never accept anything from him, except her salary, she decided. That way, when she left, if she did, he'd realize that she wanted something more than his easy conquests. She just wanted him.

He walked her back to Pine Cottage, carrying the suitcase while she clung to his other hand and guided him to the back door. Marie was still in the kitchen, almost done with her chores, when they came in.

She smiled from ear to ear. "Oh, I'm so glad you came back!" Marie exclaimed, running to hug her.

Emma grinned at her. "My suitcase got too heavy," she teased as Connor set it on the floor in the hall.

"Besides, there are probably bears," he remarked.

"There's a big grizzly one who lives here," she chided.

He grinned from ear to ear. "He's tame," he told her.

"Not so much," she returned.

"Barnes will get the cars organized in the morning for the guests to get to the airport," he told them. "For now, perhaps it would be good if we all went to bed and got a little sleep. I have contract negotiations to get through tomorrow in Atlanta. Emma, you'll stay here and deal with the mail."

"Yes, sir." She was relieved. Maybe she wouldn't have to see Ariel again.

"Stop that," he chided. "Don't call me sir again."

"Okay, chief."

He made a face.

"Boss?" she persisted.

"Harsh."

"Dictator?" she went on. "Despot? Tyrant?"

"That's no way to talk about your employer," he said, but he was grinning.

"Boss, then."

He shrugged. "I can live with that. For now," he added, and he was almost purring from the tone of his voice. "Go to bed."

"Good night," she said to both of them.

"Sleep well," he said softly.

"You, too," she replied.


"I'm glad she came back," Marie said when Emma had closed her bedroom door. "She's a great little helper, and not just in the office."

He nodded. "I almost ruined things. She isn't at all what I thought."

Marie glanced at his set features. "I could have told you what sort of person she was when she started guiding you around the plate at dinnertime. She's not like some of the other women who come here," she added deliberately.

He grimaced. "No. I should have realized that. She's never asked me for anything," he remarked.

"She never would. She works for what she gets."

He smiled. "Remember when I took her to the casino on Paradise Island?" he asked Marie. "She won five thousand dollars. She put every penny of it in the donation box at a church in downtown Nassau."

"Good heavens!" Marie exclaimed. "So much money, and

her dressing out of thrift shops…" She put a hand to her mouth. She shouldn't have let that slip.

He scowled. "Thrift shops?"

"She's very frugal," she replied. "I think it must have something to do with her upbringing. She said clothes didn't matter to her, or what other people thought about what she wore. She said that people should only look at the character of a person, not at what they had on. She said snobbery was a sad thing and she wouldn't look down on anyone, not if she had millions."

"Quite a woman," he murmured.

"She really is. Sir, you won't tell her that I gave her away?" she asked worriedly.

"I won't. But she doesn't hold grudges." His face hardened. "I do. I remember things people did to me years ago, and I still brood over them. I don't forgive easily, and I never forget." He drew in a breath. "I'm vindictive. I guess that goes back to my upbringing, as well. My father was…harsh."

Marie smiled gently. She knew about his upbringing. "You're a gentleman, for all that, Mr. Connor," she said, using the name with affection.

His high cheekbones had a ruddy color. "Thanks." He bent and lifted the suitcase. "Leave the rest of the party stuff until the morning, Marie, and get some sleep. You'll have to make breakfast for everyone before they leave."

"I don't mind. But I'll turn in, too. Good night, sir."

"Good night."

He picked up Emma's suitcase and felt his way down the hall to her room. He knocked on the door. "Special delivery," he called.

Emma laughed as she opened the door and took the suitcase from him. "Thanks."

"Don't get up until we all leave in the morning. Marie can make you a late breakfast," he said solemnly.

She realized, with a start, that he was protecting her from Ariel, who would probably be furious that Connor turned down her offer to sleep with him.

"I think I'll do that, if you don't mind."

"I don't mind." He hesitated. "I don't have plans in Atlanta that include her," he added gruffly. "In case you wondered. Sleep well."

"You, too."

He went on down the hall. Emma went back into her room and closed the door. Her eyes were wet. She'd expected a different end to the evening than the one she got. She was so relieved that she didn't have to go. She couldn't even imagine life without Connor now. If she lost him, she didn't know how she would survive. And he was a man who had nothing to offer except the occasional night in his bed. She had to keep that in mind.

But when she was bedded down for the night, all her mind kept turning to was the tenderness he'd shown her on the lakeshore, sitting on the log together. It was new and exciting, and it promised something she ached to have.

It might be foolish to stay, especially since he was getting more and more flashes of memory back following his accident. But she had to have just one more day, one more week, one more month. She'd live from day to day, hoping that he might someday want more than just one night with her.

He'd promised not to seduce her, though. That was something. It gave her the only hope she had that they might really have a future together.

# TEN

E mma was still half-asleep when she heard cars start up and doors opening and closing. Connor and his guests would be on their way to Atlanta. She remembered what had happened the night before and her heart lifted like a wild thing.

She got up and dressed in a simple sundress before she went down the hall to the kitchen. Marie was washing dishes, and she smiled when Emma came in.

"Your breakfast is right there," she said, indicating a plate sitting in front of warmers that contained scrambled eggs, bacon, sausage, biscuits and hash brown potatoes. "There's just enough left. My goodness, those folks can eat!" She laughed.

Emma grinned. "It's nice to have the house to ourselves again."

"Tell me about it," Marie said, shaking her head. "Honestly, Ariel couldn't say one nice thing about the food or me or you. She was furious. Mr. Connor just sat there and didn't say a word. He grinned, which made it worse."

"Oh, dear."

"She's a bad woman, and I don't mean just because she likes a variety of men. She's really bad, especially for him. When she was staying here, before you came, she complained about everything. She tried to get Mr. Connor to fire me and Edward, because she didn't like the way we cooked. She tried to get Barnes fired because she said he was too old to do the job." She let out a whistle. "Good thing the boss didn't listen to her."

Emma hated to think about the way it had been with Connor and Ariel. They had a history. He'd slept with her. The pain it caused her was almost tangible. She had to remember that it was before she'd known Connor, in another world.

She drew in a breath. "She's so beautiful," she murmured. She grimaced. "And he told Cort Grier that I was homely."

"He was topping cotton. He said a lot of things. I'm sure he's sorry for them now," she added. "I've never seen him so upset as he was when I told him you were leaving."

That made her smile. "He was?"

"Subdued, that's the word I'm searching for. It was so unusual. He's never subdued. But he couldn't go after you fast enough." She stopped what she was doing and turned to Emma. "I'm so glad you stayed. He needs you."

"I'm properly functioning office equipment," Emma said wickedly. "That's why."

"I was thinking of other things. You pamper him. And when he's sick, he doesn't want anyone but you around him. He's changed since you've been here, Emma," she told the younger woman. "He laughs. Honestly, I worked here all those years and it was so rare for him to be anything but somber, even when she was here," she said distastefully, and Emma knew she was talking about Ariel. "He's such a lonely man. All the family he had left was his brother. He loved him very much."

"He told me."

"That she-cat led his brother around like a dog on a leash, treated him like dirt, made him do things he'd never have done on his own. Then she deliberately got pregnant. She bragged about trapping him into marrying her. Mr. Connor hated her. He tried to split them apart, but his brother genuinely loved the woman." She shook her head. "Always amazed me, how much men respond to women who seem to hate them and treat them like dirt. Maybe that's the secret of life."

Emma chuckled, and dug into her breakfast.


Later, she sat in Connor's big leather chair and tried to organize talking points from the email messages that came in from the various divisions of his corporation. But her mind wasn't really on it. She was thinking back to last night. Connor didn't want her to go. Even if it was just that he needed her office skills, or her amateurish nursing skills for his migraines, the bottom line was that he needed her. And that made her feel warm all over.

She forced her mind back to the tasks at hand. She was learning things about aircraft corporations and the way they were organized. Some divisions made engines. Some made accessory parts. Some made wheels. Some made the computers that handled tasks in the cockpit. Another made the seats, while yet another made the metal bodies of the airplanes themselves.

Mostly what he built were corporate jets, although he'd told Marie that he maintained a research division in Arizona that worked on innovations like rockets and space-worthy vehicles. That was exciting, that he had a division working on ships that might one day go the moon or even Mars. Manned spaceflight, although Emma didn't know much about it, was a fascination of hers. She loved science fiction movies.

"Couldn't you build one like that incredible ship they had on that old TV series, *Firefly*?" Marie said she'd teased him about it.

He'd chuckled. "Sorry. Ours will be more like the NASA shuttle," he said. "Or even the Mercury series nose cone modules. Proven designs fare better than innovations. If we changed our designs, we'd also have to retool our factories to produce them. My board of directors would drown me in jet fuel if I even suggested it."

Marie had relayed the conversation with twinkling eyes. "And I told him, No guts, no glory?" she related. "He just laughed."

Emma did, too. She loved listening to Connor talk. Aviation was truly the love of his life. In between dictating letters and listening to program talking points, he liked to talk about his first days as a pilot, about inheriting the company from his father and building it into the multinational corporation it was today.

Emma enjoyed the talks. She didn't understand a lot of the terms he used, although she was getting better at that. What she liked most was that she could indulge herself when it was just the two of them, without any danger of someone else seeing the way she looked at him. She was so smitten that it would have been obvious, even to a stranger, how she felt about her boss.

By the time he came back from Atlanta, she had most of the urgent messages outlined, along with information that was about ongoing projects. Problems and complications that he had to address covered almost three printed pages, single spaced.

"It's going to be a long day," she said with a sigh as she outlined the business data for him.

"They're all long days, honey," he said softly, smiling at her. "I've had to delegate a lot of my daily routine to managers to keep things running smoothly." He shook his head as he leaned back in his desk chair and closed his eyes. "I've never had time like this. Time to just sit and go over projects, without a dozen interruptions an hour." He laughed. "I actually turn the phone off when I'm sleeping. I never did that before. I was running on five hours of sleep a night and flying all over the world to troubleshoot problems and meet with clients."

"You were a heart attack waiting to happen," she murmured, flushing at her own boldness.

He raised a thick black eyebrow. "Have you been talking to my doctor?" he teased. "Because those were almost his exact words."

Her eyes adored him. "I'm sorry you had to have this happen, to slow down," she said with genuine sadness.

"Me, too." His face hardened. "I've remembered something."

"Something?" she prodded, because he wasn't forthcoming.

"About the accident that did this." He waved a hand over his eyes.

"Oh?" she replied, hoping her voice didn't quaver.

"There was a boat," he said, and there was ice in his deep voice. "I remember seeing it come around the bend, too fast. I was on the Jet Ski, but the sun was in my eyes. It was so bright that I didn't see it coming."

"You think a boat hit you?' she asked worriedly.

"It might have," he said, his eyes narrowing in thought. "I'll have to have them check the Jet Ski and see. I assumed that I'd hit something in the water. Now, I'm not so sure."

"I can't imagine that anyone would want to hit someone deliberately," she began.

He laughed coldly. "You'd be amazed," he replied. "You haven't noticed them, because they keep a low profile. But I have two bodyguards on payroll. Anytime I travel, they're with me."

She recalled two men on the jet when they'd flown down to Nassau. She'd assumed they were just employees, because one was on the computer the whole time and the other sat up front and talked to the copilot. She'd thought he might be the relief pilot.

"Bodyguards." She was trying to wrap her mind around why he needed them.

"I've had a couple of close calls," he said gently, because he sensed she didn't understand what he was saying. "When you have to close down a facility, and people lose their jobs, you tend to make enemies. I've only had to do that once, but I've downsized other facilities. Once it was a man with a gun. Another time, it was attempted sabotage on the jet. I was lucky. They were caught before things got sticky."

"Oh, my gosh," she gasped. She couldn't have imagined that anyone would want to harm him deliberately.

"Now you see why I was concerned when you went out by yourself in the woods last night," he said. It was a lie. He was concerned because he couldn't imagine trying to make it through life without her. But it was never a good idea to tell women how important they were.

"But I wouldn't be a target," she started to say.

"You work for me," he pointed out. "Once, a disgruntled ex-employee actually kidnapped Marie and tried to hold her for ransom."

"Poor Marie!" she exclaimed. "What happened?"

"The bodyguards happened," he said with a smile. "They tracked her down. The police had to take the perpetrators to the emergency room on their way to jail."

"I see. The bodyguards got them." She chuckled.

"Actually, I got them," he corrected, and his dark eyes flashed like silver fires. "Nobody hurts my employees. Especially Marie."

"That's nice," she said. "What you did."

He shrugged. "Alistair got me off with a warning on the plea of extenuating circumstances. Privately, the judge said he'd have done the same thing. Marie was pretty roughed up."

"I'd wondered, you know," she said, thinking aloud. "She's

very careful about making sure doors and windows are locked at night, in every room."

"That's why. It was a few years ago, but we're cautious just the same." He rested his locked fingers on his chest as he leaned back, filling the leather chair that had left much space around Emma when she sat in it. "I don't advertise that I live here, and most of the neighbors think I'm just an Atlanta businessman with a lake house. I take great pains to make sure the press doesn't get wind of it. I've been hounded most of my adult life by reporters wanting to make a name for themselves by gaining a look into my private life."

He was one of the richest men in the world, she recalled, but he kept such a low profile that nobody recognized him when he went out in public.

"At the casino, nobody knew you," she recalled.

"See?" he teased. "I don't allow photos of me to be printed. Many have tried," he added facetiously. "But every attempt has failed. I don't even have a photo in our company website."

"That I did notice," she replied. She hadn't considered reporters. What if one of them found out Connor was blind and went looking for the reason? What if he traced the accident to the very woman who was working for the millionaire on the lake—Emma? Her heart fluttered like a captive bird as the possibilities smothered her.

"Emma?" He interrupted her thoughts.

"What? Oh. Sorry, boss," she faltered. "I hadn't thought about reporters."

"I think about them, all the time," he muttered. "You can't imagine the work it's cost my public relations firm to keep them from finding out that I was blinded."

"It... Would it matter?" she asked, curious.

"Stock prices would drop," he said with a hollow laugh. "Despite our politically correct society, business is war. My board of directors would have a field day trying to oust me if they could seize on a weakness that might impact sales."

"I didn't realize it would matter so much," she said, and guilt racked her.

"Think of the board of directors as a school of sharks and me as blood in the water if they had any inkling that my health was impaired," he mused. He pursed his chiseled lips. "My, my, what an image."

"Not a very nice one," she countered.

"Well, that's business, honey," he replied. He stretched and groaned. "God, I feel my age sometimes. More lately than ever before. It's not easy, coping with a world that's permanently dark."

"I guess not," she said sadly. "I'm so sorry!"

He waved her concern away. "It gets easier. You've helped more than you know," he added unexpectedly. "Teaching the staff how to tell me what's on the plate, how to let me take an arm rather than be grasped, those little things make life easier for me."

"I'm glad I've helped," she said.

"More than you know," he repeated. His face clenched. Every so often he thought about life without her, and he panicked. He didn't want her to know, but she'd become his greatest necessity, and not just because she nurtured him.

She was becoming far too important to him. He didn't want to risk his heart again, especially not on a naive young woman who had little experience with men. He could take her or leave her, but she'd never get over being intimate with him. She'd expect a commitment. He couldn't give her that. So, just as well to put some distance between them while he tried to forget how she felt in his arms.

His head lifted decisively. "I'm going to go to Germany for trade talks at the end of the week," he said. "I'll probably be gone for at least two weeks, maybe a little longer. I'll make sure Tonia knows that you might need help while I'm away. You have her number on the speed dial on the phone, right?"

"Yes, sir."

His face hardened. "Emma...!"

"Yes, boss," she said, forcing a light tone into her voice. Two weeks. Two weeks without his voice, the sight of him. She thought she'd go mad.

"I guess I can live with that," he murmured with a short laugh. "Okay, let's get things done. I don't want to leave behind a lot of loose ends while I'm away."

Time dragged. Hours seemed like days once he left. She called Tonia about a particularly difficult conversation she'd had with a low level executive at the new facility in Arizona.

"He said that I'm not qualified for the job Mr. Sinclair has me doing." Emma groaned. "And he's right. I don't even understand half the terms he uses."

"Emma," the older woman said gently, "your greatest asset is your ability to calm the boss down and keep him focused on one task at a time. Didn't you know? In the days before his mishap—" she used the term just in case she was overheard "—he could never focus on just one problem. He'd be trying to solve a fuel crisis at one facility at the same time he was coping with a staff issue at another. He got the job done, yes, but it's so much more efficient to tackle the big problems and delegate the small ones. You've helped him do that."

"Oh." Emma smiled to herself. "Well, at least I'm sort of useful," she joked.

"You're very useful." There was a faint hesitation. "He talks about you all the time. You sit up with him when he has migraines, I understand," she added with a lilt in her voice.

"Well, yes. He wouldn't let anybody else near him..."

"He thinks of it as a weakness, those headaches. He's remarkably healthy otherwise. In fact, he was in the gym four days out of seven. Working out helped with the stress. He sure has a lot of it. He's the man on top. If anything goes wrong, he's the ultimate mediator."

"I can't imagine being responsible for so many people," she replied.

"Neither can I." Tonia laughed. "He does it very well."

"He said that his public relations firm had been fielding reporters," she fished.

"Oh, yes, there's always that," Tonia said with resignation. "It wouldn't do for them to know too much, and they're always poking around. It amazes me how many people think it's their business to know every facet of a public figure's life. Privacy used to be a sacred trust. Now, it's a joke."

"He's safe here," Emma said.

"It's about the only place that he is safe," Tonia said flatly. "Every time he ventures out in public, there are rumors and gossip and the tabloids go wild." She sighed. "You watch, there'll be photos of him with an endless parade of women if he's at a party at all."

Emma grimaced. "Ariel was here for several days recently," she said in a subdued tone.

"And left very suddenly, I believe?" came the amused reply. "She's like all the others, Emma. Something pretty to keep his ghosts at bay. That's all she ever was."

"He's very attractive."

Tonia laughed. "Yes, he is. Years ago, before I married, I had a real crush on him," she confessed. "But I wasn't his type. He liked beautiful, flashy brunettes. I'm a redhead," the other woman confided.

Emma laughed with delight. "I'm blonde."

"Ouch."

"Oh, it's not like that," Emma fumbled. "I just work for him. He's a great boss. He only yells three times a day, and he's only threatened to push me into the lake once."

Tonia roared. "Ask poor Edward how often he was threatened with that when he started making creamy chicken dishes three times a week," she replied. "Boss hates chicken," she added.

"Is that why Edward's still in France?" Emma asked innocently.

There was a long pause. "You know, Edward is relatively young, and he's single. He's also something of a ladies' man."

Emma was puzzled. "So?"

Tonia laughed gently. "He was having a vacation, but before he was due back here, he remarked to the boss that he saw a photo of you that Barnes had taken and included when he messaged him about the new personal assistant. He said you were very delicious and he wanted to take you out dancing. The very next day, he was flown to the boss's villa in Nice, making nice creamed chicken dishes for the staff, before you ever got on the plane to Nassau. Edward was supposed to be doing the cooking there. Marie was enlisted instead."

Emma felt the heat rising in her cheeks. She could hardly believe it. She'd wondered why she'd never met Edward.

"He's protective of you," Tonia continued. "I don't remember him ever wanting to take care of a woman before. Not like this."

"He's afraid that I'll quit and he'll have to hire somebody else to type up his notes and answer mail and sit with him when he has headaches," Emma argued, tongue in cheek.

"I don't think so," Tonia said softly. "Now, back to business. Who gave you the hard time in Arizona?"

Emma named the manager.

"Ah, yes. That guy." Tonia put worlds of meaning into the two words. "I'll have a quick word with him and you won't have trouble again. Boss doesn't like him much, anyway," she added. "If he knows that he mouthed off to you, he may be unemployed soon."

"Don't tell the boss," Emma pleaded. "Honestly, it wasn't so bad. I wouldn't want anyone to lose their job because of me, because of something I said!"

There was a soft sigh. "Emma, you're one of a kind. All right. I won't tell the boss." There was another hesitation. "But Mr. Attitude is about to get an adjustment to his."

"Thanks, Tonia," Emma said.

There was another affectionate laugh and the line went dead.

"I didn't know Edward was supposed to be in Nassau cooking for us," Emma mentioned at supper, which she and Marie and Barnes had just finished. Barnes had gone off to watch television in his room.

"Yes," Marie said, sighing. "But there was some sort of emergency at the house in Nice that Edward had to go take care of. I don't miss the creamed chicken," she mused, "but I do miss him. He was so much fun." She frowned. "I don't understand why the boss won't let him come back," she added, all at sea. She shrugged. "Ah, well. I did enjoy our trip to Nassau, even at Edward's expense." She laughed. "How about dessert? I made us a bread pudding!"

So Marie didn't know why Edward was kept away. But Tonia did. Or was it just that Tonia had made the connection? It flattered Emma to think that Connor didn't want her going out with other men.

But she might be making assumptions. Probably it was just that Connor didn't want her distracted while she was working. Her heart plummeted. She shouldn't get her hopes up about any romance with the boss. He liked kissing her. But that was a world away from love. He'd probably kissed hundreds of women. He was a sensual, attractive man, and he would have attracted women in droves even if he hadn't been a high-powered millionaire.

He liked Emma. But he couldn't see her. If he'd known how plain she was, if he'd had his vision, he'd have walked past her on the street without a second glance. She was only useful to him because he was blind. And it never left her that the blindness was her fault. She thought of her time with him as penance. It would never make up for the anguish she'd caused him, but it eased her conscience.

The days dragged. Connor phoned once or twice to check on business contacts that might have called the house instead of the main office in Chicago, where Tonia was. But his conversation had been strictly business. In fact, he'd been more irritable than ever. It showed that he didn't want to talk to Emma at all, that he'd probably have preferred not to have to speak to her. He made it so obvious that it hurt.

She wondered what she'd done to anger him. She prayed that it wasn't his memory coming back. She didn't want him to know that she was responsible for his condition. She wanted to leave long before he knew the truth. But it was so sweet being in his house, being near him, just sitting in the office staring at him when he didn't know. She'd never known what love was until she came to work here. She'd never get over him, never want anyone else, not if it meant spending her entire life alone, growing old without a husband or children. There wasn't a man on earth who would ever be able to replace Connor in her eyes.

The days dragged on. Marie went shopping for groceries. Barnes had the car cleaned. The maid staff came to do the heavy work, like cleaning carpets and washing curtains and beating area rugs. Connor didn't like that sort of interruption when he was in residence, Marie had told her. It interfered with business.

Once, Marie and Emma had gone to the movies to see a

science fiction film that had been panned by the critics. It was one of the best Emma had ever seen.

Marie laughed. "It's just personal opinions, Emma," she remarked sagely. "Everybody has one. But it's a poor consumer who lets him or herself be swayed by someone else's opinion. I make up my own mind about movies, and books, and most everything else."

"So do I," Emma replied, smiling.

"But I do miss the older movies," Marie confessed. "The ones you could take your kids to see, and not just animated movies. The world has changed."

"Yes, it has. But I like animated movies!" Emma laughed.

"I have to confess, so do I!" Marie told her.

It had been two weeks since he'd left. Emma sat on the log by the lakeshore. It was late afternoon and warm, for mid-November. She had on a long-sleeved sweater with a V-neck and jeans, her pale blond hair long around her shoulders. She was brooding because Connor hadn't called in days.

Worse, there had been a tabloid photo of him—a distant one, because the photographer was apparently keeping his distance—with a gorgeous brunette under one big arm at some sort of benefit in Berlin. The woman had been so obviously fawning on him that the caption read Brunette Debutante Finds Aircraft Magnate Fascinating.

Emma found him fascinating. She could understand the other woman's interest. The story hadn't mentioned that he was blind, so apparently he put on a very good act in public. Marie, who also saw the story, didn't comment at all. Odd, that the boss allowed himself to be photographed like that. She'd known him to do it deliberately once or twice, to fend off aggressive women who were pursuing him too much. So perhaps there was a woman he was pushing away by allowing the story to run. Marie knew, as Emma didn't, that Connor had the power to stop a story he didn't like, especially in that particular tabloid. He was friends with the publisher.

Emma drew in the dirt with a stick, making curlicues and unconsciously tracing Connor's initials. GC. GC. She frowned. She wondered if he had a middle name. She'd never asked.

"Emma!"

Her head lifted. Marie was standing on the porch, waving.

Probably business again, Emma thought morosely. She got up with a sigh, dropped the stick and brushed off the back of her jeans as she headed toward the house.

"Am I needed on the phone?" Emma asked as she reached the porch.

Marie's eyes were bright. She grinned. "Boss is home. He wants you in the office."

The joy Emma felt was almost tangible. She glowed with it. "He's home? But I didn't hear the car!"

"He came in through the back drive," Marie said. "Hurry. He's in a temper," she added with a sigh.

"What else is new?" Emma teased.

She didn't run to the office. But she did walk fast.

The door was closed. She took a breath and opened it. "Boss...?" she began.

He was sitting on the sofa. His jacket and tie were off, his shirt half-unbuttoned over that broad chest. He looked worn and angry and irritated.

His head lifted and turned toward the sound of her voice. "Emma? Is that you? Come in and close the door," he said tensely.

Her heart jumped. He sounded furious. Was he going to fire her? Had he found out something, remembered something...?

"Yes, boss." She closed the door.

"Lock it," he said curtly.

She didn't understand but she flicked the lock.

"Come here."

She moved around the easy chair to the sofa. She started to speak when she felt his hands reaching for her, finding her legs, her hips, her waist. He tugged, so that she fell into his arms. He crushed her against him and found her mouth in one smooth motion, forcing her head back into the crook of his arm while he kissed her with such desperation that she gasped.

It wasn't practiced. It was flash fire, an aching hunger that seemed to find no satisfaction no matter how urgently he kissed her.

"Emma," he groaned against her mouth. He lifted her, turned her, so that she was lying on the couch and he was above her.

His hands slid under her, grinding her up into the swollen contours of his body while his mouth fed on her soft, trembling lips.

"Two weeks," he moaned. "Two long, damned, endless weeks without you... Kiss me!"

Her arms went around him. She clung, letting him take what he needed from her. She registered the faint tremor of his arms, the dampness of the thick, cool, wavy black hair that her fingers tangled in while he made a banquet of her mouth.

He'd missed her! She was so unbalanced by the hunger in him that her mind barely functioned, but that one thought penetrated the sweet anguish of his ardor. He'd missed her!

He hadn't wanted to. She sensed that. It might explain the irritation she'd heard in his deep voice when he spoke to her on the phone. He resented the hold she had on him; he didn't want to be attracted to her. But he was.

This wasn't a teasing embrace, as the first ones had been. It wasn't tinged with amusement at her naive response or her equal hunger for him. This was desperation.

"Next time, you're coming with me," he ground out against her mouth. "I can't...bear being away from you. Damn you!"

She melted into him. She smiled under his lips. If he could be this hungry for her, it wasn't likely that he'd been to bed with that gorgeous brunette in the tabloid.

"You're smiling," he growled. "Why? Do you think this is funny?"

"You didn't sleep with her," she managed breathlessly. "Or you wouldn't be so hungry..."

He stilled. His chest vibrated. "No, I didn't sleep with her, you irritating, nagging little innocent," he said huskily.

"I'm glad," she whispered shakily.

"Were you jealous?" he murmured as his mouth slid down into the warm curve of her throat.

She swallowed. She shouldn't admit it, even if she was.

He felt her body cooling. His big, warm hands slid up, his thumbs teasing at the lower band of the lacy little bra she wore under her long-sleeved sweater. "You were jealous," he answered his own question, and felt ten feet tall. His mouth nuzzled her shoulder. "I don't belong to you," he said roughly. "I never will."

"I know that," she said quietly.

The hurt in her tone wounded him. He let out a long, heavy sigh. "She works for a foundation for the blind," he confessed. "She went with me to make sure the reporters wouldn't notice anything amiss, to keep them from seeing that I couldn't see." He hesitated. "She's married and has three children."

"Oh."

His thumbs passed over her firm breasts, finding the hard little peaks that told him how hungry she was. "Oh?" he teased. His mouth slid down to where his thumbs were, and found her firm little breast right through the sweater.

She shivered and arched up into him. She'd missed him so

badly that she was beyond any hope of protest. She loved his hands on her, his mouth on her. Even if it was just physical, just for this little space of minutes when she could pretend that he belonged to her... It was just something, a piece of him, to take down the long lonely years with her. Surely it wouldn't hurt just to give in a little, just enough that he wouldn't take his mouth away from her warm, hungry breasts...

"Did you do this with him?" he asked angrily.

"No," she moaned. "He never...wanted to...!" She gasped, because his mouth was moving down, onto her flat stomach.

While she was trying to find just enough will to stop him, he eased her jeans down, along with her cotton briefs, and spread her thighs apart.

She came right up off the sofa as he moved his lips up the soft skin on the inside of her thighs.

"Two weeks," he groaned. "Couldn't eat, couldn't sleep. All I wanted was this. This!"

"Oh, please, you...mustn't," she whispered weakly, with one last desperate attempt at saving herself as his hand found her in a new, shocking way.

"I must," he ground out. He touched her ardently and she gave up any hope of stopping him.

# ELEVEN

The phone rang in the other room and Connor groaned. Emma, suspended in mid-heaven, lay still, stunned by the invasive sound. He stopped long enough to feel for his cell phone. He pushed the first speed dial number.

"No calls for a while, Marie. No interruptions," he added curtly. "I'm eating crow."

There was an audible chuckle on the other end. He turned off the phone and tossed it in the general direction of the coffee table, where it landed with a soft thud.

"And after crow," he whispered, bending back to Emma's soft mouth, "we have dessert."

His mouth descended on her soft breasts again. She was vaguely aware that she no longer had a stitch of clothing on to hide her body from him. Not that he could see her. But his hands were seeing her, learning her, exploring every inch of her. So was the hard, warm, sensuous mouth that was arousing sensations she'd never felt in her life.

Some part of her was aware that he felt different now. His warm, muscular, hair-roughened chest was pressing against her bare breasts. His legs, like tree trunks, had a feathering of hair that she felt as he moved in between her own soft thighs.

She began to panic, but his mouth gentled on hers and he touched her again, making her moan with sensations so joy-

ful that she felt she was going to explode with every movement of his fingers.

He probed between her thighs while he kissed her. She
felt him smile against her mouth. It wasn't going to be hard
for her. She flinched in pain, but only for a second. Then he
slowly thrust deeper, and she made a sound that seemed to
electrify him.

"That's it, baby," he whispered as her hips arched. "Do
that. Do it again. Do you feel how easy it is? I'm not hurting you, am I?"

"No," she choked. She barely heard him. Her nails were
biting into his shoulders with every slow, deep movement of
his hips. She'd been afraid of this all her life, but it wasn't hurting—only a little, just a little. Beyond pain was pleasure. So
much pleasure! The tension was tearing her apart. She ached
to have him even deeper. She loved what he was doing to her,
loved the closeness, the hunger of it, the feel of all that warm
strength under her hands. She was focused on some distant
goal, some sweet prize that hung just out of reach.

"Please," she whispered as his hips moved a little roughly,
as his knee pushed her legs apart even more.

One big hand went under her, to lift her up to the hard,
quick thrust of him.

"Soon," he whispered roughly. "Oh, God, Emma,
Emma..."

He began to shudder helplessly. He felt her body suddenly
arch under him and shiver as she cried out. Then he drove
into her furiously, his face buried in her damp throat, one big
hand supporting her neck, the other lifting her rhythmically
to the quick, rough movement of his hips.

"Oh, God!" He groaned in agony as fulfillment brought
him into actual convulsions, the pleasure so intense. His hands
were hurting her, but she hardly felt it. Her body was pulsing

with his, so racked with pleasure that she thought she couldn't live through its culmination.

A minute later, he shuddered once more and his heavy body collapsed onto hers, wet with sweat, shaking in the aftermath of something he'd never dreamed he could feel with a woman.

Emma lay under him as the sweet pleasure drained away and she was left with a cold, sick numbness in her mind. She'd given him what he wanted. She couldn't pull away in time. She'd sold out all her sterling ideals for a few minutes of pleasure, and now her conscience was going to haunt her forever. Hot tears ran down her cheeks.

He felt them against his cheek. He lifted his head and winced. "Oh, God, I'm so sorry, honey," he whispered, kissing the tears away. "Did I hurt you? Was I too quick?" He moved slowly against her, making the sensitized flesh suddenly ripple with pleasure all over again. "Here," he whispered softly. "I can hold out a little longer. Move with me. Move with me, baby, I'll make it right."

He didn't understand. She tried to open her mouth, to tell him, but the pleasure took her again almost at once. What she'd already felt was devastating, but there were apparently levels of pleasure, and the first fulfillment had only been a plateau. She went up another, and another, until she shuddered with such ecstasy that she clenched her teeth onto his broad, bare shoulder and moaned piteously as the wave washed over her again and again.

"There," he whispered tenderly, when she lay still and shivering faintly under the crush of him. "Better?"

She made a soft sound under her breath. Her nails bit into him and she buried her face in his damp throat. He rolled away from her, onto his side, and drew her close again. His big hand smoothed over her cheek. He drew in a long, exhausted breath and kissed her forehead.

She lay with her hand on his broad chest. The thick hair

was damp. His skin was cool from the sweat. The hair tickled her fingers as they burrowed into it. She was quiet.

His arm contracted. "It will have to be a civil ceremony, for now," he murmured. "We'll do it right later on. But I don't want to be surrounded by reporters eager to dig into every corner of your life."

"A ceremony?" Her mind wasn't working.

He kissed her forehead again and stretched, groaning a little. "Honey, it's like eating potato chips," he mused. "You won't be able to keep me out of your bed after this and what we feel will show." He sobered. "And damned if I'm having you gossiped about, even by my closest friends."

"A ceremony." She still wasn't getting it.

He rolled over toward her. His big hand smoothed over her firm, soft breast. He bent his head and kissed it tenderly. "A wedding ceremony, Emma," he said gently.

She felt the blood drain out of her face. "You mean, you want to…marry me?" she faltered. "But I'm ordinary, and I'm not pretty…!"

"You have a heart as big as the world," he replied. "It doesn't matter what you look like. I can't see you, anyway." He sighed. "The one regret I have is that I couldn't see your face this first time together," he added quietly. "I've never been the first, Emma. Never in my life. It's something I'll treasure forever."

"It's guilt, isn't it," she began worriedly.

He put a finger over her mouth. "It's impossible to feel guilt after an experience like that," he mused. "You were a virgin and you went off like a rocket. My head wouldn't fit through any door in the house right now."

"Oh." She laughed softly.

"So no, it's not guilt. Pride, maybe. Hunger. Delight." He yawned. "And now I'm sleepy. Jet lag is lethal if you indulge it. We'll get dressed and go tell Marie and Barnes. They'll have to come with us. We'll need witnesses."

"Where will we go?"

"Las Vegas," he said, grinning. "We'll get married, then play the slot machines."

"Are you sure?" she worried, feeling even more guilty because she knew something that she didn't dare tell him.

"I don't know why, but yes, I'm sure," he replied. He touched her face gently. "I'm very sure."

After they dozed a while in each other's arms, they dressed, in between kisses, and he slipped his phone into his pocket.

"I suppose we both look rumpled and guilty as sin," he said with twinkling eyes.

"I guess so."

"Might as well face the music." He caught her hand in his and let her lead him to the door, which she unlocked as quietly as possible.

Marie was in the kitchen, working on supper. She turned. Her eyes widened at the sight of them and she had to conceal a grin.

"We're going to Las Vegas to get married," Connor announced. "All of us." He grinned. "But nobody can know. Just us."

"Oh, sir, congratulations!" Marie said. She hugged Emma, fighting tears. "I'm so happy for both of you!"

"Maybe we should wait," Emma said worriedly.

"Not on your life," Connor said. "Barnes!"

The older man, who'd been out back, came inside. "Yes, sir?"

"We're going to Las Vegas to get married. Everybody start packing."

"Mr. Sinclair, this is so sudden," Barnes drawled. "And you haven't even brought me flowers or taken me on a date..."

"Throw something at him for me," Connor told Emma with a chuckle.

"I'll just go get you packed, then. Congratulations, miss," Barnes said with a broad grin at Emma.

"Thanks! But he'll probably come to his senses on the way and turn back," Emma teased.

Connor felt for her hand. "No. He won't," he said with affection in his tone. "Pack."

"Yes, boss," she said at once and ran to do it, pushing her conscience and her guilt out of the way. She was going to marry the man she loved. It was going to be the happiest day of her life. Complications could wait, and if there was a cost later on, she'd pay it. For now, she was going to be happy, truly happy, for the first time in her life.

# TWELVE

Emma was amazed by all the beautiful neon lights in Las Vegas. The city looked like a jeweled nebula, all decked out in every color of the rainbow. She remarked on it to Connor, sitting beside her, holding her hand, in the back of the limo he'd hired.

"It's a gaudy jewel." He chuckled. He was quiet for a minute. "Even though it's a private civil ceremony, I'd like you to wear a wedding gown."

Her breath caught. "I have a white dress," she said.

From some thrift shop, he was certain, but he didn't upset her by saying it. His big fingers contracted. "I'm fairly notorious, and one day people will find out about you. When they do, that wedding photograph is going to be our answer to any negative publicity, if they accuse me of treating you shabbily by marrying you here."

She wondered how and why, but she only smiled and said, "Okay." Actually, she was touched that he wanted her in one, despite the reason.

"There's a high-end wedding dress shop in town. We'll go there after we get the rings."

She gnawed her lower lip. She didn't want him to buy her expensive things, but this was really a necessity, she rationalized.

He leaned close to her ear. "Just don't imagine that you're

going to keep me out of your bed, ever. I'm dying for you already."

"Oh, gosh." She felt her heart running away. "Me, too," she whispered.

"Rings. Gown. Wedding. Bed. In that order," he said.

She drew in a breath. "All right."

The rings Emma wanted were less expensive than the one the clerk, at Connor's insistence, showed her.

"But fourteen karat is still gold," she began.

Connor pulled Emma close. "Eighteen karat gold is more beautiful," he said. "Look at the most decorative rings in that display case. Most of them will be eighteen karat. It's softer than fourteen karat, yes, but far more lovely." He kissed her forehead. "Humor me. You don't want people to think your husband is cheap, do you?"

She looked up at him with her heart in her eyes. "Okay, then. Whatever you want."

He pursed his lips. "Whatever I want?" he teased.

She laughed and pressed close against his side, her face on his shoulder. "Whatever," she whispered.

"Then pick out what you want and stop worrying about the cost," he instructed.

"Well, I do see a set I like," she confessed. "And the design is just incredible."

He hesitated. "Describe them to me."

"They're rubies. The wedding ring has a tear-shaped ruby solitaire. The wedding band has scrolls on it and the rubies are tear-shaped in the band. They're yellow gold. And they're just beautiful!" She hesitated. "But I only see them in fourteen karat. And that's the set I really want."

"Can you have those rubies reset in the same design in eighteen karat?" Connor asked the clerk, and pulled out a black credit card.

"We can do better than that," the man replied with a chuckle. "The artist who designed these rings lives locally. He tried to sell me the set in eighteen karat and I turned him down because it's an unusual design and I wasn't sure I could find a client who would want to buy them. I'll give him a call. I'm sure he'll be willing to bring the set in tomorrow. It will be expensive..."

Connor handed him the credit card. The man's lower jaw fell open.

"Mr. Sinclair!" he said breathlessly. "Sir, it's an honor...!"

"It's a very private honor," Connor said at once. "My fiancée isn't used to life in the public eye. I don't want her hounded by the press. So keep this quiet. Okay?"

The man smiled wistfully. "I'll do that, sir. Let me make that phone call to the artist. I'll see if he can bring the rings over today, in fact."

"Thank you," Emma told Connor. "I really love the design. I've never seen anything like it."

"I'm a lucky man, Emma," he said unexpectedly. He pulled her close to his side. "The luckiest man in the world."

She stood in his embrace and wished with all her heart that she could go back in time and stop herself from ever getting in that speedboat in the first place.

They ate in the finest restaurants in Las Vegas. They saw a Cirque du Soleil show at one of the casinos. Emma loved them because they were so musical and athletic and creative.

"And you said you didn't like casinos," he chided. "Liar."

She laughed under her breath. "Okay, I like them occasionally."

"I like crickets occasionally," he replied, responding to the private joke about his glamorous life and her sedate one.

"You should learn to fish," she said.

"Fish?"

"Yes. You know, you put worms on a hook and stick them in the water to catch fish."

"I can catch all the fish I like at the supermarket," he responded drily.

"Not as much fun as catching it yourself," she returned. "Fishing is also relaxing."

"I know something more relaxing," he said in a velvet tone. He slid his fingers into hers, tangling them sensuously.

Emma forgot about the show onstage, the other people, the whole world. "Me, too," she whispered back, her voice choked with emotion.

"Let's get out of here."

She held his hand and guided him, unobtrusively, to the elevator and back up to their rooms.

Once inside, he closed the door and locked it. His big hands slid around Emma and pulled her close. He felt her inner struggle, mind against body.

"We're getting married," he whispered as he began to touch her more intimately. "Engaged couples do this."

"I know." She leaned her forehead against him as he started removing clothing. She caught her breath when she felt his callused hands on her bare skin.

"You're sensual, Emma," he whispered against her mouth. "I love kissing you. I love touching you. You don't hold anything back with me."

"I can't," she explained shakily. "You rattle me when you start touching me. Oh!" she gasped as he found a very sensitive spot.

"Where's the damned bed?"

He leaned over her, his hands and mouth making a virtual banquet of her while she lay writhing under him, as the pleasure built and built and built.

His mouth lingered on her hard nipples, his tongue teasing them tenderly. "I love your breasts," he murmured. "Not too big, not too small. Just right."

She arched her back. She loved it when he touched them, when he kissed them. Even as she thought it, she felt his warm mouth open on one and take it right inside. He suckled it, harder than he meant to as the heat built in him. She moaned and lifted it up to him, aching for more of what he was doing.

He increased the pressure of his mouth. At the same time, his fingers touched her in a new way. She almost leaped off the bed when she felt the incredibly arousing rhythm. Her legs parted even more. She whispered to him, words that would have embarrassed her with anyone else. She writhed under him, her body demanding satisfaction.

He made a sound deep in his throat as he moved over her and, delicately, into her. He lifted his head, aching to see her face, her eyes. He could hear her hunger for him, feel it in the response of her body, the pounding of her heart, her sharp, quick breathing. He was her first lover, and he desperately wanted to see her. But it was impossible. He hated his blindness because he wanted to see Emma in the throes of passion, see her face, her eyes. He groaned as the pleasure rose in him. But he moved into her so slowly that she cried out and tried to pull him down to her.

"Patience," he breathed into her mouth as his hips moved slowly into contact with hers, and he began to enter her. "Humor me. It will be good, Emma. Very, very good!"

"Torture," she moaned, her body involuntarily moving against his.

"Yes." He shifted, the action bringing a harsh moan from Emma. "The sweetest torture there is."

His hips lifted and fell in a soft, slow rhythm, far too slow for Emma, who was building up to a spectacular release. Her mind focused only on the pleasure that was growing like a hot tide in her body. She shivered and moaned as he found

the right movement, the right touch, to bring her to absolute ecstasy.

When she cried out and sobbed, he impaled her, went in
deep, so deep that he thought he was going to pass out from
the rush of pleasure. A rough sob broke from his tight throat
as he went shooting up like a meteor, bursting into a thousand pieces, as he gave himself to the culmination.

Emma watched. It was the first time she had. It intensified
what was already almost unbearable delight. She shivered as
he throbbed, and her body undulated under him until she
went rigid again, shuddering with pleasure so incredibly intense that it was almost painful. And at the last, she almost lost
consciousness. Connor's warm mouth covered hers to stifle
her cries, which grew louder as the tension snapped and left
her trembling all over.

"You're loud when we make love," he teased minutes later
when they were curled up together under the covers.

"I'm sorry," she said at once, flushing.

"It wasn't a complaint, honey," he whispered. "I love it
when I can hear how much pleasure I'm giving you. It almost
makes up for not being able to see it."

Guilt racked her. She moved closer. "I'm so sorry, about
your sight..."

He kissed her temple. "Life happens. We can't look back.
We have to go on, however hard it is."

"I guess we do."

He stretched lazily. "Your period comes in about another
week, doesn't it?" he asked.

She was shocked that he knew. "Well, yes..."

"I want you to see a doctor and get on birth control," he
said seriously. "No kids. You know that already."

She'd hoped that he might change his mind. They'd had
unprotected sex for several days. Some women weren't regular in their periods. Emma wasn't. She usually ovulated about

this time in her cycle. It was a dangerous time to make love. But she hadn't told him. She could dream of a child. He might want it. There was always the hope that he would change his mind when it was a child of his own. He'd had one brother, and no sisters. It was highly likely that the child would be male.

"You're too quiet," he said curtly. "Are you brooding about what I said?"

"No," she lied. "I was thinking how sweet it is to sleep with you."

He laughed softly, the irritation quickly gone. He drew her closer. "Yes. It is sweet. The sweetest taste of honey I've ever had, bar none."

"Really?" she asked.

He kissed her softly. "Really. You give me insane fulfillment."

Other women must have, too. She thought of all the women he'd had in his lifetime.

His arm tensed. "It was all before you came along, jealous heart," he teased, guessing what had caused her to be silent again. "Educational experiences."

"Not your first wife," she said quietly.

He shifted in the bed. "No. I loved her." He was quiet for a minute. "I could never love anybody else like that, with that intensity." His head turned toward her, and he traced her soft face. "I love sleeping with you, Emma. I enjoy your company. But love…"

"I know," she said lightly, trying not to betray how desperately she wanted him to love her.

"It's dangerous to let a woman that close," he muttered under his breath. "Once was enough. Never again."

Emma bit her lip to keep from crying. It was hard, to hear a dream die. But there was always hope. Always!

After a minute, she yawned audibly. "Sorry. I'm so sleepy. Does making love always make people this tired?" she wondered aloud.

"When it's this good, it does," he replied. He sighed and turned her so that her soft breasts were pressed into the thick hair over his chest. He moved her lazily against him, arousing her all over again. His hand slid down her back. He pulled her closer, and moved his hips, so that they were lying side by side.

He tugged one of her legs over his hips and gently eased inside her. He heard her soft gasp, her intake of breath. He felt her nails biting into him as he moved with her. He hesitated a moment, and she moaned. He knew, then, that it wasn't weariness that produced those reactions. He caught her hip in one big hand and dragged it into his.

She felt him go into her, so hungrily that she responded immediately. He'd sensitized her to his touch already. This pleasure was beyond her meager experience. He seemed more powerful, more…intimidating. She felt him swell inside her body and she stiffened a little.

"It's all right," he soothed her, his voice faintly unsteady as he pushed her hips against his in a quick, hot rhythm. "You can take me. I'm a little more potent this time, that's all."

"Okay," she whispered. She was shivering at the sudden rush to pleasure that took over her body and made her moan as if she were dying.

He positioned his mouth over hers as he increased their rough rhythm. "So our neighbors don't hear too much of that," he teased as his mouth went down against hers.

His hips drove into her with a piston-like rhythm, quick and hard and deep. She cried out when she shot up into the stars, her whole body convulsing with such ecstasy that she was certain she was going to die.

He went with her, every step of the way. His big body shuddered over and over again as he throbbed and exploded deep in her body. For some incredible reason, he thought about a baby when he fell into the hot darkness of climax.

Emma was feeling something similar. She clung to him in the aftermath, kissing him everywhere her mouth could reach.

"It was good," he whispered.

"Yes." Her voice still sobbed with echoes of the joy he'd given her.

He held her close, enjoying her reaction to him. He buried his face in her soft throat. "It's never been quite this good for me," he breathed.

She held him closer. She didn't like being reminded that he'd had it a lot.

He knew that, but he didn't say it. He smoothed her supple body against the length of his. "My sweet girl," he whispered.

Her arms tightened. Tears burned her eyes. "I love you so much, Connor," she whispered brokenly. "More than anybody in the whole world!"

The words humbled him. Embarrassed him. He ground his teeth together. "Emma..." he began.

"You don't have to say it. You don't feel that way for me. It's okay. I just wanted you to know. I won't say it again," she promised.

Odd, how much the words pleased him. But his face set. "Don't think this is permanent," he said after a minute, feeling her sudden start. "It suited the situation, but I'm no good at relationships. I don't believe in forever. We'll be together until the passion burns out, then we'll move on."

Her heart was breaking. She'd hoped... Well, what had hope ever gotten her? She snuggled close to him and didn't say a word.

His hand brushed her disheveled blond hair. "Did you hear what I said, Emma?" he asked quietly.

"I heard, Connor. I know you're only marrying me because of my conscience."

He drew in a troubled sigh. "That's right," he said, and he was lying. He was marrying her because he wanted a visible

Hands Off! sign on her. Emma belonged to him. He didn't want
men like Cort Grier hitting on her. He wanted…possession.

He felt her softness next to him and experienced the first
real peace he'd ever felt. She'd made him slow down, enjoy
life, delegate responsibility. She'd changed his life.

But that didn't mean he'd stay married to her, he assured
himself. She wanted a family, children. And he never wanted
a child. Ever.

They were married in a small wedding chapel on the
Vegas Strip. Emma wore a couture wedding gown because
she couldn't out-argue Connor. It was a symphony of white
lace and satin and handmade white roses that embossed the
gown, and were visible on every inch of the Brussels lace that
made up the train and the fingertip veil and the lacy gloves
she wore. Underneath everything was pure silk. Emma had
never had such finery in her life. She felt like Cinderella and
worried at the possible ending to her fantasy even as she glo-
ried in the ceremony being performed.

When the minister pronounced them husband and wife,
Connor raised the veil, even though he couldn't see her, and
bent to touch his mouth gently to hers. Barnes and Marie,
standing nearby, were both misty with emotion.

A professional photographer, sworn to silence, recorded
the event. As the camera flashed, Emma laid one soft hand
on Connor's hard cheek. She was so in love with him, and
so happy, nothing could ruin this moment. And the way she
looked at him was so poignant that the photographer regret-
ted not being able to enter the shot in some competition. He'd
never seen such love in a woman's face, or such sorrow. Odd
to capture both in one split second of emotion.

"Mrs. Sinclair," Connor teased as he kissed her.

"Mr. Sinclair," she replied saucily.

He felt such a flash of possession that he had to fight it. This wasn't permanent. He couldn't let himself be caught up in that tangle. So he laughed and caught her hand in his. They finished the formalities, the marriage license was given to Emma and they went back to the hotel to celebrate.

Emma had a small trousseau—also at Connor's insistence—so she changed into a cherry-red dress to go out with her new husband. She worried about the color, but he laughed and said at least she'd stand out in a town where glitter went mostly unnoticed. Besides, he added, he thought blondes looked beautiful in red. She sighed and told him beautiful blondes probably did, but she wasn't beautiful. He just kissed her, assuring her that she was all the beauty he needed in his life. The words were so profound that she had to fight tears.

Barnes and Marie went on a casino crawl with them, all over Vegas. They saw floor shows and danced and drank and generally had a ball. Connor wasn't recognized once. In a city of strangers, it wasn't odd.

"Corrupting influence," Emma accused when they were briefly alone.

He chuckled. "You needed a little corruption," he retorted. "Everything improves with a little spice."

"I wish you hadn't gone to so much expense on my clothes," she said quietly. "I would have been happy with just a wedding dress, even if it was off the rack."

He knew that, and it humbled something inside him. "I told you why," he added. "I'm not having people say I was cheap if they find out we had a honeymoon and your clothes came out of a thrift store." He sounded absolutely horrified at the prospect.

She wasn't offended. She just smiled. "I lived within my means," she said simply. "Most people do. The ones who don't are usually in jail," she added pertly. "If I got thrown in the slammer, who'd do your typing?" A shiver went through her as she said the words. She grew cold all over. It was a possibility.

He just laughed. "You can live within my means now," he teased. "Having fun, honey?"

"The time of my life," she assured him. "I've never been so happy!"

He could have said that, too. But he didn't. She had a hold on him that he hated. He was obsessed with her body, but also with her mind and her heart. She'd changed him from a somber, indifferent, vindictive man into one who cared intensely about other people. It was a shift that she might not have been aware of. She brought out the very best in him, made him hungry for her, nurtured him. He couldn't imagine life without her, despite what he'd told her, about the marriage ending when the passion burned out. Even without passion, Emma was part of him. He knew it, even if he couldn't admit it.

"Let's find another club," he said in her ear. "This one's too loud!"

She laughed. "Okay."

They went home a week later. But it was only the first of many trips she was to take with him. He took her to Cancún, to Morocco. They spent a magical Christmas in Paris and had roast goose and all the trimmings at one of the most famous restaurants in the City of Light. Later, he booked them onto a Mediterranean cruise and remained anonymous throughout the whole thing, which wound through Italy and the Greek islands, all the way to Spain.

They stopped by his home in Nice, so that Emma could see what the ancient, elegant old home looked like, and meet his newest chef Edward, who was tall and very attractive. But her reaction to him was that of a woman madly in love with her husband, and it seemed to set Connor's mind at ease. They spent a week on the Riviera lounging on the beach, and another week touring the sites in the surrounding area aboard the yacht of one of Connor's friends. Emma had been nervous at first, but she discovered that people with money were pretty much like people without it. Some were nice, some weren't.

In the midst of the whirlwind, Emma hadn't had time to talk to a doctor. She wondered if Connor was really that insistent about not having children, because he made love to her all the time, day and night, and never seemed to care about taking precautions. It was as if his subconscious and his conscience were at war over the thought of a child.

Emma hoped that was the case, because about two months after they married, she threw up her breakfast. Fortunately, she was alone in the lake house when it happened. They'd arrived home just two days before, weary from the long honeymoon. Connor had received a phone call that left him quiet and brooding. He'd gone into town with Barnes, after saying barely a word to Emma.

"Do you know what's going on?" Emma asked Marie, and hoped she didn't sound as apprehensive as she felt.

Marie grimaced. "Something about the accident that caused his blindness, but I don't know what," she confessed, unaware of Emma's sudden anguish. "He hired a private detective. I don't know what he thinks he can find out after all this time," she added softly. "It's been months since it happened."

"I know." Emma pulled apart lettuce for a salad they were making. "What did the detective tell him, do you know?"

Marie shook her head. "He was very quiet about it. Barnes said he was smoldering, but he didn't say a word. He thinks Mr. Sinclair found out something about the accident—that maybe it wasn't really an accident."

*But it was*, Emma groaned inwardly. *It was absolutely an accident.* She'd never meant to hurt him, even when she thought he was a horrible stuffed shirt.

If he ever found out it was her...

She closed her eyes and shivered. He'd be sure that she'd played him, as he'd called it once before. He'd think she maneuvered him into marriage because she wanted what he had. Nothing was further from the truth. She loved him. She had his child growing in her body.

If he found out about the baby, she knew he'd force her to terminate it. She could refuse, but he'd said once that he'd go all the way to the Supreme Court if he had to, to stop a pregnancy he didn't want. There were ways, even illegal ways, that she could be made to give up the child.

She felt protective of it already. She wanted it, with all her heart. She knew Connor didn't love her. He'd only wanted her. But the child was part of him, a small part that she could keep and love and nurture.

The trouble was going to be keeping him from finding out. She'd have to go back to Texas and try to hide. She worried about Connor's wealth. If he really wanted to find her, if he thought he needed to find her, the Griers couldn't hide her. There would be no place on earth that would be safe for her and a baby he didn't want.

He didn't come back for hours. When he did, his face was pale under its olive tan, and he looked absolutely devastated.

"Is something wrong?" Emma asked worriedly.

His jaw tightened. "I'm expecting Alistair," he replied. "When he comes, send him into the office."

"Yes, of course. Do you want me to—"

"I don't want anything from you, Emma," he said icily. He turned and felt his way along the hall to the office door. He opened it and went in, slamming it behind him.

Marie exchanged a worried glance with Emma. That didn't sound like the happy man of recent weeks, since their marriage.

Emma had a premonition that made her sicker than the

pregnancy did. She ate a salad, noting that Connor refused any food. She heard the clink of ice in a glass when Marie had gone to the door to ask if he was coming to lunch. He was drinking, and it was barely noon. He never did that.

He must have found out something. But maybe if she was careful, she could get him to listen. She'd tell him the truth, something she should have done when it first happened. She should have told him the day she went to work for him. Now it was too late.

She wondered why he didn't call her in and give her hell. If he knew, he must want to. But he just waited.

After lunch, a car pulled up outside. Alistair Sims, his attorney, came into the house.

"What's going on?" he asked in a hushed voice, scowling. "I couldn't make heads nor tails of what he said to me. And he's made a phone call—"

The opening of the office door cut him off. "Alistair, is that you?"

"Yes, it is."

"Come in here. Now."

Alistair grimaced as he looked at Emma's guilty face. Whatever was going on it involved her, he was willing to bet. "On my way."

Then another car pulled up. A door slammed. Two men got out. One of them was wearing the uniform of the local sheriff's department. Another was with the Department of Natural Resources Law Enforcement Division.

The office door opened as they entered and Alistair invited them inside, with a painful glance at Emma.

So he knew. She was certain of it now. Why were the law enforcement officials here? Her heart stopped. Surely, he wasn't going to have her arrested. Not after all this time?

"What in the world is going on?" Marie asked, aghast.

Emma wanted to tell her, to explain. But even as the thought presented itself, the office door opened one last time.

"Emma," Connor called coldly. "Come in here."

She took a deep breath, squared her shoulders and walked slowly toward the office, feeling small in her jeans and sweater and sneakers, with her long hair down around her pinched face.

She walked into the office and closed the door behind her. Four masculine faces turned toward her. Pity was in Alistair's eyes. The others were less readable. Connor's were merciless.

"You worked for Mamie van Dyke," Connor said shortly.

Her heart fell into her shoes. "Yes, sir," she said softly.

"You ran the boat into me."

She drew in a painful breath. "Yes. But not deliberately. The sun—"

"I don't care about any more lies!" he said, and brought his fist down hard on the surface of the oak desk, shaking the floor. "You hit me. You blinded me! Then you moved into my house and pretended to be someone you weren't. You lied to me!"

She bit her lower lip. "I wanted to tell you," she said, choked with emotion. "But I didn't know how."

"You liked it here, didn't you?" he asked, his expression so sarcastic that it hurt. "Nice things to wear, expensive trips around the world, clothes you didn't find in some thrift shop!"

Her eyes fell to the floor. "Those things didn't matter."

"Hell! Of course they mattered. They're all that did matter. You played me like a violin, Emma."

She tried to speak, but he turned to the law enforcement people. "Alistair?" he prompted.

Alistair gave Emma a sad and regretful look before he produced a paper out of his briefcase and handed it to the deputy. "It's an arrest warrant," he explained.

Emma stared helplessly at the warrant. She'd never been in trouble with the law in her whole life. She didn't know anybody who had been, except a classmate in high school who'd passed a bad check. He was going to send her to jail.

The worst thing was that she didn't have a defense. It was an accident, but he had every reason to believe she'd done it on purpose. He'd called her down about speeding in the boat, he'd made her cry at Mamie's party, he'd insulted her on the shore of the lake when she'd run into him there after the party. He only knew the Emma of his earlier acquaintance as someone unpleasant. He couldn't seem to connect her with the Emma he did know.

"Come here, Emma," he said, interrupting her thoughts.

She went to him, wondering if he might change his mind, if he was having second thoughts.

He caught her arm and slid down it to her fingers. He tore off her wedding and engagement rings and threw them violently across the room. "Just so you understand," he said icily. "I'll send Alistair over to the jail with the divorce papers. You'll sign them," he added furiously. "And if you turn up pregnant, you'll get rid of it or you'll never get out of jail. Do you understand me?"

She swallowed. Her face was flour pale. "Yes, sir." He was scary like that. Scary like her father used to be when he drank, when he hit her. Connor's breath was alcohol scented. The glass on his desk was empty. It smelled like whiskey. He almost never drank hard liquor. It was an indication of how upset he was.

"Get her out of here," Connor said, turning away.

The deputy put handcuffs on her. She stood with her eyes on the floor. She never said a word, not even when they took her out the door and put her in the squad car. She was completely silent all the way to the detention center.

# THIRTEEN

It was the worst day of Emma's whole life. She was finger-printed, booked into custody and placed in the detention center with other female inmates. One of them, about twenty years older than her, gave her dirty looks that made her want to curl up and die. She accused Emma of having her locked up, for reasons Emma couldn't understand. She'd never seen the woman before.

She sat by herself, huddled up, while around her inmates in various stages of drug and alcohol withdrawal, or just plain miserable, sat on cots in their orange uniforms and wished they were somewhere else.

Emma looked at her ring finger and winced. Connor had pulled her rings off so roughly that he'd bruised her finger. He'd been drinking, she reminded herself, and he was proba-bly so angry that he wasn't thinking straight. He must hate her. He remembered a woman who didn't like him, who'd resented his warnings about driving Mamie's boat. He thought she'd hit him on purpose. Now he was getting even.

She gave a thought to the tiny life that she was certain was growing inside her. She hoped she could lie convincingly and make Connor believe that she wasn't pregnant, so that she could save her child. He'd said he was sending divorce pa-pers to her, and that would mean Alistair would bring them.

Perhaps she could convince him, so that he could convince Connor.

It was such a shock to be in jail. They'd allowed her one phone call. She'd wanted to call Mamie, but no overseas calls were allowed. So, in desperation, she called her father. He was, as usual, drunk. When she told him what she wanted, he exploded in anger. His child, a jailbird? Nobody in his entire family had ever ended up in jail. She was no longer his child. He didn't want anything else to do with her, he told her, cursing all the while. She could go to hell. And he'd hung up on her.

She wasn't without friends. She could have called Cash Grier. She had no doubt that he'd have flown to North Georgia and bailed her out himself. But that would put him up against one of the richest men in the world, and Cash had two little kids. She couldn't put him, or Tippy, in that position.

She had no money. Her checkbook was empty since she hadn't been drawing a salary since her marriage, and she'd spent the last of her savings on a wedding present for Connor, a new expensive wallet. She grimaced as she imagined him throwing it into the fireplace now. She had a little in her savings account, but she didn't have her bankbook. All her things were still at Connor's house. None of them would add up to the amount she'd need to make bond. Apparently Connor, or Alistair, had talked to the prosecutor, because bail was set high at her arraignment.

Soon after her arrest, she'd had a visit from a harried public defender. He'd gone over her case and was fairly optimistic until she mentioned who was pressing charges. Then he'd gone very quiet. Of course he knew who Connor Sinclair was. He'd promised that he'd do what he could. He mentioned putting up bond, but she told him she owned no property. A property bond was impossible. She had no money, either. That meant she'd have to sit in jail until her case was called to trial. He added that it could take months, even possibly a year, before that happened, considering the current state of the court docket.

He left her even more depressed than she'd been before. She had a cousin in Comanche Wells, in addition to the father who'd disowned her, but to involve her cousin would risk having Cash learn about her situation and come to save her. She couldn't let Connor go after him. Cash and Tippy had done so much for her. She owed them too much to let them know what a miserable situation she'd landed herself in.

So she sat in the detention center, growing more and more edgy by the day, while she waited in vain for her case to be called.

Sudie, a fellow inmate but much older, became protective of her when the antagonistic inmate she'd met on her first day at the detention center pushed her off her feet and hit her.

"You back off," Sudie told the other woman, her gray hair sticking straight out from her broad head. She was big, burly, and most of the other inmates didn't mess with her.

The other woman, Jackie by name, glared at her. "That's my damned sister." She pointed at Emma. "She put me in here, and I'm going to kill her! You won't stop me!"

"Jackie, your sister lives in Atlanta," Sudie tried to convince her. "She's not in jail."

"Yes, she is. I know my own kin when I see them. That's her. You're gonna die!" she told Emma with such venom that Emma felt sick. "I'm gonna kill you. Just wait. Nobody's going to save you. Not even her!" She indicated Sudie.

But Jackie did go away. Sudie put an arm around Emma. "Don't worry," she said when she felt Emma shaking. "It's okay. I won't let her hurt you."

Tears ran hotly down her cheeks. "Thanks. I wish I could repay you," she began.

Sudie waved that away. "We're all in here because we're in trouble. We get by if we help each other. Some of the guards are nice. Some are just pure evil. That one—" she indicated a tall male guard who was watching them "—he likes pretty women. You make sure you scream if he tries anything. He's twitchy. He'll try something if he's not under the cameras. But if you scream, he'll back off."

"I never dreamed that I'd end up here," Emma said miserably.

"What did you do, baby?" Sudie asked.

"I hit a man with a speedboat." Her eyes closed. "He was blinded. I was so scared. I didn't do it on purpose, but he thinks I did."

Sudie patted her back. "You'll have a chance to tell your story when you get in front of a judge. Ever been in trouble with the law before?"

"Never in my life," was the reply. "I've never even had a parking ticket!"

"Then you'll get first offender status. It will be okay." She frowned. "The man you hit, he wasn't over sixty-five, was he?" she added worriedly.

"No! Why?"

"Bigger penalty if you hurt somebody elderly." She smiled at Emma's surprise. "Most of us know something about the law." She rolled her eyes. "This isn't my first time around the block. I've been in trouble since I was fourteen. This latest wrangle is because I stole an expensive car and went joyriding in it." She shook her head. "'Grand Theft Auto' is a great video game. In real life, it's not so much fun."

Emma smiled. "Thanks for saving me."

Sudie shrugged. "Not a problem. Stick with me, kid. I'll keep you safe." She motioned to another inmate, one who was as thin as Sudie was hefty. "This is Emma," she told the other woman with an affectionate smile. "We're adopting her."

"Hi. I'm Delsa," the other woman said. She hugged Emma. "Welcome to the family."

Emma laughed self-consciously. "Thanks." She looked at them worriedly. "I've read books about jail. I don't have any cigarettes…"

They both laughed. "We don't smoke," they assured her. "But where we'll be going, cigarettes are a very valuable commodity. She's in for reckless driving or hit-and-run, something like that, but she's a first offender," Sudie told her friend.

"She'll be out in no time," Delsa agreed. "Have they set a bond hearing yet?"

"I don't have any money," Emma said complacently. "So I'm here until my case comes up in court."

They both grimaced.

"It's not so bad," Emma replied in her soft voice. "The food is nice, and so is the company."

They both smiled.

"Thanks, kid," Sudie said gently. "Been a long time since I've been called nice company."

"People get in trouble for all sorts of reasons," Emma said. "My parents were sticklers for going to church. They taught me that you never judge other people."

"Can't you call your parents to get you out?" Delsa asked.

"My mother's been dead a long time." She lowered her eyes. "I called my dad. He disowned me." She sighed and forced a smile. "So thanks for adopting me. I guess I'm an orphan."

"My dad threw me out of the house when I was ten," Sudie said. "I was glad to go. I got tired of getting beat up when he was high. He died of an overdose, I heard. My mom's still on the streets, making her living."

"I only had my mother," Delsa said sadly. "She died when I was eleven. I had to go on the streets to survive." She made a face. "My pimp taught me how to steal. I've been doing it ever since. Wouldn't know how to make an honest living."

"Me, neither," Sudie agreed. She shook a finger at Emma. "You didn't hear that," she said firmly. "If you're gonna be our kid, you have to turn out right. Got that?"

Emma beamed. "Okay."

"Gonna raise some eyebrows when we put that out. Her being our kid." Sudie grinned.

It was true. They were very dark-skinned with curly hair and jet-black eyes. Emma was blonde.

"We should of got married." Delsa sighed. "Not easy, being like us, even in 2017."

Emma looked from one to the other. "Are you a couple?"

They both nodded.

Emma just smiled. "I think how people want to live their lives is their business. You'll get no judgments from me."

Sudie hugged her. "Now I know you're my kid!"

Emma laughed.

It was a long process, getting used to being incarcerated. So many restrictions. In the shower room, Emma was always with her two companions. If she hadn't been, Jackie would have been on her like a duck on a June bug. She kept making threats. Emma got to know one of the detention guards, a kindly older woman named Bess. She mentioned it to her.

"She's got mental problems," Bess told her quietly. "You watch out for her. But you're in good hands." She indicated Emma's friends. "Nobody's going to risk getting in bad with them to get to you. They're dangerous."

"They're so sweet," Emma defended them.

Bess smiled. "I guess different people bring out different qualities in people. They had a rough start in life. It has an effect."

"Yes, it does."

"No chance that he might drop the charges?" Bess asked aloud.

Emma sighed. "I blinded him," she said simply. "I should have stopped to see about him. But I was too afraid. He's suffered so terribly. We have to pay for the things we do in life. God forgives. But He exacts a price when we hurt people. And that's the way it should be."

Bess grimaced. "You're a good person, Emma. I'm sorry this happened to you."

Emma smiled. "It will all come right, one day. If he could regain his sight, I'd stay in here forever. I'd do anything if he could see again. I love him...so much." Her voice broke.

Bess didn't reply. She felt sorry for the man who'd thrown Emma to the wolves. One day he'd come to his senses and realize that he was exacting punishment for an accident. But it might be too late by then.

Emma was sick every morning. Jackie noticed and it set her off. She started raging about her sister bringing a child into the world who'd be corrupt and hateful like she was. She told Emma she was going to make sure that baby didn't live.

Connor had made the same threat. He hadn't sent her any more messages, but Alistair, who contacted her through her public defender, said he'd been out of the country. Emma was sure that Connor had meant what he said. If she'd been out of jail she might have been able to find a way to hide her pregnancy. Here, confined, there was no hope.

She touched her stomach lightly and sighed. If only her life had been less complicated. If she'd had a loving father, a happy marriage...

Wishing was useless. She pulled herself up. Adversity was like the tempering of steel. It would make her stronger, better. She kept telling herself that, repeating it like a mantra while she worried about the threats to her poor unborn child. She wanted it so much. *Please, God*, she thought silently, *don't punish my child for what I've done.*

★ ★ ★

They were going to send Emma to a doctor to be checked after Bess realized that she was showing the symptoms of pregnancy. They assured her that they weren't going to do anything to harm her or the child, but Emma was worried.

She wasn't paying attention when she started back to her detention cell, or she might have noticed that Jackie had gotten up from the table with an odd smile and was following her.

Halfway down the hall, with guards all around, Jackie jumped at her. There was the flash of a small, metallic object, and Emma felt the impact of the blade in her stomach.

"No!" she screamed.

"Pregnant, are you, Peggy?" Jackie raged. "Well, you're not bringing a child in the world to be as evil as you are! I told you I'd get you, I told you!"

Emma tried to defend herself, but the older woman was uncannily strong. She kept striking at Emma's stomach with the small homemade shiv. Emma felt blood and hoped it was from her poor hands, which she'd used to help ward off the attack, and not her stomach. *Please*, she pleaded silently, *please, don't let her hurt my baby!*

Bess came running with another guard. They wrestled Jackie down to the floor and handcuffed her. She was still yelling threats and curses when they dragged her away.

Emma didn't hear her. She was on the floor, bleeding, sobbing.

"Get an ambulance!" Bess said frantically.

Connor had stayed drunk for the better part of a month. He'd moved the whole household to Nice, where he went from one business meeting to another when he was sober enough. When he wasn't, he delegated his responsibilities, talked on the phone and filled the house with people. He made sure there was enough noise to drown out his conscience.

Emma had tricked him. She'd run over him with the boat and blinded him, then she'd lured him into marriage by withholding her body until he was so besotted that he'd have done anything to get her into bed.

He hated her. She'd made herself so necessary that he still missed her. Well, she was paying for it now, he assured himself angrily. She'd be under threat of prosecution until he decided whether or not he wanted to withdraw the charges.

He wondered if she thought about him at all, now that he'd discovered her secret. Probably she was back at her father's ranch, leeching off him. He recalled that her father hated her, and rationalized that he'd forgiven her in her time of trouble and taken her back in. She might have gone back to work for Mamie van Dyke, which was why he was in Nice. He didn't want to take any chance of seeing her again, even from a distance.

He hadn't phoned Mamie. He heard through mutual friends that she was at some inaccessible spot in the Middle East now, still researching a book. She would have bailed Emma out, even if her father hadn't. Lucky Emma. So many people who would give a damn. He didn't. He hated her guts. She'd taken away his vision. He'd never forgive her for it!

He'd just come back from an organizational meeting for a new plant in France when he took a wrong step and fell down the stairs.

He heard gasps around him. It didn't hurt, really. He was very fit, despite his disability. He worked out in his private gym at his ocean property every day to make sure of it. He caught himself, even though his head took a sharp blow.

He sat up, laughing. "I'm all right," he said. And then, suddenly, light burst in front of his face.

He shivered. Light. Then blue ocean. Then sand. Then Barnes, with a shocked expression on his face.

"Mr. Sinclair?" he asked worriedly.

"I can see!" Connor exclaimed. He fought a mist in his eyes. "My God, Barnes, I can see!"

"Oh, thank God!" Barnes helped him up. "Are you all right, sir?"

"Just shaken." He ignored the bystanders. "Take me to Dr. Fouget's office, will you?"

"Right away! Sir, what wonderful news!"

"It is, isn't it?" He blinked. "The light is blinding. I can't quite focus."

"Because it's so sudden, I imagine. I'll get there in a flash, sir."


The doctor, whom Connor had known for many years, examined him and grinned. "No ill effects from the blow to the head. Except returned vision." He pursed his lips. "I told you it was hysterical blindness. You saw something coming toward your eyes, felt a blow and assumed you were blinded. I've seen several cases of it over the years. Not one of the victims was emotionally compromised or mentally unstable," he added drily.

"I still can't believe it," Connor said, his heart lifting. "I thought I'd go through the rest of my life blind as a bat."

"Just take it slow. Don't try to do too much," the doctor advised. "It may be difficult for a few days. You'll have to adjust to returned vision. It may take a little time."

"I don't care. I'll do anything. Thanks," he added huskily, and shook the physician's hand.

"I didn't do anything. Thank the staircase that tripped you," he mused. "Let me know if there are any complications. And avoid sunlight for a couple of days, just until you adjust."

"I'll do that."

★ ★ ★

Marie burst into tears. "Sir, it's like a miracle," she wailed. "I'm so happy for you!"

"As are we all," Edward agreed, grinning. "I will make a special dish in honor of the occasion."

"If it contains creamed chicken, you'll feature in a dish yourself," Barnes threatened.

"No chicken. I swear."

Connor chuckled. He drew in a long breath and went to the patio to look out on the ocean. He'd never realized how much color there was in the world, how much beauty. The transition from black to color was shocking. He felt a little dizzy and the colors were too vivid, but he knew he'd adjust.

As for being quiet…

He got on the phone and called everyone he knew, inviting them over for a huge celebration party. He instructed Edward to hire a caterer to help him with food, and he called in a party planner to manage things. He felt ten years younger. He could see. He was going to be fine.

He spared one cold thought for Emma, with the charges still hanging over her head. He might drop them. But she needed to live with them for a while longer. After all, his vision returning was a fluke. For all she knew, she'd blinded him for life. There was one thing he did have to do, though.

He phoned Alistair and had him draw up divorce papers. "Get her signature on them," he added. "You'll have to track her down. She lives in a town somewhere south of San Antonio. And find out if she's pregnant," he added, feeling a twinge of guilt because he hadn't done a thing to prevent a child. He'd been so besotted with her that, for a few days, he'd even longed to get her pregnant.

"If she is?" Alistair asked worriedly.

"Tell her we'll drop the charges if she gets rid of it, and I won't argue the point," he said icily.

Alistair sighed. "Yes, sir. Shall I send the papers overnight to you for your signature?"

"No," Connor said. "I'll be coming back to the lake house in a couple of days. I'll sign them then. Meanwhile, we're having the party to end all parties here tonight."

"I wish I was there."

"I could send the jet." Connor chuckled.

"I was kidding. I'm not much of a party person. I'll get the papers arranged and find out where to send them for Emma's signature. It may take a few days."

"No rush. Just do it."

"Yes, sir."

It was a night full of fun and frivolity. Connor flirted with the ravishing women present, kissed one or two of them, ate exquisite gourmet food and filled his glass over and over with the most expensive champagne.

But despite the joy, he still felt empty. He kept remembering Emma's comment about casinos and crickets.

He didn't want to miss her. But he did. She'd become so much a part of his life that it was like having a limb removed to be without her. He had to keep in mind that she'd lied to him. She'd hit him with the boat deliberately. She might have even meant to kill him.

As soon as that thought presented itself, he remembered Emma in the bathroom with him, holding a wet washcloth to his face after he'd thrown his guts up. She was tender with him. She couldn't have pretended that. She had a soft heart. She worried about total strangers. He remembered seeing her walking along the lake with the lost child, and it was like a knife through his guts. She'd given five thousand dollars to a church in Nassau, when she hardly had a dime of her own.

He blamed her for blinding him. But had she seen him when she came around the bend in the lake? The sun had been behind him. It might have blinded her, just in those few seconds, and he'd been too far out in the lake. He hadn't been paying attention. Was it just an accident? Had he been looking for a way out, for an end to the hunger that kept him on the rack day and night? Had he blamed her so that he had an excuse to throw her out of his life, before he was unable to let her go at all?

He hated his own thoughts. He poured himself another glass of champagne and went back to the live band. He was divorcing her. Nothing else mattered. He hooked his arm around the first pretty woman he saw and drew her onto the dance floor.

Alistair Sims was absolutely shell-shocked by what he saw when he was allowed into Emma's hospital room.

She was crying. Absolutely sobbing.

"My God," he said softly. "What happened to you?"

She swallowed. Her eyes were swollen and red. "This woman... She thought I was her sister. She said she was going to make sure I didn't bring a baby into the world who'd be just like me. I lost my baby." Her eyes were tragic.

"I'm so sorry," he managed. His throat was tight.

She lowered her eyes. "She stabbed me, over and over and over. They said the shiv had a small blade or I might have developed peritonitis and died." She hiccuped. "I wish I'd died! My baby!" She sobbed. "My baby!"

The nurse who'd checked her when she came in said they'd run tests but it was pretty certain that the baby wouldn't have survived the attack. Everyone was sorry. Emma had that effect on people, even though it was known that she'd been in jail.

Alistair didn't know what to say. "I thought you'd made bail and gone to Texas," he began.

She bit her lip. "I don't have any money, Mr. Sims," she said simply. "And I couldn't get in touch with Mamie. My father disowned me. So I had to stay in jail until my case came up. It hasn't yet."

"It's been two months." He groaned.

She drew in a shaky breath. "I know. This woman thought I was her sister. But I made friends inside. They've looked out for me. But they were transferred to another facility two days ago, and there was nobody to watch my back." Tears fell hotly down her cheeks. "I guess she'll kill me when I go back," she said with quiet resignation. She lay back in her hospital bed and closed her eyes. "I don't care anymore. Life is just too horrible. If it ends, it will be all right. Maybe I'll find peace."

Alistair was livid.

Emma opened her eyes. "Why were you trying to find me?" she asked suddenly. She knew it wasn't because Connor cared. He'd made that crystal clear.

He gnawed his lower lip. "Mr. Sinclair sent me with divorce papers…"

"Oh. That." She managed a wan smile. "If you've got a pen, show me where to sign them. It's okay, Mr. Sims. I never wanted anything from him, you know."

He was fighting some strong emotions of his own. Poor little thing. He indicated the flags that marked places for her signature.

"Is there anything I can do for you?" he asked when she handed the papers back.

She smiled sadly. "No. But thank you for asking."

He hardly recognized this wan, tired woman. The Emma he knew from Connor's lake house had been alive, full of fun and joy. This Emma had been to hell and looked as if she never expected to get out.

"I'm so sorry…for what's happened to you," he said inadequately.

"I got what I deserved, Mr. Sims," she said simply. "I blinded Connor. I did a stupid thing. We have to pay for our sins. This is my payment. It's all right. I don't blame him for hating me."

He started to tell her that Connor's sight had returned, but she closed her eyes with a weary sigh and turned her head away.

"I think I'll try to sleep now," she said drowsily. She drifted off. He stood by her bedside for a moment before he let himself out and drove back to his office.

He tried to call Connor, but he couldn't get through. Just as well, he thought irritably. If he'd said what he felt, it wouldn't help their professional relationship. Not a bit.

So two days later, Connor asked him to come out to the lake house to talk about the divorce.

"I've only been home a day," Connor remarked. He looked years younger, fit and spry. He was smiling. "It's like a miracle, having my sight back. I'd forgotten how to move. I had to learn to do things all over again. But it's great, being able to see." He grimaced. "I guess maybe they were right about the cause of it. I assumed I'd be blind, so my mind tricked me into thinking I was."

"I see."

"Okay. About the divorce. Did you find Emma? Is she back in Texas?"

Alistair clasped his hands behind his back. "No."

Connor frowned. "Why not?"

"She didn't have any money for bail."

"I didn't think about that. All her things are still here, including her purse. Well, you can take them to her... What is it?" he asked, because Alistair's face was a study in tragedy.

"Without money or property, you can't make bail," Alistair explained.

Connor's expression went taut. "You don't mean to tell me that she's still in jail?" he exploded. "Good God, it's been almost two months!"

"I know."

"Why didn't Mamie bail her out? Or her father?" he demanded.

"Her father disowned her because she'd been arrested," Alistair said. "She couldn't get in touch with Mamie. There wasn't anybody else."

Connor shouldn't have felt guilty, but he did. Emma, gentle Emma, in the company of criminals every day for weeks, with nobody to help her. Emma, who would have helped the whole world, who had a heart as big as all outdoors.

"She wasn't looking," he said. "Neither was I. It was an accident. I was blinded, or thought I was, and I overreacted. I should have thought things through. Emma wouldn't deliberately hurt anyone." He remembered her voice, choked with emotion, as she whispered how much she loved him. His teeth ground together. He turned. "Get her out of there. Get her out today!"

"It may not be that easy…"

"We'll drop the charges. I'm the one who was hurt. If I don't prosecute, they can't," Connor argued. "Find a legal precedent. Hire experts. Do whatever you have to do. Just get her out of there right now!"

"I know all that," Alistair interrupted with exaggerated patience. "What I meant was, I'm not sure they'll let her out of the hospital right now…"

"Hospital?" He moved closer. "What hospital? What happened?"

It was harder than Alistair had thought it was going to be. He took a steadying breath. "Emma made an enemy, a woman who was mentally ill and thought Emma was the sister who'd had her arrested. She had a homemade shiv. She… stabbed Emma, several times…"

"Oh, dear God!" Connor leaned over his desk, his hands white where they gripped.

"She'll live. The wounds weren't that bad. It's just...well, she lost her baby in the attack."

Connor's reaction was immediate, violent, totally unexpected. He kept a loaded .45 auto in his desk drawer. He had the drawer open and his hand on it almost before Alistair realized what he was going to do.

"Barnes!" Alistair screamed.

The older man came running. Marie heard scuffling sounds and then a gunshot. Muffled conversation followed. She went running, her heart racing, toward the office.

She got a glimpse of her employer, almost collapsed in Alistair Sims's arms. "No! Oh, God, no!" Connor sobbed. His voice was deep with torment. It was almost a sob of rage, of pain so deep that words weren't enough to express it.

"Here. Get it out of here. Hide it. And close that door!" Alistair shouted. "I'll call the doctor. He's going to have to be sedated."

Barnes came out holding the pistol. He looked at Marie, his face contorted.

"What happened?" she mouthed.

He moved closer. "Emma was still in jail. She didn't have any way to make bail. She was stabbed by another inmate. She lost her baby."

Marie didn't even try to stop the hot tears from tumbling down her cheeks. Barnes put the safety on the pistol and walked out toward the patio, fighting the mist in his own eyes.

# FOURTEEN

They told Emma that she was going to be released, that the charges had been dropped. She was happy about it, although she couldn't be sure that Connor might not have the charges pressed against her again, at some future date. She'd long since given up hope that he might relent. Memories of his hard mouth on hers, his arms holding her, had slowly faded into the same substance as dreams. It seemed so long ago that he'd wanted her, hungered for her. But the woman he thought she was hadn't existed.

She'd let him marry her, knowing he was unaware of her true identity, that she'd been responsible for his blindness. He'd thought she was honest and kind and free of any criminal impulses. But she hadn't been his ideal woman, and his private detective hadn't pulled any punches laying it out for the man who hired him.

Emma knew that she would never forget the way it felt when she saw the disbelief and anguish and rage in Connor's face. She'd lied to him, he shouted. She'd played him for a fool. She was the woman who'd caused him to lose his vision, condemned him to a lifetime of darkness. And she'd married him, knowing he hadn't had the truth. She was nothing but a cheap con artist, looking for an easy life. Well, it would be no easy life for her! He'd make sure of it!

She remembered with kindness the public defender who'd

come to see her shortly after her arrest. He had a caseload, he'd said, that looked like Mount Rushmore, but he'd do what he could for her. She'd answered his questions in a dull, uncaring tone.

He'd frowned. "This was an accident. There was no malicious intent…"

"Mr. Sinclair had warned me about speeding in the boat before," she'd said softly, not adding that he'd been her husband. "He thinks it was malicious." She looked up at the public defender. "Mr. Sinclair is one of the richest men in the world," she added. "Even a court of law is going to find it hard to go against him. He has the best attorneys in America on retainer." She smiled sadly. "I'll be convicted if he has to find a way to intervene with handfuls of money. He wants me here."

He grimaced. He knew how the system worked even better than Emma did. "All right, I'll do my best for you, anyway. But how about bail?"

"Bail is not possible," she said softly. "I have no money, none at all. I had a little in a savings account, but I don't think a hundred dollars will take me very far. My father just disowned me because I disgraced him, being in jail. My former employer is somewhere overseas. I wasn't allowed to try and call her, even if I could find out where she went. But I wouldn't want to ask her to go against Connor. She did, once before, and he cost her her career. He is—" she swallowed hard "—very vindictive."

The young attorney had stared at her sadly. "I'll do what I can to see about getting you out of here."

"Sir, I have no place to go, even if I get out. Unless I could get into a homeless shelter…" Her voice broke. She bit down hard on her pride and lifted bright eyes to his, her mouth set firmly against weakness. "I'll manage. I did blind him, you know," she added. "There's no way around that. Intent might matter, but facts are facts." She lowered her eyes. "So I'll take my licks."

Brave woman, he thought silently. He'd do what he could, if he could think of anything. Sadly, without collateral, she wouldn't make bail. He thought about going up against the attorneys who worked for the multimillionaire and gritted his teeth. A famous trial lawyer would hesitate to tackle that bunch. He'd heard rumors of men Sinclair had ruined. He really didn't want to join the ranks, although he felt very sorry for Miss Copeland. She was pure gold, despite accidentally blinding the tycoon. He truly wished he could help. Emma had watched him go with no real enthusiasm. She knew how things were. But she'd remember that the young man had wanted to help her.

She was surprised that Connor had dropped the charges. She'd been certain that he'd find a way to make sure she never got out of jail. But apparently he had no more taste for vengeance. Mr. Sims seemed to feel that way. But Emma was wary. Right up until the day she was released and Mr. Sims drove her away, she wasn't really sure she'd get out at all. She'd learned not to trust people in the two months she'd spent in the detention center. It had soured her on life. Connor might have some other purpose in mind, some darker purpose. She was grateful that she was going to be free, but she'd have to think of some way to make sure Connor never found her. Especially now.

Connor had slept around the clock, sedated by his local physician. When he came out of it, he was quiet and oddly subdued. He ate breakfast without any real enthusiasm and asked Alistair to stop by. He was on his second cup of coffee, in the office, when the attorney arrived.

"When are they releasing her?" he asked.

"Tomorrow," Alistair replied. He put his briefcase on the desk.

"Have you spoken with her about where she wants to go?" he asked.

"No. She wasn't really in much shape to talk. They stitched her up, but she's almost suicidally depressed about the child."

It hurt him, thinking how much Emma loved children. Of course she'd wanted it, and not for any underhanded reason. She must be in hell.

"I'm sorry about the child," Connor said heavily. "I accused her of being mercenary when that's the last thing she is. I was disoriented by what happened, by the shock of knowing who Emma really was. I just...went a little crazy. I never meant for her to stay in jail that long! I never wanted her hurt!"

"They're charging the other woman with attempted murder. Her public defender will probably plead it down to felony assault, but she'll do more time. The woman has mental issues that were never addressed."

"The woman stabbed Emma," Connor said icily. "She'll do time, all right. I'll make sure of it."

"Meanwhile," Alistair said quietly, "I'll get Emma out of jail."

There was a hesitation. "About the divorce papers..."

"She signed them," he told Connor. He opened his briefcase and took out the divorce papers. "She said she wouldn't accept alimony even if you offered it. A proud woman."

Connor's conscience was killing him. "Yes. Proud."

"I'll talk to you later."

He left. Connor looked at the red-and-black painting on the wall. It was called *Despair*. It seemed a very appropriate adornment for the study now, he thought sadly. He'd put Emma in harm's way, helped damage her emotions and her body and her spirit. He'd thrown her away because she was driving a boat that accidentally ran over him and caused, or seemed to cause, his blindness. He was punishing her for an accident. If he'd been looking, he'd have seen the boat coming. If she'd been looking, she would have seen him. It was just damned bad luck on both sides, but that wasn't a criminal issue. Emma would never have hurt him deliberately. He should have known that.

Anger had been riding him when he had her arrested. He was ashamed and sorry that he'd taken things so far. He didn't think Emma would be able to forgive him for what had been done to her. Imprisoned like that for two whole months with a woman after her blood. And he'd been relaxing on a beach near Nice, enjoying the sun and his new ability to see, and feeling that he had the world in his pocket. He'd had the world when he had Emma, but it had taken time to come to his senses. Now, he almost wished he hadn't.

Emma would hate him. She should hate him. He'd done terrible things to her in the name of vengeance. He could never make up for the misery he'd caused her, for not trusting her, for betraying her. She hadn't even had the money to call Mamie overseas, because he'd sent her away without her clothes or her purse.

At least Alistair could bankroll her. She could have a place to stay, money for food and necessities, while he debated ideas to get her back into his life. He'd do anything to get her forgiveness.

The divorce papers lay on the desk, unread. With a groan of self-contempt, he grabbed them and threw them into the open fire in the fireplace. He watched them burn. They'd still be married, even if Emma didn't know. He'd find a way to keep tabs on her, to make sure she was all right. If she found someone else…well, he'd let her go. What a shame, he thought, that he hadn't realized what she meant to him until it was too late, until he'd shattered her life.

He'd spent his whole life being vindictive, paying people back for things they'd done to him, even innocent things.

Now he was seeing the other side of the coin, and it wasn't pleasant. He'd lost the one person in the world who'd really cared about him. Emma had loved him. He'd told her that he only wanted her. She probably believed it now, after what he'd done to her.

Vengeance, he thought miserably, was a tragedy in itself. He wished he could go back in time and undo the anguish he'd caused Emma. He'd lost her and a child he hadn't even known he wanted, all because of vengeance.

He sat down behind his desk. He had more money than most people on the planet. But right now, he had nothing. Nothing at all.

Emma winced as she tried to walk. She had a cane, a present from Bess, the guard who liked her. She hugged the woman with tears in her eyes.

"You just get better, you hear?" Bess asked softly, her black eyes smiling like her lips.

"You take care, too," Emma said. "I'll never forget your kindness."

"It's not hard being kind to nice people. I don't meet many in this business," she added with a smile.

"If you ever hear from Delsa or Sudie, can you tell them that I got out? I'm sorry they didn't."

"I will," she promised. "We have a mutual friend. They'll be happy for you."

"They were so kind to me." Her voice broke.

Bess hugged her. "You're the kind one, sweetheart. Be happy."

"So long."

Emma followed the lawyer out to his car, an expensive sedan like the one Connor drove. She got in, favoring her leg. The wounds in her belly were still painful, and she was having gas pain like nothing she'd ever dreamed.

"What did they say about that leg?" the lawyer asked as he pulled away from the curb.

"The doctor just sewed me up," she replied. "He didn't say anything much except that I might need further surgery. I don't know for what."

"I see." He glanced at her. "Connor told me to find you a place and make sure you had enough money."

"I don't want anything from him, Mr. Sims," she said with quiet pride. "I just want bus fare to Texas and a ride to the bus station in town, and that's all. I'll be obliged if Mr. Sinclair doesn't mind lending it to me. My father doesn't want me, but I have a cousin who'll let me live with her."

He didn't look at her. He wondered if Connor had ever known this woman at all. She was fiercely proud. "Connor wanted me to tell you how sorry he was—"

She held up a hand. "He doesn't owe me a thing," she replied. "I paid for what I did to him. Not enough, maybe..."

He groaned out loud.

She glanced at him. His face was shuttered now. He looked straight ahead. She wondered why Connor felt sorry for her.

"You told him about the baby?" she asked.

He wished he could tell her how Connor had reacted. He didn't dare. That was for Connor to tell her, if he ever decided to. "Yes. I told him."

She knew something about the baby that she wasn't telling him. The wounds on her stomach had been largely superficial, because the shiv had been very small, with a short blade. The baby was still tucked safely in her womb. The doctor had smiled at her expression of joy when she knew.

But Connor wasn't going to know. He was divorcing her. He wouldn't know, so he wouldn't ask to have her get rid of the child. He'd think she was hoping for an easy life of luxury if she told him, even if he didn't insist on ending the pregnancy. So she wasn't telling the lawyer, and she wasn't telling Connor.

"What about your belongings, Miss Copeland?" he asked suddenly.

"Oh. I only had a few things at my… At Mr. Sinclair's house."

"Your purse and your cell phone and some small bills. They're here." He reached into the glove compartment and handed them to her.

"Thank you!" she exclaimed. Now she had her identification, her credit card and some cash. After the weeks of being in jail, it was like finding a fortune under a rock.

He smiled at her enthusiasm. "You had some items of clothing but…" He hesitated. Connor had thrown them out. He'd even had Marie burn the wedding photos that had been taken in Las Vegas. But Connor didn't know that Marie had saved one, the one that had captured all the love and anguish of Emma's heart in it, of her looking up at Connor. She'd told Alistair that she just couldn't throw it away. He promised he'd never tell.

"It's okay," she said, discerning what the man didn't want to tell her, about her clothes. She knew Connor and his temper very well. "I have some clothes at Mamie's house. I know where she keeps the spare key." She didn't mention that she still had her own key, in her returned purse. "She wouldn't mind. Could you drive me there on the way to the bus station, please?" she asked, wide brown eyes meeting his.

He felt guilty, just looking at her. He wondered if there wasn't more damage than surface damage on her leg. That limp seemed out of place if there had only been a shallow cut.

"Sure."

"And…could you go around, so we don't go by Pine Cottage?" she asked tautly, without looking at him.

"We can do that, as well," he agreed.

"Thanks."

He let her out at the door of Mamie's huge lake house and watched while she went painstakingly up the steps and pretended to look for the hidden key. She had it in her hand when she turned.

Emma waved it with a smile and went inside. She went to her room and looked around. It seemed an age since she'd been here. So much had happened in between.

She gathered up her things and put them in the small, battered suitcase. She didn't have much. Sentiment was expensive, space-wise. But she had pictures of her mother and the ranch, the way it had once been. She didn't have a single photo of her father. She didn't want one.

She checked to make sure she had everything and carried the suitcase into the living room. It was heavy. It hurt to walk at all, much less carry something. She'd have to call Mr. Sims and ask him to lift it for her.

On an impulse, when she saw the fancy mock-French phone on the table in the living room, she picked it up and dialed Mamie's cell phone.

"Hello?"

She hadn't expected Mamie to answer. She gasped. "Mamie!"

"Hi, baby! How are you?"

Emma burst into tears. "I married Connor but he found out that I blinded him. He had me arrested. I've been in jail, and I got stabbed…!"

"Slow down, slow down. Stabbed? Jail? My God, why didn't you call me?"

"They wouldn't let me make an overseas call." Emma sobbed.

"Dear God! My poor baby! Listen, what do you need? I can get you the best lawyers…!"

"I'm out. Connor dropped the charges. I may still face misdemeanor charges for reckless driving on the lake, though."

"You can stay at the house," Mamie said.

"Connor's still at the cottage," she said through her teeth. "I can't stay here at the lake, not now."

"Where will you go?"

"Texas. I have a cousin there. I told the investigator I spoke to that I'd make sure he knew where I was, in case they want to press charges." Her voice sounded dull. Lackluster.

"Emma, Connor will go to his house in Nice very soon. He'll stay there for several months while he does business all over Europe. He won't be back until late September. You can stay in the lake house, at least while he's gone."

"He hasn't gone anywhere and I can't risk bumping into him. Even though he can't see…"

"But he can!" Mamie explained. "Didn't you know? It was in the papers."

She caught her breath. "He can see again? The lawyer didn't tell me."

"What lawyer?"

"Alistair Sims. He's been so kind. He got me out of jail and persuaded Connor to dismiss the charges. He's going to drive me to the bus station." She hesitated. "Connor can see." She laughed as she glimpsed herself in the mirror. She didn't even look like the old Emma.

"Yes. But he'll be leaving soon. Honest."

"Mamie, there's another reason I can't let him see me," Emma said. "He thinks I lost the baby when I was stabbed, but I didn't. I don't want him to know, ever. He'll think I did it for money. He thinks that's why I married him when he was blind."

"You're pregnant? You married him? You were stabbed?"

"I'm all right. He's divorcing me. I signed the papers. I'm better, from the wounds. They let me go."

"He only saw you a couple of times before he lost his sight, didn't he?" Mamie was thinking out loud.

"Yes," she confessed. "Once at the party and once on the pier, then outside when I was sitting on a log, but he didn't get a close look at me." She laughed. It had a hollow sound. "He wouldn't recognize me now. I don't look the way I did anymore."

"Then stay at the lake," Mamie said firmly. "Listen to me, you can put a wash on your hair to make it look red. You can pretend you have a husband who works in Saudi Arabia. My godson. I hired you to house-sit while I'm working on research in Europe. Just say you're two months earlier along in the pregnancy than you really are so Connor wouldn't connect your baby with his even if he was suspicious."

Mamie was determined and Emma was weakening. Texas was a long way away. The lake had been home for a long time. This was a nice town in which to raise a child. If Connor only came home for a few weeks, maybe she could go away for that time. If he saw her only from a distance, and she dyed her hair...

"I can hear you thinking about it. Just say yes. I'll take care of everything."

Emma drew in a breath. "You're so kind to me, Mamie," she began.

"It's not hard. You're kind to the world. You know where everything is. I have credit with the merchants in town. They can deliver food every week. You just call them and say it's for me. I'll call the local limo agency and give them my credit card number, so you can get a ride to town when you need one. You could have used the car, but I loaned it to a friend. I'm so sorry, I didn't know you'd be there... But, anyway, spare cash is in a canister in the kitchen for little things you need."

"Okay."

"Don't go out at night. Don't let Connor know you're there."

"I won't. Thank you!"

"You'd do it for me," was the soft reply. "If anything comes up that you can't handle, call me."

"I will."

"Get some rest. You poor child. I'm so sorry!"

Emma fought tears. "Thank you for letting me stay here."

"Thank you for taking care of the house! I'll make sure you have a check every two weeks."

"Thank you for that, too."

"You know I can afford it. I meant to get back sooner, but I've had so much fun over here that I just didn't want to get back to work. I've got a lot of research done. I'll send my notes to you in an email. Get them in some sort of order when you have time. And keep me posted. I want to know how you do."

"I'll do that," Emma promised. "I'll let the lawyer drive me to the bus station. When he leaves, I'll get a cab back here."

"Wise woman. I'll talk to you later, Emma."

"Okay. You take care, too."

"Always."

Emma hung up. She moved to the door and called to Mr. Sims, to ask him to help her with the suitcase.

He came right up the steps and lifted it as if it weighed nothing. Emma relocked the door and put the key in her purse while the attorney put her bag in the car. She walked very slowly down the steps, using the cane the kind guard had given her. He was holding the door open for her.

"You need to have that leg looked at by a specialist," he commented.

She managed a smile. "I'll see if my cousin knows one," she replied.

"Good idea."

He drove her to the bus station. "Do you have enough money for the ticket?"

"Yes." She opened her purse and pulled out a few twenty-dollar bills that she'd found in Mamie's household money in the canister.

He smiled. "Okay."

He carried the suitcase in for her, waited while she pretended to buy a ticket and was going to wait for the bus with her.

"No. That's not necessary, but thank you for being so kind," she told him with genuine feeling. "Thank you for getting me out of jail." She choked up and had to blink the moisture out of her eyes. "I don't know what I would have done," she concluded.

He didn't, either, but he wasn't going to say so. He shook hands with her. "About those divorce papers..."

"It's okay. I don't blame him," she said. "It wasn't right, him marrying somebody like me. He needs one of those sophisticated, modern women who can hold their own at cocktail parties and fancy dinners." She smiled sadly. "It was never me, if you know what I mean. Thanks again, Mr. Sims."

He shook hands with her. "If you ever need help," he said, and fished out a business card. "I won't tell Connor," he added with a sad smile.

She returned the smile. "I'll remember." She would have thanked him again, but she felt like a robot already for having said it so much.

He nodded, turned and walked away. Emma waited fifteen minutes, then she picked up the suitcase with some effort and started toward the front door.

An elderly man saw how hard it was for her to manage the cane and the suitcase.

"Here, little lady, let me help you with that." He took the suitcase. "Where to?"

"Just out front," she said. "I have to get a cab."

He smiled. "No problem. I'm seeing my wife off to Buffalo to visit our son and daughter. She's in the snack shop."

"Thank you so much."

"No need for that. Just pass it on when you can," he said, depositing the suitcase where a taxi had just pulled up. "That's what makes us human, helping each other out. Have a safe trip."

"I hope your wife does, too. Thanks."

He waved and went back inside. The taxi driver grinned, put her suitcase in the trunk and opened the door for her. "Where you wanna go?" he asked.

She gave him the address. When they got there, she pulled out a ten-dollar bill.

"No, no, it is only three dollars," he began.

"It's a tip, for being so nice."

"Senorita, may the good Lord bless you."

"May He do the same for you," she said with a warm smile. "Thank you."

"If you ever need me to take you someplace, you call me, okay?" He handed her a card.

"I certainly will."

He deposited her suitcase on the front porch of Mamie's cabin and left her with a smile.

So Emma moved back into Mamie's house. She kept a low profile. She made sure the lights facing Connor's house were never on. She never ventured outside. She stayed in the house and organized the notes Mamie sent her, kept the house clean, did whatever she could to keep her mind off Connor altogether. In the meantime, she dreamed of her baby. She was going to love it insanely. It would never want for love, even if it never had money.

She found a midwife, recommended to her by one of the

men who delivered Mamie's groceries to her. The midwife, a nice woman in her forties, came to see her often, to make sure things were progressing well. She knew that Emma's mother had died in childbirth, so she was extra vigilant. When the baby came, she added, if she suspected any problem at all, they'd call an ambulance. Emma relaxed a little.

She wondered how Connor was, but they had no mutual friends and she wasn't about to blow her cover by calling the house or even Mr. Sims. She imagined Mamie was right, that Connor would be in France by now, living it up.

In fact, Connor wasn't living it up in France. He'd walked around the lake house like a ghost for days after he knew what he'd done to Emma. Marie and Barnes worried about him. He was so unlike himself. His suicide attempt had rattled them. Until then, they'd had no idea just how emotionally involved he was with Emma—or what losing her had done to him.

Several days later, he took one last look around the house and called Alistair to tell him to put it on the market with all the furniture included. Alistair, sadly, agreed.

Then Connor packed up the household, had their odds and ends warehoused and flew them all to his home in Nice, where Edward welcomed them with joy and some curiosity.

"What is wrong?" he asked Marie when Connor was walking aimlessly up and down the beach out back. "I understood that Mr. Sinclair had married?"

"It's a long story, Edward," Marie replied sadly. "I'll tell it to you one day. He's a mess," she added, nodding toward the solitary figure outside. "He's put the lake house on the market and he says he's never going back to Georgia. He had Mr. Sims deliver divorce papers to Emma for her to sign. I guess he's filed them already. It's such a shame," she added sadly. "She loved him almost too much. I thought he cared for her, too. If he did, it's too late now."

"But why?" he asked.

"She drove a motorboat into him and blinded him," she replied.

"It was she?" Edward exclaimed. "On purpose?"

"Of course not. She isn't the sort. But he thought she did. He had her arrested and put in jail." She grimaced. "She was pregnant. Another woman attacked her in jail and she lost the baby." She drew in a long breath, registering Edward's look of horror. "She actually told Mr. Sims that she deserved everything that happened to her, because the boss went blind."

"An exceptional woman."

"She cared so much for him. She sat up with him when he had migraines, did everything she could to keep him happy. I was sure that they'd be together forever, even when he was denying that he felt anything for her. It's such a mess," she said again.

"But she would forgive him, no?" he asked.

She nodded. "In time, yes, I think so. Right now she's emotionally raw from losing the baby, especially the way it happened. She needs time to get over it." She glanced out the window. "We have to watch him," she added. "He tried to shoot himself when he found out what had happened to her. Mr. Sims actually wrestled a pistol out of his hands."

Edward crossed himself. *"Mon Dieu!"* he exclaimed.

"He's still not quite himself. We can't leave him alone. Not until he's had time to work through it."

"What about Miss Emma? Where did she go?"

"Back to Texas, where she was from. Her own father disowned her when he knew she'd been arrested."

"Some father," Edward said coldly.

"Amen."

"She has other family?"

"I think so," Marie said. "A cousin. She'll have a place to stay. Revenge is a very sad thing, Edward. A very sad thing indeed."

★ ★ ★

Emma ventured out late one afternoon with her cane. She hadn't seen any activity down Connor's way and she was curious.

She walked to the log that had played such a part in her relationship with Connor and paused there, looking toward Pine Cottage. What she saw shocked her. There was a huge For Sale sign out front, with a Realtor's name and telephone number.

She sat down on the log heavily. So he was giving up a family home to run from the memory of her. She knew that was why he'd put it on the market. He must truly hate her to do that. He wanted to make sure that he never saw her again. He needn't have worried. Emma was never pushy. She wouldn't have gone near him, even to beg forgiveness.

Perhaps he was just tired of the place. He loved France. Certainly, that would explain it. Except that he loved Pine Cottage. He'd told her once that he never had plans to let go of it. The place held so many memories, most especially of the brother he'd lost.

He hadn't wanted to risk running into Emma, if she went back to work for Mamie. That had to be it.

It made her sad, that even with all that had happened, he bore a grudge. He was sorry for her, but that didn't mean he'd forgiven her for blinding him. He was a man who never forgot an injury. So maybe it was just as well, that he'd gone.

She thought of the long years ahead, without even a glimpse of him, and hot tears stung her eyes. But she still had the baby that he didn't know about.

One small hand smoothed over the hard little knot in her belly and she smiled sadly. At least she had a part of him that she'd never have to give up.

She turned and walked slowly back toward Mamie's cabin.

# FIFTEEN

Emma relaxed a little after she saw that Pine Cottage was up for sale. It would have made things difficult, if she'd had to be watching eternally for Connor, afraid of being seen.

She was so tired. She'd lost weight in the two months she'd been in jail. Her old clothes didn't fit anymore. They hung on her. She looked at herself in the mirror after she showered and grimaced at the scars on her belly, laced with antiseptic, and the deep, long one that slashed across one smooth, lovely thigh. The woman had been a maniac. It was a miracle that the weapon hadn't been longer. It did some damage to the muscle tissue of her leg, but hadn't hit an artery.

Thank God she still had the baby tucked inside her. She would love him and hide him from the vindictive man who'd always said he didn't want a child. He hadn't used birth control the times he'd taken Emma to bed, but she knew he assumed she was taking the pill after he'd reminded her to get started on it. He'd made his position on children crystal clear. It was just odd that he'd never really asked her if she started using the pill.

She was so tired. The past few weeks had been an ordeal that she never hoped to repeat. She looked back on her brief marriage with bittersweet tears. It was hard to forget the tenderness he'd shown her, the passionate hunger he never seemed to satisfy. It was strange that he'd hated her so much, when he knew who she was. It was like the first night she'd seen him in evening clothes, at Mamie's. He'd glowered at her, snapped at her, made her cry. When he'd found her dangling her toes into the lake from his pier, he'd been terrible. Why he hated a woman he didn't even know didn't make a lot of sense. Maybe, like that unstable woman in jail, he had her mixed up with someone who'd hurt him. It was the only explanation that made sense to her.

She put him out of her mind. He didn't want her. She'd keep to herself and have her baby. She had a job, at least, and a roof over her head. She couldn't afford an obstetrician, but she had the midwife. She recalled with bridled terror that her mother had died in childbirth, trying to give birth to another daughter, who also died. If it was a genetic thing, or a physical issue that was handed down, she could die in childbirth, too. But surely a midwife would know about such things. Of course she would. Emma knew she'd be okay. She had to be.

Connor was on a plane to Munich. The Realtor wasn't enthusiastic about finding a buyer, even for such an exclusive property, Alistair had told him. Also, the price Connor wanted for it was unrealistic.

He didn't care. He just wanted to get away from Georgia. He never wanted to go near the cottage again. It held such bittersweet memories of Emma. Emma, laughing in the muted sounds of dusk as she told him about the antics of birds on the lake. Emma, fussing over him at night when his head was splitting. Emma, moaning in his arms with such passion that he tingled all over just remembering it. Emma, sobbing and running from him when he accused her of blinding him...

He closed his eyes and shivered. Emma, he thought in anguish, sitting in a jail cell for two months and being attacked by another inmate so badly that she ended up in a hospital bed. He'd done that to her. He'd wanted to hurt her on a blind impulse of vengeance. He'd done it in the past, to other people. Now it hit home. He knew how the others must have felt. He was ashamed of himself, appalled at his own inability to control the anger.

Poor Emma. He understood her feelings. She didn't want him in her life. She was afraid of him, of the power he could wield, of what he could do to her. She'd run all the way to Texas to get away from him, to make sure she didn't see him again. It hit him in the heart like a blow from a sledgehammer. And until he knew what he'd done to her, until he knew what a hell he'd made of her life, he didn't realize...that he loved her.

It had crept up on him, like a soft fog on the lake in early morning in the fall. She'd brushed against his heart softly, so softly, her voice full of the love she couldn't hide, the desire she couldn't hide. She was the only woman he'd ever known who'd seemed to want him for what he was, not what he had.

He'd labeled her mercenary, a woman after him for a cushy life. But those terms applied to women like his lovers. They didn't apply to Emma. He remembered the time he'd seen her on the beach, sitting on the log, and he'd ridiculed her cheap clothing. It shamed him, especially when he recalled her stiff pride, despite her lack of material wealth. That woman wouldn't marry a man for what he had, or want a child for selfish reasons.

He was sorry about the child. He'd made her promise that she'd get on the pill, so that it wouldn't be a constant worry. A child. He could picture Emma holding one, loving one because it was his, too. But that was in the past, before he hurt her, before he made her run. Before he cost her the baby she was carrying, that he hadn't even known about. He closed his eyes. He would never hold her in the darkness again. He would never hear that silvery laugh that he loved so much, feel her gentle fingers in his hair, comforting him when the headaches came. He'd given all that up, and for what? For nothing. Alcohol and revenge had driven him past the point of no return. Emma, gentle Emma, in jail for two hellish months with no way out, nobody to protect her. Even then, she'd told Alistair that she deserved it for what she'd done to Connor. He almost choked on his drink, remembering that. Deserved it, for an accident that had been as much his own fault as hers!

There was an old biblical saying: vengeance is mine, I will repay, saith the Lord. He should have remembered it sooner, before he destroyed Emma's life. Too late now. He finished his drink and held up the glass for the flight attendant to re-fill. If he could get drunk enough, maybe he could forget, just for a few minutes.

Time passed slowly. Emma felt her body changing. She loved the changes. She'd put a wash on her long hair to give it a red hue, and she'd chosen very roomy dresses and jumpers that showed nothing of her figure. She didn't look like the old Emma now. She'd gained weight because of the baby. She had a beautiful complexion and a radiance about her that made people smile. She was happy.

Mamie had been away most of the four months Emma had been living at the house. She'd come home for a couple of weeks, just long enough to give another book to Emma to proof and fact-check. She kept busy.

Late in the August afternoon, she liked to sit on the edge of the lake, on that old log that she'd occupied the day Connor had come upon her. The memories were a little less harsh now with the passage of time. She still had problems with her leg. Mamie had wanted her to see a doctor, but Emma refused. She didn't tell the older woman about the midwife, either. Mamie had done enough for her. She didn't want to become a dependent. Perhaps she could find a part-time job somewhere to supplement her income and it would help pay the hospital bill when it came. The midwife, who was very knowledgeable, told her that hospitals could provide care for indigents, so she shouldn't worry. But Emma worried just the same.

She'd learned to knit. She was producing hats by the dozen. She gave them away to children she met at the stores in town, to elderly people sitting on park benches. She gave some to the midwife to pass out at the medical clinic where she volunteered. She felt that it let her give something back to the world, a spot of color to brighten people's days. She was surprised at how people reacted to the unexpected gifts. It made her feel bright inside.

She was drawing a pattern in the wet dirt near the log when a shadow fell over her. She looked up and there he was. Connor Sinclair.

"This is private land," he said curtly. "You're trespassing."

She turned, with some apprehension, because he must surely remember a little about her appearance from when he was sighted. But his pale gray eyes were hostile. There was no recognition in them.

Emma gave a sigh of relief. He didn't know her. Of course he didn't. She was wearing a shapeless tent dress that was two sizes too big for her. Her face was rounder than it had been. And her hair, tinted red, was piled on top of her head. He would remember a thin blonde woman. Emma had changed with her pregnancy. She wondered why he was back at the lake house in August, when he only came here in September. Had he come to see someone who wanted to buy the house? She didn't know.

Surely he didn't remember how she looked after all these months. He'd only really seen her once or twice. She relaxed, just a little. She got to her feet with visible effort, leaning heavily on her cane, the one Bess had given her. "I'm really sorry," she said softly. "I didn't know anybody lived here. There's a For Sale sign—"

He scowled. "Do you live on the lake?" he interrupted, and the look he gave her was disbelieving. He obviously thought she was a street person.

She should have been insulted, but she wasn't. It made things easier. She drew in a breath to steady her. She leaned heavily on the cane. "My husband's godmother lives there." She pointed to Mamie's house. "She's letting me house-sit for her while my husband is in Saudi Arabia. He works on oil wells."

He looked down at her shapeless dress. It didn't hide the thrust of her belly. "You're pregnant."

She forced a normal smile to her lips. "Oh, yes, six months along," she lied, because that was two months earlier than she really was, and it would keep him from making connections.

The pregnancy reminded him of all he'd lost. He averted his eyes to the lake. "I suppose your husband is happy about it," he said.

"He's very happy," she agreed. "We're hoping for a boy."

"They can do tests. Don't you know the baby's sex already?"

"We didn't want to know," she said simply. She drew in another breath. It was getting hard to breathe as the baby grew and pressed against her diaphragm. "I have to go. Sorry about trespassing. I won't do it again."

He frowned. There was something so familiar about her. Red hair. Six months pregnant. No way that could be Emma. But he wished...

She turned slowly and started back down the shoreline. "Who are you?" he asked suddenly.

"Mary Kathryn," she said without turning. It was her real name. She'd never told Connor.

"Mary Kathryn what?"

"Kilpatrick," she lied. "My husband is Irish."

He watched her go, every step obviously painful. "What's wrong with your leg?" he asked abruptly.

"I was in an…accident," she said. "At least I still have a leg to walk on," she added, trying to make it seem as if the accident had almost amputated her, to throw him off the track. "Good night."

He didn't reply. He shouldn't have made her leave. He wished he could will her to come back. He wanted to talk to her. She reminded him so much of Emma. He'd forgotten much about her appearance. While he was blind, he'd learned her scent, her voice, her soft hands, the feel of her body in his arms. When his sight came back, it was full of the woman who'd hit him with the motorboat.

He vaguely remembered what she looked like. Blond hair, almost platinum, straight nose, pretty mouth, medium height, big brown eyes. But the memory was fuzzy, like something out of a dream. It had been so long since he'd seen her that he wasn't sure he'd recognize her on the street. Sad, because that had been Emma. That shadowy woman whom he'd cursed as the cause of his blindness had been the same woman who sat with him when he had blinding headaches, who'd never left him until they went away. Emma. Emma!

He didn't even have a photograph of her. He'd made Marie burn them all, every single one that had been taken at the wedding. He felt that loss now, when he wanted so desperately to feed his empty heart with a picture of the woman he'd lost. But it was too late.

The photograph wouldn't be of any use, because that woman walking away from him wasn't his Emma. She was six months pregnant and married, and she had a distinct limp. Emma, if she hadn't lost the baby, would have been over eight months along by now.

So the woman on the lake was a stranger. He watched her go with mixed emotions. Her husband should be with her. He should be taking care of her. He grimaced. It was none of his business. None at all. He turned and walked back to his own house.

It was three days before he saw her again. She was wearing a sunhat. She and a little girl were putting something into the water. He heard them talking softly to each other. French. He recognized it.

"Will it sail, do you think, *mademoiselle?*" the child asked.

"*Bien sur.* It will certainly sail," was the laughing reply. "One of my great-great-grandfathers came to North Carolina by way of Scotland, and he was a shipwright. Sailing is in my blood."

The little girl laughed. "Very well, then."

Emma put the tiny boat in the water and pushed it out. It floated. She laughed softly. So did the child.

Connor moved closer. Emma saw him and flushed. She scrambled to her feet.

"Oh, dear," she said, "are we on your property? I'm sorry. We only wanted a place to put the little boat in the lake."

"It's all right," he said softly. "I don't mind."

She shifted restlessly. "It's time for us to go, anyway. Adele, can you find my stick, *s'il vous plaît?*"

The little girl handed it to her.

"Thank you," she said, and forced a smile. "We must go." She glanced nervously at Connor. He was standing on the shore, his face quiet and sad, just watching them.

She nodded at him and tugged the little girl along beside her. They made their way down the shore.

"You forgot your boat," he called after her.

"It's just made of twigs and leaves and some vine we found," Emma called back. "It will sink eventually."

She kept walking.

Connor waited until they were out of sight before he went to the water and picked up the little ship, turning it in his big hands to see the intricate method of its construction. It was pretty. He carried it inside and put it on a shelf.

Marie, his housekeeper, gave it a glare.

"Aaaaah," he cautioned. "Don't you touch it."

"It's just twigs…"

"It's a rare example of vine and leaf art," he argued. "Just leave it alone. It has…sentimental value," he added, without quite understanding why he said that.

"If you say so, sir."

"I do."

He walked to the phone he'd left lying on the table. He picked it up and dialed his lawyer.

"Sims, call the Realtor and tell her to come get the For Sale sign," he said.

"I can do that. Changed your mind about selling it?"

"I think so." He sighed. "Memories are portable. I can't evade them by selling the house where they live."

"I'll get on it first thing tomorrow."

"Have you heard anything about Emma?" he added.

"No."

"She went to Texas, didn't she?"

"Yes. I took her to the bus station myself and watched her buy a ticket."

He felt the sorrow like a living thing. He stared at the floor. The woman on the lake bothered him. There was something so familiar about her, about her voice. Red hair could be created. She could have lied about her husband and her due date.

"Why are you asking me these questions?" Sims wanted to know.

"Mamie van Dyke has a house sitter," he said. "She…looks

like Emma. I think. But she says she's six months pregnant and married. Her husband is Mamie's godson."

"Emma is in Texas," Alistair repeated with more assurance than he actually felt. He'd run into Emma only recently and felt so sorry for her that he'd sworn he wouldn't tell Connor that she was living at Mamie's and was still pregnant. She said there was no telling what Connor might do to her. He might want the child terminated, so that he wouldn't have to support it. That might be true. The man was a mystery even to his own attorney. Alistair couldn't break Emma's confidence. Not after all she'd been through.

"Yes. I guess she is in Texas. And even if she was still here, she wouldn't speak to me," Connor said huskily.

"Not likely," he agreed.

"Poor Emma," he said, his voice thready and distant. "I landed her in hell and never even looked back."

"Life is hard," was all Alistair would say.

"Hard as hell and never gets easier," came the reply. He looked out the darkening window. "This woman's damned husband is in Saudi Arabia, working on oil wells."

"A dangerous profession, although it's lucrative. I know a man who went there and now drives a Rolls."

"The point is, she's pregnant, and he's not here!" he shot back. "What the hell kind of man deserts a pregnant woman?"

"I suppose he has to keep his job, and that's the only way. Besides that, a lot of men put business before family obligations."

"Damned idiots," Connor muttered. He let out a breath. "Okay. Call the Realtor."

"I'll do that. Call if you need me."

"Count on it."

He hung up. It saddened him to learn that his neighbor couldn't be Emma. The evidence was strongly against it. Still, he was drawn to the woman. He felt sorry for her. She was all alone. Well, maybe she spent some time with that little

French girl. But she was alone in Mamie's house. What if something went wrong with her pregnancy?

It bothered him that he cared. She wasn't Emma, he had to admit that. But she reminded him of the woman he'd treated so badly. Perhaps he could find a way to help her without being obvious. He gave Emma a thought, living in Texas, with a cousin. He wanted so badly to go to her on his knees, and apologize, beg her to come back. But after what he'd done to her, he doubted that she would even open the door to him. Regrets were all he had left.

Emma walked when the pain got bad. It probably wasn't the thing to do, but her leg throbbed sometimes, despite the fact that it looked healed. Maybe the injury had been deeper than they thought. It seemed that more damage had been done than the harried doctor realized. He'd had so many patients in the emergency room the day she was brought in. But it was a moot point. She had no money for specialists. It was going to take every penny she could save to pay the midwife.

She stopped at the log she liked to sit on. It was big and roomy and somehow comforting. Long before Connor became her reason for living, she'd sat here to look at the lake in the late afternoon. There was something comforting about night sounds, lonely places. Even now, when she closed her eyes, she could hear faraway traffic on the highway, dogs barking, even a train going by.

She sat down gingerly on the log and propped her stick beside it. She loved the sounds. Heaven knew where she'd be by autumn. She would have to leave, if Connor was moving back to the lake so soon. It was curious that he'd taken down the For Sale sign. He only stayed on the lake rarely. Why keep the cottage?

"It's late for you to be out here alone, isn't it?" Connor said from behind her.

She jumped involuntarily as he came into sight around the log. He was wearing slacks and a red pullover knit shirt. He looked elegant and expensive.

"I like the lake at night," she said hesitantly.

"I like it, too," he replied. He drew in a long breath. "I've been in Europe. I thought I could outrun my conscience and my guilt." He laughed. It had a hollow, haunted sound.

"Conscience?" she asked, pretending not to understand. It shocked her that he even felt guilt. He'd been vicious when he ordered her arrested.

He nodded without looking her way. "You're too young to know it, but back in my mother's day there was a song about a big yellow taxi." He smiled to himself. "The gist of it is that we don't know what we've got until it's gone. And that is a fact."

"You lost something?" she prevaricated.

"I lost the most precious thing in my life," he replied quietly. "And I didn't know that I had, until it was gone. Until it was too late to undo the damage."

"Was it a woman?" she asked.

"Yes. I lashed out in an alcoholic daze and did something unforgivable. I thought I was justified. But I wasn't."

"That must be bad," she said noncommittally.

"Hell on earth." He turned toward her. "Have you ever lost something that was worth your own life?"

She nodded.

"A man?" he prodded.

She smiled sadly. "I've still got him. He's in Saudi Arabia."

"But you lost him?"

She hesitated. "We had a small difference of opinion. I wanted a baby. He didn't."

"Good God!" He moved a step closer, scowling. "Why doesn't he want the child?"

"He didn't say."

"I'm sorry," he said, and seemed to mean it. "So you're alone."

She stared at the lake. "I've always been alone. You get used to it."

He thought of how alone he was since Emma left. Sometimes the silence was painful. He missed her in every room of his house. Everything reminded him of her. The pain grew by the day.

"You're very rich, they say," she remarked. "I suppose you have hot and cold running women all over your house."

He laughed unexpectedly. "No. Not anymore."

"Pity."

"No. It isn't." He drew in a long, slow breath. He was looking at the lake, not at Emma. "I went through life trying not to be trapped, as so many of my friends were. Trapped into marriage by seductive women who wanted diamonds and minks and were willing to get pregnant to get them. Women can be as unscrupulous as men."

"You don't want children?"

He bit down hard on his grief. "I didn't." He hesitated. He looked down at his feet. "Regrets don't get us anywhere, really. Things are what they are. I can't go back and fix the mistakes I made. It's too late."

"That's sad."

"I suppose it is." He turned. "What are you going to do about your husband?"

"He thinks a little separation might help to work out things," she said simply. "So there's hope. He's not divorcing me. Not yet at least." She smiled. "He might want the baby when he sees it," she added wistfully.

He frowned as he looked at what he could see of her in the faint light from a quarter moon. "What a damned fool," he said softly.

She looked up at him, surprised by the remark.

He moved closer. "When is Mamie coming home?"

"I don't know," she replied. "She really hasn't said."

"When you're due to deliver, you need someone to call if you go into labor. You don't have a car, do you?" he asked abruptly, without any apparent motive. He'd driven by the house with Barnes several times. There was never a vehicle in the driveway.

"No," she said without thinking. "But Mamie left a balance at one of the limo companies, so that I could call a car when I needed it. She's very fond of my husband," she added. "She's been kind to me, too."

"I'm right next door," he told her. "If you need help, call me."

She laughed. "You're one of the richest men in the country," she reminded him. "I don't expect your number is listed in the phone book." That was a lie. She'd called the number after she'd hit him, to make sure he was all right.

"Actually, it is," he replied. "Pine Cottage is how it's listed. You'll get put through. I promise."

"Thanks," she told him, averting her face. "But I can manage."

He ground his teeth together. She was proud. Far too proud to accept help from a stranger. He didn't blame her, but he wanted to help her. It was like making up for all he'd done to Emma. He hated what he'd done. He couldn't live with it.

"My wife is alone," he said unexpectedly. "We were expecting a child. I didn't even know. She lost it, because of me. I got stinking drunk and pushed her headfirst out of my life."

Emma was shocked at the anguish in his voice. She hadn't expected that he might still feel guilty about having her arrested.

"So I have a personal motive for wanting to help you," he added quietly. "I'd like to think someone is doing for her what I'm trying to do for you. I guess that doesn't make sense."

It made too much sense. She felt his guilt. He only wanted to help. But she didn't dare let him. She got to her feet and clutched her cane. "Thank you. I really mean that. But... I don't need help."

"Remember what I said," he told her, his voice soft and low. "Neighbors look out for neighbors."

She had to bite her lip to keep from crying. He was basically a kind man. If only she'd never gotten behind the wheel of that speedboat! "Thanks," she managed in a hunted tone.

She was in so much pain that she couldn't even look at him as she made her way down the beach. What she'd lost!

He hadn't known she was still in jail. He'd never meant for her to be hurt like that. He'd even made sure that she got out and had a place to go. She drew in a long breath. She really wished she could hate him. It would make living without him so much easier.

She had to watch every word she said. She didn't want him to start asking questions about her, being suspicious about her. She knew he had doubts. But she hoped she'd convinced him that she had a husband in Saudi Arabia and the child was due in two months instead of about two weeks. If he believed those two things, he'd never suspect she was the woman he'd had thrown in jail.

Connor watched her walk, saw the pain it caused her to take each step. Something was wrong with that leg. He wondered why her doctor hadn't done more to cure her. He wondered if she had an obstetrician. She was alone at Mamie's house. What if something went wrong? It was reckless. She was reckless. There was a posture in her that he recognized. He'd seen it in his own tall form when he'd lost Emma, when he knew she hated him. It was the look of total defeat, disinterest in the world. It was the posture of despair.

He didn't know what to do next, what to say to her. He wanted to help, but she was making it obvious that she didn't want help from him. Was it really pride? Or had he gone too far with his questions? He didn't know. Sadly, he turned and walked back toward Pine Cottage.

He called Alistair the next day. "Her hair is red, but she could have dyed it," he said abruptly. "She says she's six months pregnant. But her stomach looks as if she's almost due to deliver."

Alistair hesitated.

"You know something," Connor said curtly. "Tell me!"

"If she thinks you even suspect it's her, she'll run," Alistair said abruptly.

"It's her!" Connor burst out in anguish. "It is Emma!"

Alistair drew in a breath. "She's sure that you'll insist on getting rid of it if you know she's still here," he returned. "I found out quite accidentally. I ran into her in town. She was buying a maternity dress at one of the consignment shops. She begged me not to give her away. I've never seen anyone so upset." He tamped down the pain of remembering.

Connor's eyes closed. He tried to breathe normally. Emma and her thrift shops. He was a multimillionaire, and his wife dressed out of thrift shops. "I would never, ever do anything to harm the child," he said. Emma was pregnant. His baby was growing inside her. The emotions that shot through him were unfamiliar, humbling. He was going to be a father. For the first time in his life, the thought wasn't terrifying.

"Emma won't believe that," Alistair continued. "You've never made a secret of the way you are about kids. You made a religion of protection. Emma knows all that. She thinks that you'd take her to court to make her end the pregnancy."

"I wouldn't," Connor said heavily.

"What I'm trying to get across to you," Alistair said patiently, "is what she thinks. You have to be careful."

"Does she have an obstetrician at least?"

Alistair sighed. "I couldn't get her to tell me. She mentioned that she has a midwife, though."

"Her mother died in childbirth," Connor said, anguish in his tone. "She knows that!"

"It worries me, too, Connor," Alistair replied. "I don't think she's well fixed financially, despite what Mamie pays her. If she doesn't have insurance, and many young people don't, there's no money to pay for specialists or even the pre-natal vitamins she should be taking daily."

Connor leaned back in his desk chair. Here was the fruit that his hateful seed had planted. Emma, alone, pregnant, with not even enough money for competent medical care. Emma, with his child inside her.

"I'll think of something," he said curtly.

"I did offer to help financially," Alistair confessed. "She refused. She's very proud."

"Yes." Connor drew in a breath. "Did you tell her that the divorce never went through?"

"She didn't mention it, so neither did I." He hesitated. "She's invented a fictional husband, though."

"Yes, he of the oil fields in Saudi Arabia who can't be both-ered to come home and take care of her," Connor said with biting sarcasm.

"I suppose she thought it would throw you off the track," Alistair said. "She saw the Realtor's sign on the property. She thought you were gone for good, that she'd never see you again. She said she felt safe at Mamie's house."

Connor drummed his fingers on the desk. "I'll let her think she's safe," he replied. "But I'm going to have her watched, to make sure she is. If anything happens, I'll take care of her. Whether she wants me to or not."

"I don't like that limp," the other man said. "If the inmate slashed her leg, it could mean a tendon was torn or partially severed. She needs to have it seen about. I don't know if they'd be willing to operate at this stage of her pregnancy, though."

"My best friend, Harry Weems, is a doctor in Atlanta. He's

one of the foremost obstetricians in the country," Connor said. "He has a branch office in Gainesville. I'll find a way to get her to him."

"It had better be a cautious way."

Connor laughed softly. "I'll think of something." He leaned back in the chair with a long sigh. "I'm going to have a child." He smiled to himself. "How about that?"

"I must confess, I expected a rather different reaction from you."

"Something along the lines of threats and intimidation?" Connor mused. "That might have been possible, with any other woman. Not my Emma. She'll love being a mother."

"I believe she will."

"I won't tell her that you said anything to me," Connor promised. "But thank you. I was suspicious. It was the due date and the fictional husband who threw me."

"You didn't have my advantage. I came upon her unexpectedly."

"So did I, on the lakeshore. Twice," he added with a chuckle. "But she kept her nerve both times."

"I'm glad you decided to take the house off the market," Alistair said. "I still have the house where I lived with my late wife. I can't imagine living somewhere else. I can see her in every room, everywhere I walk. It gives me comfort."

Connor was only beginning to understand how a man could feel that way. "That's why I came back," he confessed. "I never saw Emma in the house—I was blind then. But I could feel her presence, in every room. It was comforting. Life without her has been...very lonely."

"Perhaps not for much longer. If you're careful."

Connor smiled. "Careful," he said, "is my new middle name."

# SIXTEEN

Emma had a bad night. Her leg was throbbing so much that she couldn't sleep. She got up, put the lights on and went into the kitchen to make coffee. Sometimes it helped her sleep. Since she was pregnant, it was decaf, but she made it strong.

She was halfway through her first cup when she heard the knock on the door. She didn't want to answer it. It was frightening to have someone at her door at three in the morning.

She stood up, wishing she had a weapon. She didn't even have the cell phone with her. There was the landline phone in the living room. Maybe she could get to it if she needed to. She hadn't been worried about intruders before. But she'd been healthy and robust, confident in her ability to protect herself. Now, she was pregnant and nervous.

She went to the front door slowly as the knock came again. Steeling herself, she looked through the peephole.

Her gasp was audible to the man on the other side of the door.

She opened it, slowly. "Mr....Mr. Sinclair," she faltered, tugging her thick cotton robe tighter at the throat.

"Are you all right? The lights were on and I was worried," he said quietly.

It was the last thing she'd expected to hear. He was wearing slacks and a sports shirt with deck shoes. His eyes looked bloodshot and he seemed worn-out, as if he hadn't even been to bed.

"I'm fine..."

He gave her a sardonic look.

She swallowed. "My leg hurts," she said. "It keeps me awake."

"What happened to it?"

"I told you. An accident."

"Falling off Mount Everest is an accident. So is a shark attack."

She drew in a long breath. "Do you want some coffee?" she asked impulsively.

"Yes."

She opened the door and let him in. She led the way back to the kitchen, haltingly. She gasped as he bent and swung her up into his arms.

How familiar she felt. How familiar she smelled. It was like touching heaven, just to be so close to her. Even if Alistair hadn't given her away, he knew now that he had his own Emma in his arms. He carried her into the kitchen and lowered her gently into a chair.

She remembered his strength with pain. He'd carried her to bed many times during their brief marriage. She loved the way she felt in his arms. The sadness drained her of joy.

He pretended not to notice her sadness. He got a cup out of the cabinet—obviously he'd been to Mamie's house more than once—and poured coffee into a cup. "Does yours need warming?" he asked.

"No. It's fine."

He sat down at the table with her, studying her drawn young face, her soft brown eyes, the swollen contours of her body. Possession, he thought as he smiled gently. That was what he felt. Possession. Especially with the pregnancy making her body swollen with his child.

"What, exactly, is wrong with that leg?" he asked.

She grimaced. "A deep cut. I think it might have done damage to a muscle or tendon. The doctor at the time just sewed it up, but he said I needed to see a specialist."

"I see," he said gruffly. "Did you get a second opinion?"

She gave him a long, speaking look. "I don't shop at Neiman Marcus, drive a Jaguar, or spend summers on the beach," she began.

"Oh, hell."

She flushed. "Sorry, I live within my means. I was lucky to have it sewn up at all."

"What the hell sort of doctor did you have?"

"A very busy, harassed one," she said, not liking the memory of the physician who'd done the quick suture job in the infirmary. She'd been a prisoner, not a pampered aristocrat. Just the same, a nurse had questioned the resident's rushed care, but just then another accident victim from a devastating highway collision had been brought in and she was forgotten.

"You should see a specialist."

"I'll stand on a street corner with a cup and solicit donations starting tomorrow," she promised.

He laughed abruptly. The sound startled him. He hadn't realized how long it had been since he'd felt like laughing. He studied her quietly and frowned. She couldn't even afford decent medical care, and it was all his fault. His pale eyes glittered over her like seeking hands. She'd been stabbed and almost killed in an attack that could have cost her a child he didn't even know she was carrying. A baby. Emma's baby. His eyes closed. The pain was incredible.

"What is it?" she asked.

He looked down into his cup, his face drawn like cord. "My wife was pregnant," he said abruptly, hating the faint waver in his deep voice. "She lost our child. I told you about it when we met in the woods."

He sipped coffee, scalding his lip.

She didn't say anything else. She didn't know what to say.

He swallowed more coffee. "I don't even know where she is right now," he bit off.

"You've tried to find her?"

He averted his eyes. "Yes. It's a big country when you're searching for one person."

"I guess so." Her heart had jumped at the thought that he had regrets, that he'd tried to find her.

His pale eyes narrowed. "Why doesn't your husband want a child?" he asked abruptly.

She started. "He…he never said, really," she stammered.

"You're six months along, you said," he persisted.

She forced a smile. "Almost seven," she agreed. "He doesn't want it, but I do, so much!"

Almost nine. She was lying about her due date, and he knew it. He looked at her with such hunger that he had to stare down into his coffee to hide it. "I see."

Emma was nervous. He thought she was his Emma. He didn't say so, but it was there, just the same. She'd hoped that she'd thrown him off with her fictional marriage, her false due date. But she saw in his face that he hadn't believed a word. He knew who she was!

She stood up. She hadn't fooled him at all. It was her own sheer bad luck that he'd come home unexpectedly, that he'd decided to stay on the lake. And what would she do now? She backed up, holding on to the chair while she searched her whirling mind for an option, any option, to save her child.

Her long, soft hair fell out of its barrette and down over her shoulders like a red-gold cloud. Now that he was closer, he could tell that the roots were blond. Platinum blond.

She put a protective hand over her swollen stomach. "You know. Don't you?" she asked, her big brown eyes accusing and frightened on his hard face as he, too, rose.

He studied her hungrily. "Yes, honey. I know."

"I won't do it."

He scowled. "Do what?"

"I won't give up the child," she said, her voice break-ing. "I'll run. I'll hide. I'll do anything…" She was almost screaming.

He moved forward quickly and caught her up in his arms, holding her tight, enfolding her against him, rocking her hun-grily. "I've made too many mistakes already," he whispered into her throat, where his face was buried there, in the soft-ness of her hair. "I won't make that one. I swear I won't! I'd never do anything to hurt our child, Emma!"

She was shivering. He'd said "our" child. She stilled in his arms. She stopped fighting him.

He felt that softening in her. It went to his head like liquor. His arms slid all the way around her, protecting, comfort-ing. Against his stomach, he felt the thick swell of hers. "You have my child inside you," he whispered. And he sounded… fascinated. Wondrous.

"You won't…force me to do anything?" she pleaded.

"Oh, Emma," he groaned. "No! God, no!"

She let go of the fear, bit by bit, and pressed close to him. "I was so afraid," she choked.

"I know. How do I even begin to apologize for what I've done to you?" he asked huskily. "I thought you'd sold me out, seduced me into marriage. I didn't know, didn't sus-pect, that you were the one driving the boat. When I found out, I just…went crazy. There's no other way to explain it." He drew back, so that he could see her flushed face. "I was in over my head almost at once." He traced her cheek with warm, strong fingers. "You were always there when I needed you most. I got used to having you around. I wanted you. But I never considered your feelings. In fact, I ignored them.

You see, Emma, I didn't want commitment. I didn't believe in forever."

"I know that," she said, feeling her heart break. He was telling her that he didn't want her permanently. He probably didn't want the baby, either, really, but he was going to make the best of it, out of guilt.

He was trying to express feelings he'd never really had, and failing miserably. He wasn't a man who shared anything about himself, even with his closest friends. He drew in a breath.

"After I lost my first wife, I drew into myself," he said. "I felt such guilt." He bit down hard on remembered grief. "And then I did the same thing all over again. I threw you out and never considered what might happen to you. I wanted revenge."

"I know," she said sadly. "It was my fault—"

"It was an accident, Emma," he interrupted. "I was on a Jet Ski, not paying attention, and you were in a speedboat, not paying attention. I was blinded, or thought I was." He smiled sadly. "You came to work for me, trying to make amends for what you'd done. Didn't you?"

She nodded sadly. "I was coming to confess, that first day I met you on the lakeshore, after you were...blind. But I got cold feet. Then when you offered me the job, I thought, *I'll let him get to know me, and then I'll tell him, when he knows what sort of person I really am.*" She bit her lip and he looked driven. "But it didn't quite work out that way."

His eyes closed on a wave of grief. "Dear God, what I did to you...!"

Emma almost choked on her own pain. She hadn't known that he felt it was his fault as well as hers.

He drew in a breath. "We were married. I was on top of the world, even blind. Then my private detective told me I'd married the woman who blinded me." He smiled sadly. "I went off the deep end. I reacted without thinking. I had you arrested, sent to jail. I got drunk and stayed that way for weeks. Then I fell down some steps and hit my head. I woke up sighted again. They'd tried to tell me that the blindness was psychological, not biological, but I wouldn't listen. It took weeks to get used to the fact that I could see." He lowered his eyes. "As God is my witness, I thought your father or Mamie would have bailed you out the day after you were arrested. I had no idea, none at all, that you were still in jail. That you were in such danger." He swallowed, hard, to keep from strangling on grief. "I wanted to find you, to apologize. But after Alistair told me what had happened to you, I stopped looking." He studied her soft brown eyes. "Remember what I told you, about that song my mother liked back in the dark ages?" he mused, smiling. "You don't know what you've got til it's gone." The smile faded. "I didn't."

Her eyes were quiet, but troubled. He might be telling the truth, or he might not. If he truly didn't want a child, he might only be pretending that he did. He might still have ulterior motives.

She moved slowly out of his arms to clean out the coffeepot, grimacing with each step.

"You need to have that leg looked at," he said firmly. "It can't be easy, with the extra weight the pregnancy puts on it."

She ignored him, and kept on washing out the coffeepot.

"I could pay for a specialist," he began.

"But you aren't going to," she replied.

"Damn!"

She put up the coffeepot and turned. "You really are a disagreeable person."

He snorted. "Yes." He moved to hand her his cup. She barely came to his chin. He missed her so much. "Come home."

She made a face. "I am home. I live here."

"Marie could cook nutritious meals for you." He paused.

"You can have a color TV set in your room. We can buy baby furniture."

"It wouldn't be right."

"Emma, you do realize that we're still married?" he asked softly.

She almost dropped the pot. She fumbled it into the dish drainer and turned, her face pale. "What?"

"I threw the divorce papers into the fire," he said quietly. "They were never filed."

"But...why?" She indicated her floppy, cheap gown and robe. "I mean, look at me. I'm poor, I'm plain—I'm nothing. What do you want with me?"

"You're an angel, Emma," he said quietly, and his eyes were eating her. "You have a heart as big as the whole world. I'm one of the richest men in America, but I'm poor without you."

She bit her lip and fought tears. "The baby will get in your way when it's born," she said stubbornly. "You don't like interruptions. He'll cry and I'll have to be up with him all hours..."

He moved forward and pulled her close. "We'll both be up with him all hours," he said simply. He looked around. "This is no place for you. My best friend is an obstetrician. He practices in Atlanta, but he maintains an office here. He'll treat you."

"I can't—"

"If you say, 'afford it,' I'll have a temper tantrum right here," he threatened. His hands tightened around her arms. "Baby, your mother died in childbirth. I haven't forgotten that. I'm not risking your life. Don't even think about asking me to."

He sounded as if she meant something to him. But she was wary. Recent months had hardened her heart, made her uncomfortable around people, suspicious.

"I know. You don't trust me. It's all right. I don't expect

you to. Just try to believe that I want what's best for you and the baby. If you want to think I'm doing it out of guilt, fine. But come home with me. Let me take care of you, Emma."

She searched his pale eyes. "And if I want to go back to Texas and live with my cousin when the baby's born, will you try to stop me?"

"Not if I'm convinced that you really want to go." He didn't add that there was no way on earth he would ever allow that to happen.

She drew in a breath and thought for a minute. "All right, then. I'll come with you."

"I'll have Marie come and help you pack." He pulled out his cell phone.

"Connor, it's three in the morning! She'll be asleep!"

He hesitated, then grimaced. "All right. I'll help you pack," he added, acting as if he were being invited to step up to the gallows.

She couldn't resist a faint smile. "If I can go as I am, I will. I won't need anything for tonight except my heartburn medicine. It's on the cabinet."

He frowned. "Heartburn?"

"It's common with pregnant women."

He studied her with warm, soft eyes. "Heartburn."

"It goes with the overactive bladder."

He pursed his lips. "You can have the room next to mine. If you need something at night, I'll be close by."

She was surprised, and it showed. She'd never thought that he was a nurturing sort of man.

He moved closer. "You sat with me when I had migraines," he said gently. "Even when I threw up. I can't think of a woman in my entire life, except my mother, who would have done that. Certainly not my first wife."

"Oh."

He traced her soft cheek. "I'll take care of you now," he said softly. "It's my turn." He bent and brushed his hard mouth tenderly against hers. "Let's go home, Emma."

She must need her head examined, she was thinking. But she let him take her hand tightly in his and lead her out the door.

Marie was beside herself when she woke the next morning and found Emma back in residence.

"I'll go make strawberry pancakes and sausage right now!" she exclaimed, fussing over the sleepy younger woman. She knew they were Emma's favorites.

Emma laughed. "Thanks, Marie."

"Eggs for me," Connor said from the doorway. His eyes were filling with the sight of Emma in his house, in his life. He looked like a man who had the whole world. It would have been perfect if she still loved him. But he couldn't expect that. Not after what he'd done to her. He'd settle for whatever he could get in the way of affection. "No pancakes."

"Yes, sir," Marie said with a grin, and went off to cook.

"You look better this morning," Connor told her.

She pushed back her disheveled hair. "I haven't been sleeping well," she confessed. "This bed is much nicer than the one in Mamie's spare room, but don't you dare tell!" She'd been laughing, but she cried out softly, and then laughed again.

"What is it?" he asked worriedly, moving closer. "What's wrong, Emma?"

"It's just, well..." She reached for his hand, caught it and pulled it to her swollen belly. She spread it just to the side of her navel and waited.

Something under his hand bumped it. His face flushed and he jerked. She held his hand there.

"It's the baby," she whispered. "He moves. Can you feel his fist?"

He was fascinated now. He sat down beside her and spread

his big hand over the surface of her stomach. He pressed his fingers closer and felt a tiny fist moving against the stomach wall. "Good God!" he breathed. "I never knew they moved!" His face was radiant.

She laughed softly.

He met her eyes and held them. A jolt of pure electricity made her cheeks flush; it tingled all the way to her toes. He knew it, the conceited beast. But the look on his face wasn't arrogant. It was delight. Sheer delight.

He got up before she had time to savor what she was feeling. "I have to go out and make a living for us all after breakfast. God knows, when he's a few years older, he'll be eating us out of house and home."

"He?" she teased.

He scowled. "She?"

"I don't know," she confessed. "I haven't had any tests."

"I'm setting you up with my doctor friend, Harry. You don't want to take any chances, Emma. Neither do I. All right?"

She gave in reluctantly. She still didn't quite trust him. "He won't do anything to me, will he?"

"No, honey," he said. "I promise."

She relaxed a little. "Sorry," she said. "It's been…rough."

His face hardened. "You're safe now. No one will ever hurt you again."

He turned away. "I'll eat breakfast. Then I have to fly to New York for a meeting. I'd rather not go, the weather's horrible, but it's a merger and I have to sign the papers."

"I understand."

"Marie and Barnes will look out for you. Everything will be fine."

She wanted to tell him to be careful, but she was worried it might sound pushy. It was too early to start showing so much concern. She knew that he was uncomfortable with her right now. Better to let things lie for a bit.

Six days later, he was back.

She was sitting in the living room, knitting, when Marie opened the door and let him in. His black, wavy hair was damp from the rain. He was wearing a navy blue pin-striped suit with an expensive white shirt and silk tie, all under an equally expensive dark raincoat.

He grinned at Marie and went into the living room where Emma was. "I brought you something from New York," he said, handing her the bag. "How's your leg?"

"It's better, thanks." She stared at the bag.

"No need to try and use psychic abilities to figure out what's in it," he mused, shedding his raincoat. "Just open it."

She glowered at him, but she opened it. There was a small stuffed kitten inside, a marmalade kitten with brown eyes.

"Oh," she exclaimed softly.

He smiled. "She reminded me of you."

She smoothed her hand over the silky little thing. "Thanks," she said shyly. "Coffee?"

"Yes. But you need decaf, little mama," he teased softly as they walked into the kitchen.

Marie saw them coming and laughed. "Strong and decaf," she guessed. "Working on it."

"Thanks, Marie," he said, grinning.

He pulled out a chair and plopped down into it, yawning.

"I was up most of the night," he said when she glanced at him curiously. "I guess my age is catching up with me."

She only smiled. She worried that one of his mistresses had caused that lack of sleep.

He cocked his head and studied her with visible pride. "Heartburn any better?"

She laughed softly. "It never gets better. The midwife says it goes with the territory."

His face tautened. "I called Harry Weems on the way home. His nurse will call you this morning about an appointment. You'll go," he said when she tried to protest. "I won't risk your health and the health of our child with a midwife, however qualified, not with your mother's medical history."

It flattered her that he cared even that much. Perhaps he was just making the most of a guilty conscience, but she could pretend that he loved her. Once, he seemed to have come close to it. But the baby would give them something to build on. If he could love it, he might one day love Emma.

"All right, Connor," she said, her voice soft and quiet in the stillness of the kitchen, broken only by the sounds of coffee brewing.

Marie made Connor's in an espresso machine. He lived on strong coffee. But she had a small coffeepot for pods, and she made Emma's decaf in that one. Fortunately, it was a large kitchen with plenty of counter space.

"Strong and weak," Marie teased as she put thick mugs of coffee in front of them. She'd learned long ago that Connor didn't care for delicate china on his kitchen table, and he hated the formal dining room. It was only used for guests.

"Thanks, Marie," Emma said, smiling.

"You need to drink more milk," Marie chided. "And you should be taking vitamins."

The phone rang.

"That's vitamins calling you right now." Connor chuckled. He indicated Emma's cell phone, lying beside her coffee cup. "Answer it."

She made a face at him as she did. It was Dr. Weems's nurse, who sounded very kind. She made an appointment for Emma the very next day. Emma agreed and thanked her. She hung up.

"He'll see me in the morning," she said, shell-shocked. "But I thought it took weeks to get an appointment with him."

"He's my best friend," Connor replied. His eyes were all over Emma. "When I told him it was my child," he said with a smile, "he was almost as excited as I was."

Emma studied him warily. She still didn't quite trust him.

He curled her fingers into his. "Do you want him to tell you the sex of the baby?" he asked softly.

She sighed. The touch of his hand on hers was delicious. "I don't think so. I'm almost nine months," she said slowly. "We'll know soon enough when I deliver."

He brought her palm to his mouth and kissed it softly. "Whatever you want, honey," he said.

She searched over his hard, broad face with acquisitive eyes. "Did you have a sister?"

He knew what she was asking. He chuckled. "No. Neither did my father. Or my grandfather." He pursed his lips. "So a little girl is unlikely." His face softened as he looked at her. "I would have loved a little girl, Emma," he said huskily, and kissed her palm again.

She tingled all over. She could hardly catch her breath. The baby kicked, hard, and she jumped and laughed.

"What is it?" he asked, worried.

She put her free hand on her abdomen. "I think your son is agreeing that he's not a girl," she teased.

His face radiated joy.

She thought about the appointment the next day and gnawed her lower lip. "Dr. Weems…is he nice?"

"He's one of the best men I know. If you're nervous, I'll go with you," he said.

She was shocked. "But everyone will know, if you do."

"Know what? That I'm your husband or the father of your child? Or both?" he teased gently. "I don't mind, Emma. I have enough people to keep the press away from us. We won't be bothered here."

"They'll think you've lost your mind when they see me," she worried. "Stock prices will fall..."

He just laughed. "They'll think I've finally become sane," he corrected. "Then it's settled. We'll go to the appointment together." He picked up the phone and started making calls, first to Tonia.

"Yes, that's what I said, Emma's pregnant. In fact, she's due almost any day now." He smiled as he listened. "That's what I told her...Okay. Call our PR people and let them release it just to the tabloid that Kane Lombard's people own. Give them an exclusive. That should get the rest of them off our backs, at least until the baby's born...Sure. Thanks, Tonia." He laughed. "I'll tell her. Bye."

He hung up and glanced at Emma. "She said to tell you that they should put you in the book of records, considering how long I've avoided fatherhood."

Her eyes fell. "It was my fault," she said, and felt guilty. "I didn't use anything," she added, lowering her voice so that Marie, tidying the living room, didn't hear.

"Neither did I," he replied. "Didn't you realize? I went in headfirst, honey. Once, when we were making such slow, soft love, I even thought about making a baby," he whispered, burying his mouth in her palm. "I was a fanatic about prevention, but I never even asked if you'd gone on the pill, did I?"

She shook her head. The touch of his mouth on her palm electrified her. She could barely breathe.

"I can't ask you to forgive so much," he whispered. "But I'll try to make it up to you, Emma," he added softly, searching her big, soft brown eyes. "I'll do anything to make you happy."

"The baby will mean a lot of changes," she said.

He shrugged. "We'll cope."

She wondered if he had any idea what babies were really like. She'd lived with the Griers and she knew about taking care of infants. They were noisy and there would be toys spread all over the house. But perhaps he was right. He might learn to tolerate the baby even if he wasn't as excited over fatherhood as he seemed to be.

The Griers. She groaned inwardly. She hadn't told them anything. She'd been too afraid to put them in the line of fire when she was in trouble with the law, and she didn't want to impose on them when she knew she was pregnant. She corresponded with Tippy, but she hadn't mentioned the pregnancy or her marriage, or the man in her life. She'd lied and said that work was keeping her very busy and she was happy. Tippy believed her, because Emma had never lied to her.

"What's wrong? You look worried," Connor said softly.

"I have friends in Texas," she said. "I lived with them when my father…" She bit down hard on her lip.

He was recalling things from the first days he'd known Emma, when she'd talked about her alcoholic father.

"Your father drank," he recalled. His face hardened. "He hit you."

She drew in a breath. "It was long ago. The Griers took me in when I had no place to go. I lived with them and worked as a cook in a local café. I often took care of their two children while they went shopping or if she had to go on a trip with him. He gave lectures at the FBI Academy once or twice."

He frowned. "You never mentioned them."

She sighed. "I was trying to hide my past from you, while I got up enough nerve to confess what I'd done," she said sadly. "I was afraid that if you knew about them, you might take it out on them, too, if you ever found out who I was."

He lowered his eyes. His fingers tangled with hers. "I'm not a nice person, Emma," he said after a minute. "I was wrapped up in vengeance. I got even with people for the slightest offenses." He smoothed his fingers over hers. "It's hard to change the habits of a lifetime. But after what I did to you, I lost my taste for getting even with people." He smiled wanly. "I suppose it takes a hard jolt to make us look at ourselves. I didn't like what I saw. I went all the way to France, trying not to face what I did." He added huskily, "I am more sorry than you'll ever know for what I did to you." He searched her pretty brown eyes. "But I am not sorry for getting you pregnant," he added gruffly. "It's the only thing in my whole damned life that I got right."

She flushed with pleasure. "Really?" she asked.

His fingers contracted. "Really," he replied. He drew in a long breath. "Oh, baby, it's been a long few months. So long!"

The flush grew redder. He'd only called her that pet name in bed, and it brought back raging memories of exquisite passion.

He was remembering, too. His big fingers eased between hers in a slow, sensual motion. "After the baby comes," he whispered, wary of eavesdroppers, "we might lock ourselves in a room and never come out."

She laughed. "Connor!"

He brought her fingers to his lips and nibbled the ends. "It's been a long, dry spell for me," he said, his voice husky with desire. "Very long."

Her eyebrows raised. "A dry spell?"

"No women, Emma."

Her heart jumped. "You're n-not serious," she stammered.

"I'm deadly serious." His eyes fell to her pretty bow mouth. "A man who gets used to the most expensive champagne isn't likely to suddenly develop a taste for cheap beer," he mused.

"You had parties in France," she said, and her voice was faintly harsh. "It was in all the newspapers. You were dancing with some tall brunette…"

"Dancing, yes," he agreed. "Nothing but dancing. Ever.

With anyone. Not after we'd been together," he added softly, every word emphatic. "Never after you, baby. I couldn't."

Tears stung her eyes. She hadn't expected that. Maybe it was guilt, and only guilt, but it touched her. She certainly was more emotional these days, because of the baby.

He got up, picked her up and sat back down with her in his lap. He kissed away the tears. "It's all right," he whispered. "I'm going to take such exquisite care of you, Emma." His mouth was warm and slow and tender. "You and the baby. My baby. Our baby." He buried his face in her warm throat. "Dear God, I've been out of my mind with worry! I didn't know where you were, what had happened to you, if you were all right." His arms contracted, while she felt like treasure. "It's like coming home, to have you here, in my house, in my life."

It was for her, too, but just as she started to say it, Marie came back into the room and smiled with pure joy at the two of them.

"Would you like some lunch?" she teased. "I made a fresh pasta salad."

Connor lifted his head and searched Emma's eyes. He smiled. "That would be nice. Thanks."

Emma smiled back.

# SEVENTEEN

Connor did go with her to Dr. Weems. He even went into the examination room, exchanging robust hugs with the taller, thinner man.

"Harry and I went through college together," Connor told Emma. "He was smarter, though. I took my degree in business. His took brain power."

"Don't let him fool you. He's smart." Harry grinned. "Okay, when was your last period?" he asked Emma, and glanced at Connor's outrage. "She can tell me," he added with a laugh. "I'm an obstetrician, remember?"

Connor ground his teeth together. "Sorry."

Emma was faintly surprised at his reaction. She studied his face curiously.

"Women love me," Harry told her. "They fall all over me, especially in the last months of pregnancy before they deliver. One woman even proposed to me during the delivery and she'd been happily married for ten years. He's jealous," he added, his dark eyes twinkling as he glanced at Connor.

Emma was fascinated.

Apparently Connor didn't like her knowing how he felt, so he excused himself while Emma went through some tests and questions. When she came back out, she was flushed and a little worried.

"He says my cervix is tilted the wrong way," she said in

the car on the way home. The window between them and Barnes in the limo was closed, so she felt comfortable talking to Connor. "He said it was almost a miracle that I even got pregnant. The baby's okay. They did an amniocentesis to make sure. It's just…"

"Just what, honey?" he asked softly.

She drew in a breath. "I'm scared."

He knew why, without being told. He drew her into his arms and held her, his lips on her temple. "I'm right here. I'll be with you the whole time. I promise."

She relaxed. "All right."

He folded her close. At least she didn't hate him. It was something.

She slept fitfully that night. She had a nightmare. Connor was far away and she could see him, but he couldn't hear her. She was screaming that she loved him, but he just kept backing away. When she woke, and realized it was a bad dream, she still didn't feel comfortable.

The feeling got worse at breakfast when he announced that he had to fly to Arizona to sign some contracts on a partnership for his aerospace division. Emma felt chills even as he said it.

"I'll only be away a day or so," he promised.

"Are you going in the company jet?" she asked.

He shook his head. "Business class on a commercial airline, worrywart. Okay?"

She smiled. She beamed. "Okay."

"So you worry about me, do you?" he teased, although the look on his face was oddly expectant, hopeful.

"I worry about you," she confessed. "Be careful."

He smiled. "Always."

Two days stretched into five. He phoned her every night to talk. She was worried as her due date approached, but she tried not to let her fear seep into the conversation. She was being fanciful, she thought. If he was flying commercial, there was nothing to worry about. All the airlines had excellent safety records, and he built aircraft. He should know which airline was the safest.

A carpenter showed up the second day after his departure. He said there was a repair needed in Connor's office. Emma was suspicious, but Marie came into the room and greeted the man like an old friend. He was close to her age.

"This is Danny Barton," Marie introduced him. "We went through high school together. He's a master carpenter."

"Nice to meet you," Emma said, smiling. "I'm Emma."

"Mr. Sinclair's wife? Nice to meet you, too. And congratulations."

"Thanks." She put a hand over her belly. "Any day now." She sighed wistfully.

"Where's the repair needed? I want to see it to know how much material I'll need and what I'll have to do to fix it."

"It's over here, near the ceiling." Marie pointed to a spot on the wood paneling. It was a round spot, splintered.

Emma frowned. "That looks like a bullet hole."

"That's what it is," Marie said quietly. "We'll leave you to work, Danny."

He nodded, already setting up his ladder to climb up to do the repair.

"It's a bullet hole?" Emma asked when they were in the living room, with the door to the office closed.

Marie looked uncomfortable. "Yes," she said. She searched Emma's eyes. "Mr. Sinclair didn't tell you what happened?"

She grimaced. "We've been sort of tiptoeing around each other since he recognized me," she confessed. Her eyes fell. "I'd die for him, Marie, and that's God's own truth. But he never says what he feels."

Marie smiled and drew her into the kitchen. "How about a nice cup of tea?" she asked. "And I'll tell you about it."

Marie waited until they were sipping herbal tea before she began. "It was when we got back from France," she said. "Mr. Sinclair was in the office—" she nodded toward the part of the house where it was "—and Mr. Sims came by to talk about the divorce. He'd sent the papers to have you sign, you remember. So Mr. Sinclair asked where you were, and Mr. Sims told him you were still in jail." She drew in a breath and took a swallow of hot tea, noting Emma's intent stare. "Mr. Sinclair thought you'd been out on bail all that time. He could see again, and he wasn't so, well, so angry. He was shocked. He told Mr. Sims to get you out that very day, no matter what he had to do." She toyed with her cup. The memory was painful. "That's when Mr. Sims told him what had happened to you, and that you'd lost the baby—because that's what he was told."

"That's what I thought," Emma said. "It wasn't until the doctor treated my wounds that he said the shiv hadn't penetrated too deeply. I was so lucky!"

"Anyway, I heard a scuffle and the pistol shot. I ran to see what was the matter. Mr. Sims was yelling for Barnes and trying to restrain Mr. Sinclair." She met Emma's shocked eyes. "I'd never seen the boss like that. He was sobbing…" She swallowed, hard. So did Emma. "They got the pistol away from him and closed the door."

"Dear God." Emma whispered the words reverently as she realized just how deeply Connor cared for her. If they hadn't got the pistol away in time…!

She fought tears. "I didn't blame him, you know," she said brokenly. "I loved him so much. I thought I deserved what happened, for blinding him. I was sure that he hated me. And

I was afraid for my baby. You know what he always said, about not ever wanting one."

"It's certainly not the case now," Marie replied, and she smiled. "You've had your worst time, Emma. You're overdue for some happiness."

"So is he," Emma replied. She drew in a long breath and let it out. "He feels something for me, anyway."

"Something very deep," Marie agreed. "He isn't a man to talk about his feelings, but it's easy to tell from the way he is with you. I've never seen him show tenderness to a woman. Any woman. And he talks about that baby all the time." She laughed. "Imagine, the boss looking forward to being a father. It really is like a miracle."

"For me, it certainly is," Emma said. She sipped tea and felt its warmth run down through her. A similar warmth brushed her heart. He cared. He really, really cared. It was more than she'd dare hoped for.

"There are plenty of good days ahead," Marie said. She finished her tea. "I'll just go see what he thinks we need to do to the wall," She laughed. She hesitated, with a worried look on her face.

"I won't tell Connor that you told me," Emma said. "I promise."

Marie relaxed. "He might not mind. But I'd rather not find out. Oh! I saved something…"

She went to the bookcase and extricated a file folder. She handed it to Emma.

Emma, puzzled, opened it. She caught her breath. It was the photo the man had taken at their wedding in Las Vegas. The look on Emma's face spoke volumes about her feelings for the man she was marrying. The anguish she felt at her guilt was also there, and her hopes.

"I've never seen anything like it," Emma said, shaking her head. "I look…beautiful."

"You are beautiful, my dear," Marie said gently. "You glow. When you look at the boss, you don't see a millionaire. You see a man. That's what sets you apart. You keep that," she added, indicating the photo. "It's the only one left." She grimaced. "He was in such a temper, just after he had them take you away. He ordered everything burned. All those lovely photos. I saved that one. I had to. It was irreplaceable."

"Thanks, Marie," she said. She hesitated. "Has he seen it?"

Marie shook her head. "I was afraid it was worth my job to let him know I hadn't done what he told me."

"It will be all right. I'll put it in a safe place."

"Why don't you lie down for a while and rest?" Marie asked. "Pretty soon, you'll forget what it was like to lie down and rest." She laughed softly. "The baby will be a handful."

"I'm looking forward to it," Emma replied. "I can't wait!"

"The house will need some new furniture for little people. I wonder if we could persuade Danny to make you a cradle and a baby bed? He makes furniture, too. He uses oak and what he does is magnificent. I'm sure the boss wouldn't mind."

"Then please ask him," Emma said with a smile. "I love handmade things."

"I noticed, from all those caps you knit." Marie chuckled.

"I'm making you one," was the reply.

"Thank you!"

"But I'm not telling you what it will look like," she said. "It's going to be a surprise!"

Two days later, Emma got a shock. She was watching a talk show on television when a news banner flashed across the screen. It was brief and utterly devastating. It said Millionaire Aviation Magnate Connor Sinclair Feared Dead in Tragic Plane Crash in Arizona.

The news feed went on to tell of three passengers on the

plane who were well-known, one a famous singer. But Emma didn't notice that. She was screaming. Absolutely screaming.

Marie came running. She'd heard it on the small television in the kitchen. "Oh, Emma," she said, tearing up. "Emma!"

Emma didn't hear her. The hysteria had her by the throat. "He's dead. He's dead. I didn't even get to say goodbye. He's dead!"

She started screaming again. It was like the nightmare she'd had, the one where she'd tried to get to Connor and he kept going farther and farther away. Her throat was raw. Her stomach began to throb as labor set in.

Barnes came running when he heard the screams. He, too, had seen the news flash on television.

"Call an ambulance," Marie said urgently.

"Right now."

They took Emma to the hospital. She had to be sedated, not only because the baby was coming, but because Connor would never see him. She loved him more than anything on earth, and now he was gone. She had nobody.

The labor was long and difficult, and finally Dr. Weems had no choice but to do a cesarean section because she never dilated even one centimeter. The shock of the news, he imagined, had contributed to her condition.

They rolled her into surgery. Minutes later, the nurse showed the tiny creature to a dazed, hurting Emma.

"It's a little boy," the nurse whispered. "Congratulations."

"He's so beautiful." Emma dissolved in tears. "He's dead. My husband is dead!"

He put a gentle hand on her shoulder. "You still have the baby, Emma," he said softly. "At least you have a part of Connor."

She nodded, but the pain was racking her. After they gave her a sedative, she went out like a light. Harry Weems sighed.

He'd lost his best friend. It was all over the news. Poor Emma, with a new baby and hope for a happy marriage, all gone now. He turned away, hiding the ache in his heart.

Marie had cried all day. She called often to check on Emma. One of the duty nurses was a cousin of hers, and was willing to relay information. The little boy was doing fine. Emma was still sedated.

She wished she was sedated. She'd called Tonia and they'd wailed together. Nobody knew exactly what to do. The companies were pretty much autonomous, but the board of directors would have to appoint someone to head them up. Connor had been the heart of the business. Nobody could replace him. Tonia said she'd relay the news to the divisional managers, if they hadn't already heard about the crash. She'd called Edward in Nice, to inform him of the tragedy that had occurred. Edward had already heard the news. He'd sobbed on the phone, Tonia told Marie.

Barnes was morose, as well. He'd been close to Connor. He and Marie sat at the table, picking at salads and sipping black coffee for lunch. It had been a miserable day.

The front door opened. They both started, because it was kept locked all the time. Only someone with a key could get in.

"Where the hell is everybody?" Connor Sinclair asked irritably. He tossed his briefcase onto the side table and ran a hand through damp, wavy black hair. "I've had a hell of a day. My damned cell phone died." He held it up and tossed it onto the briefcase. "Barnes, can you find a charger for it? I usually keep one in the briefcase but…" He stopped, aghast at their faces. "What the hell is wrong with you two?"

Marie ran and hugged him. So did Barnes.

"All right, what's going on?" he asked. He frowned. "Has something happened to Emma?" he asked suddenly. He went quickly to her room, opened the door, and it was empty. He turned. "Where is she?" he asked with fear in every word.

"She's in the hospital, sir," Barnes said gently.

"She started screaming when she saw the report on television," Marie managed through sobs of joy. "We couldn't calm her. She went into labor. We called an ambulance and Dr. Weems—"

"She's going to be fine," Barnes added.

"You have a healthy little boy," Marie told him gently, watching the expressions cross his face, the most prominent one of absolute exaltation.

"Barnes, get me to the hospital. What was on television that upset her?" he asked while Barnes was getting the limo out.

"Sir, it's been reported everywhere that you're, well, dead," she said, grimacing. "The plane crashed."

His eyebrows arched. "The plane? Oh, the commercial plane. I missed the flight by ten minutes. Damned traffic slowed down the limo I hired. So I hitched a ride with a friend who has a private jet like mine." He made a face. "It wasn't as comfortable as mine, I have to admit, but I didn't want to wait for them to get it to Arizona. I'm not dead."

"Thank God! I have to call Tonia. She'll be so relieved. We were scared to death, sir. Especially Emma," she added. "She said her life was over."

Connor's face was so radiant that it glowed. "She did?"

Marie hesitated, but only for a minute. "I need to show you something."

She went into Emma's room and fetched the photo that Emma had framed and tucked into her bedside table. She showed it to Connor.

"I'm sorry," she said. "You did tell me to burn all of them."

He was looking at the portrait of him and Emma, his eyes misty. He'd never seen a photo capture such an expression on

288 DIANA PALMER

anyone's face. Emma loved him beyond measure. The photograph was like a statement of love.

"Thanks," he told Marie, and hugged her. "Thanks for disobeying. This once," he added in a teasing tone.

"You're very welcome. You should go and meet your son."

"On my way." He handed Marie the photo. He was smiling from ear to ear.

Emma was in a twilight state, between consciousness and unconsciousness. She was in a quiet place, free of pain and worry. But there was a voice. It was deep and slow and tender. It wanted her to open her eyes.

She wasn't eager to wake up. As she drifted closer to consciousness, she remembered why she was in the hospital. She opened her eyes and tears stung them. She thought she heard Connor's voice. It was so close...

"Baby," he whispered. He was standing over her, his face tired but radiant with joy. "My sweet baby, we have a son."

She looked at him through a mist. "Connor?" she choked. "Am I dreaming?"

He bent down and put his mouth roughly, hungrily over hers. "We're both dreaming. And we're never going to wake up. I'm real, Emma. Kiss me and find out."

She kissed him back. She tried to lift her arms, but that hurt her stomach.

He felt her wince and drew back. He smiled warmly. "Stitches," he whispered. "You'll get better." His big hand smoothed over her cheek. "You're worn-out and in pain. Go to sleep. I'll be right here when you wake up." The smile faded. "I'll never leave you. Never, as long as I live."

"You're not dead?" she whispered, and tears ran down her cheeks.

He smiled. "I missed the flight. No, I'm not dead."

"Everybody thought you were."

He brushed his mouth over hers. "Marie's calling Tonia. She'll handle the press. I'm going to see our son."

She managed a wan smile. The pain, even with the sedation, was bad. "Okay."

"What are we going to name him, honey?" he asked.

She studied his face. It was strong. Handsome. She loved looking at him. "Names?"

He nodded.

"Do you have a middle name?" she wondered.

"Jacob."

She smiled. "Jacob Connor Sinclair?"

He brushed his mouth over hers. "We'll call him Jake."

She reached up just far enough to draw her hand down his cheek. "I like that."

He put his mouth over her eyes and closed them. "Go to sleep."

"Okay."

He held his infant son in the nursery. They gowned him and handed him the little boy, who was so small. He'd never in his life experienced such emotions. He kissed the tiny forehead, looked into eyes that were a silvery gray, like his own. He wondered if they'd change as Jake grew older. He was perfect. Tiny, but perfect. He fought tears as he handed the child back to the nurse. He was a father. It was a life-changing event. He had a sudden urge to go buy out a toy store. But that would have to wait. His first priority now was getting Emma back on her feet, and home.

It took several days to accomplish that. Emma had wanted to breastfeed the baby, but the C-section pain was just too much for her. It overwhelmed her. So she bottle-fed Jake. Connor was delighted, because he could do the same for his son.

Emma loved to watch him hold the little boy. She'd never

seen such affection in those pale eyes as she saw when he held Jake. He loved the child already. He loved Emma, as well. She knew it. His reaction to her situation, the bullet hole in the office, told her things he might never be able to. But she knew how he felt, and that was enough.

Likewise, her hysteria had told him clearly that she still loved him, in spite of what he'd done to her. It was like a miracle, to know that Emma cared. She was his. He had a wife and a son. He was part of a family. He could hardly stop smiling.

They brought Emma home in the limo and Connor carried her into the house while the private duty nurse they'd hired brought baby Jake along in his carrier.

Emma was shocked when she saw that her room, next to Connor's, had been transformed into a nursery, complete with monitor, handmade crib, curtains with sailboats and every sort of baby furniture known to man. Plus a selection of mobiles for the crib and electronic toys made especially for newborns. There was a dresser, too, chock-full of onesies and socks and blankets.

"You did all this?" Emma asked with a surprised smile.

"I had a little help from Marie." He chuckled.

"It's wonderful." She kissed his hard cheek. "I love it!"

He smiled and kissed her soft lips. "I'm glad. We'll have him right next door to us, so that if we need to get up, we can."

"I can get up," she began.

"When you heal," he replied. "Nurse Pitts will do everything necessary until you can. No lifting unless it's as heavy as a handkerchief, remember?" he teased. "Babies are heavy. Ours weighs eight and a half pounds."

She sighed. "Okay, then." She'd noticed that there was a nice rollaway bed in the nursery, so she assumed the nurse would spend the night here.

"We gave the nurse one of the guest rooms," Connor said, guessing her next question. "But she'll stay with Jake at night."

"Yes, I will," Nurse Pitts said with a grin. "I'll take ever such good care of him," she promised. "So don't you worry. I raised six of my own."

Emma smiled. "Okay. Thanks."

"You're most welcome, Mrs. Sinclair."

Emma blushed. It was the first time anyone had called her that since she and Connor had married.

He noticed. He turned and carried her through to the master bedroom, nudging the door closed behind them. He put her on the bed and arranged pillows so that she could sit up comfortably and the stitches wouldn't pull.

"I gather that I'm sleeping with you?" she teased.

He sat down beside her. "I'm never letting you out of my sight," he replied seriously. "I've already put out the word that I'm taking two weeks off to be with my family. That means no travel, no business, period. If Tonia can't handle it, the divisional managers will have to." He traced her cheek lightly. "I'm the luckiest man on earth, Emma," he whispered, and bent to kiss her with a restrained hunger. "I didn't think you could forgive me..."

"You silly man," she whispered against his lips. "I love you. That never stopped. It never will." She drew back and looked into his pale eyes. "I'll never stop loving you."

His eyes misted. He drew her face into his throat and he rocked her. "I'll never stop feeling guilty for what happened, for what I did to you," he said gruffly. "But I'll do all I can to make it up to you, for the rest of our lives." His arms contracted gently. "I never knew what love was, until you came into my life. I'll love you all the way to the grave, baby," he whispered huskily. "And forever beyond it."

She let the tears fall, healing tears, cleansing tears. He held her while she wept. And for those few minutes, it seemed as if they were the only two people on earth who'd ever known love, who'd ever spoken of love, who'd ever shared love. Emma knew that as long as she lived, she'd never forget the day he told her his heart. She closed her eyes and smiled against his hard mouth. Dreams really did come true.

"Will you hurry?" Connor teased as they crawled out of the limo. "Slowpoke."

"I am not a slowpoke," she said, making a face at him as she handed Jake to him. "All you have to do is get out. I have to get Jake and diaper bags and my purse and—"

He reached in, kissed her and took Jake. "Barnes will get the bags. Come on."

"We didn't even call first," she protested as they walked down the driveway to the big, old-fashioned house right in downtown Jacobsville, Texas.

"I called," Connor replied.

"You told them who you were?" she asked, all eyes, while Jake gurgled in her arms.

"Not exactly. I told them I was your husband and we wanted them to meet our son."

She started to speak when the front door opened and Tippy Grier stepped outside with her mouth open.

"Emma?" she exclaimed. "You're married! You have a baby!"

"I'm so sorry I didn't tell you," Emma said. "It's a very long story..."

Tippy took in the very expensive limousine sitting at the end of the driveway, Connor's designer suit, Emma's couture pantsuit and all at once she recognized her male visitor. "Connor Sinclair?" she asked slowly.

"I hope so. I'm wearing his suit."

She burst out laughing. She hugged Emma. "Talk about keeping secrets!" she exclaimed, and held out her arms.

Emma put Jake into them, beaming. "I wanted to tell you, but I was keeping secrets."

"Big ones apparently," Tippy mused, sizing up Connor.

He chuckled. "We'll tell you one day."

A tall, dark man with black hair in a ponytail came out the door behind Tippy. "Damn! A husband and a child, and you didn't even invite us to the wedding!" Cash Grier teased.

"I meant to," she said.

Cash chuckled. He shook hands with Connor. "I've heard about you from my brother," he said.

"Cort." Connor nodded. "I can only imagine what he told you."

"Something about a very attractive young woman that he wanted to get to know, and you came at him like a mountain lion," Cash remarked. He was looking at Emma. "He didn't know who you were, did he?"

"I'd never met him," Emma reminded him. "He's very nice."

"That last word is why he's still breathing." Connor chuck-led. "Nice. She never calls me nice."

"You're a grizzly bear," she told Connor. "Grizzly bears are not nice."

"I married one of those, too." Tippy laughed, making a face when Cash glared at her. "Come in! I made a pound cake and there's plenty of fresh coffee! Bring your driver, too," Tippy added. "We've got lots."

"You heard her, Barnes," Connor called. "But bring the ten tons of baby equipment in with you."

"You bet!"

"Thanks for all you did for her," Connor told Cash while the women gossiped. "I've heard too much about her father already."

"He was a piece of work," Cash agreed. "Tippy and I sort

of adopted her. She didn't have anywhere to go, and she was such a nice young woman." He raised both eyebrows. "We never heard anything about any of this—the blindness, the marriage…"

"It's a sad story. It was almost a tragic one," Connor said quietly. "Life teaches hard lessons."

"Tell me about it," came Cash's reply.

"The important thing is that it all worked out," Connor replied.

"Her father just got married," Cash said. "The woman's a lot like Emma. She's got a soft heart and she loves to help people. She got him into AA and helped him sober up and sort himself out. He'd like to see Emma, but he says it's early days yet and she needs time. He'd like to call her and talk sometime. If she's willing."

Connor nodded. "I'll tell her."

"Did she tell you about Steven?"

Connor drew in a breath. "He was gay, right?"

"Yes," Cash replied. "We didn't tell her. She was so upset already. But you might mention it. She thinks they broke up because he hated her father's job. It was his mother who hated people knowing she had a gay son."

"Idiot," Connor scoffed. "Your child is still your child, no matter what."

"Absolutely."

He hesitated, and a wicked gleam came into his silver eyes. "You might mention to your cattle baron brother that Emma's permanently off-limits. Just in case he ever gets itchy feet and wanders to Georgia."

Cash burst out laughing. "I'll do that."

Emma glanced toward the men while Tippy's young brother Rory held little Jake, and Tris and Marcus, their new little boy, hovered around Tippy and Emma.

"He's pretty famous, your husband," Tippy remarked with a smile when she saw where Emma was looking.

"He's pretty sweet, too," Emma replied. "I never thought I'd fit anywhere in his life, but he made a place for me. Connor, the baby." She shook her head. "It all seems unreal."

"I feel the same way about my own life." She studied Emma. "We lived through hard times. Then we got lucky. That's life."

Emma laughed. Her eyes, brimming over with love, homed in on her husband, who was looking back at her with eyes just as loving. "That's life," she agreed softly.

★ ★ ★ ★ ★

*Be sure to check out*
*Diana Palmer's next book in her beloved*
LONG TALL TEXANS *series*
*DEFENDER*

*The man who shattered Isabel Grayling's trust is back to protect*
*her.*
*Can she trust Paul Fiore not to break her heart once again?*

*Turn the page to get a glimpse of*
*DEFENDER.*

# CHAPTER ONE

ISABEL GRAYLING STUCK her head around the study door and peered in. The big desk was empty. The chair hadn't been moved from its position, carefully pushed underneath. Everything on the oak surface was neatly placed; not a pencil wasn't neatly in a cup; not a scrap of paper was out of line. She let out a breath. Her father wasn't home, but the desk kept the fanatical order he insisted on, even when he wasn't here.

She darted out of the office with a relieved sigh and pushed back the long tangle of her reddish-gold hair. Pale blue eyes were filled with relief. She wrinkled her straight nose, where just a tiny line of freckles ran over its bridge. Her name was Isabel, but only Paul Fiore called her that. To everyone else, she was Sari, just as her sister, Meredith, was always called Merrie.

"Well?" her younger sister, Merrie, asked in a whisper.

Sari turned. The other girl was slender, like herself, but Merrie had hair almost platinum blond, straight and to her waist in back. Her eyes, like Sari's, were blue, but paler, more the color of a winter sky. Both girls looked like their late mother, who was pretty but not beautiful.

"Gone!" Sari said with a wicked grin.

Merrie let out a sigh of relief. "Paul said that Daddy was going to Germany for a few weeks. Maybe he'll find some other people to harass once he's in Europe."

Sari went up to the shorter girl and hugged her. "It will be all right."

Merrie fought tears. "I only wanted to have my hair trimmed, not cut. Honestly, Sari, he's so unreasonable...!"

"I know." She didn't dare say more. Paul had told her things in confidence that she couldn't bear to share with her baby sister. Their father was far more dangerous than either of them had known.

To any outsider, the Grayling sisters had everything. Their father was rich beyond any dream. They lived in a gray stone mansion on acres and acres of land in Comanche Wells, Texas, where their father kept Thoroughbred horses. Rather, his foreman kept them. The old man was carefully maneuvered away from the livestock by the foreman, who'd once had to save a horse from the man. Darwin Grayling had beaten animals before. It was rumored that he'd beaten his wife. She died of a massive concussion, but Grayling swore that she'd fallen. Not many people in Comanche Wells or nearby Jacobsville, Texas, wanted to argue with a man who could buy and sell anybody in the state.

That hadn't stopped local physician Jeb "Copper" Coltrain from asking for a coroner's inquest and making accusations that Grayling's description of the accident didn't match the head injuries. But Copper had been called out of town on an emergency by a friend and when he returned, the coroner's inquest was over and accidental death had been put on the death certificate. Case closed.

The Grayling girls didn't know what had truly happened. Sari had been in high school, Merrie in grammar school, when their mother died. They knew only what their father had told them. They were much too afraid of him to ask questions.

Now, Merrie was in her last year of high school and Sari was a senior in college. Sari had majored in history in preparation for a law degree. She went to school in San Antonio, but wasn't allowed to live on campus. Her father had her driven back and forth every day. It was the same with Merrie. Darwin wasn't having either of his daughters around other people. He'd fought and won when Sari tried to move onto the college campus. He was wealthy and his children were targets, he'd said implacably, and they weren't going anywhere without one of his security people.

Which was why Sari and Paul Fiore, head of security for the Grayling Corporation, were such good friends. They'd known each other since Paul moved down from New Jersey to take the job, while Sari was in her last year of high school. Paul drove the girls to school every day.

He'd wondered, but only to Sari, why her father hadn't placed them both in private schools. Sari knew, but she didn't dare say. It was because her father didn't want them out of his sight, where they might say something that he didn't approve of. They knew too much about him, about his business, about the way he treated animals and people.

He was paranoid about his private life. He had women, Sari was certain of it, but never around the house. He had a mistress. She worked for the federal government. Paul had told her, in confidence. He wasn't afraid of Darwin Grayling—Paul wasn't afraid of anyone. But he liked his job and he didn't want to go back to the FBI. He'd worked for the Bureau years ago. Nobody knew why he'd suddenly given up a lucrative government job to become a rent-a-cop for a Texas millionaire in a small town at the back of beyond. Paul never said, either.

Sari touched Merrie's slightly bruised cheek and winced. "I warned you about talking back, honey," she said worriedly. "I'm so sorry!"

"My mouth and my brain don't stay connected," Merrie laughed, but bitterly. Her blue eyes met her sister's. "If we could just tell somebody!"

"We could, and Daddy would make sure they never worked again," Sari said. "That's why I've never told Paul anything..." She bit her lip.

But Merrie knew already. She hugged the taller girl. "I won't tell him. I know how you feel about Paul."

"I wish he felt something for me," Sari said with a long sigh. "He's always been affectionate with me. He takes good care of me. But it's... I don't know how to say it. Impersonal?" She drew away, her expression sad. "He just doesn't get close to people. He dated that out-of-town auditor two years ago, remember? She called here over and over, and he wouldn't talk to her. He said he just wanted someone to go to the movies with, and she was looking at wedding rings." She laughed involuntarily. She shook her head. "He won't get involved."

"Maybe he was involved, and something happened," her sister said softly. "He looks like the sort of person who dives into things headfirst. You know, all or nothing. Maybe he lost somebody he loved, Sari."

"I guess that would explain a lot." She moved away, grimacing. "It's just my luck, to go loopy over a man who thinks a special relationship is something you have with a vehicle."

"It's a very nice vehicle," Merrie began.

"It's a truck, Merrie!" she interrupted, throwing up her hands. "Gosh, you'd think it was a child the way he takes care of it. Special mats, taking it to the car wash once a week. He even waxes it himself." She glowered. "It's a truck!"

"I like trucks," Merrie said. "That cowboy who worked for us last year had a fancy black one. He wanted to take me to a movie." She shivered. "I thought Daddy was going to kill him."

"So did I." Sari swallowed, hard. She wrapped her arms around her chest. "The cowboy went all the way to Arizona, they said, to make sure Daddy didn't have him followed. He was scared."

"So was I," Merrie confessed. "You know, I'm seventeen years old and I've never gone on a date with a real boy. I've never been kissed, except on the cheek."

"Join the club," her sister laughed softly. "Well, one day we'll break out of here. We'll escape!" she said dramatically. "I'll hire a team of mercenaries to hide us from Daddy!"

"With what money?" Merrie asked sadly. "Neither of us has a dime. Daddy makes sure we can't even get a part-time job to make money. You can't even live at your college campus. I'll bet that gets you talked about."

"It does," Sari confided. "But they figure our father is just eccentric because he's so rich, and they let it go. I don't have any real friends, anyway."

"Just me," Merrie teased.

Sari hugged her. "Just you. You're my best friend, Merrie."

"You're mine, too, even if you are my sister."

Sari drew back. "One day, things will change."

"You've been saying that since we were in grammar school. It hasn't."

"It will."

Merrie touched her cheek and winced. "I told Paul I fell down the steps," she said, when she noticed her sister's worried expression.

"I wonder if he believed you," Sari replied solemnly. "He's not afraid of Daddy."

"He should be. I've heard Daddy has this friend back East," Merrie told her. "He's in with some underworld group. They say he's killed people, that he'll do anything for money." She bit her lower lip. "I don't want Paul hurt any more than you do. The less he knows about what goes on here when he's off duty, the better. He couldn't save us, anyway. He could only be dragged down with us."

"He wouldn't let Daddy hurt us, if he knew," Sari replied.

"So he won't know."

"Someone else might tell him," Sari began.

"Not anybody who works here," Merrie sighed. "Mandy's kept house for over twenty years, since before you were born. She knows stuff, but she's afraid to tell. She has a brother who does illegal things. Daddy told her he could have her brother sent to prison if she ever opened her mouth. She's afraid of him." She looked up. "I'm afraid of him."

Sari winced. "Yes. Me, too."

"I don't ever want to get married, Sari," the younger woman said huskily. "Not ever!"

"One day, you might, if the right man comes along."

Merrie laughed. "He's not likely to come along while Daddy's around, or he'll be leaving in a body bag in the back of a pickup truck."

The dark humor in that statement sent them both into gales of laughter.

PAUL FIORE WAS ITALIAN. He also had a Greek grandmother. It accounted for his olive complexion and thick, jet-black hair and large brown eyes. He was handsome, too, tall and broad-shouldered, muscular without making a point of it. He walked like a panther, light on his feet, and he had a quick mind. He'd been in law enforcement most of his life until he took the job with the Grayling Corporation. He'd wanted to get as far away from federal work—and New Jersey—as he could. Comanche Wells, Texas, came close to his ideal place.

He was fond of the girls, Merrie and Sari, and he took charge of the house when Mr. Grayling was out of the country. He could handle any problem that came up. His main responsibility was to keep the girls safe, but he also kept a close watch on the property, especially the very expensive Thoroughbreds Grayling raised for sale.

The housekeeper, Mandy Swilling, was fond of him. She was always baking him the cinnamon cookies he liked so much, and tucking little surprises into his truck when he had to be away on business.

"You've got me ruined," he accused her one morning. "I'll be so spoiled that I'll never be able to get along in the world if I ever get fired from here."

"Mr. Darwin will never fire you," Mandy said confidently. "You keep your mouth shut and you don't ask questions."

His eyes narrowed. "Odd reason to keep a man on, isn't it?"

"Not around here," she said heavily.

He stared at her, his dark eyes twinkling. "You know where all the bodies are buried, huh? That why you still have work?"

She didn't laugh, as he'd expected her to. She just glanced at him and winced. "Don't even joke about things like that, Mr. Paul."

He groaned at her form of addressing him.

"Now, now," she said. "I've always called the boss Mr. Darwin, just like I call the foreman Mr. Edward. It's a way of speaking that Southern folk are raised with. You, being a Yankee..." She stopped and grinned. "Sorry. I meant to say, you, being a Northerner, wouldn't know about that."

"I guess so."

"You still sound like a person born up North."

He shrugged and grinned back at her. "We are what we are."

"I suppose so."

He watched her work at making rolls for lunch. She wasn't much to look at. She was about fifty pounds overweight, had short silver hair and dark eyes, and she was slightly stooped over from years of working in gardens with a hoe. But she could cook! The woman was a magician in the kitchen. Paul remembered his tiny little grandmother, making ravioli and antipasto when he was a child, the scent of flour and oil that always seemed to cling to her. Kitchens were comforting to a child who had no real home. His father had worked for a local mob boss, and done all sorts of illegal things, like most of the rest of his family. His mother had died miserable, watching her husband run around with an endless parade of other women, shuddering every time the big boss or law enforcement came to the front door. After his mother died and his father went to jail for the twentieth time, Paul went to live with his little Greek grandmother. He and his cousin Mikey had stayed with her until they were almost grown. Paul watched Mikey go the same route his father had, attached like a tick to the local big crime boss. His father never came around. In fact, he couldn't remember seeing his father more than a dozen times before the man died in a shoot-out with a rival mob.

It was why he'd gone into law enforcement at seventeen, fresh out of high school. He hated the hold crime had on his family. He hoped he could make a difference, help clean up his old neighborhood and free it from the talons of organized crime. He went from local police right up into the FBI. He'd felt that he was unstoppable, that he could fight crime and win. Pride had blinded him to the reality of life. It had cost him everything.

Still, he missed the Bureau sometimes. But the memories had been lethal. He couldn't face them, not even now, years after the tragedy that had sent him running from New Jersey to Texas on a job tip from a coworker. He'd given up dreams of a home and all the things that went with it. Now, it was just the job, doing the job. He didn't look forward. Ever. One Day at a Time was his credo.

"Why are you hiding in here?" Mandy asked suddenly, breaking into his thoughts.

"It's that obvious, huh?" he asked, the New Jersey accent still prevalent even after the years he'd spent in Texas.

"Yes, it is."

He sipped the black coffee she'd placed in front of him

at the table. "Livestock foreman's got a daughter. She came with him today."

"Oh, dear," Mandy replied.

He shrugged. "I took her to lunch at Barbara's Café a few weeks ago; just a casual thing. I met her at the courthouse. She works there. She decided that I was looking for a meaningful relationship. So now she's over here every Saturday like clockwork, hanging out with her dad."

"That will end when Mr. Darwin comes back," she said with feeling. "He doesn't like strangers on the place, even strangers related to people who work here."

He smiled sadly. "Or it will end when I lose my temper and start cursing in Italian."

"You look Italian," she said, studying him.

He chuckled. "You should see my cousin Mikey. He could have auditioned for *The Godfather*. I've got Greek in me, too. My grandmother was from a little town near Athens. She could barely speak English at all. But could she cook! Kind of like you," he added with twinkling eyes. "She'd have liked you, Mandy."

Her hard face softened. "You never speak of your parents."

"I try not to think about them too much. Funny, how we carry our childhoods around on our backs."

She nodded. She was making rolls for lunch and they had to have time to rise. Her hands were floury as she kneaded the soft dough. She nodded toward the rest of the house. "Neither of those poor girls has had a childhood. He keeps them locked up all the time. No parties, no dancing and especially no boys."

He scowled. "I noticed that. I asked the boss once why he didn't let the girls go out occasionally." He took a sip of his coffee.

"What did he tell you?"

"That the last employee who asked him that question is now waiting tables in a little town in the Yukon Territory."

She shook her head. "That's probably true. A cowboy who tried to take Merrie out on a date once got a job in Arizona. They say he's still looking behind him for hired assassins." Her hands stilled in the dough. "Don't you ever mention that outside the house," she advised. "Or to Mr. Darwin. I kind of like having you around," she added with a smile and went back to her chore.

"I like this job. No big-city noise, no pressure, no pressing deadlines on cases."

She glanced up at him, then back down to the bowl again. "We've never talked about it, but you were in law enforcement once, weren't you?"

He scowled. "How did you know that?"

"Small towns. Cash Grier let something slip to a friend, who told Barbara at the café, who told her cook, who told me."

"Our police chief knew I was in law enforcement? How?" he wondered aloud, feeling insecure. He didn't want his past widely known here.

She laughed softly. "Nobody knows how he finds out things. But he worked for the government once." She glanced at him. "He was a high-level assassin."

His eyes widened. "The police chief?" he exclaimed.

She nodded. "Then he was a Texas Ranger—that ended when he slugged the temporary captain and got fired. Afterward he worked for the DA in San Antonio and then he came here."

He whistled. "Slugged the captain." He chuckled. "He's still a pretty tough customer, despite the gorgeous wife and two little kids."

"That's what everyone says. We're pretty protective of him. Our late mayor—who was heavily into drug smuggling on the side—tried to fire Chief Grier, and the whole city police force and fire department, and all our city employees, said they'd quit on the spot if he did."

"Obviously he wasn't fired."

She smiled. "Not hardly. It turns out that the state attorney general, Simon Hart, is Cash Grier's cousin. He showed up, along with some reporters, at the hearing they had to discuss the firing of the chief's patrol officers. They arrested a drunk politician and he told the mayor to fire them. The chief said over his dead body."

"I've been here for years, and I heard gossip about it, but that's the first time I've heard the whole story."

"An amazing man, our chief."

"Oh, yes." He finished his coffee. "Nobody makes coffee like you do, Mandy. Never weak and pitiful, always strong and robust!"

"Yes, and the coffee usually comes out that way, too!" she said with a wicked grin.

He laughed as he got up from the table, and went back to work.

THAT NIGHT HE WAS researching a story about an attempted Texas Thoroughbred kidnapping on the internet when Sari walked in the open door. He was perched on the bed in just his pajama bottoms with the laptop beside him. Sari had on a long blue cotton nightgown with a thick, ruffled matching housecoat buttoned way up to the throat. She jumped onto the bed with him, her long hair in a braid, her eyes twinkling as she crossed her legs under the voluminous garment.

"Do that when your dad comes home, and we'll both be sitting on the front lawn with the door locked," he teased.

"You know I never do it when he's home. What are you looking up?"

"Remember that story last week about the so-called traveling horse groomer who turned up at the White Stables in Lexington, Kentucky, and walked off with a Thoroughbred in the middle of the night?"

"Yes, I do."

"Well, just in case he headed south when he jumped bail, I'm checking out similar attempts. I found one in Texas that happened two weeks ago. So I'm reading about his possible MO."

She frowned. "MO?"

"Modus operandi," he said. "It's Latin. It means…"

"Please," she said. "I know Latin. It means method of op-eration."

"Close enough," he said with a gentle smile. His eyes went back to the computer screen. "Generally speaking, once a criminal finds a method that works, he uses it over and over until he's caught. I want to make sure that he doesn't sashay in here while your dad's gone and make off with Grayling's Pride."

"Sashay?" she teased.

He wrinkled his nose. "You're a bad influence on me," he mused, his eyes still on the computer screen. "That's one of your favorite words."

"It's just a useful one. *Snit* is my favorite one."

He raised an eyebrow at her.

"And lately you're in a snit more than you're not," she pointed out.

He managed a smile. "Bad memories. Anniversaries hit hard."

She bit her tongue. She'd never discussed really personal things with him. She'd tried once and he'd closed up imme-diately. So she smiled impersonally. "So they say," she said instead of posing the question she was dying to.

He admired her tact. He didn't say so, of course. She couldn't know the memories that tormented him, that had him up walking the floor late at night. She couldn't know the guilt that ate at him night and day because he was in the wrong place at the wrong time when it really mattered.

"Are you okay?" she asked suddenly.

His dark eyebrows went up. "What?"

She shrugged. "You looked wounded just then."

She was more perceptive than he'd realized. He scrolled down the story he was reading online. "Wounded. Odd choice of words there, Isabel."

"You're the only person who ever called me that."

"What? Isabel?" He looked up, studying her softly rounded face, her lovely complexion, her blue, blue eyes. "You look like an Isabel."

"Is that a compliment or something else?"

"Definitely a compliment." He looked back at the computer screen. "I used to love to read about your namesake. She was queen of Spain in the fifteenth century. She and her husband led a crusade to push foreigners out of their country. They succeeded in 1492."

Her lips parted. "Isabella la Catolica."

His chiseled lips pursed. "My God. You know your history."

She laughed softly. "I'm a history major," she reminded him. "Also a Spanish scholar. I'm doing a semester of Spanish immersion. English isn't spoken in the classroom, ever. And we read some of the classic novels in Spanish."

He chuckled softly. "My favorite was Pio Baroja. He was Basque, something of a legend in the early twentieth century."

"Mine was *Sangre y Arena*."

"Blasco Ibañez," he shot back. "*Blood and Sand*. Bullfighting?" he added in a surprised tone.

She laughed. "Yes, well, I didn't realize what the book would be about until I got into it, and then I couldn't put it down."

"They made a movie about it back in the forties, I think it was," he told her. "It starred Tyrone Power and Rita Hayworth. Painful, bittersweet story. He ran around on his saintly wife with a woman who was little more than a prostitute."

"I suppose saintly women weren't much in demand in some circles in those days. And especially not today," she added with a wistful little sigh. "Men want experienced women."

"Not all of them," he said, looking away from her.

"Really?"

He forced himself to keep his eyes on the computer screen. "Think about it. A man would have to be crazy to risk STDs or HIV for an hour's pleasure with a woman who knew her way around bedrooms."

She fought a blush and lost.

He saw it and laughed. "Honey, you aren't worldly at all, are you?"

"I'm alternately backward or unliberated, to hear my classmates tell it. But mostly they tolerate my odd point of view. I think one of them actually feels sorry for me."

"Twenty years down the road, they may wish they'd had your sterling morals," he replied. He looked up, into her eyes, and for a few endless seconds, he didn't look away. She felt her body glowing, burning with sensations she'd never felt before. But just when she thought she'd go crazy if she didn't do something, footsteps sounded in the hall.

"So there you are," Mandy exclaimed. "I've looked everywhere." She stared at them.

Paul made a face. "Do I look like a suicidal man looking for the unemployment line to you?" he asked sourly.

Both women laughed.

"All the same, don't do that when your dad's home," she told Sari firmly.

"I never would, you know that," Sari said gently. "Why were you looking for me?"

"That girl at college who can't ever find her history notes wants to talk to you about tomorrow's test."

"Nancy," she groaned. "Honestly, I don't know how she passed anything until I came along!

"She actually called up one of our professors at night and asked if he could give her the high points of his lecture. He hung up on her."

"I'm not surprised," Paul said. "Better go answer the questions, tidbit," he added to Sari.

"I guess so," she said. She got off the bed, reluctantly. The way he'd looked at her had made her feel shaky inside. She wanted him to do it again. But he was already buried in his computer screen.

"There was an attempted horse heist just two days ago up near San Antonio," he was muttering. "I think I'll call the DA up there and see if he's made any arrests."

"Good night, Paul," Sari said as she left the room.

"Night, sprout. Sleep well."

"You, too."

MANDY LED HER into the kitchen and pointed to the phone.

"Hello, Nancy?" Sari said.

"Oh, thank goodness," the other girl rushed. "I'm in such a mess! I can't find my notes, and I'll fail the test...!"

"No worries. Let me get mine and I'll read them to you."

"You could fax them..."

"You'd never read my handwriting," Sari laughed. "Besides, it will help me remember what I need for tomorrow's test."

"In that case, thanks," Nancy said.

"You're welcome. Give me your number and I'll call you back. I'll have to hunt up my own notes."

Nancy gave it to her and hung up.

SARI CAME BACK down with the notes she'd retrieved from her bulky book bag. She phoned Nancy from the kitchen, where Mandy was cleaning up, and read the notes to her. It didn't take long.

"I'll see you in class," Nancy said. "And thanks! You've saved my life!" She hung up.

"She says I saved her life," Sari said, chuckling.

Mandy gave her a glance. "If you want to save two lives, you'll stay out of Mr. Paul's bedroom."

"Mandy, it's perfectly innocent. The door's always open when I'm in there."

"You don't understand. It's how it looks, that easy familiarity between you two. It will carry over to other times, in daylight. If your father sees it, even *thinks* that there might be something going on..."

"I don't do it when he's here."

"I know that. It's just..." She grimaced. "I don't know where he put all the cameras."

Sari's heart jumped. "What cameras?"

"He had it done while you girls were at school. He had three security cameras installed. He sent me out of the house on an errand while they were put in place. I don't know where they are."

"Surely he wouldn't have them put in our bedrooms," Sari began worriedly.

"There's no telling," Mandy said. "I only know that he didn't put one in here. I'd have noticed if anything was moved or displaced. Nothing was."

Sari chewed on a fingernail. "Gosh, now I'll worry if I talk in my sleep!"

"The cameras are why you should stay out of Mr. Paul's bedroom. Besides that," she added under her breath, "you're tempting fate."

"I am? How?" Sari asked blankly.

"Honey, Mr. Paul takes a woman out for a sandwich or a quick dinner. He never goes home with them."

Sari flushed with sudden pleasure.

"My point is," the older woman went on, "that he's a man starved of...well...satisfaction," she faltered. "You might say something or do something to tempt him, is what I'm trying to say."

Sari sighed and rested her head on her palms, propped on her elbows. "That would be a fine thing," she mused. "He's never even touched me except to help me out of a car," she added on a wistful sigh.

"If he ever did touch you, your father would be sure to hear about it. And I don't like to think of the consequences. He's a violent man, Sari," she added gently.

"I know that." Her face showed her misery. She was too innocent to hide her responses.

"So, don't tempt fate," Mandy said softly. She hugged the younger woman tight. "I know how you feel about him. But if you start something, he'll be out on his ear. And what your father would do to you..." She drew back with a grimace. "I love Mr. Paul," she added. "He's the kindest man I know. You don't want to get him fired."

"Of course I don't," Sari replied. "I promise I'll behave."

"You always have," Mandy said with a tender smile. "It all ends, you know," she said suddenly.

"Ends?"

"Misery. Unrequited love. Even life. It all ends. We live in pieces of emotion. Pieces of life. It doesn't all get put together until we're old and ready for the long sleep."

"Okay, when you get philosophical, I know it's past my bedtime," Sari teased.

Mandy hugged her one last time. "You're a sweet child. Go to bed. Sleep well."

"You, too." She went to the doorway and paused. She turned. "Thanks."

"What for?"

"Caring about me and Merrie," Sari said gently. "Nobody else has, since Mama died."

"It's because I care that I sometimes say things you don't want to hear, my darling."

Sari smiled. "I know." She turned and left the room.

MANDY, OLDER AND WISER, saw what Sari and Paul really felt for each other, and she worried at the possible consequences if that tsunami of emotion ever turned loose in them.

She went back to her chores, closing the kitchen up for the night.

# CHAPTER TWO

WHEN ISABEL WALKED past Paul's bedroom after she called Nancy, she noticed his door was closed and the lights were off.

She went into her own room, climbed into bed and extinguished the single bedroom lamp in the room.

She recalled what Mandy had said, about the dangers of getting too close to him, with sadness. Yes, of course, her father would fire him if anything indiscreet came to light. She also recalled the pain she felt when the older woman spoke of Paul going on dates with other women.

He didn't take them to bed, that much was clear. But it also indicated that he wasn't ready to get serious about a woman, that he wasn't interested in marriage and kids. And Isabel was. She'd gladly have given up college to end up in Paul's arms with a baby of her own.

But that seemed more unlikely by the day. She was living in pipe dreams. Paul was content to have her at arms' length. He didn't want her. At least, he didn't want her the way she wanted him. She cared more for him than she'd ever cared for anyone, except her mother and sister.

As Paul liked to remind her, though, she hadn't been out in the world long enough to know what she really wanted. That amused her. He seemed to think she was still the seventeen-year-old he'd taken to school every day in the limo. She was twenty-one, almost twenty-two now. She'd graduate from college in a few months. That made her, in the eyes of the world, an adult. Not to Paul, though. Never to Paul.

She had to start thinking about what she was going to do with her life after college. Law had always fascinated her. She'd been hanging around the courthouse after school, grilling one of District Attorney Blake Kemp's assistant DAs about what it was like to practice in a courtroom. Glory Ramirez was happy to talk to her, filling her head with thoughts of working in the DA's office.

"Blake knows how much time you spend here, on my lunch hour and after work," Glory teased.

"Oh, no," Sari began.

Glory held up a hand. "He doesn't mind. There aren't that many people blazing paths up the street to the courthouse to solicit work in the DA's office." She sobered. "It's hard work, Sari, with long hours. Sometimes defendants' families target us, because they think we've been unfair. Sometimes the defendants themselves try to attack us when they get out. Those instances are rare, but they do happen. Family life is hard." She smiled gently. "I'm qualified to know that, because my husband and I have a son who's almost four years old. Rodrigo still works for the DEA and I'm at the courthouse all hours. Sometimes we have to have the Pendletons babysit." The Pendletons were Glory's adoptive family. Jason's father had been Glory, and Gracie's, guardian.

"I don't really think they mind," Sari teased, because it was well-known that although Jason and Gracie Pendleton had a son and daughter of their own now, they still loved to watch their nephew. All the kids had enough toys to stock a nursery.

"Of course not," Glory laughed. "But I'm still missing out on time with my family to do this job. I love it," she added gently. "It's a special thing, to help keep people safe, to make sure people who do terrible things are punished and off the streets. That's why I do it."

"I...would do it for that reason, as well," Sari said, not

adding that her terror of a father was one of her own mo-
tivations. He was the sort of person who should have been
sitting in a jail cell, but never would, because of his wealth.
"Justice shouldn't be dealt according to who has money and
who hasn't," she added absently.

Glory, who had some idea of Darwin Grayling's illegal
dealings, only nodded her head.

"Anyway, what about those courses you mentioned?" she
asked, bringing Glory back to the present.

Glory laughed. "Okay. Here's what you need to consider
in law school…"

SARI WAS FULL of fire for the fall semester in law school, after
she got her undergraduate degree. Her cumulative grades assured that she would graduate, the finals from each class not-
withstanding. She already had a graduate school picked out.
Law school in San Antonio.

"You'll have to drive me, of course," Sari told Paul with a
sigh when she outlined the courses Glory had told her about.
"There's no way Daddy will ever let me drive myself. I don't
even have a driver's license."

He scowled. "Surely not."

She shrugged. "He holds the purse strings, you know. Either
I do it his way or I don't do it," she said with the complacency
of a woman who'd lived such a sheltered life. "So I do it."

"Haven't you ever wanted to break out?" he asked suddenly.

She grinned at him across a plate of cookies, which they
were sharing with cups of coffee at the small kitchen table.
"You offering to help me?" she teased. "Got a helicopter and
a couple of guys wearing ninja suits?"

He chuckled. "Not quite. I used to know a couple of guys
like that, though, in the old days."

"Oh, please," she said, munching a cookie. "You aren't old
enough to be remembering 'the old days.'"

His eyebrows rose. "You need glasses, kid. I've got gray hair already."

She eyed him. He was so gorgeous. Black wavy hair, deep-set warm brown eyes, high cheekbones, chiseled mouth; he was any woman's dream guy. "Gray hair, my left elbow."

"No kidding. Right here." He indicated a spot at his temple.

"Oh, that one. Sure. You're old, all right. You've got one whole gray hair."

He grinned, as she'd expected him to. "Well, maybe a few more than that. I'm like my grandfather. His hair never turned gray. He had a few silver hairs when he died, at the age of eighty."

"Do you look like him?" she asked, sipping coffee.

"No. I look like my grandmother. Everybody else was Italian. She was tiny and Greek and she had a mouth like a mob boss." He chuckled. "Do something wrong, and that gnarled little hand came out of nowhere to grab your ear." He made a face.

"So that's why your ears are so big," she mused, looking at them.

"Hey, I was never that bad," he argued. He glowered at her. "And my ears aren't that big."

"If you say so," she said, hiding the gleam in her eyes.

"You little termagant," he said, exasperated.

"Where do you get all those big words?" she asked.

"College."

"Really? You never told me you went to college."

He shrugged. "I don't like talking about the past."

"I noticed."

"We could talk about your past," he invited.

"And after those forty-five seconds, we could go back to yours," she teased, blue eyes twinkling. "Come on, what did you study?"

"Law." His face hardened with the memories. "Criminal law."

She frowned. "That was before you came to work for Daddy, yes?"

She was killing him and she didn't know it. His hand, on the thick white mug, was almost white with the pressure he was exerting. "A long time before that."

"Then, what..."

Mandy came into the room like a chubby whirlwind. "Where did you put the ribbons I was saving to wrap the holiday cookies with?" she demanded from Sari.

"Oh, my gosh, I was working on homemade Christmas cards and I borrowed them. I'm sorry!"

"Go get them," Mandy ordered with all the authority of a drill sergeant. "Right now!"

Sari left in a whirlwind, and Mandy turned to Paul, who was paler than normal. His hand, around the mug, was just beginning to loosen its grip.

He gave her a suspicious look.

"Sari doesn't think," Mandy said quietly. "She's curious and she asks questions, because she doesn't think."

He didn't admit anything. He took a deep breath. "Thanks," he bit off.

"We all have dark memories that we never share, Mr. Paul," she said gently. She patted his shoulder as she walked behind him. "Age diminishes the sting a bit. But you're much too young for that just yet," she added with a soft chuckle.

"You're a tonic, girl."

"I haven't been a girl for forty years, you sweet man, but now I feel like one!"

He laughed, the pain washing away in good humor.

"There. That's better," she said, smiling at him. "You just keep putting one foot in front of the other, and it gets easier."

"It's been almost five years."

"Thirty years for me," Mandy said surprisingly. "And it's much easier now."

He drew in a breath and finished his coffee. "Maybe in twenty-five years, I'll forget it all, then."

She looked at him with a somber little smile. "It would do an injustice to the people we love to forget them," she said softly. "Pain comes with the memories, sure. But the memories become less painful in time."

He scowled. "You should have been a philosopher."

"And then who'd bake cookies for you and Miss Sari and Miss Merrie?" she asked.

"Well, if we had to depend on Sari's cooking, I expect we'd all starve," he said deliberately when he heard Sari coming.

She stopped in the doorway, gasping and glaring. "That is so unfair!" she exclaimed. "Heavens, I made an almost-edible, barely scorched potato casserole just last week!"

"That's true," Mandy agreed.

Paul glowered. "*Almost* being the operative word."

"And I didn't even mention that I saw you pushing yours out the back door while I was trying to pry open one of my biscuits so I could butter it!"

Sari sighed. "I guess they were pretty good substitute for bricks," she added. "Maybe I'll learn to cook one day."

"You're doing just fine, darlin'," Mandy said encouragingly. "It takes time to learn." She shot Paul a glance. "And a lot of encouragement."

"Damn, Sari, I almost got one of those biscuits pried open to put butter in!" He glanced at Mandy. "How's that?"

"Why don't you go patrol the backyard?" Sari muttered.

"She's picking on me again, Mandy," he complained.

"Don't you be mean to Mr. Paul, young lady." Mandy took his part at once.

"He says terrible things about me, and you never chastise him!" Sari accused.

"Well, darlin', I may be old, but I can still appreciate a handsome man." She grinned at them.

Sari threw up her hands. Paul made her a handsome bow, winked and walked out the back door.

"You always take his side," Sari groaned.

Mandy chuckled. "He really is handsome," she said defensively.

"Yes. Too handsome. And too standoffish. He'll never look at me as anything but the kid I was when he came here."

"You've got law school to get through," Mandy reminded her. She sobered. "And you know how your dad feels about you getting involved with anyone."

"Yes, I know," Sari said miserably. "Especially anybody who works for him." Shivering softly, she said, "It's just, I'm getting older. I'm a grown woman. And I can't even drive myself to San Antonio to go shopping or invite friends over."

"You don't have any friends," Mandy countered.

"I don't dare. Neither does Merrie," she added solemnly. "We're young, with the whole world out there waiting for us, and we have to get permission to leave the house. Why?" she exclaimed.

Mandy ground her teeth. "You know how your dad guards his privacy. He's afraid one of you might let something slip."

"Like what? We don't know anything about his business, or even his private life," Sari exclaimed.

"And you're both safe as long as it's kept that way," Mandy said without thinking, then slapped a hand across her mouth.

Sari bit her lower lip. She moved closer. "What do *you* know?"

"Things I'll die before I'll tell you," the older woman replied, turning pale.

"How do you know them?"

Mandy ignored her.

"Your brother, right?" she whispered. "He knows people who know things."

"Don't you ever say that out loud," she cautioned the younger woman, looking hunted until Sari reassured her that she'd never do any such thing.

"It's like living in a combat zone," Sari muttered.

"A satin-cushioned one," came the droll reply. "If you want an apple pie, here's a do-it-yourself kit." She put a basin of apples in front of the younger woman. "So get busy and peel."

Sari started to argue. But then she recalled the delicious pies Mandy could make, so she shut up and started peeling.

GRADUATION CAME ALL too soon. The household, except for Darwin Grayling, who was in Europe at the time, went to Merrie's first at the high school and took enough pictures to fill an album. Then, only a few days later, it was Isabel's graduation from college. Merrie kept fussing with Sari's high collar.

"It's okay," her older sibling protested.

"It's not! There's a wrinkle, and I can't get it smoothed out!" Merrie grumbled.

"It will be hidden under my robes," Sari said gently, turning. She smiled at her younger sister. She shook her head. With her long blond hair like a curtain down her back, wearing a fluffy blue dress, Merrie looked like a picture of Alice in Wonderland that Sari had seen in a book. "I like your hair like that," she said.

Merrie laughed, her pale blue eyes lighting up. "I look like Alice. Go ahead. Say it. You're thinking it," she accused.

Sari wrinkled her nose.

Merrie sighed. "He decides what we'll wear, where we'll go, what we do when we get there," she said under her breath, her eyes on their father, standing with Paul near the front door. "Sari, normal women don't live like this! The girls I go to school with have dates, go shopping…!"

"Stop, or I won't get to graduate at all," the older sister muttered under her breath when Darwin Grayling shot an irritated glance toward them at Merrie's slightly raised tone.

Merrie drew in a deep breath. "It's Sari's collar," she called to her father. "I can't get the wrinkle out!"

"Leave it be," he shot back. He looked at his watch. "We

need to leave now. I have meetings with my board of directors in Dallas in three hours."

"That's your graduation, sandwiched in between breakfast
and a board meeting," Merrie teased under her breath. "At least
he came home for your graduation," she added a little bitterly.

Sari kissed her sister's cheek. "I was there at yours. So were
Mandy and Paul. Now shut up or I'll never graduate," came
the whispered reply. "Let's go!" She smoothed down her very
discreet black dress, regardless of her own wishes—and started
toward the door. She noticed Paul's faint wince as he saw how
she was dressed, like someone out of a very old Bette Davis
movie instead of a young woman ready to start graduate school.

She didn't answer that look. It might have been fatal to his
employment if she had.

GRADUATION WAS BOISTEROUS and fun, despite her father,
who sat through the entire ceremony texting on his phone
and then conducting a business call the minute the graduates
filed out into the spring sunshine.

"Maybe it's glued to him," Merrie teased as she and Sari
were briefly alone."

Attached by invisible cords," Sari replied. "Hi, Grace, happy
graduation!" Sari called to a fellow graduate.

"Thanks, Sari! You off to law school in the fall?" she asked.

"Yes. You?"

"I'm moving in with my boyfriend," Grace sighed, indicating a tall, gangly boy talking to another boy. "We're both
going to the University of Tennessee."

"Oh, I see," Sari said, still not comfortable with modern
ideas and choices.

Grace made a face. "Honestly, Sari, you need to buy normal clothes and go out with boys," Grace said, loud enough
for Sari's father to hear.

He hung up his phone and moved to join them, looking
expensive and coldly angry. "Are you ready to go, Isabel?" he

asked curtly. His eyes never left Grace. He looked at her as if she were some disease he was afraid his daughters might catch.

"Uh, congrats, Sari. See you around," Grace said, red-faced, and went back to her boyfriend.

"Slut," Darwin said, just loud enough for his voice to carry and Grace to look both ruffled and insulted. "Let's go." He took Sari by the arm and almost dragged her to the waiting limousine, with a flustered Merrie running to catch up.

"I'll have Paul watching," Darwin said as Paul put the girls into the back of the limo and stood aside, holding the door, so that Darwin could slide into the seat facing them. The door closed. "I'll expect you to associate with decent girls. Do you understand? That goes for you, too, Meredith!"

"Yes, Daddy," Sari said.

"I understand," Merrie added with a sigh.

The sisters didn't dare look at each other. It would have been fatal.

THE DINNER DARWIN had referred to was obviously going to be prepared by Mandy and just for the two women. Darwin had Paul drive him to the airport where his corporate jet was waiting. Sari and Merrie changed clothes and sat down to a lovely chicken casserole with homemade rolls and even a chocolate cake.

"It's delicious, Mandy," Sari said halfway through the meal. "Thanks!"

"Yes, it's wonderful!" Merrie enthused.

"Some graduation," Mandy muttered. "Should have gone out with your classmates and had fun, not be stuck here with me and an empty house."

"You know how Daddy is," Sari said quietly. "He doesn't think..."

"He doesn't care," Merrie interrupted coolly. "It's the truth, Sari, you just don't want to admit it. He doesn't want us going out with men because we might get involved and tell somebody something he doesn't want known. He doesn't want us getting married because we'd be out from under his thumb! Besides, some of that money might go outside the family!"

"I suppose you're right," Sari said, tasting her cake. "It's just, you get used to a routine. You don't even realize that it really is a routine." Her eyes twinkled. "Honestly, I thought Daddy was going to have a coronary when Grace talked about moving in with her boyfriend!"

Merrie chuckled. "I know! At least four of my classmates live with boys. They say it's very exciting…"

"Don't you even think about it," Mandy told them, waving a spoon in their direction. "There's enough wild-eyed girls out there already. You two are going to get married and live happily-ever-after."

"You make it sound like a fairy tale," Sari accused.

"Maybe, but I want more for you than being some man's temporary bed partner while he climbs the ladder to success," Mandy murmured. "Your mother wanted that, too. She went to church every Sunday. She believed that people have a purpose, that life has a purpose. She was an idealist."

"Yes, well, she waited to get married and she found Daddy," Sari said quietly. "So there goes your fairy-tale ending. I remember her more than Merrie does. She was unhappy. She tried not to let it show, but it did. Sometimes I found her crying when she thought nobody was looking. And she had bruises…"

"Don't ever speak of that where Mr. Darwin or even Mr. Paul could hear you," Mandy cautioned, looking frightened.

"I never would," Sari assured her. She grimaced. "But it's like living in prison," she muttered.

"A prison with silk hangings and Persian carpets," Mandy said mischievously.

"You know what she means, Mandy," Merrie piped in as she finished the last of her cake. "We aren't even allowed to date. One of my friends thinks our father is nuts."

"Merrie!"

"It's okay, he's from Wyoming," Merrie said, grinning. "He's in private school up north somewhere, but he visits a cousin here during the summer. His name is Randall. He's really nice."

"Don't you dare," Mandy began.

"Oh, it's not like that. We're just *friends*." She emphasized the word. "He goes through girls like some people go through candy. I'd never want somebody like that! But he's very easy to talk to, and he listens to me. I like him a lot."

"As long as you don't tell him things you shouldn't," Mandy replied.

Merrie's eyes fell. "I'd never do that."

Sari put down her fork with a sigh. "Well, it was a very nice lunch, even if it didn't come with scores of well-wishers and dancing." She frowned. "Come to think of it, I don't know how to dance. I've never been anywhere that I could learn."

"We went to that Latin restaurant once, where they had the flamenco dancers," Merrie said, tongue in cheek.

"Oh, sure, and I could have gotten up on a table and practiced the steps," came the sardonic reply.

Suddenly a door slammed. Paul came into the dining room with his hands deep in his pockets. His thick, wavy black hair was damp and there were droplets on the shoulders of his suit coat. "Well, it's raining," he sighed. "At least it held off until after the graduation ceremony."

"At least," Sari replied. "There's plenty left." She indicated the remnants of the lovely meal. "And lots of cake."

He chuckled. "I'm sorry."

"About what?" Sari asked.

"You should have gone out with your friends for a real celebration," he said, dropping into a chair. "With balloons and music and drinks…"

"Drinks?" Sari asked with raised eyebrows. "What are those?"

"I had balloons at my fifth birthday party, when Mama was still alive," Merrie added.

"Music. Hmm," Mandy said, thinking. "I went to a concert in the park last week. They had tubas and saxophones..."

Paul threw up his hands. "You people are hopeless!"

"We live in hopeless times," Sari said. She stood up and adopted a pose. "But someday, people will put aside their differences and raise balloons in tribute to those who have given their all so that we can have drinks and tubas..."

The rest of them started laughing.

She chuckled and sat back down. "Well, it was a nice thought. Daddy doesn't like us being around normal people, Paul," she added. "He thinks we'll be corrupted."

"That would be a choice," he replied. "I don't think you get one if you live here."

"Shh!" Sari said at once. "Don't say that out loud or they'll find you floating down some river in an oil drum!"

His eyes twinkled. "We found a guy like that once, back when I was a kid. Me and some other guys were goofing off near the river, in Jersey, and we saw this oil drum just floating, near the shore. One of the older boys was curious. He and a friend went and pried off the lid." He made a horrible face. "We set new land speed records getting out of there! It was a body inside!"

"Did you get the police?" Merrie asked curiously.

He gave her a long look. "Honey, if we'd done that, we'd probably have ended up in matching oil drums ourselves! You don't mess with the mob."

"Mob? You mean, real mob...mobsters?" Merrie asked, her eyes as big as saucers.

"Yeah," he replied, grinning. "I grew up in a rough neighborhood. Almost all of the kids I knew back then ended up in prison."

"But not you," Sari said, with more tenderness in her tone than she realized.

"Not me," Paul agreed. He smiled. "How about a plate?"

he asked Mandy. "I've fought traffic all the way from San Antonio and I'm starved!"

"You had the nice big breakfast that I made you this morning," Mandy taunted.

"Yeah, but all of it got used up listening to that guy who spoke at Sari's graduation ceremony. Who was he again?" he teased.

"That was one of the finer politicians this state has produced," Sari informed him haughtily. "In fact, he's your US senator."

"In that case, may he return to Washington, DC, with best possible speed and stay there from now on!" he said. "Gosh, imagine having to listen to him drone on for hours in Congress!"

"It beats having him drone on at somebody's graduation," Merrie said under her breath. "Oh, sorry!" she told her sister, but she ruined her apologetic tone by grinning.

Sari laughed, too. "I think there's some basic rule that people who speak at graduation ceremonies have to bore people to death."

"It would seem so."

"Who spoke at your graduation?" Sari asked Paul.

"The director of the FBI," he replied without thinking. His fingers, on the fork he was holding, went white.

"That must have been an interesting speech," Sari said. Not looking at Paul, she didn't see the effect the words were having on him.

"I'll bet he bored Paul out of his mind," Merrie teased.

Paul snapped out of it. He glanced at her and laughed. "Well, not completely. He had a sense of humor, at least."

"What did he... Oh!"

Mandy turned over the cream pitcher as Sari was about to ask Paul something else about his graduation.

"I'm getting so clumsy in my old age! My poor fingers just won't hold things anymore! Get us a rag, will you, darlin'?" she asked Sari.

"Of course." She paused to hug the older woman. "And you're not getting old!"

After Mandy mopped up the spill, the girls went to change out of their finery into casual clothes.

"Saved my bacon. Again. Thanks," Paul said to Mandy when they were alone.

She sat down beside him. "Whatever it is, you haven't really faced it, have you, dear?" she asked gently, laying a hand over his big one.

His lips compressed. "I came south," he said. "I couldn't stay where I was, doing the job I was doing. I wanted to get away, do something different, be around people I didn't know." He shrugged. "It seemed the best thing at the time, but I'm not sure it was. You don't face problems by running away from them."

"No," she said softly. "You never do. They just come along for the ride." She patted his hand again and got up. "But, that being said, there's no need to go rushing back to deal with them, either," she added with a smile. "We've gotten used to having you around."

"I like it here," he confessed, leaning back in his chair. "I didn't expect to. I mean, a south Texas ranch, cowboys all over the place, people with thick accents who wouldn't know a dissertation from a dessert." He glanced at her. "I got a surprise."

She laughed. "A lot of those drawling people with accents have degrees, in all sorts of surprising subjects," she translated. "And a slow voice doesn't equate to a slow mind."

He nodded. "The Grier boys changed my mind about a lot of things. You don't expect to find somebody like Cash Grier working as a small-town police chief. Or a guy who worked with the FBI's Hostage Rescue Team, like his brother Garon, heading up a local FBI office."

"Cash has been a constant surprise," Mandy said. "None of us really expected him to settle down here. He was going around with Christabel Gaines before she married his friend

Judd Dunn. Then, all of a sudden, he's married to a former supermodel and he's got two kids."

He laughed. "I know what you mean." He leaned over his coffee cup. "But the big surprise was finding Eb Scott here with a counterterrorism school. I knew him years ago. He worked as an independent contractor when I was overseas, in the Middle East."

"In the military?"

He nodded. "Spec ops. Green Berets," he added with twinkling eyes. "Eb saved my life. He went on to bigger and better things."

"So did you."

"Me? No, I'm just private security," he said, pausing to sip coffee.

"Not what you were before, though," Mandy said.

He glanced at her, frowning.

"My brother." She averted her eyes. "He...pretty much stays in trouble. He lived in New Jersey for a long time, working for some...well, some people you probably knew in the old days. I mentioned your name. Not deliberately, just in passing." She swallowed. "He knew about you."

His face went hard. Very hard. He looked up at her with cold dark eyes.

"I never tell anything I know to anybody, Mr. Paul," she said quietly. "And shame on you for thinking I would."

He grimaced. "Sorry."

"You don't know me. Not really." She sat back down beside him. "Our parents died when we were young. Grady took care of me. He worked odd jobs, did some questionable things, but he kept us together and put food on the table. When I graduated high school, I got a job working for Mr. Darwin, here. Grady figured I could take care of myself, so he went north, looking for better pay. He found it." She drew in a breath. "I keep thinking I'll hear one day that he's been found in an oil drum," she added with a wan smile. "I can't

stop him from doing what he pleases. The best I can hope
for is to make sure Mr. Darwin doesn't ever have a reason to
turn him in to the authorities."

He scowled. "Would he?"

"You know he would," she replied quietly. Her eyes met
his levelly. "It's why I never tell anything I know. And you'd
better make sure you do the same. You may not have people
he can blackmail you with, but Mr. Darwin could plant evidence and have you put away. It wouldn't be the first time,"
she added in a whisper, her eyes looking all around.

"There's no surveillance equipment in here," he whispered
back.

"Would you care to bet on it?" she returned.

*Don't miss*
*DEFENDER*
*by* New York Times *bestselling author*
*Diana Palmer,*
*available in paperback June 2017*
*wherever HQN Books books and ebooks are sold.*
*www.Harlequin.com*